TURMFALKE

TURMFALKE

CASE 387B

JOHN WILSON

HarperCollins*Publishers*

The *Turmfalke* Project referred to in this book did not
exist, nor does the island of Röhmer Insel. Apart from
historical people, none of the characters in the book
resembles or is meant to resemble anyone living or dead.
Apart from historical organizations, none of the
organizations in the book resembles or is meant to resemble
any real organization.

HarperCollins*Publishers*
77–85 Fulham Palace Road
Hammersmith, London W6 8JB

Published by HarperCollins*Publishers* 1996
1 3 5 7 9 10 8 6 4 2

A catalogue record for the book is
available from the British Library

ISBN 0 00 225360 7

Photoset in Linotron Sabon by
Rowland Phototypesetting Ltd,
Bury St Edmunds, Suffolk

Printed in Scotland

To Charlie and Mabel

Turmfalke, *n. (Orn.) Kestrel*

Cassell's German Dictionary

Hysterical amnesia: The failure to recall past events ... to escape the memory of an exceptionally distressing or frightening event.

Encyclopaedia Britannica

Loki: A Teutonic god who worked zealously for his fellow gods but who also wreaked mischief and undermined their works, eventually bringing about their downfall.

Larousse Encyclopaedia of Mythology

Deep into that darkness peering, long I stood there wondering, fearing,
Doubting, dreaming dreams no mortals ever dared to dream before.

Edgar Allan Poe, 'The Raven'

FALKENSCHLOSS, RHINELAND, APRIL 1945

The four men in the conference room overlooking the valley of the Rhine were still at war. Colonel Fred Newman was a member of the American Army administrative staff, following the front-line combat troops to collect military and civilian intelligence. His unit had established a temporary base in Andernach, a town on the west bank of the river, a few kilometres from the front line. The other American Army officer was a captain called Oswald Wise, whose uniform boasted only his captain's decals and no other insignia. He had arrived at Newman's office that morning, unannounced and armed with top-level clearance signed by one of General Eisenhower's senior commanders from a security division at Supreme Headquarters Allied Expeditionary Force, SHAEF. With this authorization, and assurances that there was no danger of combat, Wise 'persuaded' the colonel to take a trip into an area that was still in German hands. He took a minor road leading north along the river, drove the Marmon Jeep onto an old self-powered cable ferry to the east bank, then along a road through the thickly wooded hills, still heading north and at times pushing the Jeep near to its top speed. Newman was surprised at the captain's familiarity with the locality, but was too busy hanging onto the grips and keeping his eyes peeled for Germans to make any comment. Wise concentrated on his driving. The only words he uttered were at the end of the journey, when he swung the Jeep off the road and past a heavily fortified stone gatehouse with mediaeval battlements, where Newman was shocked to see four German guards pointing guns at him. His hand dropped automatically towards the Browning at his hip.

'Take it easy, Colonel,' the captain told him as they drove past. 'They're expecting us. Everything's been arranged.'

He swung the vehicle expertly round the drive to the imposing front entrance and led the way up the stone staircase and into the building. Two SS Oberschützen clicked into a salute, which Wise casually acknowledged. Newman felt the hair on his neck bristle as they entered a huge reception room overlooking a magnificent terrace. What the hell was going on?

The middle-aged German civilian sitting at the table opposite Newman was introduced by Wise as Professor Blintz, until recently in charge of the general hospital at Andernach. The fourth man was dressed in the uniform of an SS-Standartenführer, a rank equivalent to Newman's. Newman stared at him with undisguised hostility.

'Colonel Newman, this is Colonel Muntz,' Wise said.

Muntz clicked his heels and gave the American a slight bow.

Newman turned his gaze to Wise.

'Give me one good reason why I shouldn't shoot this son-of-a-bitch in the head.'

The professor sighed and said to Muntz in German, 'I told you this wouldn't work.'

'*Sprechen sie Englisch*,' Newman snapped at him.

'Take it easy, Colonel,' Wise said for the second time.

'Someone better tell me what's going on around here,' Newman said tightly. 'On the other hand, let me guess. These two *Wunderkinder* are looking for a way to save their miserable hides, am I right?'

'Not exactly, Colonel,' Muntz said in impeccable English. 'But it would be foolish to pretend there was nothing we wanted from you. In time of war we must be realists, would you not agree?'

'You should have thought of being realists before you started this thing,' Newman said disgustedly.

'Listen to him, Fred,' Wise said. 'What he's got to say makes a lot of sense to our people.'

'Sense? I'll give you sense. We've got the bastards on the run. We've taken Koblenz, Worms, Saarbrücken and now Ludwigshafen. Montgomery's crossed the Rhine up north. The Russians are pounding their way towards Berlin, for Christ's sake. The beloved Führer is counting his hours away in an underground privy. People like this should be shot on sight. That's what makes sense to me.'

'It's not as straightforward as that,' Wise said patiently. 'Just listen to the man, will you.'

Newman stared at Muntz. 'OK, Colonel. The captain is trying

hard to convince me about something, and he's come all the way from Ike's people at SHAEF. So, what can I do for you?'

Muntz pursed his lips, considering how best to approach the irascible American.

'You must be aware that your government entered the war for what it could get out of it,' he said. 'Among the benefits of victory will be access to vital information. In particular, you are concerned to acquire the best German brains for America. The last thing you want is for our rocket scientists to end up in Russia or Britain. Am I correct?'

Newman nodded. 'Sure you are, but as far as I know that doesn't include SS colonels or hospital administrators.'

'Of course not,' Muntz said affably. 'Although you should know that my good friend Professor Blintz will take a senior position in the ministry of health in the post-war German government.'

'Congratulations,' Newman said sourly to Blintz, who nodded blandly.

'The point is this,' Muntz continued. 'My family has owned the Falkenschloss estate for generations. It was the pre-war head-quarters of the Freyer Institute, founded by my father. The institute's origins and purpose are charitable and educational, and in the past three years it has been the home of an exciting project. Our work has generated an immense amount of valuable information about the human response to stress.'

Newman looked at him blankly. 'So what?'

'Such information as we have gathered would be of little use in America, and there are those of us who believe your government would not object if Germany retained information of a non-military nature to help build up its own peacetime industries. In fact, some of your Congress people actively wish to encourage such a development. In this particular case, we are talking about pharmaceuticals, the industry in which you yourself worked before you accepted your commission in the Army.'

'Let me get this right,' Newman said. 'You made contact with Captain Wise and his security goons at SHAEF because you have information here that you need to make drugs, and he dragged me behind German lines because I used to work for a drug company?'

Muntz smiled. 'Precisely, Colonel. Needless to say, if you are able to find a solution to our problem, my colleagues and I would ensure that any expansion of our company into the USA would be undertaken directly through you, or through whichever company you cared to nominate.'

'So what's your problem?' Newman asked bluntly. 'Why don't you just take your information and set up shop when the shooting stops?'

'Transport,' Muntz explained. 'Or rather the lack of it. Our depository in Falkenschloss contains over two hundred and twenty tons of equipment, documents and associated materials, and our trucks have been requisitioned by front-line combat divisions. Inevitably the Allies will take possession of everything we have here. If we can work with you to ensure that the material can be returned to our organization at an early date, everyone can benefit. Otherwise I will order it to be destroyed.'

Newman thought quickly. As success piled on success for the Allies in their race to Berlin, many of the retreating German authorities were leaving behind mountains of documents, and a major exercise was being mounted by the Allied Command to collect everything they could lay their hands on. Muntz was clearly reluctant to destroy something that was of value to him and his professor friend. He wanted Newman to hijack his material from Allied possession and to accept an inducement in return for this service. In principle Newman had no objections, especially as the presence of Captain Wise implied government approval. If he did agree to help this smooth-talking bastard of an SS colonel, it would boil down to a simple matter of logistics. What did he have to lose? And Muntz was right about one thing. The US government was worried that a weakened German economy would allow the Commies to gain a secure foothold in western Europe. But there was a point that bothered him.

'This information. It's medical research, isn't it?'

Muntz pursed his lips. 'Not within our exact understanding of the term, no.'

'What the hell does that mean?'

'I take it you are concerned about, shall we say, the proprietary nature of our work here.'

'All I know is, we keep hearing reports of Waffen-SS medical experiments being conducted on prisoners. I want no part in anything like that.'

4

Muntz's mouth tightened. 'I can assure you that nothing so barbaric has taken place at Falkenschloss. The work was of a highly classified military nature involving a cadre of highly qualified young student officers who were subjected to the most rigorous of training methods. You will find nothing in our records to indicate otherwise. Rest assured, Colonel, no one will emerge from the shadows to point an accusing finger at anyone who has had the privilege of being part of this establishment.'

Newman felt sure about one thing. Muntz was not the kind of man to leave any tracks behind. If he was preparing to build a business on the work he had carried out, everything would be squeaky clean. But it still didn't make sense. Why should Uncle Sam be so generous with this kind of information if it had any value? Why let the Germans keep it?

'No,' he said. 'I want no part in it.'

The other three men stared around the table at each other. Blintz sighed and walked to a window, deep in thought. Muntz raised his eyebrows at the captain, who turned to Newman.

'OK, Colonel. What's the problem?'

'It's a load of chicken shit, Captain. On one hand you tell me that we're in this war for what we can get out of it, on the other you're telling me that we're prepared to let these Krauts walk away with valuable information. I don't rate that as a realistic scenario.'

'You better tell him, Ernst,' Blintz said in English.

'Tell me what?' Newman demanded.

'What do you know about Unit 731?' Muntz asked him.

'Hey,' Wise interrupted. 'He's not cleared for this.'

'I think it's fair to say that clearance procedures are of no relevance here, Captain,' Muntz said. 'If we want Colonel Newman to make the correct decision he is entitled to know exactly what the situation is, am I not correct, Colonel?'

'Damn right, you are.'

'What you must understand,' Blintz said in his strained English, 'is that everything we have done here has been in accordance with the strictest of medical and humanitarian procedures. Great care has been taken of our patients, at all times. So much so that certain results have been called into question by those of your people who are responsible for assessing the value of what we have done. This is, of course, nonsense, but it suits our purpose.'

'What's he getting at?' Newman asked Wise.

The captain shuffled uncomfortably. 'All you need to know is that there's a damn good reason for this to happen, and we need you to make it happen.'

'Come now,' Muntz said suddenly. 'We have answered your question, but there is something else. Would you kindly look out of the window.'

Newman joined him at the casement and looked out to the extensive terrace. He saw a table at which three people were drinking wine. Two of them wore Russian uniforms. The third was a startlingly beautiful blonde woman.

'My sister,' Muntz said proudly.

'If we don't deal, the Russkies will, Fred,' Wise told him. 'You want that?'

Newman didn't know whom he hated more, the Nazis or the Communists, but at least the Nazis appreciated the capitalist system. 'Hell no,' he said. 'You can count me in.'

As soon as he said it, the atmosphere in the room relaxed. Muntz pressed a bell, and a young SS officer came in and stood to attention while Muntz murmured something in his ear.

The officer snapped his heels. '*Jawohl, Herr Standartenführer,*' he said, and left the room.

Muntz carried on looking out of the window. Blintz joined him, and so did Wise. The young officer appeared on the terrace and said something to the woman. She smiled and stood up. The Russians did too, but she waved them to sit down again, and two servants who had been waiting to one side came forward and refilled the Russians' glasses, which they lifted to toast the woman. Without a pause in their movements, the servants pulled machine pistols from their jackets and emptied the magazines into the Russians' backs.

Newman swallowed hard. The message was not difficult to interpret. It certainly looked like he'd made the right decision. Half of him felt mad as hell about it, but he knew that people throughout the US military machine were busy oiling the wheels to make sure that they won the peace as well as the war.

'How will my people identify your property?' he asked.

'There will be no difficulty,' Muntz said. 'Everything to do with the project is clearly stamped with the codeword *Turmfalke*. That's Kestrel, in English,' he added.

Newman juggled all this information around, trying to assess the implications, the risk. 'I don't know,' he said. 'You say I'll be your route into the States if this drug company of yours is successful. What if it ain't?'

Professor Blintz looked at him shrewdly. 'The company cannot fail, Colonel Newman. Even without the information in Falkenschloss, we have the backing of all the necessary authorities. With the information, we will be five years ahead of our competition. Have you any idea what that is worth in financial terms?'

Muntz pulled a thick envelope from his pocket and put it on the table. Newman looked at it, but before he could say anything, Captain Wise said, 'We could do this the hard way, Fred. You know, put in requisitions, legal stuff, but it would take years. These guys'll be out of here in hours. Everything they want is crated and marked. All you have to do is keep your eye on it and channel it through when I tell you.'

'OK,' Newman said slowly. 'OK. But what guarantees do I have?'

'Best one of all,' Wise said solemnly. 'We can all drop each other in the shit, anytime.'

Newman reached out and opened the envelope. Its contents made him catch his breath.

'Operational expenses,' Wise told him. 'Pay yourself a salary and use the rest to smooth things along.'

Newman stared at the money, then slipped it into his pocket.

'I guess we're in business, gentlemen.'

As they turned down the drive leading back to the public road the colonel shook his head. 'You son of a bitch. Did you know about those Russkies?'

'I had every faith in your judgement,' Wise said impassively.

'Goddamn,' Newman muttered. 'I don't believe I'm doing this.'

'Think of it as your personal contribution to the future of America,' Wise said. 'Unless the Germans establish a healthy industrial base, the Commies will be all over Europe, next stop Washington.'

'Bullshit,' Newman said.

'Maybe, maybe not,' Wise said equitably. 'So think of it as the best chance you'll ever get to be rich.'

'Oh yeah? What's to stop me throwing this dough over the side, arresting you and making myself famous instead?'

Wise chuckled. 'Greed, Fred. Plus another thing.'

'What's that?'

'We took a photo of you grabbing that envelope. Wouldn't look too good in the Advocate General's office, now would it?'

'Goddamn,' Newman muttered again. 'Anyway, I still don't trust that Blintz guy. All that crap about the quality of their results. What does that mean?'

'What he means is that their patients were given medication during the course of some of the experiments. This might have interfered with certain analytical procedures.'

Newman looked blank. 'So what?'

'This is strictly for your ears only, but we don't have the same problem with Unit 731,' Wise said. 'They didn't bother with the medical niceties, so none of their results are affected by anaesthetics or any of that stuff. It's all going Stateside. Which is why we let Colonel Muntz and his colleagues hang onto their stuff to use in the German domestic market. Both sides win, Fred.'

'What the hell is Unit 731?'

'I'm not authorized to pass you that information. Plus, I didn't want to make an issue out of it in front of our German friends. But I can tell you it's a Japanese army medical unit. Our guys believe their research data is better quality than the Krauts'. When they operate on patients, they don't use anaesthetics or antiseptics, so all the body organs are in a natural state. That's the stuff our guys want back in the States.'

'Nice people,' Newman muttered ambiguously.

Wise slowed the Jeep to let a horse and rider cross the drive in front of them. It was Muntz's sister, dressed in a severely cut jacket, her blonde hair tied into a tight bun under her riding hat. The captain waved and received a smile in return. Cool blue eyes appraised Newman, and then she spurred the horse into the forest. Newman could not stop himself turning to watch as she vanished among the pines.

'That is something else!'

'Her name's Irena,' Wise said. 'She's Muntz's twin. He thinks a great deal of her.'

'You seem to know a hell of a lot around here.'

'We're second cousins, on my mother's side,' Wise told him. 'Welcome to the family, Fred.'

CHAPTER ONE

I

As David backed the car into a parking space, Kate's mother Pamela opened the front door and stood waiting for them. He prepared himself for another Sunday afternoon of reproachful glances and pointed questions about starting a family. Leaving things a bit late. Problems of a mature woman's pregnancy. Testing for Down's syndrome. Unfair to the children to have such old parents (meaning an old father) . . .

Pamela disapproved of David Lewis, and he had every sympathy with her. He didn't stack up too well as a son-in-law for a number of reasons. She had sacrificed everything for a single child, paying money she could ill afford for ballet and modelling lessons, convinced that her daughter could pirouette Fonteyn off the stage and strut Cindy Crawford off the catwalk. And Kate had certainly been making her mark in fashion and advertising as a model, until she met David on the pavement outside Morton's club in Berkeley Square. Due to a misunderstanding they both tried to get into the same taxi, and when David realized his mistake and stepped back he dropped his briefcase on her foot. The briefcase contained a laptop computer, two spare rechargeable batteries and several files of work-in-progress from the engineering company he worked for. It broke three bones in her foot and took her out of the fashion circuit for ten weeks.

He went to see her almost every day. After an initial politeness, she told him not to bother, but he kept turning up with flowers and chocolates. She became so exasperated that she made enquiries about getting a court injunction to keep him away. But his persistence, his dry sense of humour and, above all, the fact that he never made a pass, began to fascinate her. When she asked him about his job he explained he worked for a firm of consulting mechanical engineers called Halkyn and Partners, and when she asked what the hell that was he explained about machine tools and injection-moulding processes.

'Take these carbon-fibre tennis rackets,' he said enthusiastically. 'They had to make them hollow, or they'd be far too heavy to use. So how d'you think they did that? Wax core, that's how. They form the racket over the wax, then they melt it out. The trick is to heat the carbon-fibre resins without damaging the moulding. It's the same process you use to make baked Alaska sponge with ice-cream . . .'

His business card had PhD after his name. She asked what it was for, and he told her he had a mechanical engineering doctorate from Cambridge University. This entitled him to be called Doctor Lewis, but few people knew this, and he didn't bother to tell them.

'What's the point,' he grinned. 'As soon as they hear "doctor", people assume you can set a broken leg or cure a fainting fit. The only way you'd get me into a real doctor's surgery is in a straitjacket. The last thing I need is to be mistaken for one, so "Mister" Lewis is fine by me.'

He was curious about everything, from the workings of a camera lens to the rampages of soldier ants in South America. He amazed her with his breadth of knowledge and his constant curiosity. For the first time in her life she felt that someone was interested in her, as a person and not as a performing clothes horse. Genuinely interested. And so a friendship took root and blossomed. Her friends were surprised and then astounded. In a world where beauty was everything, many of her colleagues took it as a personal insult that she could take up with a man who did not embody masculine perfection. Things reached crisis point at a photo session.

'Christ, darling,' one of the other models exclaimed, 'he's three inches shorter than you, and he's twenty years older. Plus he's . . . well, all right, he's ugly, I mean, that grey streak of hair . . . and he's Jewish, isn't he? I mean . . .'

Kate finished the photo session, then phoned Margaret Burnside, her agent, and took herself off the agency books. That done, she drove to David's house in Ealing, waited in her car until he arrived home, and tried to seduce him. Even this didn't work out as she thought it would. His shyness to her overtures became a reluctance and developed into a firm resistance. When she realized that he was a virgin, she fell in love with him. They married in a registry office two weeks later. And although she had never discussed with David her mother's clear resentment of their relationship, she too mentally squirmed during their Sunday duty calls at the motherly hints and comments.

'I hope you're trying for a baby, now that Kate's given up her career,' was an early shot across David's bows.

Or, to Kate, news of an old schoolfriend: 'I see Patricia Jordan's had another boy.'

And here she was again, hugging her daughter possessively and giving David fleeting access to a reluctant cheek.

'How nice to see you both. It seems such a long time.'

'It was two weeks ago, mother,' Kate said. 'We couldn't come last week because David had to go to Birmingham for a weekend course, and I –'

'It seems to me that David should have finished with all these courses by now. I mean, he's very highly qualified already, isn't he? And why couldn't you have come over on your own?'

'David wasn't on the course, mother, he was giving it, and he needed the car.'

'Well, you're here now, and that's all that matters. I'll put the kettle on.'

David wandered into the living room while Kate followed her mother into the kitchen. Pamela was not much older than him, and he appreciated how difficult their marriage was for her. She tried, of course, and from time to time he thought she might be learning to deal with it, to accept him, maybe even to like him a little. After all, they had something in common. They both loved Kate.

He stood staring at the photographs of Kate's father, Alex. A head-and-shoulders portrait in his Army captain's uniform. Wedding groups outside the church. The mother and child. The family at the seaside. Alex looked nice, and Pamela's expressions were softer then, he thought. And yes, he and Kate had been trying for a baby, thank you, Pamela, and they'd had all the check-ups. But the Great Conceptualizer in the sky was keeping things pretty quiet on that front, and he had to confess that their bedroom activity had slowed down, too. Pressure of work, you know . . .

His mobile phone pinged an interruption from his overcoat pocket in the hall.

'That's your phone, isn't it?' Kate called.

'Sorry. Should have left it at home.'

It was Peter Halkyn, founder of the engineering consultancy.

'David, glad I caught you. Can we talk?'

'Hello, Peter. No problem.'

'Well, I've got some good news and some bad news. The bad news is, we've promoted Stephen to full partnership.'

Halkyn liked a joke. Everyone thought David would get the promotion. Stephen Carrickworth was a good choice, though. He'd done excellent work in Europe.

'Thanks for breaking it to me so gently,' David said drily. 'Can't wait for the good news.'

'We've merged with Anstat Konsult in Frankfurt,' Halkyn told him. 'Keep it under your hat, though. We're making the announcement tomorrow afternoon. For the time being we'll each trade under the existing names but do a bit of technology transfer on a quid pro quo basis.'

David knew the company, one of Germany's most prestigious engineering design firms. Quite a coup. But who got what out of the deal?

'We want you to take over for us in Europe,' Halkyn said. 'For one thing, we already have Sacht Engineering in Frankfurt, and Anstat has a new project for a major pharmaceutical company in Munich. Just up your street.'

David stood, absorbing this.

'Hello, David. Are you still there?'

'Yes.'

'I've no need to tell you what a wonderful opportunity this is,' Halkyn said enthusiastically. 'Deutsche Arzneiwissenschaft Werke is so blue chip it makes SmithKline Beecham look like a bunch of hippies. Their chairman is one of the most eminent businessmen in Europe, one of the old school. Built the business up from scratch after the war. I've asked Carla to messenger full details across to you.'

David interrupted him. 'Peter, I made it quite clear when I joined you that travel overseas wasn't part of my career plan. We agreed –'

'I know what we agreed, old son, but Europe isn't exactly overseas, for God's sake.'

14

'As far as I'm concerned it is. I'll stay on this side of the water, if you don't mind.'

There was a pause. 'It's not a question of minding, David. Let's put it this way. You're the best man for the job, but you're not the only man.'

'So choose someone else.'

'We have to shed bodies. Our man in Europe will also be responsible for UK projects. Why don't you sleep on this? I want you at the partner meeting at eight sharp tomorrow. We'll meet in my office at seven thirty.'

'There's no point . . .' David said, but Halkyn had disconnected.

'Who was that?' Kate asked as she and her mother carried in the trays of afternoon tea.

'Peter Halkyn,' he told her. 'Nothing urgent.'

Kate gave him a thoughtful look, but knew that David would get round to telling her about the call eventually.

'Those damn things,' Pamela said, glaring at the mobile phone. 'Never give you a moment's peace. There was a man using one in the library the other day. Gave him a piece of my mind, I can tell you. I'd be exceedingly grateful if you would leave it at home next Sunday, David. I see little enough of my daughter as it is, without you and your business friends spoiling everything.'

'Sorry, Pamela,' he said contritely.

'Have some of mother's lemon curd, darling,' Kate suggested.

'I'll give it a miss, if you don't mind.'

'Mind? Why should I mind?' Pamela said. 'It's not as if I've gone to any trouble.'

It wasn't the worst afternoon they'd spent with Kate's mother, but it was close. David was unusually pre-occupied and ignored almost everything that Pamela had to say. It obviously had something to do with the phone call, but when Kate asked what Halkyn had wanted, he wouldn't discuss it. When they arrived home, he found a motorcycle courier waiting with the packet from Peter Halkyn. David said he had work to do and vanished into his office. Twice Kate tapped on the door during the evening and asked him if he wanted something to eat, but he refused, with increasing irritability. The third time, she opened the door anyway.

'For Heaven's sake, what's wrong?' she asked.

'It's bloody nothing, all right?' he snapped. 'Something I can sort out in the morning, if you'll just give me some peace and quiet.'

He had never spoken to her like that, and it hurt.

The packet contained a confidential briefing document about the merger of Halkyn and Partners and Anstat Konsult, together with a list of potential joint ventures. Anstat's Deutsche Arzneiwissenschaft Werke project was top of the list. A summary outlined a range of improvements that DAW wanted to make in various fabrication processes, including plastic moulding, David's speciality. DAW's corporate brochure explained that the company prided itself on its ethical standards and on the consistently high quality of its pharmaceuticals. It claimed a product range having fewer side effects than any of its competitors. The chairman's mission statement expounded the philosophy that man was a decision-making creature and that all human and commercial endeavour should be directed to enhancing this attribute. Stress was a major factor in inhibiting decision-making, and DAW's products were directed at the problem. Care of the customer came before any other corporate or operational consideration. Everything was subservient to and supportive of this statement, including the activities of DAW's 'trading partners', meaning its suppliers. The overriding message was that DAW was wealthy, focused, successful, tough, demanding and scrupulously fair.

II

Peter Halkyn was waiting in his office when David arrived. He closed the door and poured them both a tea.

'A word to the wise, old son. I won't mention yesterday's conversation to the others. We're looking for total commitment on this. As far as I'm concerned, this is exactly the right job for you, and you've got to go for it. You might as well know that your name came up for the Nigerian project last year, not to mention Oman, and I blocked them both because of your aversion to foreign parts. But Europe, for Christ's sake! It's like working in your own bloody back yard. If you turn this down, I won't be able to protect you.'

Halkyn opened the boardroom door, and they went in. David nodded to Stephen Carrickworth, who smiled back. Halkyn took the chair, then looked towards his deputy, George Morrisey.

'As everyone here knows, David was my appointee to the firm,' Halkyn said to his fellow board members, 'so once I've run through the preliminaries, I'd be grateful if George chaired this meeting.'

There were murmurs of approval from the dozen partners.

'I have asked David to be at the meeting because his expertise is crucial to the way forward for our company in Europe. As you know, he has project managed the technical developments we've been working on for Sacht Engineering and other clients in Germany from the UK. I am sure we're all hoping that he will consider the benefits of a closer physical link with our European clients, old and new. Later today we will be greeting Anstat's senior partner, Herr Mullner, and his colleague Herr Kloss, who is Stephen's counterpart. I'd like to think that we can meet them with all the elements in place for a successful future. The one remaining piece of the jigsaw involves David's future role, and I'd now like George to take over and formally interview David for the position of the company's European representative.'

Morrisey had a reputation for going straight for the jugular.

'Frankly, David,' he said, 'I'm not sure about your capability for this work. For one thing, you haven't got any overseas experience. How would you set about convincing me that you're the right man for the job?'

'You already know I'm the right man, George,' David said. 'What you really want to know is, am I interested?'

Morrisey's lips turned slightly up at the corners, which was the nearest he came to smiling. 'Have a shot, anyway,' he said.

David felt Peter Halkyn's eyes burrowing into him. It was clear from the type of work involved in any joint venture that his acceptance of the job was crucial. Halkyn was right. If he didn't take the position, he was out.

'A key problem throughout the European plastics moulding industry is the increasing competition from the Far East,' he said. 'One way of countering this without high capital expenditure in the short term is to set up machine lines with new plasticizers operating at higher throughputs. One of my fields is high-pressure injection of high-density polymers. The key lies in precise control of temperature, and that, in turn, depends on controlling the spinner environment. You also have to deal with complex low-energy ultrasonics that can adversely affect product density. I cracked that problem at Cambridge. I can get new lines up and running in such circumstances three months earlier than anyone else here, and that means the partnership makes twice the target profit. I'd like to think there's a bonus element in there for me.'

'I see you've given the matter some thought,' Morrisey said.

'I've also taken note of Stephen's report about marketing in Europe,' David continued. 'I'd like to develop his ideas on attending more professional functions. What's more, many key German and Italian firms have committed themselves to eastern Germany's development problems. That leaves gaps in their home markets that we can exploit.'

After some more questions, Morrisey said, 'OK, David. Give us a few moments to talk things over.'

When they called him back into the boardroom, there were smiles all round. George Morrisey shook him warmly by the hand, and Peter Halkyn pushed a sheet of paper across the table.

'It's the basis for your new contract. I hope we can reach a fast agreement on this. In fact, I'd like your approval before our guests arrive.'

David scanned it. The first paragraph offered him a junior partnership with the firm, provided he accepted the remaining terms, all of which were geared to accepting full responsibility for company business in Europe. There was a large salary increase, stock options and various improvements in pension rights, car and health care. It was the kind of opportunity that did not come round a second time.

'There's only one thing wrong with this,' he said. 'If I'm to take over European activities, what's Stephen going to do?'

Carrickworth grinned. 'Pacific Rim, old chap. I'll have plenty to do there, don't worry.'

'Where do I sign?' David asked wryly.

Halkyn leaned round the door of David's office and beamed widely. 'Congratulations. But why the about-face from yesterday? You seem positively eager to take it on.'

David shrugged. '*Ich bin ein Europäer*,' he said.

'Don't tell me you actually speak another language,' Halkyn said. 'You're full of surprises today. All good ones, I'm happy to say.'

'My parents were originally from Germany,' David said. 'I picked it up when I was a kid.'

'I'm sure it'll stand you in good stead,' Halkyn said. 'They'll appreciate a Brit who can talk their lingo.'

'There's one thing,' David said. 'This bloke Helmut Kloss. My counterpart in Anstat.'

'Very capable chap, according to Stephen.'

'I'm sure he is, but I've read Stephen's reports, and Kloss crops up everywhere with irrelevant objections. I don't want him cramping my style. When I work on a project, I do it my way. Every time I've spoken to him on the phone he refers back to his senior partner. If I'm any judge, he'll want everything in triplicate before I even talk to the client.'

'I'm sure there'll be no problem,' Halkyn said. 'In fact, we made you a junior partner so that you'd have the necessary clout to get your points across with these people. But we all have to keep a grip on our egos in a new situation.'

'It's nothing to do with ego, and you know it, Peter,' David said. 'It's all to do with getting the job done within European standards, within budget and within my lifetime. I can spot a panic merchant when I see one, and I want him off my back.'

'Fair do's, old son,' Halkyn said amiably. 'So long as you deliver the technical goodies you'll have total support. Now why don't you let that lovely wife of yours have the good news.'

Halkyn shook his hand and left his office. David picked up the phone. His home number was engaged for several minutes.

'Hi,' he said when he finally got through. 'The line's been busy.'

'Margaret called me for a chat,' Kate told him.

'How is she?'

'Fine.'

'Great,' he said. There was a pause. 'Look, I'm sorry for being such a bastard, but everything's sorted now.'

'I don't want us to argue. I can't stand it.'

'Me neither. I'm really sorry. It's just that there's been a merger with a German firm. Peter offered me a job looking after Europe, and you know what I feel about overseas work.'

It had been one of the mysteries in her life with David. How could a man with such a brain and so many wide-ranging interests block out all idea of travel? She'd lost count of the number of times she'd tried to persuade him to take a couple of weeks in Portugal, or a trip to Mauritius or a weekend in Paris or Amsterdam. She had friends they could stay with almost everywhere, but he wouldn't budge. In the end they agreed that if she really wanted to go to such places she could, and he'd take some time in Cornwall or Scotland. It worked reasonably well, but she always missed his company.

'I wish you'd told me,' she said. No wonder David had been so upset. 'I suppose you indicated where to stick it, as usual.'

'Not this time. I'm taking it on.'

'You're kidding me!'

'Let's just say they wrote me a contract I couldn't refuse. Another ten grand, plus Stephen Carrickworth's Carlton. He gets a Jag, but I also get cunning bonus deals. So apart from me apologizing for being such a sore-head, we've got some celebrating to do. How about tonight? You, me and a couple of bottles of fizzy stuff.'

'Ah,' she said. 'Bit short notice.'

He remembered the engaged tone. She'd arranged something with Margaret. 'No problem. We can carouse tomorrow, or whenever.'

'No,' she said. 'I'll put Margaret off.'

'Rubbish. You've missed seeing your old chums. I've been monopolizing you lately.'

'It's all right. Honestly.'

'Why don't we compromise? Ask her to join us. What's her bloke called? The photographer. Cockney chap. We'll make up a foursome.'

'Ted,' she told him.

III

They booked in at the Brasserie in Wandsworth. David liked Kate's friends and thought it was a pity they didn't see more of each other. Margaret Burnside had been her agent since she began in the business, and Ted had taken award-winning photographs of her for *Paris Match*. The three of them began talking about the good old days, with a succession of amusing anecdotes. As they finished the main course, Margaret broached the subject of Kate's modelling career and how one of her agency contacts had a new client with a project that was simply screaming for someone with Kate's looks, and would she consider coming out of retirement? At that point they both looked at David, and he realized that the dinner was something of a set-up.

'I think it would be a great idea,' he told Margaret. 'It's likely I'll be spending more time away from home, so I won't be needing so much of Kate's slippers-and-pipe routine. Be something useful for her to do, for a change, instead of looking after an unappreciative husband.'

'Are you sure you wouldn't mind, darling?' Kate asked.

'Absolutely not.'

Margaret and Ted began arranging for Kate to visit Ted's studio to bring her portfolio up to date, while David sipped his wine. The waitress came to take their order for sweets, followed by a youth dressed in Lederhosen and a Tyrolean hat who was wheeling a trolley.

'G'day folks. The name's Brian from Wines of Germany, and we're doing this wine promo, so I'd like to invite you all to take a sample with our compliments,' he said in an Australian accent. 'They go down remarkably well with puddings, or so I'm told. Still, what have you got to lose, hey?'

'Sure, why not,' Ted said.

'Great,' Brian said, uncorking a bottle and pouring out four glasses.

'Not for me, thanks,' David told him.

'Aw, come on, mate. You'll enjoy it.'

'No thank you,' David repeated.

'I've got to get rid of this lot tonight, sport, or I don't get my commission.'

'Quite frankly, I don't give a tuppenny fuck about your commission, sport.' David's voice had risen, and several people looked over to see what was happening.

'Leave it out, David,' Ted muttered. 'The bloke's only doing his job.'

'Oh really. You call poncing about in that ridiculous get-up doing a job, do you?'

Kate wanted to tell David to shut up, but she was rendered speechless. He had never reacted like this to anything before.

'I'm sorry,' Margaret said to the young man. 'Perhaps we've all had a bit too much to drink.'

'Fair enough, but there's no need for him to take it out on me,' he said reasonably.

'Just get the fuck away from me, will you?' David said in a low voice.

The manageress came to the table and quietly motioned the young man to leave.

'What seems to be the problem?'

'Problem! I'll tell you what seems to be the problem.' David was having trouble controlling himself. 'I'm having an enjoyable meal with my wife and my friends, and this schmuck comes prancing round dressed like a bloody Nazi and waving bottles of bloody German wine in our faces.'

Kate's face was white with a mixture of anger and astonishment. 'Will you bring us the bill, please,' she said in a whisper.

David stared at her, a blank look on his face. 'Yes, let's pay up by all means.'

He got to his feet and stumbled. Ted put his arm round him.

'Come on, mate, let's get you home.'

They left the restaurant in one of those appalled silences that happen when people witness a total breakdown of normal behaviour.

Kate drove David's car. Ted and Margaret followed them home and helped her put him to bed. She made coffee and they sat staring at her.

'Shit,' Ted said. 'What brought that on?'

'I've no idea,' Kate said tiredly. 'He hates going abroad, and I think this new European job is worrying him.'

'So, why did he take it?'

'I rather think it was Europe or bust,' Kate told him.

'All the more reason for you to get back into the business, love,' Margaret said brightly. 'If he's going to be gallivanting across the Continent, you'll be bored out of your skull. Tell her some more about the new account, Teddy.'

'Right,' he said. 'You won't be able to resist it. There's this men's fashion outfitters. Can't mention the name, yet. They're planning to open up a woman's section in all their shops, aren't they! What they're looking for is the right kind of woman to get the image across. Sexy. Sophisticated. Not too young . . .'

'Thanks a lot, Ted,' Kate forced a laugh.

'One day, he'll learn how to be diplomatic, won't you, lover,' Margaret said.

'. . . but not too old,' Ted continued with a grin. 'Just right, in other words.'

'I've sold the agency an interview,' Margaret said. 'Ted'll set up a screen test. Nothing to lose, plus the money's fabulous.'

'Why not,' Kate said.

The scream from upstairs was ear-splitting.

'Papa! Papa!'

'Jesus! What was that?' Ted asked.

Kate stood up quickly. 'Oh God. It's David. He must be dreaming. I'll go and see if he's all right.'

'That's a really freaky guy she's married to,' Ted said when Kate had left the room. 'Quite a wobbly he threw on us.'

Margaret nodded. 'It's certainly been a night to remember. I like him, myself. Very clever. Intellectual. Probably a bit highly strung. He was very kind to Kate when she hurt her foot. Flowers. Visited her in hospital. I like that, in a man.'

'Considering he broke her bloody foot in the first place, I should think he was kind. Only why she had to go and marry him beats me. I mean, he's not exactly the most photogenic son-of-a-bitch, is he?'

'Looks aren't everything a girl wants in a man,' Margaret said pointedly.

'Me?' he said. 'I'm a dead ringer for Tom Cruise. Everybody says so.'

'Name one,' Margaret said acidly. She looked towards the ceiling. 'I wonder if they're all right up there.'

'Probably got the DTs, I shouldn't wonder.'

Margaret went to the door and listened. 'I'm going up.'

'Leave well alone, my girl,' Ted said. 'You might find yourself stumbling into a kinky nocturnal romp.'

'You're disgusting,' she told him.

She tapped on the bedroom door and pushed it open to see Kate cradling a limp David in her arms.

'Are you OK, love?'

Kate nodded. 'I think so. He must have had some sort of bad dream.'

'You look absolutely shattered,' Margaret said.

'Last couple of days have been a bit of a worry, to tell the truth. He'd been working all the hours God sends, and then some.'

'If I were you, I'd take him to see a shrink.'

'Don't be silly. He'll be all right.'

Margaret shrugged. 'If you call screaming in your sleep and going completely off your bloody rocker all right, I suppose he is. On the other hand there's a bloke in Harley Street I see when I'm at my wits' end called Reed. Dry old sod, but he seems to be able to sort me out. You'll need to get your GP to refer you to him.'

'He'll be all right,' Kate said.

Later that night, Kate woke from a disturbed sleep and lay blinking. As her eyes grew accustomed to the darkness, she wondered what had wakened her. Then she realized that David was sitting upright, and the sheets had been pulled away from her.

'Is anything the matter, darling?' she asked sleepily. When he didn't answer she leaned across and put her arm round him. His body was hot and rigid. 'David, are you all right?' When he still didn't answer, she reached for the bedside lamp. 'David! What on earth's wrong?'

He was staring straight ahead at the wall, his breath rasping and shallow. The expression on his face horrified her, and she pulled at his arms.

'David? For God's sake say something.'

His eyes started moving wildly, and he began a high-pitched moaning. He was clearly in the grip of some kind of nightmare, and Kate tried to calm him by holding him protectively, pressing her breasts against his back and whispering frantically in his ear, but nothing had any effect. Sweat was soaking his pyjamas, and his breath was short and rasping. He started shuddering, then half a minute later he gave a sudden shrill cry. The sound of a child in fear. That's what it was like. A terrified child.

24

'Papa! Papa!' He slumped in her arms, and when she let him go he rolled back onto the bed and lay unnaturally stiff, his skin clammy and waxlike. She leaned over him, but she could feel no breath. Desperately she tried to remember which side of the wrist his pulse would be, but there was no response there, either. Panic set in, and she tried to blow into his mouth, then banged his chest. He still didn't respond, so she struggled to calm herself, went to the phone and dialled 999, but before the emergency operator could reply, David made a small whimpering noise. She slammed the phone down and took hold of him again, willing him through his nightmare. He remained still for a long time, then pulled sharply away.

'Christ, darling. I can't breathe.'

'Sorry, David.' She loosened her grip, relief flooding in. 'You were dreaming.'

He sighed and moved a little further from her. 'Oh come on, Kate.'

'You were. Can't you feel how wet you are? Your pyjamas are soaking.'

'No wonder, with you hanging on to me like that. Are you sure it wasn't you doing the dreaming?'

It happened the next night and the night after that. Kate listened to the rasping breath and the shrill, piping cry. When she tried to wake him during the nightmares she found it impossible. The worst thing was not being able to talk about it. David insisted it wasn't happening, that she was imagining things in her own dreams. The sequence of events lasted about half an hour, from the time he sat bolt upright, through the trance-like period, to the awakening. On the Thursday night she sat at the dressing table until he fell asleep, than waited for the nightmare to begin and run its course. When he came out of the trance and returned to normal sleep she shook his shoulder.

'Are you awake?'

David sighed and blinked sleepily. 'Not so you'd notice.'

'Margaret says we ought to see a doctor.'

'Doctor? What about?'

'These nightmares.'

25

'Not again,' he complained. 'Anyway, how come you're discussing our personal affairs with your agent?'

'You know very well Margaret's not just my agent. She's one of my best friends. I have to talk to someone. You're leaving at seven and getting back from that damned office of yours after ten, then we go to bed like two bloody strangers, and we're not getting any sleep. It can't go on like this.'

David groaned. 'I'm sorry you're upset, but do we have to go through it now? I've got a hell of a schedule tomorrow.'

'And I've got a hell of a schedule getting ready to meet someone who might think that a thirty-five-year-old hausfrau who's had no sleep for several days is good enough for an advertising job, only by the time I get to see them I'll be looking like a zombie because you and your bloody dreams are keeping me awake all night.' She only half regretted the outburst.

David got out of bed and reached for his dressing gown.

'What are you doing?' she asked as he opened the wardrobe cupboard and took out a bundle of blankets.

'I'm keeping you awake, and you're keeping me awake, so we'll both be better off if I'm in another room.'

She followed him to the door and held his arm. 'Hey, this is no way for two married people to carry on. I don't want you to sleep in another room. I want you to sleep with me.'

He stood stiffly while she pulled gently at the back of his neck. 'You've got a funny way of showing it,' he said. 'These days neither of us seems to be getting much sleep, or much of anything else, come to think of it.'

'Well, you know how it is. Either I'm too shattered, or you're as limp as over-boiled spaghetti.'

'I love your way with words.'

'Word power is one of my obsessions.' She tugged the blankets from his arm and dropped them on the floor. 'Want to find out what the other one is?'

'For Christ's sake, it's three o'clock in the morning, and I'm serious about tomorrow. I'm meeting some of the chaps from our new German tie-up. They may well ask me to grab my passport and go back with them.'

'That's just the point. No self-respecting hausfrau would let her husband go to Germany without some kind of preparation. What do they call that street – the Reeperbahn? My motives are purely selfish, so you won't have any energy left when you get there.' She untied his dressing gown. 'You know, you have a lovely body.'

'Their offices are in Frankfurt, not Hamburg,' he said. 'Anyway, don't patronize me. I'm five foot bloody five, for God's sake.'

She put on her husky playtime voice. 'It's quite magnificent.'

Half resignedly, he let her guide him back to bed. 'You mean, apart from the fact that you have to wear flat shoes so you don't tower over me, not to mention my candidature for the Grecian 2000 School of Hair Recovery?'

'I like your grey streak. It turns me on.'

'Yes, but grey streaks should be round the ears, not sprouting out of the middle of the forehead.'

'You're far too sensitive. I've told you that before.' She pressed him onto his stomach and began kneading the muscles in his shoulders. 'My God, you've got knots in here big enough to tie up the *Queen Elizabeth*.'

'Seriously, I have to get up at six thirty.'

'I was hoping you could make it sooner than that. Say, in about two or three minutes.'

'How could I have married such a vulgar woman!'

'Because she was the best bed partner you ever had in your life. Admit it.'

She rolled him onto his back and moved her mouth slowly down his belly to meet her hands, already cunningly at work. Helplessly, David watched her dark head as it nuzzled him. What she said was logically true. She was the best partner he'd had, but she was also the only one he'd had. Lots of fumblings, but he never quite made it. She'd been very open about her own sex life, relationships with photographers, account executives, advertising managers. She didn't want anyone from the past springing surprises on them, she'd said. He still didn't understand why she'd given up life in the fast lane to marry him.

He was under her control now, waiting for the sinuous, heavy-breasted body to snake upwards, for her mouth to fasten wetly over his while her legs curled forward to ease him inside her.

But she held away. He thought she was teasing until she said, 'I want us to see a doctor, David. I really do.'

'Sweet Christ.' He was verging on hysteria, anger vying with an absurd impulse to giggle. 'You can't do this to me. It's not fair.'

'I'm not a fair person. You know that.' She lowered herself on him and drew back again. 'What about it?'

'This is obscene.'

'Maybe, but it's the best weapon I've got, and I am very, very serious about seeing the doctor.'

'How do you know I won't say yes, then change my mind after I've let you have your evil way with me?'

'Because apart from having such a magnificent body, you are the only truly honourable person I know. So, how about it?'

IV

The parking spaces in Harley Street were full, and so were the spaces between them, with Rolls Royces and Mercedes, chauffeurs lounging against shiny bodywork, bored, waiting for the return of their medically debilitated employers. David drove round several blocks to find a space for the Carlton, muttering bad-temperedly, finally stopping on a yellow line outside a pub in a mews off Devonshire Place.

'We'll probably need a drink afterwards,' he said as they climbed out.

Kate didn't say anything. She was feeling guilty about the way she'd bludgeoned him into this. He was losing a morning's work, and doing so with an extremely bad grace. They walked into Harley Street and up the marble steps to the imposing door and its brass name plate. Over twenty names to scan before seeing 'Mr J.E.P. Reed' halfway down the list. David pressed the ivory bell button, and a small, mousy woman in a white overall let them in.

'Mr and Mrs Lewis to see Mr Reed,' David told her.

She peered at them and checked her notebook. 'Yes, if you'll take the lift to the fifth floor, Mr Lewis.'

The owners of the building had managed to squeeze an elevator into the well of the staircase. He noticed that it was an original mechanism for the old hydraulic mains system installed at the turn of the century, now converted to electricity. Wonderful bit of engineering. Just enough room for three thin people.

When Mr Reed's fifth-floor door opened they were faced with a dour assistant who quickly took the initiative.

'Your appointment is for eleven o'clock, Mr Lewis. You're fifteen minutes early.'

'Sorry.' David smiled tightly at her. 'Perhaps you'd like us to wait on the pavement.'

'We are very limited for space. It would be helpful on future visits if you can keep more closely to the time of your appointment.' She led them to a poky, unprepossessing room where they waited in silence until the consultant's door opened at one minute to eleven o'clock. A short, nervous-looking man came out, and the door closed again. A few seconds later the receptionist said, 'Please go in now, Mr Lewis.' They both stood up, but the woman frowned and shook her head. 'Mr Reed sees his patients separately. Mr Lewis first, please.'

Kate protested. 'We both need to see him. Together. And we're not patients. We've come for advice. Surely our GP explained that to you.'

The dourness tightened into disapproval. 'I'm sorry. It must be one at a time.'

David shrugged and pushed the door open.

'Mr Lewis, do come in.' Mr Reed was a distinguished-looking man in an expensive suit, but his consulting room was not in keeping with his personal appearance. Faded wallpaper and peeling paintwork surrounded a worn Indian carpet. A green metal filing cabinet stood incongruously next to a leather chaise longue in front of his wooden desk. 'Now, let me see. Your general practitioner referred you to me. Marital problems . . .'

'I beg your pardon?' David said stiffly. 'We are here because my wife is worried about our dreaming habits, not our sleeping habits. Her friend comes here. Margaret Burnside.'

'Any problem that jointly affects a husband and wife must, of its nature, be a marital problem.' Mr Reed peered through gold-framed reading glasses at David's letter of referral. 'Now, let us begin at the beginning. I have your name. David Lewis. Your address. London SW18. Married, yes, with how many children?'

'No children.'

'And your wife is Kate, aged thirty-five. And you are fifty-five. A consultant engineer. You play squash. Don't smoke. Don't drink

29

unduly. Good physical health. Now, Mr Lewis, some family background about your parents. Father's name?'

'Jacob.'

'And mother?'

'My mother's name was Edith.'

'Are they still alive?'

'What's that got to do with anything?'

Mr Reed paused and looked at David over his half-moon lenses. 'We'll progress more expeditiously if you merely answer my questions, Mr Lewis. Rest assured I have no wish to waste either your time or mine.'

'They were killed in a car crash in 1953, when we were driving from a friend's bar mitzvah to a football match. I was thirteen.'

'I see.' Mr Reed noted this down. 'Am I to take it that you are Jewish, Mr Lewis?'

'Depends how you look at it. My parents were Orthodox, but I'm only a little bit Jewish. Almost Anglo-Saxon. In fact, one of my best friends is Anglo-Saxon.'

If Mr Reed understood the joke, he didn't show it, but carried on asking what appeared to David to be irrelevant questions, occasionally coming back to the car crash, dwelling on their sex life. Was it frequent, satisfying, adventurous, orthodox, or not? Did David get on well with Kate? With other women? How was his business? Eventually the psychiatrist put his pen down and said he would like to see Mrs Lewis.

'You haven't asked me about these dreams I'm supposed to be having,' David said.

'According to what your wife told Dr Watkins, you have no recollection of any dreams. I see no point in asking questions for which you have no answer. On the other hand, Mrs Lewis does experience them, or rather she believes that she does.'

'He kept on about your parents' car crash,' Kate said as David pulled the parking ticket from under the windscreen wiper.

'Christ, look at this,' he said. 'Sixty bloody pounds, for God's sake.'

'Then he latched onto the fact that I used to be a fashion model. Did I miss the freedom?'

David sniffed. 'Meaning, did you miss your sexual freedom!'

'Right, the dirty old sod. Then he gave me a prescription. Jesus Christ, David. I complain about your dreams and he gives me a prescription for tranquillizers. On top of all that, he even asked me if I had ever contemplated suicide. Bloody cheek of the man!'

'It was your idea, after all,' David said smugly. 'And let's face it, you're the one losing sleep, not me. I'm perfectly healthy, especially on the sex side. Apparently, once every three or four months is average for middle-aged professional couples.'

Kate kept quiet as the Carlton pulled out of the mews and turned north towards Marylebone Road. David reached out and squeezed her hand. 'Sorry.'

'That's OK,' she said quietly. It wasn't like David to say mean things. Not typical. Probably strain. 'He wants to see us again.'

'Does he, indeed? He didn't mention it to me.'

'We've got an appointment in two weeks.'

'No way! I only came along because you were so upset, and I'm damned if I'll let that old fart turn this into some kind of marathon. You've got your pills, and I've wasted three hours of working time. That's it.'

'He only wants to see if there's been any change, any improvement.'

'Improvement in what? In you? In me? Look, darling, let's not get sucked into the old bastard's clinical case notes. If there's really anything wrong with our relationship, we don't need a bloody Harley Street psychiatrist to screw things up even more. Next time you think I'm having one of those dreams, you kick me awake, pour cold water on me, connect me to the national grid – whatever it takes – and we'll see what's disturbing the old slumber, OK?'

'Yes, David.'

Connecting him to the national grid was about the only thing she had not tried, but Mr Reed had insisted that on no account must she wake him during a dream. It might be dangerous, he said. He's reliving the car crash that killed his parents. Not unusual in a man of his age. Guilt complex. Best to let his crisis work itself out during sleep. With professional help, of course. It would take possibly half a dozen appointments, he said.

But what about her crisis, her sleep? She felt like screaming the question, but managed to keep her voice reasonably steady.

31

'Your husband has a very stressful job, and we must give him all the help we can. I can comfort you with the thought that Time is the Great Healer. Your husband's problems can be overcome if he can be given a chance to relax. He has assumed responsibility for the accident that killed his parents, as the cry for his father indicates. He persuaded them to take him to a sports function on the Jewish Sabbath, and if he had not done so they would not have been killed. Irrational, of course, but then so many human reactions are irrational. Rest assured that with your help and understanding the problem will ameliorate. A little wifely tender loving care. And now I'm afraid it's time for my next appointment.'

The patronizing old shit, she thought as David turned off the Westway and headed south towards Wandsworth Bridge. Rest assured! If only she could. Tender loving care, indeed! It's a wonder the old bastard didn't specify the pipe-and-bedroom-slippers routine. Maybe she'd land this modelling job. That would help. She certainly needed something to take her mind off all this.

David drove automatically but well, anticipating changes in traffic and avoiding Rambo couriers on high-powered motorcycles with an accustomed ease. He admitted to himself that he had not handled things sensibly with Mr Reed. Kate was obviously losing out on her sleep, and sleep deprivation would strain the patience of an angel. Even so, Reed appeared to be completely out of touch with the real world. On and on about sex. If that sort of questioning was supposed to help, how come it made Kate so angry? And that bit about contemplating suicide. Well out of order! Her problem was all to do with sleep deprivation. The thought reminded him of an engineering colleague from Houston, Walter Bratski. He'd introduced David to one of his Army chums, a hippie-looking fellow who specialized in rehabilitation therapy. He'd fascinated them by describing how the Viet Cong could turn a platoon of disciplined marines into raving lunatics by keeping them awake for a few days and then reversing the command structure. Sleep deprivation was the key. And he had been too preoccupied with his own business problems to give Kate the attention she needed. What an asshole. What was the man's name? Joe Something-or-other.

'That'd be Joe Carrigan,' Bratski's Texan voice drawled over the phone. 'Some kind of CIA goon before turning to Hippocrates. Knows more about war-washed brains than the guys at Bethesda Medical.'

'Have you got his number?' David asked.

'Nope. Lost touch. Believe he was over in Europe, couple of years ago. Paris, maybe, but it could have been London. Or Frankfurt. No, it was definitely London. If you track him down, say Hi to him for me, will ya!'

V

David followed the principle of looking in the easy places first, and for once it worked. A Joe Carrigan MD was listed in the London business directory at an address in Wimbledon. David keyed the number, and an American voice answered.

'This is David Lewis, Dr Carrigan. We met briefly when I was staying with Walter Bratski in Houston.'

'Sure, I remember. How're things with Walt?'

'He's fine. Says hello,' David said. He paused, thinking what to say next. How to start.

'What can I do for you, Mr Lewis?' Carrigan prompted.

'It's not me. It's my wife. Kate. She's having problems with her sleep, and I'm getting quite worried. I remembered that this is something you talked about. Your kind of thing.'

'Sure is, but my area is more business and military than domestic. Have you tried a conventional counsellor?'

'Of course we have,' David said impatiently. 'Some cretin in Harley Street. He just made things worse.'

'I can't take over someone else's case,' the American voice said. 'Wouldn't be ethical.'

'It's no one else's case,' David said. 'My wife needs help, and if it's your line of country I'd appreciate a chance to talk to you about it.'

'How about next Tuesday?' Carrigan asked.

David parked his car on the pavement and checked the number on the broken gate. The house was large, with unkempt briars flopping over a dilapidated fence. An elderly but immaculate BMW motor-bike with rechromed silencers and a new metallic paint finish stood by the steps leading to the front door, a tempered steel chain wound several times round both wheels and secured with a massive pad-lock. Next to the bell push a sign carved in redwood said: JOE CARRIGAN — PRESS, AND GIVE YOUR PROBLEMS THE WORST TIME THEY'VE HAD IN YEARS.

Underneath this exhortation a set of tiny letters told those who cared to squint closely that the sign had been hand-crafted by Frank Corola of Sausalito in Marin County. As David stood staring, Carrigan opened the door. He still sported shoulder-length dark hair, a well-trimmed moustache and tinted glasses, as David had remembered.

'Saw you arrive,' he said in a West Coast accent, holding out his hand. 'Good to see you again, David. I hope I can call you David.'

'Indeed you can, Mr Carrigan. Or is it Dr Carrigan?'

'It's Joe.'

'Joe,' David said.

'The first barrier, overcome!' Carrigan said, leading David into the house. 'Did you know that many primitive people keep their names secret, in case someone gets one over on them? They tattoo a name symbol on their scalp so it's hidden by their hair.'

'Fascinating,' David said.

Carrigan led him into an untidy but comfortable-looking room filled with ancient furniture and antique bric-à-brac. 'I'd lay odds you're not too sure about coming here. Am I right?'

'You tell me. You're the psychiatrist.'

Carrigan sat himself carefully into a red leather bean bag. 'Why are you so up-tight? You don't know if I'm a charlatan or not, yet. Sit down and relax, for Christ's sake.'

David took the proffered chair. 'Frankly, I don't really know anything about you at all, beyond a eulogy from Walter. He thinks very highly of you. As I said on the phone, my wife is having problems with her sleep. She's in a bad way, blaming me for every-thing, and she's been insisting that we see someone about it. I thought it would be a good idea to check you out. To be quite honest, I'm not sure I should even be here, without her knowing.'

'Put your mind at rest, David. Mrs Lewis, Kate, was pretty keen on having us meet.'

David stared at him blankly. 'But how . . . ?'

Carrigan held his eye, guilelessly. 'I called her.'

Anger rose like bile. 'You what?'

'What would you have done, in my position?' Carrigan asked. 'I get a call from a guy I dimly remember meeting when I was working at Langley, and the old stress analyser goes off the scale when your voice hits it. For all I knew, you could have been an agent yourself. A hitman, even. They never really let you off the hook, y'know.'

'Let me understand you,' David said, cold as ice. 'Am I to understand you analysed my voice, then called my wife to check up on me?'

Carrigan seemed pleased. 'Exactly.'

David stood up. 'Well fuck you.'

'Sit down, David, why don't you,' Carrigan said unconcernedly. 'The fact remains, your wife is seriously disturbed. You're quite right about that. I'm sure I'm not revealing a confidence when I say it all seems to point towards a problem you have, rather than one she's started out with.'

'I presume you're referring to my so-called dreams.'

'That's right. Of course, there may be nothing to it, even if you could remember what it's all about. Frankly, I'm not sold on Freudian dream analysis and stuff like that. The ancient Egyptians had a much better system, and the Cretans were best of all. They linked dreams with everything. You might have offended a god, for instance, or swindled Pharaoh out of some taxes. Or it could be the result of a metabolic imbalance. Too much feasting.'

'You mean, perhaps I've been eating too much Gorgonzola?' David didn't bother to keep the sarcasm from his voice.

Carrigan sighed and eased himself off the bean bag. 'I can understand your antagonism, David. As far as you're concerned, this is all a waste of valuable time, am I right?'

'Bull's eye!'

'In that case, let's cut the crap. Your wife claims you have bad dreams, and you can't remember any of it. Your main priority is to make a living, and anything that interferes with that is a pain in the ass.'

'I underestimated you. That is one hundred per cent accurate.'

'Good! Now we're travelling together. I can't stand time-wasting,

35

either, so let's get down to cases. First off, I'd like you to listen to this.' Carrigan opened a cupboard and switched on a tape recorder. In a few second the room was full of highly amplified noises. The strange muffled sounds of a bedroom. Irregular breathing. Creaks from a bed. Rustling covers. Breath coming in harsh, painful rasps. Violent movement. Then a soul-splitting high-pitched scream.

'*Papa! Papa!*'

David looked blankly at Carrigan. 'Is this some kind of shock therapy?'

'We have to diagnose the complaint before we recommend treatment. Indulge me.' Carrigan reversed the tape and played it again. 'Any comment?'

'Indeed I have. I fail to see the significance of playing me a tape of some poor kid yelling for his father.'

'What about the accent?'

'If you want an opinion, I'd say it was German. How much should I charge you for my opinion?'

'How much d'you think your time is worth?'

'My company hires me out at a thousand pounds a day. How much do you cost?'

'Let's not tear each other's throats out. I'm trying to help, I really am. Bear with me.'

'What's this – the Sympathy Sell?' David sneered.

'No,' Carrigan said blandly. 'You have a problem, and I want to help you to get to the bottom of it.'

'I haven't got any fucking problem. You should be interviewing my wife. She's the one with the problem.'

'I have interviewed her.' Carrigan looked thoughtfully at David, then changed the cassette in the tape recorder. 'And you're quite right. She does have a problem.'

Kate's voice came over the speakers.

'. . . and I went there again last week. David wouldn't come. It was awful. That horrid old man ignored everything I said about David's dreams and kept asking me about our sex life. When I told him we had sex about once every three months he started writing me another prescription for sleeping tablets. Told me not to wake David, because the bread-winner needs all the sleep he can get. Can you believe it? Told me it would be all right in the end. But I can't

36

stand it, I really can't. It tears me apart when David goes through it. He's suffering, really suffering, only when he eventually wakes up there's nothing. He doesn't remember a thing. Not the shuddering. Not the screaming. You've no idea what it's like . . .'

'Take it easy, Kate,' Carrigan's voice said. 'We can get to the bottom of this, believe me. The first thing is for you to take this and stick it by the bed. All you need do is press this red button. It's a sixty-minute tape, so it'll get everything we need. But you mustn't play it to David. Bring it straight back to me.'

When Carrigan switched off the tape recorder, David exploded. 'You lousy bastard.'

'Not according to Marin County marriage records,' Carrigan said briskly. 'But that's beside the point. The fact is that you are suffering from frequent nightmares. They leave you unaffected, but they are shredding your wife's nerves. I don't need to tell you about divorce statistics, David. Unconsciously or not, you are putting your domestic relationship under a terrible strain. Not to mention your job. Now. Do we get down to business?'

'You've got some bloody nerve,' David snapped. 'Tape-recording my wife when she was clearly unaware that you were doing it. And I suppose . . .'

'Exactly,' Carrigan said pleasantly. 'It's all going down on tape, so I don't overlook anything important.'

David stood up. 'I've had enough of this. You can stuff your tapes. And if I catch Kate pressing your red button I'll come back here and ram the bloody thing down your throat.'

Carrigan held up the first cassette. 'In that case, old buddy, you better start ramming.'

David stared at him, shocked. He swallowed, hard. 'Me? That's my voice?'

'I'm afraid it is, my friend. So what say we calm down?' David stood for a moment, then sat in the chair again. Carrigan went to his desk and opened a notebook. 'OK, let's start at the beginning. Your full name is?'

'David Lewis.'

'No middle names?'

'No.'

'Date of birth?'

'First of January 1940.'

'Kate tells me you're an engineering consultant. What kind of engineering?'

'Mechanical and process. I do a lot of work in the machine-tool industry. Plastic injection, stress factors, corrosion, fatigue, that kind of thing.'

'Are you any good?'

'Very good. I earn a lot of money. Trouble is, we spend a lot, too.'

'I know the feeling. Have you any qualifications besides engineering?'

'Computer sciences, languages – German, with smatterings of French and Spanish.'

'I suppose that accounts for the accent on the recording. We can get more personal details later, but right now I'd like you to tell me about the thing that your Mr Reed latched on to.'

'What thing?'

'Your parents' car accident. Anything you can remember. How it happened, any injuries.'

'I can't remember anything about the accident itself. It was all over in a flash. I woke up in the hospital. It wasn't . . . It wasn't very nice.'

'What wasn't?'

'The whole thing! As soon as I opened my eyes, this enormous policeman starts asking me bloody fool questions. How fast were we travelling? Had we been to a party? Did my father drink a lot? Then a nurse came in and played merry hell with him for not calling the doctor when I woke up. She kicks him out and then starts crying, tells me that my mother and father are both dead.'

Carrigan was studying David intently, and scribbling notes. 'It must have been rough. Only thing is, why should Mr Reed conclude that you were suffering from a guilt complex over it? Do you feel guilty?'

David blinked fast, several times. 'Lord deliver me, a sinner,' he intoned. 'Of course I feel guilty. They were saints, those two. Where do I begin to tell you? School? Apparently, I was what they called a slow starter. They spent hours every week helping me with my reading and writing, buying books, making sure I caught up with the other kids. They weren't exactly wealthy, y'know. And in all those years of getting their love and care, in all that time of sacrifice, you know what? I never once told them I loved them. Not once! And then they die, taking me to a bloody football match they didn't even want to go to, and it's too late . . . too late, to tell them . . .'

Carrigan went into the kitchen and brought back a glass of water. Waited while David composed himself.

'You were brought up in the Jewish faith, yet you talk about saints.'

'Ah well, I missed my bar mitzvah through circumstances beyond my control, and the orphanage was, to put it mildly, multi-denominational.'

'Bit strange, isn't it, going into an orphanage?' Carrigan commented.

David shrugged. 'No living relatives. You know what it was like for European Jews in those days.'

'How did you get on in there?'

'How does anyone get on in an orphanage?'

'Hey, come on, David. That's my trick.'

'What's your trick?'

'Answering one question with another. That's how we charlatan psychiatrists make all our money. Didn't you know?'

David smiled faintly. 'No, but I do now.'

Carrigan closed his notebook, pulled a number of business cards from his desk drawer and selected two of them. 'I'd like you to make an appointment to see a couple of friends of mine. Marty Clarke is standard psychology and IQ stuff. Half of it's crap, but we don't know which half. More to the point, give this lady a call and tell her I sent you for a week's sweat. I'll see you on the fifteenth. Shall we say four thirty?'

'Should be OK.' David looked at the card. 'Diana Shrimply. What's her bag? Sex therapy?'

'Nope. She teaches fine art at the Hornsey College of Art. Best in the business, so don't waste the time you spend with her. Take advantage. Enjoy.'

'What the hell am I going to an art teacher for?'

'Let's call it occupational therapy.'

David felt as if he were being sucked along a slippery tunnel, but behind his resentment he sensed something he couldn't quite put a name to. Relief? Hope? Confidence in someone who seemed to know what he was doing.

39

'What about fees?'

'Fred will charge you fifty pounds for his standard tests. Diana may not charge you anything. I'm not sure about me. Let's say we keep the slate clean until I get their comments. Then I'll quote you.'

When David left Carrigan entered his notes into his computer.

Client Case Note

CLIENT'S NAME: David Lewis
BIRTH DATE: 1 January 1940
BIRTH PLACE: London
OCCUPATION: Engineering consultant
MARITAL STATUS: Married. Wife: Kate. Children: None.
PARENT STATUS: Father: Jacob. Mother: Edith. Both deceased.
HEALTH: No previous indication or history of medical or mental illness
BACKGROUND: David Lewis and I were introduced four years ago by Walter Bratski in Houston. He phoned me and complained that his wife was suffering from a sleep disorder and accusing him of causing the problem. She persuaded him to seek medical advice, and they were referred to a Mr Reed, who practises in Harley Street and who is a visiting consultant at the Maudsley Hospital. Reed appears to have followed a conventional line of psychiatric enquiry. David exhibits mild symptoms of ambulatory schizophrenia based on guilt associated with the deaths of his parents. He is shorter than his wife and older, and is self-conscious about a wide streak of frontal grey hair. She is an attractive woman, an ex-model who retains an active libido. They have adapted to their physical differences in a seemingly balanced way, although they copulate infrequently. David holds a doctorate in mechanical engineering from Cambridge University. He is modest about his academic achievements, which include fluency in German and a working knowledge of two other European languages. During the first part of our meeting he was tense and antagonistic. He believes his wife is being over anxious. He could not recall having dreams, neither does he seem to be suffering stress that is dream-related. However, there are signs underlying these indi-

cations that are difficult to quantify. David is a deeply troubled person, and his dreams may be an integral part of his problem. NEXT STEP: Assess IQ. Combine art and hypnotherapy to test David's eidetic memory of his dream sequence.

CHAPTER TWO

I

David drove into the country and wandered deep into a forested area, his head spinning with the events of recent days. He sat on the trunk of a fallen elm, deep in thought. Two squirrels scampered their way down a beech tree and peered at him with bright eyes, looping closer to see if there was any food on offer. He gazed back at them vacantly, and after a few minutes they lost interest and rustled off through the dried undergrowth. Part of his mind was just as it had always been. Aware, analytical, precise. And this part of his mind found itself living uncomfortably with an altogether different mind. He knew as much as any reasonably informed lay person about stress, and he recognized that he was in the middle of a stress-related crisis. But knowing is one thing, being able to deal with it is another. It was time for some self-analysis. Some honesty. To start with, his outward show of intellectual humility was a sham. He was intensely proud of his doctorate, his capabilities and his achievements. He was proud of having married such a beautiful and, yes, let's admit it, sexy woman. And something was threatening all this. It could be this dream Kate was so worried about, or the new responsibilities he had at work. It could be anything at all. It could be, for instance, the fact that Stephen Carrickworth had been appointed to a full partnership, while he had been given Stephen's left-overs. The only reason he had been given his junior partnership was because Anstat Konsult wanted his expertise to clinch the deal with the German pharmaceutical company. That hurt, did that!

Whatever the problem, there was something going on in his head that was impairing his performance. How to sort it out?

He once heard a professor of mathematics from Warwick University give a lecture that rejoiced in the title of 'The algebraic topology of the human brain', an hour of untrammelled delight for the learned audience. The professor's suggestion was that human experiences are somehow recorded in the brain in a series of layers, similar to the surfaces of long-playing records. Like consciousness, these layers do not have a physical existence in the brain cells. But the process of being conscious about something works like the needle of a record player. The needle passes along a groove in a layer of vinyl. The groove contains bumps, and the sound that created the bumps is reproduced by the vibration of the needle. The music of the London Symphonia or Louis Armstrong is brought into awareness. And if something happens to make the needle jump, it produces a break in that awareness. One moment it's playing Bach's Toccata and Fugue in D Minor, the next, 'Potato Head Blues' by Louis Armstrong. Same with consciousness. Same with dreams.

David felt very much at home with that idea. All kinds of things can make the needle of consciousness jump, and then you might forget something or make a poor decision. When David recalled what the professor had to say about dreaming, he really felt excited. During sleep, the conscious mind loses control of the needle of consciousness, and it rambles among the memory layers, sometimes in a logical sequence and sometimes at random. It can lead to the kind of nonsense dream in which a golfer finds himself playing down an aisle on a Jumbo jet with the President of the USA as a partner and the Count Basie orchestra blowing golf balls at him through their instruments. Or it can focus on some hidden fear, so sharply that nightmares are created.

David had to accept the fact that he was dreaming, not Kate, and that the dreams, whatever else they were, were not at all pleasant. Kate and Carrigan had gone to a great deal of trouble to prove it to him. He could either walk away from this thing, or find out what was going on. As he sat among the leafless trees listening to the squirrels and the birds he was honest enough to admit that his personal arrogance would not let him walk away. It was intolerable that something out there had affected the smooth running of a keenly honed brain. So he'd go along with Carrigan. He'd see this bloke Clarke and the watercolour woman. More to the point, he had some serious apologizing to do.

43

When Kate heard David's key in the lock she switched off the television and poured him a cup of coffee. David slung his briefcase onto a chair and sat down beside it, flexing his hand.

'What's she like?'

'She's a slave-driver, that's what she's like. I haven't had cramp like this since the sixth form.'

'You know what I mean.'

'Ah, you mean, has she got big knockers and a shapely bum, and does she ravish new male art students like my good self? Ten years ago I'd have said the answer would have been in the affirmative. Now, I'm not so sure.'

'Well,' Kate said, holding out her hand. 'Let's see the masterpiece.'

'You won't believe this, but there is no masterpiece.'

'You're kidding. A whole evening, slaving over a hot palette, and no masterpiece!'

He sipped the coffee. 'Absolutely not. And there's no palette with watercolours. When I got there, with charcoal sticks at the ready, this octogenarian biddy gives me hand exercises, while she rabbits on about form and perspective. She had me squeezing an India-rubber ball for twenty minutes. In the end I speak up for my rights. I say, "Miss Shrimply, I believe there has been some kind of mistake. I have, in fact, been referred to you by Dr Joe Carrigan, who has sent me to learn to be an artist in one week." And she says, "I know exactly why Joe has sent you, young man, so if you'll kindly pay attention!"'

Kate laughed at his mimicry. 'Are you sure you can afford the time, David . . . really sure?'

'Now she asks me! Listen, my beauty, if you want me to go through this performance to win some kind of spurs, I'll squeeze rubber balls and converse with trendy American head-shrinkers for as long as it takes. Anyway, there are some tasty young students at the college. I could get to like it there.'

'You'd better not,' she warned, jokingly. 'And Joe isn't a head-shrinker. He prefers to call himself a phenomenologist.'

'What's that — a synonym for expensive?'

'Why are you so worried about the money? You're insured for medical treatment, aren't you?'

'Not this kind of stuff.'

'Oh well, after this you'll have a brand new career. Paintings by David Lewis. It could be the start of a whole new way of life.'

III

Carrigan looked at David's portfolio with satisfaction. 'She's absolutely brilliant, isn't she? Look how the sense of perspective has developed over just a couple of weeks. And the detail. It's amazing.'

'I'm glad you like it,' David said. 'And now perhaps you'd be kind enough to let me know what this art business is all about?'

Carrigan opened a cabinet and pointed at the bottles inside. 'A drink first. Scotch, gin . . . whatever?'

'Scotch'll do fine, thanks.'

When they had settled down Carrigan looked thoughtfully at David. 'First off, Marty Clarke has you down as a near genius with no apparent mental disorders. I want to tell you that I do not subscribe to Reed's guilt theory. Sure, you feel guilt about your parents, but so do lots of us after our folks die. We remember all those times we didn't bother to phone home, all the weekends we were too busy to visit them. There's no reason to believe that this dream of yours has any connection with their accident. Something else is bothering you.'

'And what might that be?'

'I'm hoping we can find out. Have you heard of eidetic memory?'

'Yes, but I don't know much about it.'

'It's a fancy name given to someone's ability to conjure exact images from things they have seen. It's like having a good memory for words, only in this case it's entirely visual.'

'Got you. It's like that parlour trick where you try to describe a tray of objects after it's been taken away.'

'It's no trick. The image is locked into the brain, and some people manage to gain access to it unaided. All of us have an eidetic memory, but we haven't all got a natural ability to get at it. Not without some kind of help. Like hypnosis, for example.'

45

David shook his head. 'You disappoint me. I thought you'd come up with something more original than that. There's no way you can hypnotize me.'

'It's not so much hypnosis as ultra-relaxation. Why not give it a try?'

'And my new-found skill with a sketch pad will no doubt be called into play, at this stage.'

'I hope so. If there are any images in your dream, maybe we can get them down on paper.'

'I've come this far, so why not?'

Carrigan pushed a form across the desk. 'First thing to do is to OK this. It's the usual nonsense about you permitting me to stick needles in you. Don't worry. Among my many attributes is a medical degree from Stamford, plus I'm a state registered nurse.'

'I can't sign that.' David's voice was strained.

'It's just a routine precaution. Part of the standard regulations. And it's only a tiny needle.'

Carrigan took a kidney bowl out of a small sterilizing box and showed David the hypodermic syringe. David shook his head violently, face taught with fright. 'No. I can't stand injections.'

'But you must have had all kinds of jabs in your time.' Carrigan watched David carefully and saw that his eyes never left the needle.

'No!'

Carrigan put the bowl back into the sterilizer. 'That's OK, David. I've got pills that'll do the same job. It'll take a little longer, that's all. They're just mild sedatives.'

'No needles?' Sweat was running in streams down David's face.

'Who needs them. Just relax and leave everything to me, and to your subconscious.'

David swallowed four pills. Ten minutes later he was sitting at Carrigan's desk with the sketch pad and charcoal sticks in front of him. Carrigan talked to him quietly and soothingly, taking no notice of David's occasional comment. Eventually there were no more comments, just the sound of even breathing, and Carrigan switched on the tape that Kate had made in the bedroom, filling the room with the sound of violently disturbed sleep, punctuated by the piping scream. There was no visible reaction from David, so Carrigan played it again, and a third time. On the fifth playback, David began to twitch uncontrollably.

46

'David,' Carrigan whispered. 'Can you show me what you see? Can you draw the things you see on the paper?'

After several minutes of coaxing and replaying the tape, David picked up some charcoal and began moving it over the paper, making a low mumbling noise as he did so. By the time they finished, David had covered a dozen sheets with meandering black lines. Carrigan stared at them, thoughtfully.

'OK, David, let's try again.'

Client Case Note

TREATMENT: hypnotherapy/regression, enhanced by art expression.

As we proceeded into deep hypnosis, the images that David Lewis drew became more precise. At a subconscious level he may be obsessed by fantasies relating to the Second World War, and the dream he experiences may well be a symptom of a psychosis that has its origins in the persecution of Jews. At the moment it is not possible to ascertain if and how his marital situation might be involved. I am continuing interviews with Kate Lewis.

IV

Carrigan showed Kate into his private reception room, decorated to keep the original Victorian flavour, with jardinières holding potted plants. The marble and tiled fireplace contained a log fire, which spread a warm flickering glow over the chintz-covered easy chairs. Bun-haired ladies and waistcoated gentlemen stared formally from dozens of sepia-toned photographs in wooden frames that were scattered about the room.

'I detect a woman's touch.'

'A sexist statement, if ever I heard one,' Carrigan said. 'I claim total responsibility for this work of art. Victorian England is a passion of mine. Gas-lit streets, hansom cabs. Just look at the tiles in the fireplace. No one makes things like that any more. Works of art, every damn one of them.'

'Quite a contrast to your consulting room,' Kate commented.

'I keep that in a mess, so the poor souls who wander in feel comparatively well organized.'

'That's sneaky. Mind you, your technique seems to have worked wonders with David. He's more relaxed than he's been for ages, and he hasn't dreamed for over two weeks. I'm sleeping much better, too, so I suppose we can stop coming to lay ourselves on your dissecting table.'

'Sit down there for a moment. There's something I want to show you.' He pointed at a pile of charcoal sketches on a table by her chair. 'Look through those while I get us a coffee.'

'David's?' she asked. He nodded. 'I was wondering when I'd get to see his handiwork.'

When Carrigan came back with the tray of coffee she was still sifting through the drawings. 'He's not exactly a budding Klein, is he? And they're so sinister. I wouldn't want these hanging on my living room wall.'

'He did this lot in his first few visits,' Carrigan said. 'The more we get into it, the more precise he's getting. I'm particularly interested that you think they're sinister.'

'He is getting better, isn't he, Joe?'

'There are no simple yeses and noes in this business, Kate. Not for Freud, Jung or Eysenck, and certainly not for Carrigan. I'm going along with my guts on this one, and my guts tell me that David is a very disturbed person. Don't ask me how or why disturbed. Stress is a combination of many things. It could be triggered by something physical, like an imbalance in the neuro-endocrine system, or it could be mental, like his reaction to the car accident in 1953.'

'What are you trying to tell me? Is David mentally ill?'

'In the clinical sense? To be honest, I've no idea.'

'If you'll forgive me for saying so, that's not the kind of answer I'd expect from a professional person.'

'I'm sure your Mr Reed would come up with some relatively acceptable clinical description, given the opportunity. I'm equally sure he'd be wrong. We're in an area where certainty is impossible to achieve. I'm giving it to you straight. Something's wrong with David, and I don't know what it is.'

Kate put her coffee cup down and gathered her handbag. 'Well,

I must say I'm disappointed. We seem to have been wasting each other's time, and at no little expense, I might add.'

'I explained to David that I wasn't charging my full fees for our meetings. I have a grant from a charitable foundation that lets me develop the combination of hypnotherapy and art and my interpretation of the results.' He put his arm out and took her hand as she stood up. 'Before you go there's something else you must see. These sketches were just the beginning.'

'You mean they get better? Maybe we can get a hanging at an art gallery.'

Reluctantly she followed him into another room where there was a video recorder set up for viewing. He dimmed the lights.

'After a time I noticed that the sketches repeated themselves, and they did so in a particular order. Each one was relatively vague, but I decided to see what would happen if I linked them together in sequence. Like a movie.'

The TV screen showed a caption for a few seconds: 'D.L. Dream Sequence No. 8'. Then movement began. When it was over, several minutes later, Kate found she had been holding her breath and clenching her hands tightly.

'What is it?' she whispered.

'I can only tell you what I think it may be,' he said. 'It's a view of some kind of room, a section of a room, as if we're looking through a window. Figures come through a door on the left. Three of them. They remain still for a while as if they're talking, then one moves forward, does something with his arm or hand, and falls to the ground. The other figures move forward too. Finish.'

'It's horrible, Joe.'

'I'm sorry this is upsetting, but I have to show you why I'm so worried. The next sequence is a repeat of that video linked to the sound recording you made of David's dream two months ago.'

'I don't want to hear that again.' She tried to quell the panic.

'The only way we can help David is by trying to understand what's disturbing him,' Carrigan insisted. 'The fact that he is not dreaming now in no way indicates that his basic problem is solved.'

Blinking back tears, Kate stared at the screen as it showed: 'D.L. Dream Sequence No. 9'. David's spasms and moans provided a nerve-racking counterpoint to the shadowy movements, lending the figures a terrifying reality that was lacking in the silent version. The frenzied, high-pitched scream rang out as the central figure dropped from view. *'Papa! Papa!'* Kate was crying openly now, sobbing into her clenched fists. Carrigan pushed a glass of whisky at her.

'Come on. We've got to finish this, or the whole damn thing will be a waste of time.' He pulled some more sketches in front of her. 'These are his latest. He seems to be focusing on particular parts of the sequence, and many of the features are much clearer.'

Kate wiped her eyes and looked at the drawings. There were two men and a woman with the kind of faces a portrait artist would produce as a preliminary sketch. One of the men was wearing a white laboratory coat over a black uniform and the woman wore a white overall. The other man wore shapeless overalls covered with stripes. Another sheet was completely covered with military-looking insignia, some of which featured swastikas.

'Notice that all his sketches of the room contain something on the wall,' Carrigan said, pointing. 'This turned out to be a portrait, possibly a photograph. We worked very hard to get a likeness.'

He showed her three developing drawings. The first was an indistinct blob with a wavy line underneath. The second was clearly a face. When she came to the third she looked at Carrigan in shocked surprise.

'It can't be.'

'There's no doubt about it.'

The clearly recognizable face of Adolph Hitler stared arrogantly at her. A squiggly line represented what must be a caption.

'I believe that David has invented his own holocaust horror story,' Carrigan continued. 'Maybe it's got something to do with his new work in Germany. Maybe it's all this anti-Semitism. Who knows. Whatever the trigger, this is the result. The period of quiet after the dream is more like coma than natural sleep. Medically speaking, that's the most disturbing feature of all. It's like a state of deep shock, so you see why I think we're still in trouble.'

Kate shuddered and drained her glass. 'What does David make of all this?'

'I haven't shown him the video yet. He's not ready for it.'

'I don't want him to see it,' she said emphatically.

'I'll prod around for a while to see how things develop, but sooner or later I'll have to confront him with this,' Carrigan said. 'It may be the kind of catharsis he needs to sort things out.'

V

David lay quietly in the dark, Kate snuggling warmly beside him. The sex had been good, and he felt relaxed, ready for his effort. He hadn't told Carrigan, but when he concentrated he could summon the dream without the pills or the prompting of Carrigan's hypnotic voice. It had been very difficult at first, because he had to overcome a sense of dread and the sickening odour of carbolic soap. He cleared his mind and waited for the images. He wasn't sure what happened during his sessions with Carrigan, except that he had been helped through some kind of barrier. He hated the place on the other side, but he had to carry on. There was something he had to remember, something he had to do.

Now, as he relaxed next to Kate, he began to see them: three faces moving in and out of his vision in a room containing some kind of scientific equipment. The woman stayed in the background until the end. The man in the black uniform seemed happy, but his father was very frightened. It had taken David a long time to recognize his father, because his face was different. Younger than he remembered. There was someone else in the room too, if only he could turn to see who it was. But his head was paralysed, so he could only stare straight ahead. He didn't think it could be his mother. They had left her on the train, and his father had cried.

The photograph on the wall was easy to see, just by moving his eyes. Tonight he wanted to concentrate on this, so that he could make out the fine details at the bottom. He had recognized the face the last time he had summoned up the dream. It didn't make any kind of sense to see Adolph Hitler, but there he was, black hair slicked down, staring arrogantly into space.

The dream sequence repeated itself, while he lay silently bathed in sweat, careful to keep away from Kate so he wouldn't wake her. He ignored the door bursting open and his father rushing in, pleading with the man in uniform. Just kept his mind on the photograph, on the scrawled lines underneath the staring eyes. He focused his entire being on the caption under Hitler's face, while the dream bathed him time and time again in its terror. After half an hour he got quietly out of bed, went to his study and wrote it down on his note pad, the words flowing down his arm and through his fingers.

'*An unseren lieben Freund, Ernst. Lass Diesen "Turmfalke" uns den Weg zeigen – Adolph.*'

For more than an hour he stared at the words. They were not in his handwriting, but he gave no thought to that. In fact, he gave no thought to anything in particular. But deep in the recesses of his mind he heard a low resonating sound as if a large crowd of people were murmuring encouragement at him. There was something he had to do, but he had no idea where to start. Then he thought of his father's old friends. He felt sure one of them could help in some way. Throw some light on it. A group of them used to meet once a month before the Sabbath. Itzak Rabin. Isadore Absolom. Old people, talking about the old days. And one in particular. David remembered an intense man with a scar on his face to whom the others seemed to defer. What was his bloody name?

He sat for several minutes, racking his head to remember. Then he smiled. What an idiot!

He reached for his pencil and sketch pad, and began to relax again, as Carrigan had taught him. When he finally re-focused, the name was written clearly on the paper.

VI

The synagogue was in a street behind Marble Arch, a featureless brick building with a double staircase leading from the pavement to a large wooden door. A discreet sign told passers-by that non-orthodox worshippers were welcome. The April sun shone brightly into the street as the congregation gathered at the top of the steps to say their goodbyes after the morning service. David had introduced himself to the rabbi before the service, and when the congregation began to leave the rabbi beckoned.

'This is Mr Absolom,' he told David, indicating a frail old man

52

in a black homburg hat. 'Mr Absolom. Do you have a moment? This is Mr Lewis. Jacob Lewis's son.'

The old man peered at David. 'Jacob Lewis? A long time ago, Jacob and I were friends. This must be little David.'

David took his hand, a trembling collection of thin bones, covered with dry, translucent skin. 'I wonder if I might have a word with you, sir.'

'He doesn't join us for worship, this little David,' Absolom confided to the rabbi. 'The young ones go their own way these days.'

'I'm sure Mr Lewis is aware of God's place, Isadore,' the rabbi said. 'It would, of course, be good to see you here again, Mr Lewis. Mr Absolom's car is waiting over there. Perhaps you would be kind and escort him, when you've finished.'

When the rabbi had gone back into the synagogue, David said, 'Mr Absolom, I need to know about my father. It has something to do with the Holocaust, and I understand you are friendly with a man who may be able to help me. Albert Levy. I was hoping you know how I can get in touch with him.'

Absolom nodded slowly. 'Still they search, still they collect their information, but what good does it do? The Jew is bombed and burnt from his home and his synagogue. New York. Paris. London. Israel in turmoil. We came from Lithuania, your father and I. We arrived in 1939, together on a steamship. Two frightened jewellers fleeing from the Terror. They thought we were rich. They smashed our windows. They beat us. They pulled up floorboards looking for gold, but the only gold we had was used to make wedding rings and small articles of jewellery such as young girls might buy. The only wealth I had was my family, my loved ones, my good friends such as Jacob. I still say Kaddish for him. Do you?'

'No, sir. But I think of both my parents every day.'

A black limousine slid silently to the bottom of the steps, and a chauffeur got out and looked expectantly at Absolom, who started to walk carefully down. David followed, a hand cupped under a trembling elbow. 'If you know the man I mean, sir, I would be grateful to know how to make contact with him.'

The old man paused and looked at him, the watery eyes suddenly clear and piercing. 'Albert Levy. A number can be found under the name of C.P. Bansil in the telephone directory. Tell him Isadore says Shalom.'

53

* * *

Loki Threat Assessment

SUBJECT: *Levy, Albert*
NATIONALITY: *Jew*
SEX: *Male*
DOB: *1915*
LOCATION: *Believed living near London*
DISTINGUISHING FEATURES: *Scar on face. No. 439261 tattoed on left forearm*
KEYWORD AFFILIATIONS: *Anti-Nazi; Nazi hunter; Nuremberg; World War II investigation; Treblinka; Auschwitz*
COMMENT: *Subject elderly and in poor health; gone to ground; still active researcher; usually accompanied by members of militant Jewish Youth Movement; has Mossad connections*
ASSESSMENT PRIORITY (0—10): *10*
DATA ON SUBJECT: *Participated in research into Aryan superiority. Developed investigations into alleged war criminals (German); responsible for arrest and execution of 15 Party members and imprisonment of 45.*
CROSS REFERENCES: *Wiesenthal, S; Müller, H; Bormann, M*
ACTION: *Report information on Levy direct to Loki One. Members of Neuvolkgruppe are authorized to kill on sight.*

* * *

A woman answered after the second ring. 'Yes.'

'I need to meet Mr Levy,' David said.

'Who is this calling?' The voice gave nothing away.

'My name is David Lewis. I was given this number by Isadore Absolom. Mr Levy knows him, I believe.'

'Just a minute.' David heard the click of a recorder. 'Mr Levy doesn't live here any more. Perhaps I can get a message to him, if you leave me your address and telephone number.'

David dictated slowly.

'I'll pass on your message, Mr Lewis,' the woman told him.

VII

As Carrigan continued his hypnotherapy sessions, David learned how to control the experience. He slowly pieced together his dream and determined its causes. His father had experienced an ordeal at the hands of the Nazis which he had described to David during early childhood. David's dream was the result of the mature mind trying to convert the childhood story into graphic imagery in which the most important single clue was the caption on the photograph.

'To our dear friend, Ernst. May your "Kestrel" show us the way – Adolph.'

Ernst, Kestrel and Adolph Hitler. Three slender clues to a mystery. David was sure there would be a way to unravel the problem, and meeting someone like Albert Levy was a natural first step. He knew the name from articles in newspapers, and an hour spent in the local library and on-line to the Internet revealed a great deal about the man. Levy was a legend, a leader in the resistance in the concentration camp at Treblinka. When the SS closed this camp Levy was sent with hundreds of comrades to Auschwitz for elimination. He survived, as many had done in this notorious death factory, because the SS discovered he had a useful ability, sculpting. They put him to work preparing exhibits for the camp museum. His most popular work among visiting Nazi luminaries was a range of model skulls. The Aryan skulls were carefully sculpted in plaster of Paris. The others were real. Levy's captors expected him to show the superior brain capacity of the Aryan, compared with lesser forms of human life such as Jews, Gypsies and blacks. He did this by exaggerating the measurements he took of the heads of SS guards. It was Levy's way of staying alive.

After the war Levy, like Simon Wiesenthal and other victims of the Nazis, devoted his life to the search for war criminals. He amassed and indexed a huge volume of information on the SS and Gestapo, and his files were a major source of information for the Israeli hit squads that operated in the 1950s and 1960s and more recent activities of Mossad, the Israeli secret service. Unlike Wiesenthal he had managed to avoid the spotlight, concentrating his efforts in the accumulation and interpretation of archival information rather than becoming involved in arrest and capture. His name was connected with a number of unpublicized acts of retribution including the execution of the Gestapo chief Heinrich Müller and Hitler's deputy Martin Bormann, both of whom disappeared after the German surrender.

The Friday after David had telephoned the mysterious C.P. Bansil, Kate took a phone call from a man speaking in a foreign accent who asked to speak to Mr David Lewis. When she said David would be home later, the man abruptly disconnected. Thinking this was extremely rude, she remembered the caller identification service and on impulse asked the BT operator for the number. When she returned the call, a woman answered, so she rang off. No matter, she'd tell David, and he could deal with it if the man called again.

The phone rang just after they finished dinner, and David took the call in his study, closing the door behind him. When he identified himself, the man asked him why he wanted to meet Levy.

'I'm not prepared to discuss that over the phone,' David said emphatically. He could sense the animosity at the other end of the line.

'Be at the Fox and Grapes on Wimbledon Common tomorrow lunchtime,' the caller said.

He arrived at the pub sharp at twelve o'clock and sat nursing a beer until three. Bitterly disappointed, he left the bar and walked to his car. He was unlocking the door when two young men approached him.

'Mr Lewis. Would you be so kind as to use our vehicle. It will be more convenient. My name's Leon, and this is Uri. We'll bring you back here after you have met Mr Levy.'

The speaker had a friendly enough expression, but his companion, a tall black-haired youth, stared unblinkingly at him with flat dark eyes. David walked between them to a fawn-coloured Jeep with tinted windows, slightly disconcerted by their appearance after such a long wait. Once in the car the friendly one, Leon, held out a blindfold.

'I'm sure you'll understand that we do not wish to advertise where Mr Levy lives.'

'Is it far?' David felt ridiculous. It was all so melodramatic.

Leon ignored the question. 'He can see you for half an hour. You'll be returned here at four thirty.'

'I wish you'd come earlier. My wife will be worried.'

The silence indicated that neither of them cared much about a worrying wife.

David tried to trace the route by the turnings and the stops at traffic signs. At one stage they speeded up, and he guessed they were travelling along the Kingston by-pass, but by the time the vehicle had turned one way and then another for several more minutes, he gave up the attempt. Eventually they stopped, and he heard gates being opened before they rolled forward a few more yards. Uri pulled his mask off and motioned him out of the vehicle and into an enclosed yard at the back of a large detached house. A tall girl with short dark hair and a serious face was waiting at the door.

'Good afternoon, Mr Lewis. My name is Anna.' She led him inside and through a kitchen to the hallway. 'I must ask you to consider that Mr Levy is not in the best of health. Please do not excite him.'

The walls of the hallway were lined with metal filing cabinets and shelving stacked with bulging folders and box files. Every conceivable space was taken over with cupboards and packing cases with file numbers scrawled on them in black marker ink. The landings above each flight of stairs were also packed with documents and wartime memorabilia. Anna showed him into a small room at the top of the house furnished with a bed, a desk and more filing cabinets.

'If I were a younger man, I would put all this into one of these wonderful data processing machines that would sit silent and obedient in a corner and give us space to move around. Man is a creature set upon the ruination of his own environment, would you not agree, Mr Lewis?'

Albert Levy was a small man with straggles of white hair running across a partially bald head. A deep scar ran across his nose from his eyebrow to his chin, disfiguring both lips and causing his voice to hiss slightly over the strong German accent. He was sitting hunched over a pile of papers, looking intently at David with luminous dark eyes.

'It's very kind of you to see me, Mr Levy. Isadore Absolom asks me to say Shalom.'

'That is kind of him. I believe you have something to tell me and some questions to ask. It is my business to listen and to speak about such things. Anna, perhaps our guest would like some refreshment. I take weak lemon tea, myself, Mr Lewis, but we have a selection of other drinks.'

'Lemon tea would be fine, thank you.'

When the girl left the room Levy invited David to sit. 'Please tell me what is troubling you.'

Under Levy's steady gaze, David began to feel less sure of himself. Ernst, Kestrel, Hitler. Three words in a nightmare, and in this house he was surrounded by millions of words of reality and more nightmares than any rational human could imagine.

'I've been having dreams . . .' He stopped, but the silence forced him on. 'They are extremely vivid. Frightening. They have something to do with the war, with the Nazis. And my father. It's difficult to explain, but there are words I can see in my dream. Words and three names. "*An unseren lieben Freund Ernst. Lass Diesen 'Turmfalke' uns den Weg zeigen . . . Adolph*". They are written underneath a photograph of Hitler. And I can see people in a kind of laboratory. My father is there, with a woman and a man in uniform . . . and someone else that I can't see. That's all. I want to find out what it means.'

'I am not a clairvoyant, Mr Lewis. The interpretation of dreams is best left to those who study aspects of the human mind other than the depredations of National Socialism. I regret, but I do not think I am the one to help you.'

David sighed and stood up. 'I'm sorry. I didn't mean to waste your time.'

Levy waved him back into his seat. 'Forgive an old man's rudeness, Mr Lewis. Anna is always complaining that my manner is too abrupt.' He paused while the girl came back with two steaming glasses of tea. 'There is more for you to tell me?'

David sat down again, feeling sweat break on his forehead. 'I don't know. I haven't tried a clairvoyant, but I've been to a psychiatrist. Two of them.'

'And what did they say, these two psychiatrists?'

'The first one didn't say anything useful. When I saw him I didn't even know I was having dreams. My wife insisted I see a doctor, you see. My nightmares were very disturbing to her.'

'And the second?'

'He calls himself a phenomenologist, whatever that means. But he's good at his job. He managed to get me to draw what I see. I say dreams, but it's one dream. Always the same.'

'And did you get an explanation from either of these two people?'

'The first one said I felt guilty about my parents' death in a road accident. The second one, Joe Carrigan, is more intelligent. He has no idea what's at the bottom of it.'

Levy smiled at the distinction. 'Mr Lewis, it is not unusual for Jews to dream about the Holocaust, whether they experienced it or not. We see books, photographs, films of the horror. We recall snatches of conversation. And this can be woven into a fantasy, with great clarity and conviction, often with members of family or other loved ones in positions of danger.'

'I know you're right,' David said. 'But there is someone else in the dream, someone that I know is there but can't see. If I'm deluding myself subconsciously, why don't I at least delude myself totally?'

The old man looked at him thoughtfully, then gestured at David's briefcase. 'You have something to show me?'

David hesitated. 'I made sketches. Joe Carrigan has most of them, but I made these at home. They are more detailed.' He opened the case and passed a bundle of papers to Levy who leafed through them slowly. When he came to the last one he gazed at it for a long time.

'... *Diesen Turmfalke* ... You wrote this in your own hand-writing?'

David glanced at the inscription. 'That's how I saw it. I just wrote it down that way.'

'And these ...' Levy held up a paper with drawings of military insignia. 'Have you at any time studied the regalia of the Schutz-staffel, perhaps from books that you have?'

'No. I've never been interested in things like that.'

'What about your friends? Perhaps one of them keeps books that you might have read at some time.'

David shook his head. 'Maybe I saw something years ago, here and there, but I can't be sure.'

59

Levy stood up stiffly. 'Would you excuse me for one moment. I should like to show you something.'

When he was out of the room David was aware of Anna staring at him. 'I'm sorry,' he said. 'I didn't mean to stay for so long.'

'That's OK,' she said. 'It's good for him to see a new face from time to time. We worry about over-tiring him, that's all.'

The old man came back a few minutes later with a folder bound with a green ribbon.

'What I am about to show you is almost certainly unconnected with your problem,' he said. 'Nevertheless, I have learned not to overlook even the most remote possibility in any avenue of enquiry. If your dream has any basis in reality, the Kestrel of your photograph might be a codeword. This file contains summaries of many projects that were given codewords by the Gestapo and the SS. Few of them were investigated by the Allies or any other organization. The problem was that we had too much information to sift. Millions of tons of captured documents. Thousands of hours of testimony at Nuremberg, much of it conflicting, misleading or simply untruthful. In some cases, an investigation was started, only to be postponed and then terminated as priorities were changed for one reason or another. There is one such investigation listed in this file with the name *"Turmfalke"*. A clerk at the Government Code and Cypher School on secondment to the American Advocate General's office in Berlin in 1947 began examining the documents under this name, because he assumed they were connected to a Wehrmacht army and Luftwaffe co-operation key in the Enigma code. But that "Kestrel" was in fact one of a series of British codenames for German Air Force Enigma encryptions. After cross-checking he realized that the *Turmfalke* in his file had nothing to do with that. It was a secret SS project, and he was not authorized to deal with these, so he passed it back down the line. There is no record of what happened next.'

'But what does it mean?' David asked.

'All it says here is that the word is connected with an unspecified staff college for selected SS officers. However, there is an index of the documents involved, compiled by the clerk when he began his search, showing the depositories to which they were taken for copying or storage. The entire project was shrouded in the most unusual secrecy. You can see here, for example, his final comment: none of the personnel involved in *Turmfalke* is referred to by name, only by their own codenames.'

'I thought the Nazis had a reputation for putting their names to everything they did in the War,' David said.

'They did at first. A kind of insane arrogance.' Levy sipped his tea. 'But as early as 1940, the more perceptive of the leading Nazis could see the implications of being associated with some of the orders and operations being carried out. They began to be more cautious. For example, the location of the college associated with the *Turmfalke* project is never mentioned. And that is all I can tell you, Mr Lewis.' He leaned back and rubbed his eyes.

'May I have a copy of the index?' David asked.

'Anna will prepare one for you.'

David gathered his belongings. 'I don't know how to thank you, Mr Levy.'

'For what are you thanking me, young man? A list of numbers? The names of a few libraries?'

'No, sir. I'm thanking you for this . . .' David tried to make his gesture embrace a lifetime of devoted work.

Levy sighed. 'Each day I ask myself, what is the significance? Have I wasted my life? Look at the streets of Europe, Mr Lewis. The Nazis are back, where they started in 1920. Does anyone care more now than they did then?'

As David was leaving the room he turned. 'Do you dream, Mr Levy?'

'Dream? No, not since a certain day in 1943. My memories attack me in the open, where there is no place to hide.'

Anna looked affectionately at the old man in his rickety chair. 'I shouldn't have let him stay so long.'

'No matter,' Levy said. 'It was good to break the routine with a visitor. I see so few people, these days.'

'Is he genuine?'

'Oh yes, my dear. He is genuine. But his dreams, are they also genuine, I wonder?'

'He left these photocopies of his sketches. Why did they interest you so much?'

Levy took the copies and pulled out the one with the military

61

insignia. 'He claims never to have studied the SS, yet look at these drawings. They are remarkably accurate. This one on the uniformed man's lapel is the rune of an SS-Standartenführer in the Florian Geyer cavalry division. And this writing . . .' He turned to the caption from the photograph. 'This is the real mystery. A curious problem. Perhaps he will solve it; perhaps there is nothing to solve.'

Anna looked at it. '*To our dear friend Ernst. Let your Kestrel show us the way. Adolph.*' She frowned. 'What does it mean?'

'I know no more than I told him. It is not so much the words as the writing itself. It is unmistakably Hitler's handwriting. Ask yourself how or why a Jew brought up in England should be able to reproduce the scrawl of that degenerate fiend.'

'He has seen Hitler's writing published somewhere and adapted it, consciously or unconsciously, for his own reasons.'

Levy leaned back and closed his eyes. 'I suppose that is the explanation. In any case, our Mr Lewis seems to have got himself involved in a Nazi paper chase.'

'You should have warned him that it's quite possible that he will stumble into something best left to the professionals. What if he upsets somebody?'

'They won't take any notice of someone browsing through library archives. Hundreds of people do it every day, in Washington, Berlin, Koblenz . . .'

'Maybe. I still say you should have warned him.'

'But would he have taken any notice? I think not. He is being driven too hard. In a short time, a few days, a few weeks, he may come back with information that we can file for others to worry about in the years to come. Or he may go home quietly to his wife and forget the entire matter. It is not our concern.'

'Well, at least we should circulate a note to the others about Mr Lewis and his *Turmfalke* obsession,' she insisted. 'It can't do any harm, and it might prod a few memories.'

Client Case Note

David's recall of his dream is now very precise. His drawings fall into a continuing sequence of events, with much detail. But I can't seem to get beyond this. It's almost as if he's blocking me out. Need to find a way to shake him up a little.

CHAPTER THREE

I

David could see Kate through the living-room window as he parked the car in the driveway, vacuuming the carpet. Inside the house the roar from the machine drowned the sound of his footsteps, and when he tapped Kate's shoulder she gave a squawk of fright before switching it off.

'I didn't know you were home. Thought you'd emigrated.'

'Sorry,' he said. 'Something came up, and I couldn't get to a phone.'

'Joe Carrigan phoned to see how you were, and I asked him over. He's bringing a girlfriend.'

'Phoned to see how I am! Why should he care? We've paid his bill, haven't we?'

She glared at him. 'That's a rotten thing to say.'

He bit his lip. 'Sorry. You're right. I have been out of sorts lately. No need to take it out on you. All the same, I don't think I'll be very good company.'

'Shall I call him back and put them off?'

'No. I quite like him, really. It'll make a change.' He opened the cabinet where they stored the drinks and peered inside.

'I stocked up this morning,' Kate said.

'So I see. We'll have to keep a rein on the old housekeeping bill, you know. Never sure what the future may bring.'

She watched him staring vacantly into the cabinet. 'David. I do love you.'

'What's that?'

'I said I love you.'

'Yes,' he said. 'I love you too.'

*

Carrigan's girlfriend was called Alice Cranley. She was outstandingly beautiful and interested in everything, talking about Tassajara cooking with Kate one minute and asking David about the problems of corrosion in offshore platforms the next. The conversation moved effortlessly through theatrical productions, World Cup football, motor racing and windsurfing. Alice had a degree in psychology. She had climbed in the Himalayas, flown solo across Australia and spent a winter in the Antarctic as human resources adviser to a scientific expedition. She was the kind of woman who should make other women feel inadequate, threatened and envious, but never did. She was very entertaining, and by the time they were sipping brandy David was more relaxed than he'd been for a long time. Consequently he reacted rather more slowly to her comment than he would otherwise have done.

'By the way, David,' she said, 'Joe showed me the film he made of your drawings. You have an amazing ability to recall.'

'Film . . . what film?'

'You know. The one with all your sketches linked up. Fascinating.'

There was a silence. David looked at Kate and Carrigan.

'For Christ's sake, what is this? Have you been discussing me behind my back?' Kate looked down at the table, but Carrigan held his eye steadily. 'Oh, I get it. Yes. This is all part of it, isn't it? Get the patient nice and relaxed on his home ground, and trigger him off to see what happens. Well, I must say I like your choice of trigger. She certainly knows her stuff.'

Kate looked pleadingly at Carrigan. 'I can't stand this.'

'You're exactly right, David,' Carrigan said quietly. 'I tried to use Alice as a trigger. I'm sorry about that, but I hit a block. I know we started this as a professional relationship, but it's become more than that for me. We're here as friends, and we want to help you.'

Something snapped. 'You can help me by getting the fuck out of my house.' David was almost screaming with rage. Nobody moved.

For several seconds David glared at them, unable to spit any more words out. Then his expression began to change, slowly at first. A smile twitched the corners of his mouth. 'Jesus Christ, you should see your faces.' He began to laugh. 'I've never seen such a guilty bunch of conspirators.' His laughter increased in gusts, until he sank in his chair, holding his stomach. 'Oh Christ, look at you,' he kept saying, whenever he could catch his breath. In the end it was infectious, and they all joined his laughter in an uproarious and rather self-conscious release of tension.

'Look,' David said eventually. 'I'm sorry about the outburst.'

'Don't be,' Carrigan said. 'I had it coming.'

David turned on the TV and video recorder. 'Well you might as well show me what you've taken so much trouble over.'

They sat silently, watching the images form and swirl on the screen in a sinister dance, expressing an unknown horror. David silently chalked one up to Carrigan. It was bloody clever to link the images like this, but they showed him nothing he didn't already know. His current crop of drawings were way ahead of this. Way ahead.

'What d'you think?' Carrigan asked him.

'Frankly, it's all a bit of a mystery, but it doesn't seem worth bothering about now. I'm not having any more of those nightmares, am I, Kate?' She shook her head. 'I appreciate what you've done, Joe, and I'd like to settle up with you. There's no need to worry about me, honestly. I'm perfectly all right. In fact, I feel on top form. Better than I've done for ages.'

'That's good to hear,' Carrigan said lightly. 'If you're sure, I'll let you have my bill for services rendered.'

'That'd be great. I must admit that things were getting me down, but I've decided to get my finger out. I haven't had time to tell you, Kate, but I have to go to Germany next week to start work on my new projects. I'll probably stay over the weekend to blow some cobwebs away, mix a little pleasure with business.'

'I think that's a great idea,' Carrigan said, turning to Kate. 'Don't you?'

'Yes,' she said. 'A great idea. Really.'

II

Albert Levy's list contained over two hundred references, long alphanumeric file names, with dates and the last recorded location of the original documents. After several phone calls to the US Army repository in Alexandria, Virginia, and to the Ministry of Defence, the Public Records Office and the Imperial War Museum in London, David discovered that documents indexed under *Turmfalke* had been returned to the archives in Berlin and Koblenz during the 1950s. Koblenz was a short journey from Cologne where he had arranged to see a number of potential clients. The decision he faced was whether to pack the list in his briefcase or throw it in the waste bin and forget the whole thing.

Kate had a Scotch and soda waiting for him downstairs. 'What time did you book the cab?' she asked.

He looked at his watch. 'It'll be here in about twenty minutes.'

'Are you sure you've got everything? Razor, toothbrush, socks, underwear?'

'When did I ever forget anything?'

'Just about every journey you make.' She gave a short laugh, then said, 'David. I wish you weren't making this trip.'

'You'll be all right, won't you?'

'Of course. It's just . . .'

'I know,' he said soothingly. 'But I'm fine. Never felt better.' He wondered if he meant it.

'You're sure you're not worried about what Joe said, and Alice?'

'Come on! We all got over that, didn't we? I was a bit upset at the time, to be honest. But the art sessions seem to have done the trick. And you've been a tremendous help. You know you have. A lesser woman would have walked away from it. I'll never know how to thank you.'

It was a natural reply, but it did nothing to ease her mind. David was keeping something from her. She could sense it in every movement his body made and everything he said to her. He leaned to kiss her, and she held him tightly. A car horn tooted outside the house.

'Cab's here,' he said, pulling away. 'I'll phone you when I've booked into the hotel.'

III

Kate dialled Carrigan's number and waited fretfully for him to answer. After six ringing tones she heard a click, and his voice said, 'Hi there! This is Joe Carrigan. Leave your name and number, and I'll get back to you.'

There was a high-frequency bleep, and Kate groped for something to say into the hollow silence. 'Joe. This is Kate Lewis. God, I hate these machines. Can you call me please?'

She sat by the phone for half an hour before it rang.

'Kate. It's Joe.'

'Thanks for calling me back. I have to talk to you. About David.'

'How's he doing?'

'Well, he's just phoned to say he's staying in Germany for some extra days.'

'And you're worried?'

'I know it sounds silly, but it's not like him to change his plans.'

'Did he say why he was staying?'

'Only that it was business, but . . .'

'Kate, let's not forget that you've been under considerable stress yourself for quite some time. Lots of guys have to extend their business trips. Happens all the time to me.'

'But not to David. Honestly. He usually manages to finish things early.'

'I don't think you should be too concerned about this. He'll be back soon, and then I can keep an eye on things as we discussed, but if there's anything I can do . . .'

She hesitated. 'Can I come over and talk?'

'Of course. As a matter of fact, I'd welcome that. There are a couple of gaps in David's file, and you might be able to fill in some background for me.'

'At least he isn't having any more of those awful dreams. I just pray that he's better.'

'Better? Cured, solved, healed? I wish things were as straightforward as that, but they seldom are. David is still reacting to an enormous stress. Maybe he's coming out of it, and getting stuck into his work might help. In any case there'll be a period of readjustment, and it's quite possible he'll need a little outside help from time to time, that's all. When can I expect you?'

She checked her watch. 'I can be with you at nine.'

CHAPTER FOUR

I

Frankfurt. Sitting in the Sacht Engineering boardroom, David should have been able to see the mediaeval town centre and the river frontage of the Sachsenhausen district, but the low cloud and drizzle restricted the view to the Commerzbank and the nearby head office of Anstat Konsult, where he had spent the previous day discussing how to take the merger of Halkyn and Anstat further forward in terms of new projects. They were particularly keen for him to meet their contacts in Deutsche Arzneiwissenschaft Werke, and he had promised to make arrangements to do so as soon as possible. In fact, he had no intention of meeting anyone from DAW with Anstat tagging along, and particularly not the excitable Helmut Kloss. He wanted to start with a clean sheet. As he gazed out of the window, he became aware of a silence and looked up to see Sacht's chief engineer, Herr Weerts, looking questioningly at him and tapping the computer screen.

'I beg your pardon?' he said quickly.

'These drawings of the inlet manifold, Dr Lewis.' German proto-col demanded the reference to his doctorate. 'If I am not mistaken, they are the same ones you sent us some weeks ago, whereas we understood that there should be modifications to the flanges to cater for the change in the coolant system.'

David checked his hard copy of the drawings. They were two months out of date. The amended disk was on his bureau at home. Damn.

'You're quite right, Herr Weerts,' he said. 'I'll have the correct ones sent over here by courier immediately. I do apologize.'

Luckily, Kate was home to take his call. She did not know enough about his computer to send it on-line, and he made the necessary arrangements for an immediate pickup. It would cost him over two hundred pounds for the express delivery, but if Weerts didn't get them within twelve hours Sacht would miss the deadline to their own client and charge any loss to David's company under the terms of their contract. It was a bad mistake, and David knew it would be logged into the communication system and duly reported back. When he returned to the table, they carried on talking about other components, but he found it difficult to keep his mind on the job.

The meeting dragged on until six o'clock, and when he was packing up his belongings Weerts's secretary came over to him. She was tall, elegantly dressed, the kind who took care of their figures by constant attendance at fitness clubs and saunas. He had spoken with her many times on the telephone.

'Good evening, Dr Lewis. May I introduce myself. I am Maria Frozell.'

'Good evening, Fräulein. It's good to meet you in the flesh – I mean not on the phone – well, you know what I mean.'

She smiled. 'Indeed so. Did you book a room at the Interconti-nental?'

'Sounded too grand for my taste. I'm at the Plaza.'

'That's a fine hotel, too.'

'All I know is, it's a ten minute walk from here. Twenty minutes by taxi. They drive you all round the city. I'll ignore the rain and take a walk.'

She laughed and said quietly, almost conspiratorially, 'Well, if you need to break the monotony of an evening by yourself, please tell me.'

Before he could reply, Herr Weerts beckoned her over, and he took advantage of the break in conversation to say goodbye. He had finished his schedule in Germany, and the rest of his week was free. The information officer at the Imperial War Museum had confirmed that most of the files he wanted to see had been returned from the universities of California and Columbia to the Bundes-archiv in Koblenz, and he planned to take an early-morning train there. Quite apart from the practicality of having a restful night, he found the secretary's obvious invitation rather offensive.

II

Next morning the rain and clouds had cleared by the time David arrived at the station. The train journey took him through Mainz and down the western bank of the Rhine, among pine forests and the spired castles of erstwhile princes. At Bacharach and Boppard the train skirted the river, past cargo vessels and barges fighting the current towards Basel and speeding downstream to Koblenz at the junction of the Rhine and the Mosel, then on to Cologne, Düssel-dorf, Arnhem and the seaport of Hamburg.

He arrived at Koblenz at midday and booked into a small guesthouse off Bismarckstrasse, close to the city centre. After dump-ing his bag on the single bed he went to the receptionist and asked the way to the Bundesarchiv building. Twenty minutes later he was standing in front of a clerk, a fat man with a sullen face, who handed him an application form without looking up. He filled in his name and gave the guesthouse address, putting Management Consultant in the space under 'Profession'. There was a section at the bottom of the form asking for the reason for the enquiry. He wrote, 'Research into the administrative techniques of the Third Reich', and in the space left for the desired reference he wrote 'Kestrel'.

The fat clerk scanned the completed form and pointed to the last entry.

'*Kestrel? Was ist das?*'

'*Turmfalke,*' David replied in German.

'Is this the only reference you can give us?'

'I have many file numbers listed under that name. I need to sort through them all.' David handed a copy of Levy's list across the counter.

The clerk sighed and pointed to a row of wooden armchairs. 'Very good, Herr Lewis. Be so kind as to wait over there.'

David sat down, and spent the next fifteen minutes watching the containers of an automated document-handling system move steadily along a service counter. Eventually a young woman came over to him, holding the application form.

'Herr Lewis, I regret there is a delay, but we cannot trace this reference. Is there no more information you can give us?'

He felt a pang of disappointment. 'I don't understand. I was assured in London that these files would be here. There must be some mistake.'

'I am sorry, but the only reference for *Turmfalke* is under its British translation, *Kestrel*, which appears in a number of British Intelligence documents. However, the file numbers you gave us are totally unconnected. Perhaps you have been given the wrong reference.'

David remembered what Levy had said about the Luftwaffe signals and the Enigma code. 'I'm sure this is correct. The files went to America for copying and examination but were returned here before that took place. Apparently they were not considered important.'

The assistant smiled. 'I see. If that is the case they will be held in our annexe in Hermannstrasse. All the documents in this building were actually copied by the Americans before being sent here.' She handed him back the application form and gave him a card with directions to the annexe printed on the back. 'You can use the same form, but they have a manual retrieval system, so things generally take longer.'

The annexe was an old building, full of narrow corridors, stained-glass windows and musty reading rooms. David sat impatiently in one of these for over an hour before the attendant returned with a trolley piled high with boxes and coloured folders, gave him a disgusted look, and limped back into the oblivion of the main storage rooms. Disconcerted by the sheer mass of documents, he began checking the file headings. He had just set aside a thin one marked with the US State Department badge when the attendant returned with a second trolley, equally loaded.

'I think I'd better take up residence,' he said to the departing and unresponsive back.

The first folder contained a file note from a US Army sergeant who had worked on the information.

For the attention of Colonel S.D. Stamford

FROM: Alpert, R. (Sgt)
DATE: 5 June 1955

The files arranged under the heading *Turmfalke* were collected May 1945 through September 1947 under the direction of the

Advocate General (Cmmd SIGINT 45083/KESTREL/0845). It should be noted that the Advocate General's list of documents included a section labeled *Medizinisch: Extrahieren* (Medical Abstracts) that were not checked against the inventory lists. I conclude they were not passed to Investigation Branch. The remaining *Turmfalke* files were passed to this office with reference to the codeword Kestrel; that is to say, to the German Army/Airforce Enigma key given that name by the British Government Code and Cypher School at Bletchley Park. I have established that *Turmfalke* and Kestrel are not connected. None of the documents relating to *Turmfalke* refer by name to any SS personnel and neither is the geographic location of any associated facility mentioned in the documentation. Because of this, although *Turmfalke* was designated as a *Hulle* (Top Secret) operation, investigation is considered to be a low priority. Under Command INTCOM/SSDOC/765/0946 signed by Colonel Fred Newman of the Army Documentation Inspectorate, I have down-classified the *Turmfalke* documents from Priority 3 to Priority 6. The documents, films and other materials relating to this project will be returned for filing to the archives at Koblenz.

The files bore the dust of forty years' neglect, but each was clearly labelled with a number and a date. The first few were orders from department heads of various Nazi organizations giving authority for setting up the *Turmfalke* operation, described briefly as a Waffen-SS staff college with facilities for training batches of fifty junior officers for six-week periods. There were requisition lists of items ranging from construction materials and transportation to office and laboratory furniture. Desks, chairs, projectors, blackboards, surgical tools, centrifuges, glassware, medical and building equipment were tabulated with manufacturers' names, costs and delivery schedules. Another batch of files contained references to the SS directing staff. Yet another contained listings for several hundred student officers. The entries comprised rank, initials and a four-figure code number. No names were given. The nature of the project was summarized in a handbook containing notes on the induction of student officers. One chapter was entitled 'Commandant's Address to Student Officers'.

'Ladies and Gentlemen. On behalf of the Directing Staff I welcome you to *Projekt Turmfalke*. You have been selected to come here as part of your continued training as future leaders of the Fatherland, and your presence has been personally approved by the Führer himself. It is my duty to remind you that your work here and all that you will see is subject to the strictest confidentiality. I am sure you are all eager to discover what lies in store for you, and we have arranged an introductory tour of the facilities. This will impress upon you that although our work is inspired by the purest of philosophical thought it is also based on the proven findings of our highly qualified research staff from the Waffen-SS Institute of Hygiene. In short, you are here to enhance a quality that each and every one of you has demonstrated you already possess in abundance: the ability to make military decisions. Man is a decision-making creature, set aside from the animals by this great gift. It follows that the man, or woman, who can make the fastest, most ruthless decisions will be supreme in action. Yet even within the Germanic peoples there are forces that inhibit this process of pure decision-making. Ill health, lack of concentration, personal and family relationships, stress, subconscious desires, contamination by contact with an inferior being . . . these and other factors can adversely affect your ability to make decisions. You are here to overcome such inhibitions. We are here to guide you. I believe you will find the process both rewarding and enjoyable. The course is intensive. However, we shall not neglect your leisure. These lovely grounds, so near to the river, are ideal for hunting and riding, and I have indulged myself by installing a lodge for my own favourite sport of falconry. There will be time in your otherwise busy schedules for you to relax in such pursuits. But never for one moment forget the reason you are here. And never doubt the absolute importance placed upon your presence, by the Reichsmarschall and by the Führer himself. I thank you for your attention. The Obersturmbannführer will now escort you on your tour. I look forward to meeting each of you individually at dinner this evening.'

A detailed itinerary followed this speech of welcome. Lecture and discussion rooms, library, dining rooms, living accommodation and recreation rooms were all seen during the first hour, and the file contained a plan for the movement of small groups of the new-comers through what appeared to be a large mansion. The groups were then taken into the grounds to other facilities, for which maps and brief descriptions were provided. This was followed by a speech by one of the medical staff on the physiological effects of decision-stress on the human body. Finally they reassembled to be treated to a demonstration of work selected from the research programmes, which covered such topics as instinctive behaviour, rational and irrational decision-making under varying degrees of stress, response to authority, the abdication of personal priorities, sacrifice and self-sacrifice, and the choice between alternatives.

By teatime, David had come to the conclusion that *Turmfalke* was simply a fancy name for a traditional if rather esoteric staff college for an officer elite. The first indication that this was not the case came when he opened a file containing award-winning essays by graduating students.

We were conducted to a gallery above the main teaching labora-tory and were met by the Standartenführer Director. He intro-duced a male subject who had received instruction in a test of manual dexterity in which the subject had to keep an electrical conductor within certain boundaries on a rotating metal drum. Control was by means of an adapted motor vehicle steering wheel, and the exercise was not dissimilar to an aptitude test for Luft-waffe pilots. Care had been taken to ensure that the subject was in good physical condition, and I noted that he was treated with consideration by the attending staff. In five minutes he scored maximum points; that is, he managed to avoid electrical contact during three complete sequences. He was given refreshment and allowed to rest for one minute. After that time a woman, whom we later learned was his wife, was wheeled into the laboratory in a metal chair. Contact was made via a transformer between this chair and the rotating drum. The subject was then asked to repeat the experiment. At first he disobeyed, but the drum was started and the woman began receiving electrical shocks. The subject was obliged to continue the experiment. The speed of the drum was increased during a number of sequences until the woman no longer reacted. The subject was humanely killed by a laboratory assistant. Both bodies were removed for detailed

75

physiological examination. I was particularly impressed with this demonstration, in that it provided an excellent example of what little resilience under difficult circumstances is possessed by a Jew. The subject behaved in a most degrading manner. I noted that he exhibited a number of involuntary and severe facial movements and venture to suggest that work might be done to ascertain the connection between facial muscles and mental stress during decision-making. Quite apart from a certain value among players of games of chance, it might prove possible, for example, to mislead interrogators by the cultivation of suitable expressions.

STUDENT APS 6758, HAUPTSTURMFÜHRER,

XIV WAFFEN GREN DIVISION

Someone had scrawled in handwriting under this essay, '*An excellent appraisal.*' Next to this comment another hand had appended, '*Agreed. But check whether this student is known to participate in the games of chance to which he refers.*' Under the second entry was a set of initials. David stared at them for a long time before he decided that they were the letters 'E.M.'.

* * *

Loki Threat Assessment

SUBJECT: *Lewis, David*
NATIONALITY: *UK*
SEX: *Male*
DOB/AGE: *45–55*
LOCATION: *Guesthouse, 54 Farbenstrasse*
DISTINGUISHING FEATURES: *Grey streak in hair*
KEYWORD AFFILIATIONS: *Kestrel; Koblenz; Management studies*
COMMENT: *Subject studied files of Allies' Kestrel project at archives. This is cross-referenced in Loki system to Projekt Turmfalke.*
ASSESSMENT PRIORITY (0–10): *1*
DATA ON SUBJECT: *None*
CROSS REFERENCES: *None*
ACTION: *Maintain scan*

III

At the sound of the doorbell, Carrigan looked carefully around. The evening was warm, but he had turned on the living-flame gas fire anyway. Kate had liked it so much on her first visit that he felt it would create a good atmosphere. He realized that his feelings for Kate were beginning to reflect more than a therapist-client relationship. On the other hand, he was both professionally and personally interested in David's problem and had grown to like the man. From a psychiatric point of view he could only enhance his reputation in this particular case, with its innovative method of revealing hidden dreams. So his reasons for agreeing to see Kate were professional. At least, that's what he told himself as he opened the door.

She was wearing a high-necked blouse under a soberly tailored jacket and a skirt with a low hemline. Although she looked strained her face was perfect, lips picked out with a dark liner that emphasized symmetrical curves. When he offered her a drink she chose coffee.

'Thanks for letting me come over at such short notice,' she said. 'I feel a bit silly, really.'

'No need for that. I'm glad you came.'

'He's never done this before. I knew he had something on his mind before he left. He even forgot some important papers and had to get them flown to Frankfurt with a courier. He just doesn't do that kind of thing.'

'I don't think you need to worry, even if it's not typical. His stress has been severe, and I believe it still is. The hypnotherapy has helped to relieve it in some respects, but we still have no idea what lies at the bottom of his problem. Maybe we never will.'

She shuddered, remembering the images of the video recording. 'It certainly brought something into the open. Surely that's all that matters.'

Carrigan nodded. 'Well, it's a start. There are several aspects of David's case that I need to fill in to get the whole picture,' he said. 'Maybe you know some of the answers. D'you mind if we go through it?'

She remembered what David had said about settling Carrigan's account.

'Provided we do it on a professional basis. I just want to get this over with so we can carry on with our lives.'

'Fair enough.' Carrigan pointed at the whisky bottle, but she shook her head. He poured himself a stiff one and sipped it appreciatively. 'Academically, he's brilliant, isn't he?'

'Oh yes. Mind you, he seemed to have been a slow starter. His primary school reports make pretty grim reading, I can tell you, but things seemed to improve when he went to secondary school. His parents spent a great deal of time, helping him with schoolwork. He said his teachers were amazed when he decided to go in for engineering. They felt it was beneath him, that he could have been a scientist, or a lawyer. Maybe a language teacher. He's always been marvellous at German. Anything but an engineer.'

'That ties in with what he told me. In one of our first discussions he mentioned how his parents helped him. Do you know anything about that?'

'He talked about it sometimes. Just that he was behind in everything. In fact, I gather that when he was very young he had to go to a special school. Apparently he found it difficult to speak, let alone read and write.'

'Yet now he's bilingual,' Carrigan mused. 'I'm no specialist in child education, but it sounds peculiar to me. If he is so intelligent, what could have repressed him like that?'

Kate unbuttoned her jacket. 'Joe, would it be possible to have that drink now?'

'Sure. What'll it be?'

'A small gin and tonic.'

'Is that fire too hot for you? I'll turn it down if it is.'

'No, I'm fine, thank you.'

As she moved he was acutely conscious of her breasts stretching the fabric of her blouse. He knew she had seen him watching. When he came back with the drink he asked, 'Would you like me to put on some music?'

'Look,' she said, suddenly nervous. 'I'm intruding into your evening.' She began drinking quickly, then put the glass down and stood up.

'How could you be intruding? If you look around you'll notice that I haven't exactly treated your visit like a random event. Bach-

78

elors don't normally stick daffodils around the place, you know. Puff up the cushions . . .'

'That's one of the reasons I think I should go.'

Coming to him like this was a mistake. She wanted his help, but was that all she wanted? He knew why she'd chosen to wear a formal suit. A warning to him. A defence for her. And he just stood there, watching, waiting.

'If you mean that, I'll drive you home,' he said at last.

'Thank you, but there's absolutely no need. I've got the car outside.'

'I'll drive you in your car and take a cab back. No problem.'

There was a problem, she thought. In her isolation she would have given her soul for one touch of a human finger, and Carrigan was standing so near she could smell him. A wave of anger at David for being so bloody thoughtless swept over her. She had never needed anyone as much as she needed her husband at that moment, and the bastard was wandering about Europe indulging in Lord knows what! The anger directed itself at Carrigan. There he stood, waiting for Nature to take over. Waiting for her to turn to him in her distress. He was the bastard, not David. Carrigan and his West Coast morality. She knew all about the relationships between shrinks and their patients. And that's all he was, after all. An arrogant, conceited shrink. She smiled at him brightly.

'I wouldn't dream of it, Joe,' she said. 'But you never know. David might phone, and I'd prefer to be on my own. You understand, don't you?'

Of course he understood. They both knew exactly why she was leaving.

IV

David spent Saturday in his room in the guesthouse in Koblenz, reading the photostats of files from the annexe, unable to take in the enormity of coming so close to horror. Personally close. Several times he crossed the small landing to retch into the lavatory. By Sunday morning he was empty of everything but a deep-rooted disgust that began as a sweeping indictment of the human race

79

and ended focused here in Germany, the land that had emerged so effectively from the chaos of the last European war. At lunchtime the proprietor's wife knocked on his door to enquire whether he would join the other guests in the small dining room. His curt reply and the state of the lavatory were taken as a sign of gastric flu, and they called a doctor. David pulled himself together long enough to convince them that he was recovering from a sudden chill, closing the door firmly in the doctor's curious face and returning to the document he'd been reading, one of several dozen reports on student achievements at the camp.

STUDENT:	T.P. 9744
RANK:	Obersturmführer
DESIGNATION:	Amt VI
BATTLE ORDER:	9th SS Panzerdivision, Hohenstauffen
PARTY AFFILIATION:	NSDAP (2 February 41), Napola (1940–41)
DATE OF COMMISSION: 13.01.45	

This student is on secondment from his battle unit to the Reichs-sicherheitshauptamt. During the entire course he performed with exceptional vigour and passed out as Sword of Honour Student. Detailed course comments are attached. (Attachment 2c)

The student has several brothers and sisters younger than himself. Because of this he was given access to children from the medical facility, and it was noted that he became particularly friendly with Case 341/F. This Case was selected for the student's *Dolchstoss*, which was performed after the student had worked through a number of educational exercises with the Case. Timing from Anordnung to Gnadenstoss was 1.25 seconds.

RECOMMENDATION: This student is recommended for accelerated promotion. His understanding of European languages and international affairs plus his ability to perceive the underlying philosophy of both military and civil action make him a suitable candidate for service under BSS.

The literal meaning of *Dolchstoss* is: to stab in the back with a dagger. David looked again at the explanation given in one of the standard SS reference books: 'The initiate is encouraged to develop a relationship with a living creature. A suitable animal is a dog, a non-Aryan woman or a non-Aryan child. Once the relationship is established the initiate is given an unexpected order to stab the subject with his or her SS dagger. The initiate's reactions and timing are noted and used as a guide to his or her loyalty to the SS Oath of Allegiance.'

The meticulous SS records contained the information that Case 341/F was a twelve-year-old Polish girl called Nadia Retza, the child killed by Student Obersturmführer T.P. 9744.

David collected his photocopies and pushed them into his suitcase, then recovered a small round package wrapped in silver foil from a hiding place under the ramshackle chest of drawers and slipped it carefully into his briefcase. After that he sat in the darkened room, eyes closed, mind racing. Towards the end of the afternoon he stood up stiffly and ran a hot bath which he followed with a shave. There was nothing more he could do in Koblenz, and he had a progress meeting with Sacht the following morning. After packing away his belongings he checked out of the guesthouse, took the train back to Frankfurt and booked into the Plaza Hotel.

V

At ten o'clock that evening he tried to put the revelations of his visit to the archives from his mind and began reading his notes in preparation for his morning meeting. He expected quite a grilling now that the Sacht engineers had had a chance to examine his design amendments in detail. He did not anticipate any trouble, but they would be uneasy about his lapse of memory over the blueprints. They'd be wondering what else he might have forgotten. Fair enough. He would feel exactly the same, in their position. At ten thirty, he was surprised to hear a knock on his door.

'*Ja! Wer ist da?*'

A woman's voice called something, softly. He went to the door.

'*Ja?*'

'It is Maria Frozell. May I come in?'

He opened the door.

'Dr Lewis.' She smiled, a little nervously, he thought. 'I hope you don't mind my calling around at such an hour. There are some papers I thought you might like to see before you meet Herr Weerts tomorrow.'

Very strange, this. 'Perhaps you'd better come in, Fräulein.'

She stepped into his room quickly, as though she didn't want to be seen.

'If you're quite sure.'

'I was about to go through my own papers. If I've overlooked anything, I'll be only too grateful for your help.'

The last thing he needed was another fiasco like last time. If she had any information that could be useful, he'd like to know about it. The question was, why was she doing this?

She sat on the chair by the shallow desk and pulled a file out of her briefcase.

'These are reports on the current situation between our two companies. You will see that Herr Weerts is entirely in favour of your work, but some of our other senior engineers are pressing him to consider using another consultancy. I would, of course, be grateful if you would treat this information in the strictest confidence.'

She put the files on the desk and pushed them towards him.

'You've gone to a great deal of trouble for a stranger, Fräulein.'

'But you're not a stranger. We have known each other for, what is it, almost a year on the telephone and by the facsimile. I can now look forward to your visits in person.'

'If my company and Sacht continue to do business, you mean. Can you tell me exactly why you brought this information to me, Fräulein?'

'Indeed. But why are we being so formal?' She smiled. 'Perhaps in private you could call me Maria.'

Her face was oval, slightly Eastern, with dark, almond eyes and pale skin. She had the fine, sexy features he associated with high-class call girls. Alert. Aware of her capabilities. Slender body, swelling breasts.

He glanced through the files. They were reports on the meetings that had taken place during the Sacht project with comments from various departments, much along the lines she had described.

'I must repeat, Fräulein, why did you come here?'

'I find you very attractive,' she said seriously. 'I want to help you.'

82

'Really.'

'Is that so strange?'

He felt a flush of irritation, but answered as lightly as he could. 'I'm not exactly the sophisticated woman's answer to Tom Cruise or Al Pacino. Woody Allen, maybe.'

'I can't help the way I feel.' She rose from the chair and stood in front of him, tense. 'Do you not feel something for me?'

David was suddenly overcome with an intense sexual longing. It came out of nowhere and made him shake with its intensity, but he was unable to make any movement towards her. She moved forward slightly, so her breasts were touching him.

'Do you not feel something?' she repeated. When he didn't answer she put her arms round his neck and pulled him towards her, pink tongue flicking his lips slightly, pushing her hips into his crutch. When she felt his erection she gave a little gasp and slid to her knees, unbuckled his belt, pulling his trousers down to his shoes. When his legs were free she took hold of his genitals, holding him as if he were a precious statue.

'It's beautiful,' she whispered. 'So strong and unhidden.'

He looked down, utterly detached, feeling the physical pleasure as if it belonged to someone else. She rose and eased off her own clothes, then pulled him onto the bed and began stroking him again. He tried to concentrate on what she was doing. Part of him wanted sex with an unthinking primitive passion, but the musty stench of the SS documents from the Koblenz vaults filled his skull. He was split in two separate parts, one linked to the terror of the past, the other swimming in a sea of erotica. He was caught in an irresistible paralysis, not able to stop her, nor to assist, nor to respond.

After she had played with him for a few minutes she snuggled close and asked, 'Tell me, how does someone become what you are? You know, a consultant in engineering.'

He gazed into blackness. 'I'm too highly qualified to work on staff for most manufacturing companies. Started in research laboratories in the oil industry and then branched out on my own. The Halkyn partnership head-hunted me.'

'That was BP's research centre at Sunbury, wasn't it?'

'Yes.' He was surprised. 'How did you know?'

'We collect information on anyone who negotiates with Sacht at your level.'

He moved uneasily. 'Really?'

'Shhh.' She took hold of him again and was silent for a few minutes. Then: 'Presumably there are many things in the files that might be of interest to you.'

In a dark corner of his mind an alarm clanged. Was she referring to his visit to the archives? No. She couldn't be. How would she know where he'd been over the past couple of days? But the alarm kept sounding. 'Files? What d'you mean, files?'

'You know.' She giggled. It sounded forced. 'Things about contracts. Your competitors. What they are offering Sacht, for example.'

'Oh, I see. Are you saying that you'd let me look at them?'

Her fingers cupped him in a rhythmic caress. He was completely detached from what she was doing.

'Well, it's possible, is it not?'

'I presume you'd want something in return.' Her naiveté amazed him. If she were prepared to tell him her company's secrets, would not the reverse be true? Did this sexual encounter provide her with the security that he would not report her to Sacht? He could imagine her outraged reaction if faced with such a thing: 'But Herr Weerts, Dr Lewis took advantage of me. He invited me to his hotel. He asked me questions about the company.'

On the other hand, maybe she wasn't doing this on her own. Maybe someone in Sacht paid her to set up this kind of thing. Maybe it was a trap for him. A test of his integrity.

The air weighed down like a lead curtain, lifeless, holding the sickening odour of burning fat and carbolic soap. It took a super-human effort for him to fight the billowing sickness. How old was Maria – thirty, thirty-five? One of the post-war children, born of parents who had stood and watched *den Führer* rise to power, turned blind eyes to the crowds herded out of tenements, to the cattle wagons rattling though darkened suburban stations, perhaps taken part in what followed. She belonged to a generation that had grappled its recent history with a disturbed and disturbing mixture of guilt and defiance.

Sensing his change of mood, she stopped caressing him and got out of bed. 'Does your cabinet have cold drinks? Wouldn't you like that?' When she came back with two glasses of cold champagne she said, 'It's expensive living in Griesheim. Many people try to get

84

flats by the river where I live. The rents go up all the time.'

So that was it. He felt very cold. At school he'd been given a copy of a magazine called *Picture Post* that contained award-winning photographs. One, taken in Dresden in the winter of 1945 outside a pavement café, showed a dozen thin young girls staring at the camera with flat eyes, waiting for GIs to come with chocolate, cigarettes, stockings and other items from the PX stores. There was no suggestion that the GIs were being anything other than generous to a vanquished and hungry population. It had taken many years before he realized what they wanted in return, and he understood how children could sell their bodies in return for the necessities of life during such times. Maria, well groomed, sensual . . . Maria was different. She had no such needs. Not really. She was simply a whore.

When she bent across him with his glass he knocked it violently from her hand and began dressing. She did the same in angry silence before grabbing the files from the desk and stuffing them into her case. As she opened the door he called her back.

'Here,' he said, holding out a hundred-Deutschmark note. Her whisper floated over him from the coldness of space.

'You bastard Jew.'

CHAPTER FIVE

I

Albert Levy handed the final photocopy of David's Koblenz files to Anna and rubbed his eyes. David remained silent while the girl finished reading.

'This is a frightful story, Mr Lewis. You have been most meticulous, and we shall certainly add your work to our records,' the old man said wearily. 'We owe you our thanks.'

The implied finality alarmed David. 'But this isn't all of it. Just the beginning. I've a lot more work to do, and there's something else I want to show you.' He opened the round flat tin that he'd collected from a photographic laboratory in the West End that morning. 'This was among the boxes and files in Koblenz. The original is an old eight-millimetre reel, and it's rather brittle. I had this sixteen-millimetre copy made so we could look through it together.'

'You took this from the official files?' Levy sounded scandalized, offended by the impropriety of such an action.

'It's been gathering dust for fifty years,' David said forcefully. 'None of these damned files has got the name of a single person who was involved in this *Turmfalke* thing, and whatever is on this film might give us a clue.'

'Albert is concerned to act within the law, Mr Lewis,' Anna said, 'even though it is sometimes tempting to do this kind of thing.' She turned to Levy. 'Now that we have a film, we must see it. Mr Lewis is right; you might recognize something. We can always return the original to the archives, if need be. I'll ask Uri to set up the projector.'

Anna called down the staircase, and Uri came up a few moments later carrying an ancient film projector. Following Levy, they made their way slowly to another room where Uri plugged the projector into the mains and threaded the film through the sprockets.

'There is no soundtrack,' he observed.

Anna drew the curtains.

The film had been made by an amateur who started by splicing a few seconds of a Nazi banner into the beginning. Then the camera showed a large mansion, built like a castle, with a terrace overlooking a wide river, and woods and tall mountains in the background. Several people were riding on horseback towards the building with something on their wrists. When they drew close the audience saw that each of the riders was carrying a hunting bird. At a distance of about twenty metres from the camera they reined in their horses and released the birds which shot upwards and out of sight. The riders waved and pivoted expertly over the gravel path. Two of them dismounted, and the camera moved jerkily towards them to show a handsome man and a blonde woman smiling and hugging each other. The man looked into the sky and held up a gauntlet, and a kestrel stooped onto it, its curved beak open wide, waiting for the titbit of red meat that was its reward.

The next sequence was shot indoors. After showing what appeared to be lecture rooms, the camera moved into a bare chamber with whitewashed walls. In the foreground a man and woman stood under a wooden beam, facing each other, with nooses round their necks. A number of people in white laboratory coats sat at a desk behind them, with pens and notebooks. Water was running into a tank arranged as a counterbalance over a series of levers between the two trapdoors of the gallows. Suddenly, the man grabbed the lever nearest to himself and gave it a jerk. He dropped almost out of sight, head twisted like a broken doll under the coils of the noose. A black uniformed SS man appeared and unhooked the rope, lowering the man's body to someone out of sight below the floor. Then he casually kicked the woman's trapdoor free, sending her plummeting down too.

After another crude splice the screen showed a post-mortem in progress, with gowned and masked figures cutting into a male corpse and extracting items from the skull and chest. This shot cut away to a laboratory with centrifuges in operation, and this was followed by a scene in which the tall young man who had flown the kestrel smilingly held a number of glass test tubes in front of a wall chart of the human endocrine system. A close-up on three tubes showed the labels *Hernanhang*, *Thalamus* and *Schilddrüse*. The screen went black, and the film chattered its way through the projector, the top reel spinning for several seconds before Uri cut the power with a sharp movement. He turned and stared at David, his eyes blazing with anger in the flickering camera light.

Anna opened the curtains, and Levy said, 'Mr Lewis! Are you all right?'

David took a breath and pushed himself upright. 'Thank you. Yes. I'm sorry about this . . . so much trouble.' Something about the film was thundering into his temples. A link from one thing to something else. But what was it? Something in the lecture rooms. If only he could relax, as Carrigan had taught him.

'Would a cup of coffee help?' Anna asked him.

The photograph of Hitler swam into his mind, with the caption. Then he remembered the background documents that Peter Halkyn's secretary had sent him when the German project came up. The corporate brochure, with the chairman's introduction. *Our dear friend Ernst* . . . The scrawled initials on the SS student's appraisal, E.M. . . . Ernst Muntz. No. It was absurd. A coincidence.

'Uri, get Mr Lewis a brandy, would you,' Levy said. 'Perhaps we should all have one.'

When the dark-eyed young Jew left the room Levy smiled wanly at David. 'I am using this as an excuse, you understand. I am allowed an occasional brandy by my physician. He insists that it puts a strain on my heart, but at my age one should not place too much importance on what physicians say, do you not agree?'

And something else the film had in common with Deutsche Arzneiwissenschaft Werke. Oh yes. A laboratory! Links, links, links.

Uri came back with a bottle and four glasses. He poured generous helpings and handed round the glasses. Anna added some mineral water to hers and insisted on doing the same to Levy's drink.

David, still staring at the blank screen, said, 'Professor Muntz.'

'No,' Levy said. 'His name is Leopold. I have been a patient with Dr Leopold for many years.'

'The man with the test tubes. The one on the horse, with the kestrel. Professor Ernst Muntz. The chairman of Deutsche Arzneiwissenschaft Werke.' He began searching feverishly through the photocopies until he came to the Hauptsturmführer student's award-winning essay and stabbed his finger at the last set of initials.

'E.M. There you are! E. Muntz — ". . . our dear friend Ernst . . ."
In Hitler's photograph. Can't you see? Muntz was the director of
Turmfalke. He flew falcons, kestrels. It all fits into place.'

'The man with the test tubes certainly bears a resemblance to
the horse rider,' Levy nodded slowly, 'and I can accept that the
establishment shown in the film is connected with the *Turmfalke*
project, else it would not have been in the archives. It is also possible, but not certain, that the man in the film was the director. But
there is no reference to the name Muntz anywhere. It is all conjecture, Mr Lewis.'

'Muntz was the director of the *Turmfalke* project, I tell you,'
David said emphatically. 'The Commandant. Professor E. Muntz.
Ernst Muntz, the man in my photograph. He is now the chairman
of Deutsche Arzneiwissenschaft Werke. I'm pitching for a project
with his company. My god!'

Levy shook his head. 'Conjecture, conjecture. But there is something rather curious here. Anna, the battle order of SS divisions.
Can you bring the references.'

He turned a few pages, then nodded to himself, reading slowly
with his finger running down the printed lines. Anna looked over
his shoulder.

'Don't tell me Ernst Muntz was actually in the SS,' she said.

'Oh yes,' Levy nodded. 'His military designation is listed in the
order of battle. SS Standartenführer Ernst Muntz, Florian Geyer
Kavallerie Division, Regiment 18. One of the Führer's high-fliers.
Here is the Cornflower collar decal that you drew from your
dreams, Mr Lewis. Two buds and an opened flower. Just what
Muntz would wear on his uniform. This is all very strange.'

Levy pulled a large hardbound volume from a bookshelf and
looked through the index.

'Here, you see, we have a transcript of his testimony at Nuremberg. As a senior officer of the Schutzstaffel he was accused with
many others of war crimes, but he argued that in the early stages
of the war he had been on secondment to the Nationalpolitische
Erziehungsanstalten in charge of secondary-school education in
Bavaria. In 1943 he moved to take charge of medical training at a
military hospital in the Rhineland. As he was a noted academic, a
brilliant young Heidelberg medical graduate before the hostilities,
his case was dismissed for lack of evidence. We had our suspicions,

as we did for all such men, but there was nothing further we could do. We had to concentrate our meagre resources on projects that had at least some likelihood of success. From time to time I filed information about him, as I did with so many others. After the war I believe he was indeed the leading light behind a pharmaceutical company. The name is here somewhere . . . Ah yes. Deutsche Arzneiwissenschaft Werke. You are correct about this, at least. But then you will have seen his name in the company's literature, will you not?'

Levy passed the reference book to David, who stared at the runes and insignia, the decals, the uniforms, the lists of Waffen-SS officer ranks and the Order of Battle.

'What I cannot understand, Mr Lewis, is this,' Levy said slowly. 'How could you have known he was in this particular SS regiment? This is not common knowledge. Where did you first see this name Muntz? Where did you first come across it?'

Levy's voice echoed along a dark tunnel. Images from the dream, from the pages of DAW's corporate brochure, from the address by the Director of *Turmfalke* to his new students: '*Man is a decision-making creature . . .*'

A woman's voice said in German, 'Excuse me, Professor Muntz, but there is something of interest.' David couldn't move his head.

'Here, sip your brandy,' Anna said out of the mists. 'It's all right. You fainted, that's all. It's very hot in here.'

Albert Levy watched through an upstairs window as Leon and Uri helped the blindfolded David into the off-roader with tinted windows.

'It's very clear that he's unearthed an atrocity, but I can't see why he's trying to implicate this professor,' Anna said. 'You said yourself that Muntz's name doesn't appear in any of the wartime documents he studied.'

Levy rolled his brandy round the bowl and sighed. 'I know you told Uri to dilute the bottle, Anna. And then you insult me further by giving me even more water. If Dr Leopold is correct, I shall no doubt live to be a hundred. Frankly the prospect appals me.'

Anna hid a smile and took the glass from him.

'You should marry,' he told her. 'It is a waste to have you caring for an old man.'

'So why did David Lewis come up with the name Muntz?' she persisted.

'He has no doubt read about Ernst Muntz at some time, a few facts and figures absorbed many years ago, perhaps, and he has fallen victim to speculation. Why he has picked Muntz out of all the many hundreds who might have been involved, don't ask me. But if he is honest about these dreams of his, then we are witnessing a remarkable series of coincidences. We shall just have to wait and see if Mr Lewis decides to continue his research. And now, my dear, it is time for my siesta.'

Uri stopped the car near a train station. Leon told David to remove the blindfold, and they watched him buy a ticket and walk up the steps to the platforms, then they scanned the street for signs of anything unusual, an instinctive practice.

'Why does Albert continue to see him?' Leon pondered.

Uri shook his head. 'He brings trouble, that one. I can smell it in his sweat.'

'Anna says he has evidence of a Holocaust atrocity, but is this anything special?'

His dark-eyed friend recalled the flickering images of the old cine film. 'Every atrocity is special.'

'Of course, but we can't deal with them all, can we?'

Uri's smile was chilling. 'No. But when something presents itself to the hangman, all he need do is release the trap.'

'It won't come to that,' Leon assured him. 'He's a wild card, following his nose and unearthing a couple of coincidences. If he turns up anything useful, well and good. Otherwise, there's no harm done. That's what Albert thinks. Seems a waste of time to me.'

'He stinks of trouble,' Uri repeated.

David returned home tiredly, to find that Kate had left a note saying that the fashion company liked her video, and she was meeting Margaret Burnside to discuss the next step. He absorbed the information and pushed it into the background. He was glad that things seemed to be going well for Kate, but there were more important things for him to do than worry about his wife's resurgent interest in modelling, and one of them was to phone the US Army Information Directorate. According to the archives, everything related to *Turmfalke* seemed to have passed through US Army hands. If there were any more links to discover, he could think of no better place to start. Except, maybe, the People's Library in Berlin, one of the largest repositories of SS records.

II

Kate and Carrigan strolled to the bow of the river-cruiser as the deckhand slipped the ropes securing them to the landing stage and coiled them on the deck. In the small wheelhouse the captain expertly used the strong current to bring the boat into the middle of the river.

'All these years in the city, and I've never been on a river boat,' Kate said. 'Dreadful, isn't it, to be here so long and miss this kind of thing?'

Carrigan smiled and laid his jacket over an empty seat in front, stretching in the sunshine. 'I needed a break. You called me just in time to stop me collapsing over my case notes.'

They sat in a relaxed silence, and Carrigan let a few hundred yards of historic riverbank pass by. 'So. How are you?'

She pushed her hands deep into the pockets of her denim jacket and looked down at her shoes. 'Joe, I don't know if I want to talk about me.'

He waited, careful not to look at her closely, letting her decide what the distance between them should be.

'Christ, Joe,' she whispered fiercely. 'I should be devoting all my thoughts to what's happening to my husband, and every five minutes I have to fight an urge to pick up the phone and beg you to let me come round and see you. I even told him a lie today. Said I was seeing my agent. I've never done anything like that before. You know what I'm saying? This is the last thing I need.'

When he still didn't answer she rounded on him, speaking louder than she meant to, causing heads to turn their way.

'Say something, damn you.'

'What can I say? I'd be a liar if I gave you any crap about improper professional behaviour. I don't believe in all that. In my book there's nothing better two humans can do than add sex to their relationship when they're fond of each other. The only consideration is, does a third party get hurt? In this case, the answer's got to be yes. And there's a good chance one of us would get hurt as well. Probably both of us. So I'm up a gum tree, same as you. But the way I feel, I'm willing to take a chance.'

She shifted nearer to the railing and watched the waves created by their passage lap against the banks.

'You're a cold-blooded bastard.'

'Maybe. I'm certainly careful when it comes to the emotions of my friends.'

His use of the word touched her, and she stood up, holding tightly to the rail.

'Whatever happened to clients and patients?'

'I work in a strange area. The relationships change. Quite apart from my feelings for you, I like David. You take that risk when you get close to someone in therapy.'

'What risk are you taking, for God's sake? I mean, when you're tired of this place you'll go back to Los Angeles or somewhere else nearer to home.'

He nodded. 'Maybe. But I like it here. If I can find a way to stay permanently, I will.'

'I don't want you to think that there's anything wrong between David and me,' she said.

'I can accept that, and with a little patience and some luck there's no reason why you can't both get back to a normal, happy relationship. We seem to have licked his dream problem, and that means we're on the way to discovering what's underlying his tensions. When we know that, maybe we can fix it.'

'You make him sound like a broken-down car that can be mended by a mechanic.'

'I didn't mean to, but there are techniques for relieving stress that I think we can apply here. I need all the input I can get, such as your feelings about him right now.'

She hesitated. 'He's changed. Ever since he began seeing you he's been behaving oddly.'

'Do you mean oddly or differently?'

'Both. He's letting his business slide, and that's not David. He's let a couple of clients down, and he's planning another visit to Germany. It's only three weeks since he was in Frankfurt, and he should be developing the detailed project work in the office before going back.'

'I presume you've asked him about it.'

'He says it's something to do with a new project. Confidential. He's been making a lot of phone calls from his study, with the door closed. He never does that. And twice he's disappeared for practically an entire Saturday. He came back looking quite ill the last time. I asked him to get in touch with you, but he said there was no need.'

Carrigan gazed thoughtfully at the river. 'From what you say he's starting another phase of whatever's troubling him, and I need to clear up these points in his biography that I mentioned before we have another session together.'

'I'll help if I can. What's missing?'

'His place and date of birth.'

'You're going into a lot of detail, aren't you?' she asked.

'Old habits die hard. I was taught to examine Square One before believing in Square Two. It's routine, but when I checked at Somerset House I couldn't find any record of a David Lewis being born in London on 1 January 1940 to Jacob and Edith.'

'I think his parents lived in Islington. Would that be classified as London?'

'No idea. Anyway, I can ask him next time I see him. When'll he be back from Germany?'

'Friday.'

'So, what'll you be doing on Thursday?' he asked.

'I've got an interview in the afternoon. It's for the new fashion campaign I told you about.'

'Anything planned for the evening?'

'Not at the moment,' she said.

'In that case, why don't we have dinner, and you can tell me how you got on with the fashion people.'

Kate stared at the water. She wanted to have dinner with him very much indeed.

'I don't think that would be a very sensible thing to do, Joe.'

94

III

The US Army Information Department gave David the names of several World War II veterans' organizations that might be able to help. He drew blanks with the first five, but the woman who answered the phone for the Berlin Buddies Association in San Francisco sounded more promising.

'We have seven gentlemen named Alpert on our books. Would you happen to know the first name of the gentleman for whom you are looking, sir?'

'All I have is his name, rank and initial. Alpert, Sergeant R.'

'Well,' the slow voice commented, 'We have two R. Alperts, and both of them held the rank of Sergeant. You say that the gentleman was stationed in Berlin in 1956.'

'That's right,' David said.

'I'd have to check that out, sir. In any case it is the policy of the association never to reveal personal details of membership. If you would be so kind as to give me a contact address I will write you if either of the two gentlemen was stationed in Berlin during the year in question.'

'I'm in a bit of a hurry on this,' David told her. 'Is it possible for me to leave a contact number with you? I'd be very grateful for anything you can do to help.'

IV

Even in spring the eastern districts of Berlin looked dismal and drab to David, despite efforts to spruce the place up after re-unification. After they had been bumping over the uneven paving for several minutes, he caught sight of the taxi driver watching him in the mirror. The man looked quickly away, concentrating on steering a course between the potholes. Old habits die hard.

When David checked into his hotel he tried to phone Kate, but the telecommunication computers were down and there was a three-hour delay. Fighting a growing sense of depression, he walked the six blocks to the massive People's Library where the War archives were stored, checked his details at the counter and handed the assistant his list of requirements: training records for all officers under the rank of Sturmbannführer in the seven elite SS divisions listed in the Koblenz archives for the period February to April 1945. He hunted through documents as they arrived at his reading desk throughout Friday and Saturday, slept most of Sunday and found what he was looking for halfway through Monday afternoon when he was working through a section on SS education.

For obvious reasons, few German officers had been seconded to training courses after the D-Day invasion, so the lists were not as long for the latter stages of the war as he had feared they would be. And there it was, a section marked *Unter dem Siegel der Verschwiegenheit. Projekt Turmfalke.* Under the Seal of Secrecy. He took a deep breath as he stared at the pages, placing his hands on the wooden desk until they had stopped trembling.

Students seconded to *Turmfalke* were listed in the project documents by rank, a set of initials and a four-figure number which, he suspected, was a shortened version of each officer's Nazi Party number. All he had to do was cross-reference the two sets of documents.

And so, on 10 February 1945, Untersturmführer H.W.K. (2359) had been given leave of absence from SS-Panzer-Division Frundsberg for unspecified training lasting six weeks. So had Untersturmführer G.R. (1609), D.F.K. (6455), W.T. von R. (8321) and R.R.W. (1658), together with Obersturmführer T.P. (9744) and three Hauptsturmführer. He listed these details in his notebook, then he checked the four-figure codes against the library's Nazi Party records and added the students' full names and date and place of birth to the list, repeating the exercise for all seven SS divisions.

By Tuesday afternoon he had identified more than three hundred young officers who had trained at the top secret SS college code-named *Turmfalke.* Today they would be men and women in their mid-sixties and early seventies. The records showed, for example, that Obersturmführer T.P. (9744), who had been awarded his course's Sword of Honour, was Theodore Pökke, born in a small town outside Stuttgart on 14 January 1925. David sighed and rubbed his eyes. Armed with such detailed information he would be able to track at least some of them down using the public record office. This Pökke would be as good a place to start as any, he thought.

Despite a growing headache and sore eyes, he spent several more hours trying to discover something that would help him to identify the location of the college or names of the project's directing staff. This proved to be impossible, and he was about to close his notebook when one of the items he had seen among the countless documents suddenly jerked his consciousness. Feverishly he shuffled back through the files for SS-Panzer-Division Hohenstaufen. He was right. Each of the student entries contained a movement record, and halfway down the page was a reference for a rail travel warrant. Every student in the division had the same destination, and the same was true for officers in the other divisions: *Ziel Andernach (Fähre). Andernach!*

* * *

Loki Threat Assessment

SUBJECT: *Lewis, D*
NATIONALITY: *British*
SEX: *Male*
DOB/AGE: *40*
LOCATION: *Hotel Grunweiss, Berlin*
DISTINGUISHING FEATURES: *Small in stature*
KEYWORD AFFILIATIONS: *SS studies; management*
COMMENT: *People's Library enquiry report from counter staff*
ASSESSMENT PRIORITY (0−10): *1*
DATA ON SUBJECT: *None*
CROSS REFERENCES: *None*
ACTION: *Place in database*

V

Kate had invited Carrigan round on the afternoon David phoned from the railway station at Wiesbaden. She gripped the telephone hard as he told her that he needed to spend more time away. 'This is crazy, David,' she said, trying not to shout. 'We can't go on like this. You should have been back on Friday for a conference at the Institution of Mechanical Engineers. The secretary phoned and said you were supposed to present a paper, and on Monday Peter Halkyn called and asked where you were –'

'Look, I'm sorry, but something's come up, and I had to go to Berlin and then –'

'Are you listening? I'm worried sick about you. I don't need this. I love you, and I don't know what the hell is happening to us.'

'I love you too, but there's something I have to do over here. I'll be able to tell you all about it when I get back.'

'Over here? I don't even know where "here" is, for God's sake. You were supposed to come back from Germany five days ago, then you go to Berlin. So where are you now?'

'I'm still in Germany. Wiesbaden. I'm on my way to a place called Andernach. I just need a couple of days, then I'll be back. Thursday. Friday at the latest.'

'But what about –'

'Tell people I'm sick, can't you? Get Joe Carrigan to write out a note, or something. Christ, Kate, I've never taken any sick leave. They can stand a few days without me. I haven't even had a proper holiday for six years, so I'm taking a few days off. What difference?'

His question summed up the futility she felt for herself. Everything was falling apart, and such things couldn't be stuck back together. What difference, indeed? Whatever his problems, David could bloody well deal with them himself from now on.

'You're right. You're entirely right. What bloody difference!'

David heard the tears as she slammed the phone down, the unaccustomed epithet ringing in his ears.

Carrigan took her hand, but she pulled it away and dabbed at her eyes. 'Would you like me to leave?' he asked. She shook her head. 'Where is he?'

'Still in Germany, for God's sake. He was supposed to be in the UK this week, but he rushes off to Berlin and somewhere called Andernach.'

'Maybe he's taking on new clients.'

'Maybe he is, but he's never let anyone down before, and you know what it's like in business. You can't do that kind of thing. They start looking for someone else.'

'I'll make us some more coffee.' Carrigan took the cups into the kitchen. 'Where d'you keep the sugar?'

Kate followed him and took a red tin labelled 'India Tea' out of a cupboard.

'Now why didn't I think of looking in there?' he said.

'Because you're a phenomenologist.'

He took her face in his hands, wiped away tears with a finger. 'Not many people can actually get their tongues round that, y'know.'

'Don't, Joe. Please don't do this to me.'

'I'm trying not to do anything to you. You can't imagine how damned hard I'm trying.'

She went back into the sitting room, leaving him standing awkwardly. When he brought the coffee she said, 'I'm sorry.'

He made an effort to recapture his earlier light-heartedness. 'It's me that should be saying that. So much for professional ethics. The doctor's falling in love with his patient's beautiful wife.'

She looked at him intently. 'Is he, Joe?'

'Sure he is. Head over heels.'

'No. I mean, is David still your patient?'

Carrigan paused. 'Yes. Very much so.' He sipped his coffee and concentrated on David's problem, trying to take his mind off his own, wondering how much he could sensibly tell Kate about his concerns. 'As a matter of fact the situation has developed into an area I'm not sure about. I wanted a few more sessions with him before I discussed it with you.'

'But he's been much more settled in himself, I mean apart from all this running around. He seems more . . . more directed.'

'Maybe. But all this running around, as you put it, might well be part of the problem. And there's something about Germany, I mean apart from work. I think that David has convinced himself that his dreams are based on reality. Something his father told him, in all probability. I've no idea what he's looking for, but it seems he's looking for it in Germany.'

'I don't understand. Why did he tell you this, and not me?'

'You don't have him in deep hypnosis for an hour at a time.'

She bit her lip. 'I can't handle this, Joe, I really can't. Is he going crazy, or what?'

Carrigan shrugged. 'What's crazy? All I know is that David is

99

obsessive, and if we go carefully I have a chance to uncover what the obsession is all about. Maybe those phone calls you mentioned have something to do with it.'

She thought about that. 'He got one call from a man with a foreign accent. Very rude. David was out, but he called back that evening. I thought he sounded a bit weird, so I got his number through the caller identification service.'

'Any idea who he was?'

'I called back, but a woman answered. She just said Hello, and I rang off.'

'It's not much to go on, but you never know. Have you kept the number?'

Kate began fumbling in her bag. 'I wrote it down somewhere. Yes. Here.'

Carrigan looked at it and picked up his phone.

'Hello,' he said when he heard a woman answer. 'Who is that speaking, please?' The woman disconnected, and he keyed another number.

'Who was it?' Kate asked as he waited for the call to go through.

'No idea, but a pal of mine at Langley can find out. Hello. Put me through to Wayne Hartwell on 9873 . . . Wayne? Hi. Joe Carrigan . . . Fine, old buddy. And you? Great. Need a favour. Subscriber name and address for a UK number, probably on BT's Customer Service System. Try that first, plus anything that comes up against the subscriber's name in your system. Sure. No problem. I'm on a tone phone.' After a couple of minutes he began tapping numbers on the telephone pad in response to an automated call-enquiry system. Then he began scribbling on his notepad. 'Great stuff, Wayne. I owe you one.'

He held the notes out to Kate. 'Bingo! David's been talking to this guy. Albert Levy. Now we're getting somewhere.'

'Albert Levy? I don't understand.'

'He's quite famous in certain quarters. One of the old-fashioned Nazi hunters. I'll be damned. It seems as if David's been holding out on me and working ahead of the game.'

VI

Early morning sunlight streamed through the window as the train rounded a curve on the river, forcing David to blink and rub his eyes. They were passing Namedy and approaching the viaduct on the autobahn from Cologne that sweeps round the hills on concrete stilts to the north of the town of Andernach. As the carriages swung to the right and under the viaduct he saw the squat round mediaeval tower used as a crane by generations of lightermen, with the town's general hospital looming above it. Then the train slowed into the station, and he stood up to collect his luggage. Throughout the journey he had been oppressed by a growing nausea, and as he lifted the suitcase he had to fight back an impulse to retch. A woman ushering three children towards the door looked at him curiously.

'Are you feeling ill, sir?' she asked in a strong Rhineland accent.

'Thank you, I'm all right. I need some breakfast, I think.'

As he left the station, the fresh air had a calming effect, and he decided to walk through the town to the hotel. He wondered about the nausea. He felt inclined to put it down to stress. Things had been piling up at work, and he believed the diversion of his Kestrel project would help to take his mind off things. Regardless of Levy's cynicism, David was convinced he would unravel the mystery of who had been responsible for what was obviously a major atrocity. In addition to that, he was prepared to reveal the names of all those people who had taken part as students in the macabre exercise. Perhaps some of them had returned to the area, maybe to this very town that was now opening for business on this brilliant spring day. He began staring at passers-by, trying to see in their faces some connection with the depravations of the Third Reich. But apart from slight changes in fashion he could have been looking at a crowd in any provincial town. If anything, they were a more cheerful lot, smiling as they took their bags of fresh vegetables from the stallholders in the cobbled market place.

He checked in at the Stadtschanke Hotel and asked the clerk for directions to the 'Fähre' identified on his tourist map, the ferry to the village of Leutesdorf. According to the SS records, this would be the route taken by the young officers with travel warrants from their operational units to the site of the secret staff college with its associated concentration camp. Ignoring the fact that his stomach was now demanding food, he set off to walk the few blocks towards the ancient Round Tower and the old crane house he had seen from the train, landmarks for the ferry terminal.

Several cars had already jammed themselves onto the loading deck by the time he arrived, and he hurried to pay his fare in time to catch the next sailing. As he took his seat in front of the wheelhouse, a young boy on the quayside pulled the ropes off their bollards and threw them to one of the deck crew, an old man with a shiny peaked cap and a bright yellow sweater. Free of its restraints, the boat eased away from its moorings and was caught by the strong current, looping back to face upstream and force its way crabwise to the opposite bank. A trio of cargo barges rushed past, en route to Hamburg, self-powered vessels loaded with crates of electrical machinery from Switzerland.

David stared past them to the opposite bank, a peaceful stretch of green behind which the village of Leutesdorf nestled primly in the sunshine. The closer they sailed the more convinced he became that something was wrong. The old Nazi film had not shown much, but the young men on horseback had come riding from among tall trees, with steep-sided mountains in the background. The land behind the village they were now approaching was flat for several kilometres, and the nearest mountains were upstream to the south. He was convinced that the SS planners would have arranged the final transport terminus to be near the college itself. If they had taken this route and then been driven by lorry, the college could be anywhere within a large area. Not only that, but at least some of the students would have been given tickets to Linz or Neuwied, nearby towns on the east side of the Rhine. Something was terribly wrong.

Bitterly disappointed, he watched as the old man with the peaked cap threw his ropes to the Leutesdorf ferry keeper, and sat down as the cars and passengers began to disembark. As the last one rolled over the slipway the old man came up to him.

'Excuse me, sir, but are you not going to Leutesdorf?' When David shook his head he said, 'Then I must issue a ticket back to Andernach.'

David gave him a ten-Deutschmark note, and as the old man groped for change in his leather bag he asked, 'How long have you worked on the ferry?'

The ferryman took off his cap and wiped away a sheen of perspiration. 'Your parents could have married on my first ferry. Lots of people did in the old days before the War.' He looked closely at David. 'But you don't come from Rhineland.'

'I've lived most of my life overseas,' David replied honestly, before adding, 'My parents were from Innsbruck.'

The old man spat into the water and watched as cars and people began to move on board from the quay. 'Never had much time for Innsbruckers.'

'Neither did my parents,' David said, 'else why do you think they left?' An idea struck him. He waited for the guffaw to die down and asked, 'Is this the only ferry out of Andernach?'

'It is these days, but the time was when you could cross to Neuwied and beyond. The autobahns and bridges put an end to all that.'

'And you used to sail to these other places?' David prompted.

The old man sniffed. 'Not me. This is my route, man and boy. Andernach . . . Leutesdorf. Leutesdorf . . . Andernach.'

When they arrived back at Andernach, David left the ferry and went to the town hall where he asked the assistant if she had maps of Andernach that had been published in the 1940s. His hunch proved to be correct. There had been a crossing from a pier by the old Bollwerk building in the south of Andernach to the town of Neuwied and an occasional service from this jetty to an island called Röhmer Insel further up-river lying close to the east bank. With growing excitement he compared the old map with his modern large-scale version. He found that the island had been linked to the main bank by a small bridge and a track leading through woods to a large estate. The entire area was marked on the map by a thin broken line and the word *Privat*.

Back at the hotel, David ordered a light lunch to be sent to his room, and after nibbling at it he lay back on the bed and closed his eyes. In a few minutes the dream came. He could handle it now, all but the features of the three people who burst into the room. They were indistinct, as if seen through a veil of tears, but he saw one of the two men jump forward and collapse, and then the woman pushed a needle into the man's arm. David racked his brain to try and remember which movie he had drawn upon for the nightmare. Or perhaps the horror came from captured post-war photographs of the Holocaust that he had seen as a child, as Levy had suggested. What had amazed and horrified the Allied community was the discovery that so many atrocities had been filmed by the Nazis. Strutting Waffen-SS Totenkopf officers standing proudly by mutilated Russian corpses on the way to Kharkov and Kursk. Sequence shots of Jews being gassed in Dachau. Bearded professors of medicine watching as Polish Gypsy children with twisted limbs staggered past them during research into the healing of fractured bones. Either way, he didn't care where his recollections came from. He had stumbled onto yet another Nazi obscenity, and he was determined to drag the stinking thing into the open and to expose the creatures involved. Up to now, the clues had pointed to this attractive and prosperous Rhineland town of Andernach. Where would they guide him next?

In the afternoon he hired a set of fishing equipment and a motorboat and set off up-river, battling with the current and covering the ground at about three kilometres an hour along the steepening hillsides. Beyond the village of Neuwied the river turned, and as it did so he saw the long, low Röhmer Insel, its dark trees cast momentarily in a cloud's shadow. Some metres before the northern tip of the island a large stained notice on the main bank proclaimed *Eingang Verboten*, and he saw that the creek between the bank and the island was blocked from navigation by a rusty iron chain fence. The island extended two kilometres upstream, and at the other end of the creek was a similar chain and notice, partly obscured by willows and beech trees. Carefully he guided the boat behind the foliage and drove a mooring stake into the earth. When this was done he unpacked the fishing tackle and cast a line into the waters of the creek, propping the rod firmly against the cabin door. Satisfied that his arrangement would look natural to a casual observer, he slipped his camera round his neck and pushed through the undergrowth. For a hundred metres or so he encountered small saplings and briars, and then he came to the remains of a barbed-wire fence, with concrete uprights standing almost three metres high. Pausing only to take a photograph, he carried on, once again finding himself victim of a bout of nausea.

After weaving and ducking through saplings for several more

minutes he came to a clearing. It was about fifty metres wide and three times as long, surrounded by tall trees that hid the nearby mountains. The ground was covered with rectangular concrete foundations, cracked and sprouting with weeds, typical of an abandoned military establishment. The place was littered with the remains of brick walls, and at the far end he could distinguish the only substantial ruin in the area, a pile of collapsed bricks with a square structure in one corner. He picked his way over the rubble, taking photographs as he did so, until he was standing in what looked like a boiler room, with the lower portion of a chimney in one corner and a large gap in the fabric where the boiler had been. Bits of rusting ironwork lay partly hidden in the earth and grass, and he tugged at the most complete piece he could see, a circular casting with the maker's name and the broken shafts of two hinges. He lay this against a wooden post to catch a good side light and took a photograph. This brought him to the end of the film cassette, so he unloaded the camera and inserted a new one and took more photographs of the area, to be on the safe side.

There was a track leading towards the mainland side of the island, and he followed it, taking more photographs as he did so. Further on he found what appeared to be the remains of an adventure playground or military obstacle course, with balks of timber reared into fractured climbing frames and large concrete pipes set in now-disjointed tunnels. Finally he came to a gate and a ramshackle guardhouse, on the other side of which was a stone bridge linking the island to the private estate on the eastern bank of the river. As he took several more shots he was overcome by a fit of vomiting, rasping shudders that emptied his already depleted stomach. When it was over he began to stumble back to the boat.

The two men waiting by the mooring rope were thickset and threatening, dressed as gamekeepers with green jackets and feathered hats, one wearing lederhosen and the other plus-fours, both sporting stout sticks.

'This place is forbidden,' Lederhosen called aggressively. 'What are you doing here?'

David waved to the boat. 'Fishing. I thought I could hook a few carp in the creek, but I don't seem to be having any luck.'

'If you are fishing, why are you not on your boat?'

'I felt sick. In fact I have been quite ill in the woods.' David pointed at his lapel, which had not remained unaffected by the retching. 'Made a bit of a mess, as a matter of fact.'

The man with the plus-fours stared unpleasantly. 'And you took a camera to record this?'

'Oh, my camera. I always take it with me. I'm very interested in wildflowers.'

'I'm afraid you must give me the film.' Lederhosen stretched out his hand.

'I beg your pardon!' David tried hard to sound scandalized, desperately fighting another swelling sickness. 'I shall do no such thing.'

Plus-fours grabbed the camera and jerked it painfully from David's neck, opened the back, and ripped out the cassette. As he pushed it into a leather pouch his companion repeated, 'This place is forbidden. You have no right here.'

'I really must protest,' David rasped, rubbing his throat. 'I shall complain to your superiors about this ill-mannered treatment. I regret if I have trespassed, but this is intolerable.'

The two men merely stared at him, unmoved and uncaring, so he struggled to pull the mooring stake from the ground and stepped onto the boat which immediately began floating with the current further down the creek. They watched dispassionately as he battled to start the engine, face red with anger and embarrassment. It was only when he was back at Andernach that he remembered he still had the first cassette of film safely in his jacket pocket.

VII

The next morning David hired an elderly Opel from a small garage behind the market place, determined to see the private estate at closer quarters. He took his place in the queue for the ferry to Leutesdorf and was soon driving towards the forests that overlook Röhmer Insel. The narrow road twisted and turned as it climbed into the hills, giving occasional views of the sun-dappled peaks on the far side of the Rhine. At the beginning of a high stone wall, it turned away from the river and zigzagged higher into the forest. After several kilometres he came to a road junction and the entrance to the estate, where a small white sign told him that this was the headquarters of the Freyer Institute of Advanced Management Studies. The squat stone gatehouse with its crenellated battlements was deserted, so he turned the Opel into the drive and made his way through the thickly clustered pine trees. As he drove deeper into the grounds, the estate took on the appearance of a well-kept park, with tidy gravelled paths leading into arbours of rose trees and flowering shrubs. The stream that ran from the hills passed over sculpted waterfalls and into deep rock pools on its way to the Rhine, and on the far bank he caught a glimpse of deer grazing in the long grass. Rounding an ornate marble fountain he saw the building. It was an eighteenth-century castle with towers at each corner, the imposing frontage facing the river over a series of steeply descending balustrades and terraces. He stopped the Opel by the entrance, and as he turned off the engine an attractive dark-haired girl strode out of a doorway.

'Good morning, sir. Can I help you?'

David eased out of the car. 'I'm sorry to trouble you, but I saw your gardens from the road and wondered if they are open to the public.'

The girl shook her head. 'They are beautiful, aren't they, but I'm afraid that they are open only to residents. The Director is very strict.'

'I can understand that. Otherwise you'd be crowded out with sightseers. It really is extremely attractive. By the way, I've not heard of your Institute. I'm a professional man myself, and I wonder if we might have a mutual interest.'

'We are a privately owned organization, sir. What is your own interest, apart from horticulture?' She smiled slightly.

'Engineering management. Organizing capital projects. That kind of thing.'

'We do have some engineering companies among our clients,' she said, 'but their concern is mainly with the philosophy of business management at a rather advanced level.'

'Well, it certainly sounds very interesting.' David paused. 'Perhaps you have some information you can give me. A brochure, or a syllabus.'

'There is a history of the Institute that we give to new arrivals. I can get you a copy of that.'

'Thank you,' David said. 'And perhaps you wouldn't mind if I enjoyed this magnificent view before I leave.'

'I shall bring it to you on the terrace,' she said.

He strolled to the nearest balustrade and made his way along the side of the castle, past huge curtained windows. At the far end he turned, and the corners, the angles, trees and mountains of the old black and white film from the Bundesarchiv hit him like a physical blow. It was at this exact position that the cine photographer had stood. The only thing missing was the group of carefree horsemen with their hunting falcons. He half ran, half walked back to the Opel to get his camera from the glove compartment, jamming a new film in with shaking fingers. Feverishly he returned to the balustrade and began taking photographs of the drive and the buildings. When the girl reappeared carrying a small booklet he stuffed the camera back in his pocket.

'Here we are, sir. I hope you will find this of interest.'

'Thank you very much,' he said. 'I wonder if there is any chance that I could see inside this beautiful place.'

'I am afraid the Director has asked if you would leave now. We are expecting some guests, and as you can see there is not much room in the drive.'

'Of course, of course. I'm sorry to have intruded on you like this.' He at least had photographs of the castle approaches, irrefutable evidence that he had discovered the actual site of the *Turmfalke* project – unless Levy put it down to another coincidence!

The girl waved to someone as he turned towards his car, and when he looked up the drive he saw the stocky man in plus-fours who had taken the film out of his camera the day before. The man was accompanied by two Dobermans and carrying a hunting rifle, and as David slammed the door and jabbed the accelerator he squinted into the car's windscreen in an effort to see who was driving. Panic took over as the vehicle bumped and hammered its way past shrubs and small trees and out of the estate, leaving a hubcap on the ground and shards of body paint along the stone gateposts to mark his passage. Back in Andernach, the damage cost him his three hundred Deutschmark car hire deposit.

Loki Threat Assessment

SUBJECT: *Unknown*
NATIONALITY: *Unknown. English accent.*
SEX: *Male*
DOB/AGE: *45–55*
LOCATION: *Unknown*
DISTINGUISHING FEATURES: *Small in height; grey streak in hair*
KEYWORD AFFILIATIONS: *Fishing; horticulture*
COMMENT: *Subject found trespassing on Röhmer Insel; also possible visit to Falkenschloss. His film confiscated and found to contain random photographs of plants, flowers and debris in the environment of the* Turmfalke *camp.*
ASSESSMENT PRIORITY (0–10): *4*
DATA ON SUBJECT: *None*
CROSS REFERENCES: *None*
ACTION: *Maintain cross-referencing*

VIII

David had one more task to complete in Germany before he returned home. The telephone directory for Stuttgart contained only one family named Pökke living in Esslingen. The number was listed under the name Alfred Pökke, but one call was enough to discover that Alfred's brother Theodore was alive and prospering as chairman of a plastics company with headquarters in Frankfurt and branches throughout Europe. Experienced in this kind of engineering, David had no trouble in formulating a plan to get himself a personal interview with Theodore. He called the company and asked to speak to the chairman, giving his name as Davies. He was put through to a secretary.

'Yes, Herr Davies. Perhaps I can help you.'

'I asked to speak to your chairman, Herr Pökke.' David made his voice crisp with authority.

'Herr Pökke is in a meeting, sir. If you could give me some idea of the nature of your business . . .'

'Certainly, young lady. The nature of my business is to represent a number of Saudi Arabian businessmen. The nature of their business is to find someone competent to establish a plastics manufacturing facility in their country on a partnership basis. I have a strict personal itinerary that requires me to see your chairman at nine o'clock tomorrow morning on his own and in confidence. You now have one minute to discover if this is possible or not.'

She took thirty seconds. 'Herr Pökke will see you in his office at nine o'clock, Herr Davies.'

Pökke was short and stocky, with a ready smile and black, expressionless eyes. He stood up when David was ushered in by the secretary but did not offer to shake hands.

'You will excuse me, Herr Davies, if I seem less than polite, but we do not have many people appearing on matters of business without duly arranged appointments.'

'Forgive the manner in which I made contact, sir, but the matter is extremely confidential, and my clients have stipulated that the less correspondence I engage in at this stage, the better.'

'Nevertheless, I trust you can provide me with credentials.'

'My credentials are confidential, but my authority will be established by the nature of the questions I will ask you, Herr Pökke. In the interests of brevity I should like to start with your technological capabilities and finish with some questions about your own experiences.' David knew very well that senior company men liked to take the initiative, but he did not intend this man to follow that course.

Pökke looked irritated but motioned towards a circular plastic table, and they both sat down. David pushed a notepad towards the chairman.

'It will help if you take notes, Herr Pökke. The parameters of the project are as follows. My clients plan to convert two thousand metric tonnes of raw materials a year into a variety of high-value plastic products. In the short term this will be for distribution within Saudi Arabia and other Arab states. In the long term they plan to expand the process for export. In the first year their objective is to build a factory and get the first five product lines into production. Two of these will be die moulded and the rest injection moulded. They will, of course, need the appropriate tools and machinery. They want their facility to be the best that modern technology can achieve, and money is quite literally no object.' David paused while Pökke scribbled.

'Have you proof of this project, Herr Davies?' Pökke asked him.

'Naturally,' David snapped. 'I would not be here otherwise.'

'Of course, of course, but . . .'

'I have on their behalf conducted an evaluation of European firms that could enter into a joint partnership,' David interrupted. 'Three, including your own, have been shortlisted. I need hardly remind you that your absolute discretion remains a vital consideration.'

'You may rest assured that we conduct all our business with the utmost security, but I shall need more details.'

'At this stage I merely wish to establish your interest in principle and to investigate your own personal standing. Perhaps you would be good enough to let me have your biography, and biographies of your senior staff.'

Pökke's black eyes bored into him. 'Surely you would have gathered such information during your initial evaluations, Herr Davies.'

David felt sweat break out in the palms of his hands. Pökke was tough and shrewd, but you didn't rise to the top of a successful German engineering company by being a patsy. 'Of course, Herr Pökke. I hold information on what your customers and competitors think about you, not to mention the various institutions to which you belong and the usual credit agencies. What I do not have is your own view of yourselves. I would have thought that was obvious.'

'Naturally, naturally.' Pökke seemed satisfied with that. He nodded ponderously and spoke briefly into his intercom. 'My secretary will give you these documents as you leave.'

David pressed ahead. 'In the meantime, a few background details of your own career. I understand you were a commissioned officer during the war.'

'Yes. The 9th Panzerdivision to be exact. I was commissioned in December 1944 at the age of nineteen years.' Pökke did not attempt to keep the pride from his voice.

'Did you see active service?' David asked.

'Unfortunately not. I was sent straight from officer training to a course of further study. At the time the war finished I was undergoing specialized training.'

'Isn't that unusual? There was a great demand for newly commissioned young officers at the front lines in the spring of 1945. Young officers would normally have been sent straight into battle at such a time.'

Pökke settled back in his chair. 'In most cases, yes. Others, like myself, were selected for specialized development.'

'In view of the fact you are now a senior and successful businessman, would you say that this experience was of personal value?'

The ex-SS officer looked at him thoughtfully. 'Are your clients interested in such information?'

David stared back at him. 'No major enterprise in the Middle East is without military connections, Herr Pökke. My questions are entirely relevant to my briefing, otherwise I would not be asking them. I might add that what we know of your military background is a definite bonus in this regard. Perhaps you would be so kind as to tell me about this training period.'

'I don't remember much about it.' Pökke paused. 'It was to do with administration.'

'You said it was specialized development. What was special about it?'

Pökke stood up abruptly. 'Herr Davies, I must bring this interview to an end. If your clients decide to go ahead with their project you must submit a full proposal for our consideration.'

David's nervousness vanished. He felt as if someone had turned on a powerful light to guide his steps into a dark and evil place in which erstwhile terrifying monsters scuttled to avoid him.

'Herr Pökke, are you acquainted with Professor Ernst Muntz? He was a Standartenführer in the SS Institute of Hygiene at the time you were undergoing your training.'

Pökke stiffened. 'I don't know anybody called Muntz. Herr Davies, I think you have perhaps been wasting my time. I think you don't represent any Saudi Arabian people.'

'Your caution is understandable. But the project will be worth several hundred million Deutschmarks to the European partner. We must choose our own way of assessing who that will be.' He could see that Pökke was torn by suspicion and doubt on one hand and cupidity on the other.

'Well,' said Pökke shortly, 'we are always keen to examine such developments, but in future I must ask you to conduct this business with written confirmations. I bid you good-day.'

He jabbed the intercom, and his secretary opened the door for David to leave. He thanked her for the biographies and pushed them into his briefcase. As he went out he turned to Pökke with a final question. 'Do you remember Nadia Retsa?'

'Nadia Retsa? No. Why should I remember Nadia Retsa?'

'She would have been about fifty-five years old now, but she was sent for special training, too. Unlike you, she did not survive the experience you shared on Röhmer Insel. I thought you might remember her.'

Pökke's expression froze and his skin turned white. For a moment he could not speak, but finally the words came tumbling out. 'Fräulein Linten, instruct security to escort this person from the building. He is on no account to be permitted entry again, not under any circumstances!'

'Why don't you call the police, you bastard? Don't worry, Fräulein. I'll see myself out.'

David stalked past the startled secretary and out of the building. Back on the street, his knees began to shake. This excrescence had taken part in the *Turmfalke* project. David saw all the confirmation he needed in Pökke's contorted face. On the order of SS-Standartenführer Ernst Muntz, this captain of German industry had coldly used his SS dagger to stab to death a little Polish girl who had grown to depend on him for her last brief friendship on Earth.

* * *

Loki Threat Assessment

SUBJECT: *Davies (No forename known)*
NATIONALITY: *British (by accent)*
SEX: *Male*
AGE: 45–55
LOCATION: *Not known*
DISTINGUISHING FEATURES: *Greying hair*
KEYWORDS: Turmfalke, *Engineering, Plastic, Management, Middle East*

COMMENT: *Source of report: Pökke, Theodore. Subject revealed detailed knowledge of* Turmfalke *project.*
ASSESSMENT PRIORITY (0–10): 6
DATA ON SUBJECT: *None*
KEYWORD MATCHES: *589 low level; 215 medium level; 0 high level*
ACTION: *Instigate search; maintain cross-referencing; circulate reports for further consideration by Loki administration*

CHAPTER SIX

I

There were three people in the interview suite. The short, vibrant woman with a gamine hairstyle introduced herself as Helena Whycroft, the director in charge of women's merchandise for Michaelson. The casual but flamboyantly dressed man on her left was Cy Duluth, an American casting consultant. On her right was Mike Holroyd, creative director of the advertising agency. The Michaelson chain of fashion shops for men aimed at being more upmarket than their competitors. They provided a full range of clothing, shoes and leisurewear for the successful businessman, aiming to retain the loyalties of the yuppies who made money in the eighties but who did not lose their jobs in the nineties. The company was well established in the marketplace, very successful but very traditional. The board had appointed a new chairman, Paul Adderley, whose brief was to expand business and create excellence in every aspect of trading. Introducing a range of women's goods was in keeping with this strategy and with the fact that eighty per cent of men's clothes are chosen or bought by female partners. 'Women come into our stores with their partners, so why not sell them something while they are there,' Adderley maintained.

The Michaelson account was one of the plums of the advertising game, and three executives from a leading advertising agency had left their firm to run the Michaelson business on a five-year 'SOB' contract that was reputed to guarantee them earnings of a million each, provided the business targets were reached. The 'SOB' in this case meant Shit Or Bust. Kate felt quite in tune with that approach, under the circumstances.

'Good morning, Mrs Lewis,' Holroyd said. 'This will take about half an hour, and we want you to feel relaxed and at home.'

'Thank you, Mr Holroyd,' Kate said politely.

'I'd like us to be on first-name terms,' Helena Whycroft said brightly. 'And to get right down to it, Kate, we've been carefully through the portfolio and video that the Burnside Agency sent us. We're very impressed with your work and your capability.'

'We are indeed.' Mike Holroyd nodded his agreement. 'Establishing the Michaelson Woman is a vital part of our marketing strategy, in the same line of country as the Nescafé campaign and similar personality-based series. We have a shortlist of three, all of whom we believe could do a first-rate job. It's nice for us to have such a choice, but maybe a little nerve-racking for you.'

'On the other hand, you don't look particularly nerve-racked,' Cy Duluth observed with a smile.

You should be sitting where I'm sitting, she thought.

'Thank you,' she said. 'I take that as a compliment.'

'The thing is,' Helena said seriously, 'this kind of project could put you under a great deal of pressure. Could you cope? That's the question.'

Kate was about to offer up an appropriate cliché, but found herself thinking about the agency's SOB contract. What was good enough for them was good enough for her. And what had she got to lose?

'I'm pretty good at coping, considering I'm married to an absolutely brilliant man who is on the edge of a nervous breakdown,' she told them. 'The main problem I have right now is wondering which side of the edge he's on. Compared to that, the opportunity to work on a new series of TV ads isn't quite as awesome as it might otherwise have been.'

There was a blank silence, then Duluth gave a huge guffaw. 'Very good,' he spluttered. 'That's the first completely honest reply from an actress I've heard in my entire career. Jesus!'

As he sat wiping his eyes, Helena Whycroft said, 'Well fine, Kate, but we'd certainly like to believe that whoever becomes the Michaelson Woman will be able to bring one hundred per cent to this, and it sounds like you have other things on your mind.'

'Helena,' Kate said. 'We all have other things on our minds. The morning I did the screen test which you like so much, my husband's company rang up to ask why he wasn't wasn't back in the UK. I told them he'd been delayed in Germany. His therapist believes he's suffering from delusions about the Nazi Party. With things like this bubbling in the background, I believe that I can bring an added insight to the task of convincing women whose lifestyle is not altogether dissimilar to mine that spending some time and money on Michaelson fashions has got to be great for self image.'

Duluth carried on chuckling and Mike Holroyd was trying to hide a smile. Helena Whycroft struggled on. 'We have to ask you about the possibility of having children, Kate. As I am sure you realize, creating the Michaelson Woman will be a considerable investment, and . . .'

'Helena, I want this work. I can do it, and there's nothing that can stand in the way of my doing it successfully, including babies.'

'How did it go, darling?' Margaret Burnside asked expectantly.

'I blew it,' Kate told her.

'Oh god, I'm sorry. They loved your work. What went wrong?'

'I did. I just couldn't sit there and get involved in all the old crap, so I told them about David.'

'You did what?' Margaret's voice screeched from the earpiece.

'I told them the truth. I mean, what's the point of pretending that everything's rosy, when your husband is acting like some kind of demented Sherlock Holmes clocking up Air Miles. If I'd got the job, they'd have found out sooner or later. It's not the kind of thing you can hide from people you work closely with.'

'But it would have been too late by then. You'd have been perfect.'

'I'm sorry, Margaret. I know how much hard work you put into this. I just couldn't bullshit them, that's all.'

Two hours later, Kate received a special delivery of flowers and a magnum of champagne from Cy Duluth. His note said: 'You were great, but I was out-voted. If anything else comes up, I'll get in touch. Hope you sort things out.' She put the flowers in a vase, and drank a reasonable proportion of the champagne. By the time the telephone rang, she was feeling relatively mellow and quite relaxed.

'May I speak with Mr David Lewis, please.' It was a woman's voice. American.

'And whom might I say is calling him?' she said, enunciating her words carefully.

'This is Maria Alpert. I'm telephoning because the secretary of the Berlin Buddies Association told me that Mr Lewis has been trying to contact my father.'

Kate reached for a note pad and ballpoint. 'Maria Albert . . .'

'That's Alpert, with a pee. Is Mr Lewis available?'

'That's a very good question,' Kate said. 'If you find out, let me know.'

'I guess I've phoned at an awkward time,' the voice said.

'Oh no, not at all,' Kate said. 'If I can contact my husband I'll say you called, shall I?'

'Maybe he'd like to call me back,' the voice said. Kate noted the phone number, and the caller rang off. What on earth, she wondered, was the Berlin Buddies Association?

II

After his confrontation with Pökke, David was drained of energy and emotion, but in his exhaustion he found a driving force of pure hatred for Professor Ernst Muntz. He took the train to Berlin and phoned Kate to let her know when he would be home. She told him she had a message from some buddies in Berlin. She sounded smashed.

On the flight back he turned things over in his mind. Muntz was the villain of the piece. That was the focal point. The fact that Albert Levy had a file on the man corroborated what he already knew: that the distinguished professor and the sadistic director of the *Turmfalke* project were one and the same. Now it was simply a matter of building a case that would stand up in court. He would use the same methods as he did in developing an engineering project. Select and maintain the objective, painstakingly examine all known facts, logically evaluate the situation, develop a creative proposition that would lead to a practical solution. No problem.

By the time he arrived home, he felt like a hunter who has trained for weeks and now has a quarry in his sights.

When she heard the car in the drive, Kate opened the front door and waved to David as he switched the engine off. He looked a little tired, which was only to be expected, but apart from that he looked remarkably cheerful.

'You made good time,' she called.

'Tail wind, no nosy Customs officers, clear roads all the way in. What more could you ask?'

He kissed her cheek, and she hugged him hard. 'Good trip?'

'Yes,' he said. 'Yes, it was.'

'I thought we'd have a quiet night in. There's a shoulder of lamb in the oven.'

'Mmmm, I can smell it,' he said appreciatively. He put down his bags and hung up his coat.

'Bottle of your favourite plonk on the table.'

'I don't know what I've done to deserve a treat,' he said. 'In fact, I was going to rush you off for a night out, to apologize. I've been acting like a pig lately, haven't I?'

'You want the truth?'

'Not really,' he said sincerely. 'I just want to make things up to you.'

'I can't pretend over things like this,' she told him. 'I don't know what's been happening to us. I didn't think I could be so unhappy.'

He led her into the living room and poured drinks. 'OK. Let's start with the dreams. I was well out of order about that. I had no idea what was happening until Joe Carrigan got to grips with it. He's good at what he does. I've been bloody awful to him, as well. Owe the man an apology.'

'I don't think that's necessary,' she told him. 'He's a professional, after all. He must be used to things like this.'

'Well, I must at least write to thank him for all he's done to sort things out for me.'

Kate remembered that Carrigan was convinced that David was in the middle of some kind of crisis, but her husband seemed more relaxed and self-assured than he'd been for a long time. She wondered how to broach the subject.

'He seems to think you've worked out what the dreams were all about,' she said.

'I have, in a way,' he said. 'It's a bit complicated, but it's all to do with my father. Not the car accident. Something else. Something he must have told me when I was very young. I'd pushed it into the back of my mind, and the prospect of having to go to Germany must have triggered it off.'

'Is it something to do with these friends of yours in Berlin?' she asked.

He remembered that she had mentioned this when he called her.

'What exactly was that message?' he asked.

'A woman phoned to tell you about something called the Berlin Buddies Association. She was American. Miss Alpert, with a pee.'

'Great. I was expecting a call,' he said. 'I thought I could track down a few people my father might have met at some time. You know, the nostalgic family odyssey. Did she leave a message?'

'She said you could try calling back. I wrote the number on the pad. She lives near Los Angeles.'

'They're nine hours behind us,' he said casually. 'I'll leave it till later.'

He explained to Kate that another trip abroad was essential for him to settle things once and for all, and she seemed to accept that.

Over the next few days, he sorted things out with Peter Halkyn, worked round the clock to get his projects back on target, then organized a few days' holiday. She offered to go with him, but he said he'd be moving around too much to take in the sights. This, at least, was true. His first stop was Los Angeles.

III

Maria Alpert was a pleasant woman, about David's age. She lived in a modest house, not far from Malibu Beach. She showed him into a room filled with the memorabilia of a military family.

'I didn't wish to discuss family business over the telephone, but my father died two years ago, Mr Lewis,' she said. 'As you can see, I work to keep his memory alive.'

David tried hard to hide his disappointment. 'I'm very sorry. I didn't realize . . .'

'If you have a genuine interest in what happened in Berlin, he would have made you very welcome. He kept contact with all his friends from the Army. They were proud of what they did in Germany, so different from the poor boys who were sent to Vietnam. The BBA secretary told me you needed some information. I thought I might be able to help. That's why I phoned.'

'It's a long shot coming all this way,' David said. 'But my project is very important to me.'

'Perhaps if you tell me what you're looking for, I may be able to help.'

Her father must have dealt with tens of thousands of Nazi files during his Berlin tour of duty, and David had not held out very much hope that he would recollect a particular group. The chances his daughter might know something about *Turmfalke* were astronomically small.

'It's a bit complicated,' he told her. 'I saw your father's name on a document that referred to a project I'm working on called *Turmfalke* – that's German for Kestrel – and every detail could be important.'

She did not react to the name. 'Dad worked in Colonel Stamford's unit most of the time he was in Berlin,' she said. 'They became good friends after the war and went to Association meetings together, whenever they could.'

David remembered the name from the sergeant's file note. 'Colonel S.D. Stamford.'

'That's right. Sam Stamford. He lives in Santa Barbara now. His number should be in the book. I'll look it up for you.'

Sam Stamford was a grizzled but fit-looking man in his early seventies and, like Maria Alpert, he quickly made David welcome.

'Roy and I were good friends. It can get like that with enlisted men in wartime. He made Master Sergeant after Berlin, and we stayed in the same team for about ten years. Then I retired from the army to practise law in Oakland. We formed the Berlin Buddies Association to make sure we all keep in touch. We didn't think so at the time, but they were great days, y'know. Jesus, we put some vodka away with those Russian bastards before the politicians got busy! They weren't such a bad lot, the Russkies . . .' He paused reflectively. 'So, what did you think Roy could help you with?'

David handed his copy of Sergeant Alpert's file note to Stamford. 'I'm looking into this *Turmfalke* project, and I was hoping he would recollect something about it. Fishing in the dark, really, but any piece of information would be a help at this stage.'

Stamford peered at the document and shook his head. 'We must have gone through thousands of tons of this stuff. The Second World War was the most documented conflict in history. We thought our paperwork was thorough, but the Germans! Christ, they made out chitties for making out chitties. Mind you, it was a great help when we started nailing the bastards.'

'I wondered about this reference to missing medical abstracts,' David said. 'There might be something in them that could help me.'

'*Medizinisch: Extrahieren*,' Stamford read, nodding slowly. 'Yeah. We came across a lot of this kind of stuff from the Waffen-SS Institute of Hygiene and other sources. They're not the kind of abstracts you're thinking of.'

'I'm not sure I understand,' David told him.

Stamford sighed. 'It was a hell of a long time ago, but there's no way you can shake it off. The things they did! My group was restricted to the examination of documentary evidence of suspected war crimes. Physical evidence such as extermination centres, surgical equipment and suchlike were handled by other specialist teams. Have you heard of the Strasbourg trials?'

David shook his head.

'They were also called the Doctors' Trials. Bit like the Nuremberg trials, only they dealt with Nazi doctors who had conducted medical experiments on concentration camp inmates and prisoners of war,' Stamford told him. 'For instance, there was a professor called August Hirt who headed up the Anatomical Institute at the university in Strasbourg. The Nazis had this thing about racial superiority, and Hirt murdered more than a hundred Jews and other racially inferior prisoners so he could get measurements of their skulls. Their heads were kept in hermetically sealed containers so they could be compared with sculptures of Aryan heads made by some Jewish guy in Auschwitz. Then he extended the process to take in whole skeletons. His medical team was still working on this when our guys were advancing on Strasbourg. They tried to cover up their traces, but our Seventh Army units and some guys from a French armoured division found the bodies in a storeroom. In other places we came across stores of human skin and hair . . .'

Stamford stopped as David swayed in his chair, overcome with nausea.

'Gee, I'm sorry. I keep forgetting how this stuff upsets people. Let me get you a drink.'

He reached for a bottle of Scotch, but David shook his head.

'A glass of water, please. Sorry. Not used to all this.'

He couldn't shake the images from the archive film that showed the good-looking man – he knew it was Muntz – in a laboratory coat over his SS uniform holding up files labelled *Bauchspcheldrüse*, *Thalamus* and *Schilddrüse*.

Pancreas, hypothalamus and thyroid.

He struggled to control himself. 'You're saying that this doesn't refer to documents?'

'That's right,' Stamford said briskly. '*Medizinisch Extrahieren* means medical extracts from bodies, not abstracts from medical papers. That's why Roy Alpert couldn't find cross-references in the *Turmfalke* files. He thought that was strange, of course, considering how meticulous the Krauts were. Hirt recorded in great detail how many people were processed in his laboratories, when they were killed, how their skulls were de-fleshed . . . I know this is kind of upsetting, but how else can I tell you?'

'It's all right, Colonel,' David said. 'I really need to know all this.'

'My own theory, for what it's worth, is that the Strasbourg trials were bullshit.'

'How could anything like that be bullshit?' David asked.

'It's obvious. Guys like August Hirt and the others who were tried there were butchers, and the results of their experiments were so much crap. On the other hand, there were other medical facilities conducting experiments that never saw the light of day. When the war ended, I reckon the results were parcelled out among the victors. You know how it is.'

David shook his head. 'No, I don't know how it is, Sam. I don't know how any human being could do this kind of thing. But I think I might have a lead into one of the bastards involved.'

'It's not for me to poke into your affairs,' Stamford said, 'but if I knew what you were after, maybe I could be more specific.'

Listening to Sam Stamford made David realize how difficult it was going to be to get the hard evidence he needed to prove Muntz's implication. So many paths to follow, with no signposts to help. Yet everything he unearthed was interconnected in some way. He was convinced of that.

'It's difficult to know where to begin,' he said at last. 'When I was a boy, my father told me about something that had happened to him before the war. For some reason I pushed this into the back of my mind. Maybe because it was so horrendous. I don't know why, but it started coming back to me a few weeks ago, and I'm trying to get to the bottom of it. I know it's connected with *Turmfalke*, and I'm convinced a man called Ernst Muntz has got something to do with it. He was an SS Colonel, and now he's the chairman of a German pharmaceutical company. He did all right for himself after the war.'

'Didn't they all,' Stamford said dryly. 'Well, Mr Lewis, I don't think I can help you, but a pal of mine ran one of the sections responsible for investigating SS documents. Fred Newman. He's over in Boston, and he used to work in pharmaceuticals. Maybe he knows something. It's late there, but I might be able to reach him.'

Stamford went into his study and keyed a number, beckoning David in to listen.

'Fred? Sam Stamford. Great, you old buzzard, how about you? Look, I have some Buddy business you might be able to sort out. Got a Britisher here called David Lewis. Wants to know about a case we worked on in Berlin. Got time for a word? OK. Me too. I'll pass you over.' He handed the phone to David.

'Hello. Newman here, Mr Lewis. What can I do for you?' The voice was cool, businesslike.

'I'm trying to find out about a man called Ernst Muntz, Professor . . .'

'Sure I know about him,' the voice interrupted. 'SS-Standartenführer Ernst Muntz. We thought he might be implicated in a few things, but he turned out to be squeaky clean.'

There was a silence.

'Can you tell me anything about him, anything at all?' David asked.

'Not much. He and his pal Werner Blintz ran training courses for young Waffen-SS medics at a place called Andernach. Blintz was in charge of the General Hospital, and Muntz backed him up. Seemed straightforward to us, so we dropped it.'

'I've got a file note from Colonel Stamford's records that refers to some medical extracts that went missing from a project called *Turmfalke*. He thought you might be able to throw some light on this . . .'

There was a silence. 'I've no wish to be rude, Mr Lewis, but it's late. Pass me back to Sam, would you?'

David handed the phone to Stamford who listened hard to what Newman was saying, glancing at David from time to time.

'Sure, Fred. I agree, it was a helluva long time ago. OK, maybe we should discuss this later.' Stamford put the phone down and turned to David. 'I guess that's all I can do for you, Mr Lewis. Not much help, I'm afraid. Now, if you'll excuse me, I have a great deal to do.'

Was it David's imagination, or had the bluff welcome suddenly dissipated?

* * *

Loki Threat Assessment

SUBJECT: *Lewis, David*
NATIONALITY: *British*
SEX: *Male*
DOB/AGE: *40–50*
LOCATION: *London home address*
DISTINGUISHING FEATURES: *No visual description available*
KEYWORD AFFILIATIONS: *Muntz,* Turmfalke
COMMENT: *Telephone contact through Sam Stamford, of the Berlin Buddies Association. Stamford unaware of* Turmfalke *significance*
ASSESSMENT PRIORITY (0–10): *8*
DATA ON SUBJECT: *None*
CROSS REFERENCES: *568 keyword links*
ACTION: *Urgent. Possible breach of Loki security. Maintain cross-referencing.*

* * *

It was there again. A feeling of being on the right track in an obscuring mist, each step taken in a panic, each secure foothold bringing an intoxicating sense of triumph. Then the dismal realization that the mist is still there, with an unknown number of steps remaining . . .

Newman's voice had started out being quite friendly on the phone, and he had actually reinforced the location of *Turmfalke* by referring to the town of Andernach. But something happened when David mentioned *Turmfalke*. The voice changed. The friendliness vanished to be replaced by other things. Coldness? Anger? Fear, perhaps? Or was he imagining something that didn't exist? Either way, Newman had cut him off short and said something to Sam Stamford that had the same effect. The previously hospitable ex-colonel couldn't get him out of his house quickly enough. David had taken another step into the mist, but as he wrestled with the problems he began to see where his next step would lead.

CHAPTER SEVEN

I

David did not volunteer any information about his American trip, and Kate did not ask him about it. She was simply relieved to see him back home again and applying himself to his consultancy work. He also found time to commiserate with her loss of the TV campaign opportunity.

'I'm not sure I wanted it in the first place,' she said. 'Meeting those people reminded me that while it seems like fun to get into all that, it's a real grind.'

'Maybe, but I'm sure you'd have enjoyed it. Plus the money would have come in handy. Maybe something else will come along.'

She smiled. 'I did get the tiniest hint that you weren't too keen on my modelling again.'

'I'm sorry. I've not exactly been the perfect and supportive husband, have I?'

'Not exactly, but you've been under a lot of pressure. I just hope that everything's settled down.'

'Absolutely.'

'I know someone else who'll be pleased to hear that.'

'Ah yes,' he said. 'How is our hirsute phenomenologist friend?'

'He's hoping you can get together to tie up a few loose ends.'

'There's no need for that. I'm fine, really I am.'

'So I see,' she told him. 'I suppose Joe just wants a kind of signing-off session, like a doctor would.'

David looked thoughtfully at her. 'You're probably right. I'll give him a call.'

'Well it can't do any harm, can it?'

*

Carrigan welcomed David into his consulting room and after some small talk asked how he was feeling. David had expected the question. The truth was, he felt very much better. Better and different. He knew he had gone through what the agony aunts call a rocky patch, especially with Kate. But somehow it didn't really touch him. Not deep down. What was important was to honour the memory of his father. It was clear that Jacob had suffered at the hands of Muntz before he and his wife escaped from Germany to England. What would be more natural than a father telling a son of such things? The fact that these things were of such enormous horror that they were blanked out by amnesia simply made matters worse. David's duty was to avenge his father's ordeal. To do that he had to get close to Muntz, and the great thing was that his job would take him into the heart of the company that the man himself had founded. You couldn't get much closer than that.

He didn't really care what Joe Carrigan thought about him personally, but he had every respect for the American's intelligence, and he didn't want him worrying Kate with any more fears about his mental health. He just wanted to prepare himself to track down the truth about Muntz and *Turmfalke* without any interference, and that meant convincing Kate that he was OK. Mended. Fixed up. That's why he was happy to let Carrigan conduct one more hypnotherapy session. He was confident that he could control the results, which would be far more convincing than any verbal reassurances. In fact, he was so confident about all this that his fear of hypodermic needles seemed to have vanished. He even managed to visualize the point sliding through his skin and into the vein, and it didn't disturb him in the slightest. He was really on top of this thing.

'I feel great,' he said. 'But why take it from the conscious horse's mouth when there's a subconscious horse to deal with.'

'You mean, you'd like another hypno session?' Carrigan was pleasantly surprised.

'Seems the best way of tying up loose ends.'

'It certainly is. So let's get you ready.' Carrigan opened his drugs cabinet and took out the sedative tablets he used to relax David.

'Didn't you tell me that a jab would save time?' David asked.

Carrigan was even more surprised. 'Yes, but you said no needles, remember?'

'That's not a problem,' David assured him, holding out his arm. 'Jab away.'

'Fine,' Carrigan said. 'If you're sure.'

He prepared a syringe and put a thong round David's upper arm to make the vein swell. He dabbed the area with antiseptic solution and placed the needle on David's skin. David looked up at him and smiled, watching calmly as the sharpened plastic tube indented his flesh then popped into the blood vessel.

'No problem at all,' he murmured, and drifted into sleep, still smiling.

Carrigan put a drawing pad in his hands and started the process of prompting and suggesting that had produced such dramatic results over the past weeks. In return, David replied easily to his questions and began producing a series of excellent sketches of Kate, smiling, seductive, thoughtful, displeased, forgiving, relaxed . . . Everything he did, every reaction, was perfectly normal. He had also been more relaxed before the injection, as if he had settled something, solved a problem.

Overcoming a phobia of the needle was remarkable enough. But far from feeling pleased with his patient's progress, Carrigan was extremely worried. In the early stages of therapy, he had realized that David of the dream was a different person to David the engineer and loving husband. One personality that had been hidden by another was beginning to emerge. Such a change could be a sign of schizophrenia, but in addition to that there was now a fatalism about David which Carrigan had seen many times in seriously disturbed patients. Before committing an extremely violent act, they often go through a period of tranquillity. Carrigan wondered how he was going to tell Kate that her husband was exhibiting all the signs of a schizoid psychopath. Worse still, what was he going to do about it? His work did not conform to any recognized diagnostic procedure, so the medical authorities would not accept his conclusions. Indeed, they might take grave exception to his procedure. There was a dramatic difference between providing services as a registered nurse and using drugs for unorthodox medical research. He looked down at the still peaceful David and waited for him to wake up.

In one sense, David was awake. He was floating in a sea of semi-consciousness in which Albert Levy and Peter Halkyn were both asking him to do the same thing: to continue his search for the commandant of *Turmfalke* – and to expand the partnership's business in Germany. He felt very lucky that two such vital activities were in harmony with each other.

II

The commercial relations manager at Deutsche Arzneiwissenschaft Werke's head office in Munich was a woman in her early thirties called Helga Winter. She greeted David in the imposing reception area and took him via an executive escalator to a conference room on the tenth floor. The walls were lined with framed reproductions of advertisements for the company's range of pharmaceuticals, each captioned with the year of its launch. The first one said: '*Schlafgutex* – *1947*'. From the literature that Peter Halkyn had sent him, David knew that this was the wonder drug that had launched DAW into the international pharmaceutical scene just after the war, the first in a series of successful sedation-related products. Pride of place was given to an older photograph showing the founders of the firm.

'It's a pleasure to meet you after our correspondence, Mr Lewis,' she said as they sat in front of a demonstration screen. 'Your new colleagues at Anstat Konsult have impressed us with their description of your firm's capabilities.'

'That's very gracious, Fräulein,' David said. 'And I am grateful that you could see me at such short notice. You must be preoccupied with tomorrow's shareholders' meeting.' He had timed his visit to coincide with the annual event. Although it was a closed meeting, the press reports of the annual returns would provide useful analyses and descriptions of the company.

'I will take you through a short history of our company, and after some refreshment perhaps you would be kind enough to explain how your field of activity could assist our project in Rosenheim.'

The screen glowed with the company's logo and a blast of Wagner, then some fast mixes showing product packs, currency signs of the world, award-winning drugs, and newspaper coverage. It settled down to long shots of the Bavarian countryside and pastoral music, with a commentary extolling the virtues of the DAW Way. Then came a series of historical black and white photographs leading into colour shots of laboratories and manufacturing facilities. There was a face-to-camera monologue from the company's chief executive Otto Dolland followed by more Wagner to round things off, but David did not hear it. He struggled to keep his emotions under control as a maid came into the room wheeling a trolley with coffee and cakes.

'These gentlemen,' he said to Fräulein Winter, pointing at the photograph of the two company founders, 'are they still active in the business?'

'Professor Blintz left at an early stage to take a senior appointment in the Health Ministry,' she told him. 'Professor Muntz is still very active with us, but he is spending more of his time with the Freyer Institute.'

'I don't think I know of it,' David prompted. 'But I have, of course, heard of the professor.'

'The Institute specializes in political and management studies,' Fräulein Winter said, with enthusiasm. 'The re-vitalization of Europe. Professor Muntz is in great demand as a lecturer. Indeed, he is preparing a tour of major European cities before the May festival at his home in Switzerland. It's a regular routine for him each year. He will be in London at the end of this month. You should attend his lecture, if you are able.' She opened a drawer and passed a brochure across. 'This is his itinerary . . .'

The idea filled David with a mixture of elation and fear. Was it so easy for a hunter to approach the prey? And if he managed to get near to the monster, what then? Perhaps he would prove inadequate for the job of exposing the obscenity who had organized such terror and pain. On the other hand, maybe the hunter's instinct would take over. Man was, by tradition, a hunting animal.

'. . . which I think might be of interest to your firm,' Fräulein Winter was saying. 'The extension of our packaging units in Rosenheim. The director in charge of that facility can provide you with our pre-tender qualification requirements.'

'Presumably they comply with EU regulations,' David managed to keep the excitement from his voice.

'Naturally,' she said. 'Everything here at DAW is done strictly according to European standard procedures.'

131

He forced himself to concentrate as Fräulein Winter asked him to describe his firm's history and how they expected to build on the Anstat Konsult relationship. And as he laid out his documents and brochures, he felt like a pilot watching a Head Up Display of an enemy aircraft, his missiles locked on, closing in for the kill. Or, yes, this was more like it – like a kestrel that had seen its prey from a thousand feet in the air, beginning its shattering stoop, talons outstretched. How about that for turning the tables on the monster Muntz? He'd get to the man by navigating back through the skein of lies and deceit he had built around himself since the war, and what better place to start than in the company for which he was responsible?

III

The manager of security at DAW was an ex-policeman called Moritz Hubermann. In addition to the physical security of DAW property and installations, Hubermann's department dealt with standard credit reports on companies applying to do business with DAW and for checking their trading credentials. Like many European companies concerned about kidnap and assassination, DAW was sensitive about the safety of its senior personnel, and Hubermann was personally responsible for the operational integrity of the company's on-line counter-terrorist system. This was a syndicated system, set up by his predecessor, an American computer *wunderkind* called Harry Downer who had left his position in DAW to run the security organization that coordinated the information, Loki.

All Hubermann knew about Loki was that the company had an extremely low profile, an enormously powerful data system and a great deal of influence at the top level. His receptionist staff entered information about all visitors to the firm into the DAW computer which stored details of the visit and printed out a visitor's pass. Unknown to the receptionists and to the visitors, this information was also sent down a dedicated data line to the Loki computer and compared against lists of organizations, criminals, terrorists and any individuals whose activities could imperil the company's security.

A few days before David's visit to Munich, the Loki system matched the name Lewis with an instruction from the chairman's office that contact with anyone called Lewis must be reported immediately and directly to the chairman under confidential cover. When Fräulein Winter's secretary informed reception of David's appointment, Hubermann followed this instruction and had been ordered by the chairman's personal assistant, Oskar Hind, to activate the surveillance equipment in one of the tenth-storey conference rooms and take no further action. Such a break from official procedure was an affront to his standing in the company, but he did as he was ordered.

The chief executive watched the video screen as Fräulein Winter showed David out of the conference room, turned to his assistant and gave him a puzzled look.

'You thought I should see this, Oskar?'

The assistant, a high-flying young Heidelberg graduate, returned his look steadily. 'Yes, Herr Dolland.'

'All you show me is a boring English engineer trying to make his entry onto our client list. Our procedures will, no doubt, ensure that his firm will receive a contract only if they adhere to all our criteria. This is hardly a matter for the chief executive officer.' His tone was indulgent rather than critical. Bright young DAW high-flyers did not risk wasting his time on trivial matters. He was not to be disappointed.

His assistant handed him a memorandum from the firm's Philadelphia office. As he read it, his lips turned white.

'This arrived ten days ago,' Dolland said quietly. 'Are you aware of its significance?'

'I assumed the message meant that the security of Professor Muntz might be compromised for some reason, Herr Dolland. Accordingly, I alerted Herr Hubermann, and when this fellow Lewis arranged a meeting with Fräulein Winter his name came up on the Loki system. I started an investigation of his company and reported the matter to you. I have also arranged for a video of the meeting to be sent to Philadelphia so that they can check if this is the same David Lewis who called on Colonel Newman's friend in order that no mistakes are made. As you will observe, the memorandum indicates that this was the correct action to take. Have I made an error?'

Dolland sighed. 'You acted perfectly correctly, Oskar, but I must ask you something. What relevance do you give to this reference to *Turmfalke*?'

'None whatsoever, sir, but I assume that Herr Newman is concerned with the security of Professor Muntz and that this David Lewis might be, in some way, a threat to him.'

'Yes, in some way,' Dolland murmured. 'And he might be a threat to all of us. After all this time. Who the devil is he? Oskar, I want you to meet Mr Lewis and press a few buttons. See if you can find out what he is doing, who he is working for besides this English engineering consultancy. Get him off balance. See who he contacts.'

As David was handing his visitor's pass back to the receptionist her phone bleeped. She listened for a few seconds, then turned to him. 'Mr Lewis, I wonder if you would mind waiting? Our chief executive's personal assistant Herr Hind would like to see you before you leave.'

'Of course not,' David said, surprised. He had agreed with Fräulein Winter to make his own arrangements to see the director of the factory in Rosenheim. He wondered what other business needed discussion.

The elevator doors slid open, and a keen-looking young man came towards him.

'Mr Lewis? My name is Oskar Hind. I was hoping to join your meeting with our commercial relations manager, but unfortunately another commitment prevented me from doing so. Do you have a few moments?'

'Of course,' David told him as they shook hands. 'I have no more appointments in Munich today.'

Hind led him into a dining area where an array of machines offered micro-waved snacks and hot beverages.

'This is not Michelin quality,' he said smilingly, 'but the meals really are quite good.'

'A black coffee will be fine, Herr Hind.'

David wondered where all this might be leading, as Hind took him to a table in the corner, away from other staff.

'Your consultancy is keen to gain contracts in the European Community, I believe,' Hind said.

'Yes. We already have a good client here in Germany. Sacht Engineering of Frankfurt. You might know them. And we also have several clients in Italy, the Middle East and Nigeria,' David said. 'We believe our recent agreement with Anstat Konsult will provide clients such as DAW with a much enhanced service.'

'We know Sacht. Also we know the Odonga Group in Lagos,' Hind nodded. 'A continuous process for reconstituting old car tyres.'

'I'm impressed with your thoroughness, Herr Hind,' David said sincerely.

'I believe you English have an expression, "The feeling is mutual". You are clearly a man who takes his work very seriously indeed.'

'Thank you.'

'The point is,' Hind said, leaning towards him slightly, 'we have a peculiar situation in our Rosenheim facility. I believe Fräulein Winter mentioned the project to you.'

'She told me that I should make contact with the engineer in charge. I'd like my company to get on his pre-tender list.'

'Quite so,' Hind said, his voice dropping almost to a whisper. 'Herr Doktor Abel Frinkmann. The matter I am about to tell you is most sensitive, but I have reason to believe that someone in Herr Frinkmann's staff is making financial accommodations with our suppliers.'

David stood up. 'Herr Hind, I am shocked!'

Hind interrupted him. 'Bear with me, Mr Lewis. How else can we check such a thing unless we involve someone totally new, such as yourself? I understand your admirable concern, but it is my job to use all means to ensure that DAW interests are never compromised.'

'All I'm interested in is using the correct procedures to gain mutually profitable work with your company,' David said. 'I can have no part in any activity that will jeopardize that objective.'

Hind nodded. 'But if I help you to follow those procedures, I will save you a great deal of valuable time. You would still be in a competitive situation, and there would be no impropriety. If you provide me with information that will enable us to root out any malpractice unconnected with your firm, we will each have benefited without compromising ourselves ethically.'

David thought hard. This was too good to be true. But it was typical Teutonic logic. Using a newcomer to the corporate scene like this made sense. If it worked, everyone was a winner. If it crashed out for any reason, DAW could throw him to the wolves. Nothing ventured, nothing gained. It would give him a fantastic opportunity to get closer to the company, closer to Muntz, and how ironic it would be if he grabbed a contract out of it! It was irresistible.

'I really don't think I can help, Herr Hind,' he said solemnly. 'Much as I personally might like to, my partners might not. Professional code of practice, and all that.'

'I quite understand,' Hind said. 'Why don't you call and ask them to consider the matter? Meanwhile, I invite you to stay in Munich as our guest. We are holding our annual shareholders' meeting tomorrow. After the meeting we host a gala for major customers and suppliers. We would make you most welcome.'

IV

The shareholders' meeting was held in a mediaeval hunting lodge in the forest outside the city. The owners had turned the lodge into a conference centre, a series of wooden buildings connected by glass-enclosed walkways and set against a hillside. The welcome that David received on his arrival was warm and seemed sincere. Fräulein Winter took him under her wing and introduced him to senior company managers, local politicians and influential people in German banking and the European Commission. Rooms were set aside as restaurants, with food from various European countries laid out on trestles. Other rooms had been cleared for dancing, with traditional German music, a dance orchestra and band playing Dixieland jazz.

Despite the carnival atmosphere, David had the impression that everyone was on their best behaviour, as if they were aware of a higher scrutiny. People came up to him and pumped his hand, smiling, full of a bonhomie that didn't ring true. One in particular, a stocky man called Streichner, latched onto him and insisted on plying him with white schnapps and canapés, most of which he managed to empty into one of the plentiful pedestal ashtrays. By eight o'clock he had run out of business cards. At nine o'clock the oompah band broke away from a polka and created a cacophonous drum roll and fanfare, after which the public address system crackled and announced the entrance of the DAW shareholders and company officers. Doors leading from the conference hall were opened by liveried servants, and a double file of men marched into a space created by the dancers, who set up a rhythmic hand-clapping.

'These are the men of the past and of the future, Mr Lewis.'

David turned to find Streichner at his side again.

Streichner nodded to himself. 'How many of us could establish a company such as this, eh? Germany owes much to these men, the shareholders and founders of Deutsche Arzneiwissenschaft Werke.'

'I'm sure you are right,' David answered politely.

Streichner pointed as the clapping changed tempo and broke into a frenzy of applause. Two tall, distinguished elderly men were standing in the centre of the room, smiling at their admirers.

'Herr Professor Muntz and Herr Professor Blintz,' Streichner said proudly.

David stared, while the cameras flashed and the music rolled over him. Muntz and Blintz were moving round the circle, shaking hands and exchanging words with favoured guests. A familiar face came into David's strained focus, a face bearing an expression akin to worship. Theodore Pökke. The ex-SS officer drew himself stiffly to attention and clicked his heels as the two men approached him, right palm snapping upright in the short salute used by top Nazis. Muntz returned the salute, and the greeting was repeated by several men in their sixties and seventies. Further down the line he saw two more faces that he recognized with a shock. The gamekeepers from Röhmer Insel. But they did not seem to have noticed him. They were gazing at Muntz with expressions that he had last seen on the faces of crowds meeting Adolph Hitler. Adoration. Worship. But what the hell would they do if they recognized David?

Easing himself nervously backwards, David managed to keep his focus on Muntz. Despite his years, the chairman of DAW was still a handsome aristocratic man with an upright military bearing, keen blue eyes radiating confidence and authority. As Muntz and his colleague moved down the line of guests towards him, David felt as if the room was narrowing and that he was being crushed by heavy weights.

'Perhaps you wish me to present you to the Herr Professors . . . ?' Streichner was saying, turning round to find where David had gone.

'Excuse me, Herr Streichner,' he managed to stutter. 'I am not feeling very well . . .'

He pushed his way through the crowd to the men's room and spent some minutes voiding the contents of his stomach into a pristine WC with an electronic flushing mechanism, before rinsing his face with cold water. He realized that the old David Lewis had reappeared on the scene: the careful engineer, the weak David Lewis, who had just been sickened by the sight of Ernst Muntz collecting the plaudits of an adoring crowd of murderous right-wing sycophants.

The new David Lewis, the hunter with a mission, was struggling to overcome such weakness, was trying to get out there and deal with the situation. He rubbed his face vigorously with a cotton towel and went back into the reception hall.

Fräulein Winter was waiting for him by the lavatory door, her expression one of concern.

'Herr Streichner said you have been overcome by sickness, Herr Lewis,' she said in English. 'Perhaps we have inadvertently served you with items of poor quality.'

'No, no,' he reassured her in German. 'Your hospitality is wonderful. I have been suffering from a mild attack of gastroenteritis for the past few days, although to admit such a thing in the heart of one of the world's leading pharmaceutical companies is, perhaps, an unforgivable indiscretion.'

Fräulein Winter missed his attempt at light-heartedness. 'Deutsche Arzneiwissenschaft Werke does not manufacture products for the digestive system, Herr Lewis, only those suitable for alleviating stress and anxiety.'

'Of course,' David said, 'but in any case, I seem to be fully recovered. Sorry if I alarmed you.'

'That is good,' she said. 'I had come to search for you, because Herr Hind has asked me to introduce you to the manager of our Rosenheim factory, Herr Frinkmann. He is over there, talking with some colleagues. But only if you feel capable, of course.'

'Never felt better,' said David Lewis, the hunter. He looked around for his prey, but Muntz was nowhere to be seen, and luckily neither was Theodore Pökke, nor the two gamekeepers.

Moritz Hubermann moved casually among his colleagues keeping David in sight, watching the Englishman's face as the two founding fathers of his company entered the reception, noting the attention that Streichner paid to the Englishman. Josef Streichner was not a DAW employee. He was listed in the database merely as an associate of Herr Professor Muntz. Hubermann had once tried to discover through the company files what 'associate' meant, but there was no other information. And when he entered the man's name into the Loki system, the report came back that nothing was known. Which was very strange, because Hubermann's contact in the Bundespolizei internal affairs unit told him that Streichner was a leading light in *Volkssozialistische Bewegung Deutschlands*. VBD. Not a nice bunch of people to run up against. Especially if you were a Jew, like David Lewis. Or like Hubermann. One of the company's pet Jews, employed by a fascist management to satisfy European regulatory requirements. So he kept his mouth shut and his head down. He had his retirement to consider. But all this was most curious.

At one point the Englishman seemed to be taken ill. At any rate, he made a dive to the lavatory, and while he was in there Herr Dolland's personal assistant Herr Hind whispered something to Josef Streichner who immediately had words with two VBD thugs employed at the chairman's Falkenschloss estate in the Rhine valley. They left the room. Hind then moved across to a group of DAW guests, and one of them also left. Hubermann recognized him as an old SS chum of the good Herr Professor, a factory owner from Stuttgart called Pökke.

When this fellow Lewis returned, looking very much as if he'd just emptied a kilo of bratwurst from his belly, Fräulein Winter took him over to a group of senior managers.

What the hell was going on?

Whatever it was, Hubermann decided, he didn't like it. Not one bit. His instinct told him that this David Lewis was heading into trouble and that he, Hubermann, had better keep his eyes and ears even wider open and his head even lower down.

He was about to replenish his wine when Herr Hind snapped his fingers from across the room.

'Herr Hubermann,' Hind called out loudly. 'Our guest is leaving us. Please arrange transport for him to his hotel.'

'Certainly Herr Hind,' Hubermann replied impassively. He walked across to David. 'Where shall the driver take you, sir?'

'Please don't trouble yourself,' David told him. 'I can make my own way back.'

'Not from the middle of a Bavarian forest in the middle of the night, I think.' Hubermann smiled at him. 'This is no trouble. No trouble whatsoever.' He used his short-band radio to instruct the security guards outside to allocate one of the company cars to David.

'Thank you, Herr Hubermann,' David said, holding out his hand. Hubermann took it, thinking how strained the Englishman looked. No. Strained was not the right word. Haunted.

'I trust you enjoyed your evening with us, Mr Lewis,' he said politely in passable English.

'Yes,' David told him. 'Most enjoyable.'

As he watched the guest make his way to the entrance, Hubermann became aware of a strange emotion, something that confused his normally ordered mental processes. He found himself hurrying after David to hold the door open for him, watching to see if the thugs from Falkenschloss were waiting in the shadows, making sure that the Englishman was settled in a car with a driver he knew personally. It wasn't until he returned to his widower's flat on the outskirts of Munich that he realized what the emotion had been. It was fear, fear mixed with shame.

He had no illusions about the men who controlled companies like DAW. They were the ones responsible for crimes beyond the imagination, and he, like so many others, was prepared to turn away to avoid involvement. Even prepared to work for such companies, with the ready excuse that if he didn't someone else would. And he had no doubt whatsoever that he had just witnessed a perfectly decent person being stalked by these bastards. He had no idea why, but as he was lying in bed something began niggling. One of his friends had received a message from London just before their last weekly meeting. There was a reference, a word that he had also seen on a recent company document.

He got out of bed and dialled a number, letting the distant phone ring until his friend woke up and answered.

Keeping his head down was not going to be easy.

CHAPTER EIGHT

I

The facsimile machine was a novelty for Albert Levy, making it easier to communicate with his friends and business contacts around the world. It was connected to the networks through a new cellular phone system. This was untraceable to his address, a decided advantage in his kind of work. On the second morning after David Lewis's visit to DAW headquarters, the fax tray held a respectable pile of incoming messages.

'I told you this would improve matters,' he said to Anna as she sorted them for him to read. 'People don't always like talking on the telephone, and no one sends letters these days.'

'I hope we can afford it,' his assistant said seriously. 'It's much more expensive than an ordinary fax.'

'Not if we don't make the calls,' Levy said, his eyes twinkling. 'Our friends will use it to send us information. You'll see.'

Anna was pleased that the old man had found a new interest. Contact with his colleagues and with various sources of information had diminished over the past few years. Some had died, and many were turning their attentions towards the current problems of anti-Semitism. World War II atrocities did not excite the same passions as they did in the old days. Nevertheless, she had sent a note to the network of Jewish organizations with interests in war crimes to tell them of their new facility. As an afterthought she had asked if anyone could supply information on an SS project called *Turmfalke*.

They received a considerable number of replies, more by way of greeting than with any information. Most of the in-coming faxes omitted the sender's identification. In some countries this is illegal, but not everybody wants to broadcast the origin of a message. So it was not the sender of the fax that caught her attention, but its title, and the fact that it was in German. She pulled it from the pile.

142

I refer to your recent request for information relating to a wartime
Nazi project referred to as Turmfalke. I am able to inform you that
an enquiry about Turmfalke was originated a few days ago in the
USA by a person called David Lewis. He was interested in any
connection between this project and Professor Ernst Muntz who
is a co-founder of Deutsche Arzneiwissenschaft Werke in Munich.
A warning about his enquiries was sent from the DAW subsidiary
in the USA to the company's headquarters. Meanwhile, an engineer
called David Lewis had already arranged an appointment with a
senior manager in the DAW buying department. This meeting
was reported to Herr Dolland, Chief Executive Officer of the DAW
group, who by-passed the normal security procedures to monitor
the meeting privately. Mr Lewis is now the object of a surveillance
operation involving members of the Volkssozialistische
Bewegung Deutschlands. In addition, there is an organization of
which you must be aware called Loki which circulates security
reports to which I have limited access. A number of these contain
the name Lewis. The Loki system seems not yet to have made
the link, perhaps because Lewis is a common British name. I believe
that all these reports refer to the same person and that he is in
danger. As both yourself and Mr David Lewis have originated
requests for information about Turmfalke, I decided to bring the
matter to your attention. I myself have no knowledge of Turmfalke.
I trust this is of use to you.

A Friend of Justice

'I wonder who is this friend of justice,' Levy mused, turning the
fax round and round as if this would somehow reveal a name.
'Someone who works for the pharmaceutical company, by the look
of the disgruntled insider references. Our Mr Lewis is certainly
beginning to make his presence known.'
'What is the Loki organization?' Anna asked him.
'It is a highly secretive and ultra-right-wing group that protects
war criminals who established themselves in successful industries
after the Second World War,' Levy told her. 'Loki has great wealth
and immense influence. Much of its efforts are concerned with
maintaining surveillance and security around those whom it pro-

tects. Needless to say, it has links with other Nazi organizations, such as VBD and Neuvolkgruppe. Apart from that, there's not much I can tell you.'

'We should have warned him, Albert,' Anna said seriously.

'Nonsense. He is merely causing a few eyes to peer his way. It happens all the time. There is no reason to believe he is involved in anything of significance.'

'But what if you're wrong?' she insisted.

Levy sighed. 'If it helps to soothe your concern, my dear, we'll take a look at Deutsche Arzneiwissenschaft Werke.'

Two days later, Levy called Anna into his office. His desk was buried in a mountain of paperwork, ranging from decades-old documents to modern company brochures. He was holding a new fax towards her.

'Just look, Anna,' he said excitedly. 'I asked our friend in Addenbrooke research laboratories to see if she could identify the research that led to the production of best-selling DAW drugs. You know how these people rejoice in their learned journals. The company was incorporated by private shareholders in 1943, and she could find no research that related to products launched between 1945 and 1952. That was the period in which the company produced the first three of their wonder drugs. These were aimed at the tranquillizer market, for stress relief, anxiety and sleeplessness. Despite the lack of research reports, they were fully documented with regard to factors such as dosage rates, side effects and something called . . .' Levy peered at the fax. 'Can you read this?'

Anna took the fax. 'LD_{50},' she said.

'Ah yes. Be so kind as to read it for me, my dear. My eyes are playing up today.'

'"In view of the time spans involved,"' Anna read, '"the presence of such data is surprising, to say the least. It takes several years of research to establish this kind of information, yet in the case of DAW's first three ethical products they submitted detailed figures for studies that could only have taken place prior to 1946, the year of the company's launch. I am particularly surprised with the LD_{50} data. Such values are normally associated with small mammals, such as rats and beagles, but the pre-normalization figures in the raw data are large enough to suggest that experiments were carried out on higher primates such as Capuchin monkeys, and these animals were not generally available in Europe at the time . . ." She doesn't say what LD50 is,' Anna remarked.

Levy shuffled through the papers on his desk. 'It's the amount of a drug that kills half a test group of animals,' he said absentmindedly. 'LD. Lethal Dose. Fifty, meaning fifty per cent. Ah, here it is.' He held out another sheet of paper. 'It's the composition of the company's shareholders. The voting shares of DAW are held by an organization called the Freyer Institute. This is a private foundation with closed books. However, the names of the members are available for scrutiny by the public.'

His assistant scanned down the names. 'I suppose it's not surprising that Muntz appears here.'

'Not at all,' Levy agreed. 'Nor Professor Blintz, with whom Muntz claimed he worked during the war at a hospital in Andernach. But these other names are not familiar to me – Pökke, Dollman – perhaps you recognize them?'

Anna shook her head. 'Only Dollman. He's the chief executive of DAW. What's the connection with David Lewis?'

'Right now, that is the least of the problems,' Levy said. 'There's something here that I should see, but I can't.' He shook his head angrily. 'I'm getting too old for all this, Anna.'

'Nonsense,' she said firmly. The old man's energies had been revitalized over the past few days, and he was enjoying a new lease of life. She felt a flow of affection and admiration as he brought his considerable intellect on the problem.

'I wonder . . .' he said quietly.

She didn't speak, fearful of breaking his concentration.

Levy turned to a bookshelf and pulled down a book that Anna had read and re-read many times: *The Rise and Fall of the Third Reich*, by William Shirer. She watched over his shoulder as he turned to a section near the end of the book entitled 'The Medical Experiments', which she knew was a harrowing account of work carried out on prisoners at concentration camps in the name of medical research.

'What if Shirer and the others were wrong about this?' Levy murmured. 'The Allied authorities thought that all these atrocities were carried out by a few deranged and sadistic doctors on various flimsy pretexts and that the results were of little or no value. But what if . . . ?'

He pulled down another book, the official history of Dachau, the camp at which many of the medical experiments took place.

'You see, Anna. It was certainly sadistic, but it was also very well organized. The work of these animals covered aspects of medicine that were of vital interest to Germany's war effort. Malaria, cholera, the effects of high altitude, freezing conditions and broken limbs, poison gases, explosions, bullet wounds, the condition of human blood . . . By 1945, any SS doctor of suitable rank could order human specimens with almost any kind of physical characteristics . . . young, old, male, female, fat, thin, dark-eyed, blue-eyed. They just sent in a requisition, and the specimens arrived, dead or alive, as requested.' Levy paused for a moment, lost in a reverie. 'The Allies discovered many documents relating to this disgusting work, and the perpetrators were brought to trial at Strasbourg, but did it end there? Perhaps these madmen were merely sacrificial lambs, left to suffer the hangman's rope by others more cunning. What if Mr Lewis has stumbled onto something that evaded Allied justice and survived to perpetuate evil?'

CHAPTER NINE

I

David hired a car and drove from Munich to Rosenheim for his meeting with DAW's factory manager, Herr Frinkmann. Despite having been introduced to David at the company's annual general meeting, Frinkmann rudely kept him waiting in the reception area for more than an hour before sending his secretary to guide him to his office. He was a thin-faced man in his fifties, with a hollow smile and a wet handshake, and David had already taken a dislike to him. He waved casually at a chair and opened a file, flicking a glance at David every now and again.

'It seems that my colleagues in Munich believe your firm has the potential to undertake work in the impending refurbishment of my factory,' he said.

'They were kind enough to let me present credentials, Herr Frinkmann,' David said. 'But they were careful to point out that the appointment of design consultants and other contractors was your responsibility.'

The factory director nodded. 'Such decisions are for the experts who know how to get their hands dirty. The head offices of all manufacturers are full of people bulging with theory, and not a minute's worth of practical experience between them.'

It was an odd thing for a senior company man to say to a stranger. David interpreted the remark as a deliberate attempt on the part of Frinkmann to distance himself from his colleagues. He wondered why.

'In my experience, those who produce the goods are able to address the most important problems of manufacture,' he said diplomatically. 'My firm is used to working directly with the producers to get the best results. All I want is the opportunity to compete for those parts of the work for which we have proven capabilities.'

'Naturally,' Frinkmann said. He stood up and opened the door. 'Herr Brinden will show you the area affected by our plans and describe some of the problems we face. He will bring you back here in one hour.'

A pimply young man with a serious expression was waiting for David in the corridor. He politely shook hands and led the way to a changing room, where they donned sterile gowns, caps and face masks. They began the tour on a metal gantry that ran round the production area.

'For reasons of security and quality control, we manufacture everything here. Pharmaceuticals, plastic containers, boxes, printed instructions, cartons. The entire system is controlled and coordinated by a single computer,' Herr Brinden began. 'Orders and projected orders for our products are entered into our system through a wide-area data network. These orders initiate a raw material acquisition procedure for products, containers and packaging. Each process is timed carefully so that there is neither undue storage nor wastage of any material. Costings are thus kept to a minimum. However, we are finding that certain machinery is unreliable, and we are expecting a considerable rise in throughput over the next few months. This is the reason for our expansion.'

'Which production line causes the problems?' David asked.

'Not the pharmaceuticals themselves,' Brinden answered. 'It is the manufacture of containers, and in particular the security screw tops. Despite our stringent specification to the suppliers, there are slight differences in the quality of delivered feedstocks that cause disruption to the moulding process. It wastes materials and delays the fulfilment of orders. In our view, this is unnecessary, but we have yet to solve the problem.'

The engineering side of David's mind began mulling over what Brinden was telling him. Determining the cause of the problem was the easy bit. Probably a combination of infinitesimal amounts of impurities in the feedstock coupled with slight but significant variations in temperature and pressure in the injection-moulding equipment. If these could be detected and measured as they were happening, he could solve the problem by advanced feed-back and feed-forward techniques based on laser sensors and control programs that he had developed. He began asking Brinden questions about timing and cost parameters.

Frinkmann looked at David thoughtfully as Brinden withdrew from the office.

'Perhaps you have already gained some first impressions, Mr Lewis,' he said.

'I'm impressed with the thoroughness of your operation, Herr Frinkmann,' David said, 'although I believe I can understand your concern for quality.'

'Herr Brinden has pointed out the problems we are having with security caps for our medicine bottles,' Frinkmann said. 'The failure rate is not satisfactory. Have you any ideas on this aspect of our work?'

'I believe so,' David said, 'although it is rather too soon to come to conclusions.'

Frinkmann pushed a large document towards him, but kept his hand on it.

'Here is the application for our pre-tender qualification. You will understand that merely passing this to you involves my staff and myself in considerably more work than we had anticipated.'

David had seen hundreds of such documents. They outlined the essential requirements of the work to be done for the client and asked questions about the company that wanted to quote for the job, including information about the people who would work on the contract, the methods that would be used, the time-scales involved and how they intended to finance their part in the operation. If these questions were answered to the satisfaction of the client, the company would be placed on a short list of companies that would be invited to tender for the work. At this stage, they would be given more details of the job and asked to provide a firm quotation. It was a routine familiar to all concerned, and David was surprised at Frinkmann's comment. However, he did not remain surprised for long.

'As you have clients in the Middle East and Africa, I take it you are in a position to authorize contingency expenses.'

There was no doubt in David's mind what Frinkmann was getting at. Many countries in these areas were notorious for the bribery involved in commercial contracts. 'Contingency expenses' were a typical way of providing money for corrupt officials through the legitimate operating budget.

'Provided these are agreed in principle with our client beforehand,' he said.

'The sort of thing I had in mind was Club Class open return airfares between Munich and London,' Frinkmann said. 'We would expect at least four such journeys per week throughout the duration of the work. Some of these would be for my people, and this would naturally be part of your company's operating budget.'

So that was it. Neat, simple, and very difficult to trace. Each return ticket plus airport taxes costs about $800. On average, less than two such journeys would be needed in a week. But Frinkmann could authorize four payments and ask for the extra tickets to be handed to him, then cash them in prior to the flight dates. He would be putting the same proposition to each applicant. It would therefore appear as if the estimate for air journeys had come from everyone but Frinkmann, so there would be no come-back for him. In effect, he would be stealing over $7000 cash a month on this one project alone. And he would be stealing it from his own company, not from the consultants, so why would they bother to rock the boat, especially if they'd lose the job by doing so?

'We would certainly need many meetings,' David said innocently, 'and that seems an efficient way of managing things from our point of view, as well.'

Frinkmann took his hand off the document, and David put it in his briefcase.

'I can see no problem in your company passing our initial hurdle, Herr Lewis,' Frinkmann said.

II

Oskar Hind had asked him to report on his meeting with Frinkmann immediately he left the factory, so he made his way across the company car park to a set of public telephone booths by a street subway. In many business dealings, situations like this can arise. Double-whammies. You duck one problem and run straight into another. If he reported to Oskar Hind that his meeting with Frinkmann was an attempted bribe, Frinkmann would simply deny it. There was nothing illegal or even unusual in having his staff's travel expenses included in a consultant's budget. It made for easier accounting. On the other hand, if he failed to say what happened, Hind may well find out and pull the plug on his attempt to get work. And he had not overlooked the possibility that he was being set up, as a test of his own honesty. He reached the phone booths and rummaged in his pocket for some fifty-pfennig pieces.

The two youths who came up behind him were dressed in the calf-length laced-up boots and quasi-military uniforms favoured by right-wing organizations throughout Europe. Shaved heads and single earrings completed the picture. They came up close, standing either side as he thumbed the coins into the slot. He felt rather than saw them.

'I think the other phones are in working order,' he said in German. 'If they're not, I shouldn't be too long.'

'*Leck mich am Arsch, Engländer*,' one of them said casually.

The other reached out and took hold of David's briefcase. David pulled it back, and the first one punched him in the kidneys. The pain caused him to buckle at the knees. The second one kicked him in the stomach and emptied the contents of his briefcase over his head.

'Keep out of our country, *Engländer*. We don't want your kind here.'

The words were accompanied by a vicious kick in the back. By the time he pulled himself to his feet, they had vanished. Across the street, a woman who had been watching averted her eyes and hurried away. In the 1990s as in the 1930s, it didn't pay to get involved in anything that wasn't your business. David breathed deeply and waited until the pain had died away a little, then keyed in DAW's head office number and Hind's extension. Hind answered the telephone on the first ringing tone, and David chose his words carefully.

'Herr Frinkmann behaved in an exemplary manner,' he told Hind. 'Of course, as with all major contracts there are opportunities for malpractice. However, I certainly have no reason to believe that he or anyone else in his staff could be involved in such a thing.'

'Perhaps you could be more specific about such opportunities, Herr Lewis.'

David knew he had to tell Hind about Frinkmann's airfare suggestion, whether the exercise was a test of his honesty or not.

'In many companies, international air travel requires approval from head office,' he said. 'I presume this is true for DAW.'

He left a silence for Hind to fill.

'Yes, if a flight costs more than five hundred Deutschmarks.'

'Oh, that explains it.' David hoped his voice expressed relief. He could report his conversation with Frinkmann without implying that the factory manager had tried to bribe him. If he was on a hook, this should get him off it nicely, he thought.

'Explains what, Herr Lewis?' Hind sounded puzzled.

'I think Herr Frinkmann is concerned that his staff will have the ability to liaise with my company whenever necessary. Sometimes there is no time for approvals, so Herr Frinkmann asked if we would be prepared to cost that into our own expenses to avoid this risk. This is an administrative ploy. No more than that.'

There was a silence. 'You think not?'

'I think that Herr Frinkmann is simply trying to ensure that his liaison with his consultants proceeds efficiently.'

After another silence, Hind said, 'You seem a little breathless, Herr Lewis. Not yet fully recovered from your indisposition, perhaps.'

'A touch of indigestion, Herr Hind. No more than that.'

'I am glad that you are able to come to your conclusions. My company will be pleased to receive your pre-tender application in due course. Call me if there are any sections about which you need advice or guidance.'

David put the phone down and made his way back to the subway leading to the metro. His stomach felt as if it were on fire. In a sudden panic he felt for his wallet and passport, but they were safely in his pockets. Nothing seemed to be missing from his brief-case, either. It was just his luck that a couple of racist thugs were looking for a bit of action. Jews, Turks, English . . . anyone was fair game for the new breed of neo-Nazis.

He could see no point in reporting his misadventure to the police. It would take far too long and get nowhere. In any case, things were working out very well. He was learning more about Muntz's company, and his own company had a good chance of picking up a lucrative contract. Most exciting of all, Fräulein Winter had told him that Muntz was due to give a lecture in Westminster in a few days' time. Another chance for the hunter to get close to the quarry.

CHAPTER TEN

I

The chubby young man with the twisted spine was already cruising the data superhighway that politicians had been dreaming about for several years. All he needed to drive through the databases of thousands of organizations was an ordinary telephone line and the racks of equipment that lined his living room. An ISDN link was better, of course, and sometimes he had time to arrange a high-speed data line or even an optic-fibre cable. For his kind of work, the effect of this was like turning on the re-heat of an F-111 fighter. Tasks that took up to three boring minutes of data transfer time on a twisted copper pair were completed in a thousandth of a second. Wonderful stuff. The ultimate turn-on.

The racks were on casters, and the young man could load up his adapted van, move from one rented apartment and set up his system in another a hundred miles away in less than three hours. His personal identification on the highly encrypted computer bulletin board service that connected him with over a hundred countries was Loki Ten. He happened to be operating in a small town in the north of England, but he could just as easily have been in America or New Zealand.

Loki Ten was able to monitor David's phone conversation with Oskar Hind because Hind had filed a report to Loki One informing the network that he expected a subject to call him from a telephone booth outside the DAW factory in Rosenheim and instructing Loki One to arrange an Introductory Level beating. Loki Ten was interested in this kind of thing. Not beatings, as such, but any activity that resulted from the machinations of the high-technology data organization. Some operatives were only concerned with the computing aspects of the work, but Loki Ten considered himself on a more advanced level than that. He liked to understand how his organization's work was put to use by its clients, otherwise what was the point? An on-line map of German towns and streets provided an exact reference for the three booths, and a quick hack into the DeutscheTelekom database revealed the phone numbers of each one. A small box on one of his racks mimicked the DeutscheTelekom digital switching protocols, and as soon as David made his call Loki Ten was able to hear the conversation.

He was particularly intrigued by David Lewis because reports circulating the network referred to the appearance of a subject at locations that were sensitive to Loki. In some the man's name was given. Others included physical details such as grey hair and short stature. What so intrigued Loki Ten was the failure of the network's computing system to recognize this as a cumulative threat to the organization he served. *Turmfalke* was one of several names for which a perpetual surveillance was carried out. The safety of dozens of influential men and women associated with these names depended on total security.

Loki Ten knew nothing about *Turmfalke*, and neither was he particularly concerned with the security of the people involved. His loyalty was to the Loki community, linked together by the web of cable and satellite links, and to the Loki organization which paid him large sums of money for which he had little use and provided him with the best information-technology equipment on the market. He could browse through the libraries of the Massachusetts Institute of Technology one minute and switch to interactive pornography on his virtual-reality headset the next.

As far as Loki Ten was concerned, David Lewis's only value was as a signpost to errors in the network's programming algorithms. In this case, the errors led to failures in the cross-referencing of security reports. He had already identified, solved and removed the problem on the parallel system he had set up secretly to ghost the Loki database. His next task was to construct a way for the system to ignore irrelevant report data. It was incidental to Loki Ten that such an enhancement would increase Loki effectiveness and profitability. If he could achieve his objective, he would be the envy of all other Loki operatives.

David Lewis provided him with the perfect opportunity for his development. He would use his own system to track the man's activity and compare his results with the official Loki reports. The logical place to start such an investigation was with Lewis's use of the telephone. He tapped in the codes that connected him to BT's Customer Services System and instructed his computer to search for records of calls made from David's home to numbers that were recognized by the Loki network. This drew a blank, so he tapped into David's phone and activated a digital recorder with instructions to search for sensitive keywords. When he had done this, he began hacking into bank and major charge-card databases to search for financial information about his subject. Was he receiving payments from any source listed as a security risk, for example, or was he making payments to any such source? Another blank. Loki Ten set his systems to run automatically and returned to his scheduled work.

CHAPTER ELEVEN

I

Peter Halkyn was already at his table in Langan's as Kate paid off the taxi and entered the restaurant. He rose and shook hands as the waiter pulled the chair out for her.

'I'm so sorry, Peter. The King's Road was a bloody nightmare.'

Halkyn smiled. 'I've only just got here myself. Bubbly's on its way.'

'Sounds like a celebration,' she said.

'It is, in a way. I'm sorry I was so cryptic on the phone, but an office is no place for private utterances.'

An ice bucket arrived, and the champagne was poured. He raised his glass.

'It seems a long time since we were able to have a chat like this,' Halkyn said.

'Two Christmases ago, if I remember rightly. You welcomed me into the fold and warned me that a consultant's day finished when most other people had gone to bed. I didn't believe you.'

They both laughed. Halkyn thought that Kate was forcing it.

'I suppose you know better now,' he said.

She nodded. 'It can be tough, but there are compensations. I'm not one for a totally domestic routine.'

Halkyn put his glass down. 'In a way, that's why I wanted to see you. You'll think it frightfully impertinent, but I'm concerned that this spate of work in Europe means that David is away from home far more than usual. Family relationships can be placed under considerable strain.'

'Everything is fine, Peter, really,' she said.

He didn't believe her.

'Look,' he said, 'this really is a celebration. David is opening up a great many leads for projects. We have five pre-tender applications in the pipeline in Germany alone and two serious enquiries from Italy as a result of his contacts. But he's working round the clock. The scourge of the interactive laptop. I've told him to get back to London by Friday, or we'll pull his Gold Card.'

'That won't stop him, if he's in the middle of something,' she said.

'I know. But I thought you'd like to tell him that if he gets to my office by nine o'clock on Monday morning, he'll find himself standing in the shoes of a full partner. That should do the trick.'

He politely buried his head in the menu, while Kate pretended her mascara was stinging her eyes.

'I can recommend the poached salmon,' he said, when the waiter came to take their order.

'That's great,' Joe Carrigan said, when Kate phoned the news to him. 'I think he was more cut up by being overtaken by that guy Carrickworth than he showed. Maybe the two of you will be able to take a couple of days in the country next week. Do you both the world of good.'

'If only!' she said. 'I can't remember when we last had a break.'

To her astonishment, when David returned to London he agreed to take a few days away from work.

'Let's go to the Lake District,' he suggested. 'I haven't been there since I went on a school trip. I've still got my mountain boots somewhere, and you'll need some kit.'

'I wasn't exactly thinking of the great outdoors,' she said.

'Come on, Kate. When did either of us last get any proper exercise? You'll enjoy it.'

II

David booked into a small hotel in Keswick, and they began a set of walks that started on the first afternoon with a deceptively easy stroll along the shores of Grasmere. The next day he took her up the 'easy' climb of Cat Bells, overlooking Derwent Water. She could see that he was as out of condition as herself, but he refused to give up. More than once she tried to turn back during the first few hours' torment, her legs aching from the constant climbing and descending, but David simply watched as she sat and complained, waiting for her to get back on her feet and follow him. But by the end of the week the pain and strain faded, and she began to enjoy the clear air and the magnificent views between the ever-present clouds. In the evenings, they dined on food prepared to a remarkably high standard before collapsing into bed and into a deeply satisfying sleep.

The day before they returned to London, he took her along the notorious Striding Edge that leads to the top of Helvellyn. The path among the rocks is no more than two feet wide in places, with an almost sheer drop of a thousand feet each side. The final climb of a few hundred feet to the summit brings one of the most rewarding mountain views in Britain. As they stood panting from their exertions, David took her hand.

'I love you, Kate,' he said simply.

'I know you do,' she said. 'And I love you.'

III

When they returned home, David went into his study and put a call through to the number listed as C.P. Bansil. When the same woman answered he gave his name and asked for Albert Levy to call him back. He said it was urgent. Within minutes the phone trilled and Anna's voice greeted him.

'Good afternoon, Mr Lewis. I trust you are well.'

'Good afternoon, Anna. May I speak with Mr Levy.'

'He's taking a nap right now. Is there something I can do?'

David thought for a moment. 'I just wanted to let you know that Professor Muntz is giving a lecture in Westminster tomorrow evening at eight o'clock. I intend to go, and I wondered if Mr Levy might be persuaded to come with me.'

'I doubt if that will be possible,' Anna said. She remembered the possible danger that Lewis might be facing. 'Is it important that you should go?'

'Yes,' David said. 'Everything I do leads to the fact that Muntz

159

was in charge of *Turmfalke*. This is a God-sent opportunity to see the man in action. Something else might fall into place, and I wanted to make sure Mr Levy witnessed it.'

'When and where is he speaking, Mr Lewis?' she asked.

David gave her the details, and she covered the mouthpiece to talk with someone. He could hear voices being raised, as if in objection.

'Either Leon or Uri will meet you on the steps of the hall at seven o'clock,' she said.

Later that day, Albert Levy's fax machine began chattering, and the old man watched as the paper curled its way into the document basket. Anna straightened it out and handed it to him.

'It's from our contact in Munich,' she said. 'The one who sent us the fax about Mr Lewis's visit to Deutsche Arzneiwissenschaft Werke.'

TURMFALKE

Following the recent visit of Mr David Lewis to our head office in Munich, instructions were passed to members of the Neuvolkgruppe to deliver a Level 1 warning to him. Level 1 is interpreted by the group as a minor chastisement involving humiliation with minimal violence. This was carried out when Mr Lewis visited our Rosenheim factory. I may be able to clarify why this was done, provided I know what to look for. Kindly furnish guidance.

A Friend of Justice

Levy gazed at the paper for several minutes, then wrote something in his notebook and handed it to Anna.

'I want you to send this to the same circulation group as last time.'

Anna took it to her computer and began typing.

REFERENCE: TURMFALKE AND LEVEL 1

The results of experiments on Jewish and other people carried out towards the end of the war by the Waffen-SS Institute of Health and Hygiene may have been used in the manufacture of ethical pharmaceutical products launched between May and December 1947. Documentary evidence of research for company products will no doubt be archived in library files. Copies would be appreciated.

Before printing this for the fax, Anna paused. 'It's hardly likely they would have kept anything incriminating.'

Levy shook his head. 'It may be what our American friends call a long shot, but old habits die hard. Researchers generally keep sets of raw research data close to the reports they produce. If the basic research for these products was carried out on humans, this information had to be transcribed to more acceptable documents before submission to the drug approvals board. The normal procedure would be to maintain copies of both sets of documents in the same files. If our source finds nothing, then nothing is lost.'

IV

David took an Underground train to Westminster and walked the short distance across Parliament Square to Central Hall. It was drizzling and quite cold for the time of year. His train had been kept waiting outside Westminster station because of signalling problems, and by the time he approached the entrance where Anna had arranged for him to meet Uri or Leon he was almost ten minutes late. Muntz's lecture was entitled 'The Size of an Organization as a Factor in the Decision-Making Process', and posters around the hall informed passers-by that the function was part of the Freyer Institute's programme of European industrial revitalisation, with free admission to bona fide management students. He saw Uri standing underneath a huge solus poster of Muntz to one side of the steps leading into the building, hands shoved into pockets, collar turned up against the rain. Even from a distance David could see the scowl on his face. The traffic was moving steadily, so he had to wait until a furniture van forced its way into the line of cars and buses and caused a gap. As he made his way towards Uri a large black motorcycle with a pillion passenger appeared from behind the van and accelerated down the narrow road leading past the hall. There was a string of popping sounds, and Uri's head exploded into a reddish-grey cloud.

It seemed an eternity before anyone noticed, and then a woman screamed. Not the pure sound produced for a theatre play or the movies, but a raucous, choking noise. Shock and fear mixed with disgust. Uri remained standing, as if his legs were incapable of realizing that no more messages were being sent through the defunct nervous system, then he pitched forward onto the woman in a bloody embrace, and she screamed again.

The furniture van drove slowly away, a face at the passenger window gazing into the crowd of people surging away from the still twitching body. David stood in the middle of the traffic, unable to move, hearing police sirens blasting a route from the Palace of Westminster on the other side of the square. In no more than three minutes the area was swarming with police on foot and motorbikes, forcing people away from the bloody mess that had been Uri Betmehl and preventing anyone from entering or leaving Central Hall.

David edged back across the road to the central area of the square, his mind numb with shock, watching the panic slowly subside as the forces of law and order took control. A paramedic patrol car arrived, followed by an ambulance, cutting its way against the flow of traffic under police direction. A police inspector took charge of the scene, directing his officers to take statements from witnesses. The blood-drenched woman was still making hoarse, grunting sounds, while a young constable tried in vain to get her to answer his questions.

An official from Central Hall appeared and had a few words with the police inspector before raising a loud-hailer to his mouth.

'Please cooperate with the police, ladies and gentlemen. Give your details to the constables if you saw what happened here. If you are waiting to attend the lecture by Professor Muntz, please form an orderly queue to my right.'

David Lewis the engineer was overcome by fear. David Lewis the hunter would have to wait his turn until this could be dealt with. He made his way to a café next to Westminster Underground station and ordered a cup of tea, forcing himself to think logically about what had happened. The question that hammered at him was whether he too had been a target for the assassin. Was his kicking in Rosenheim by the two skinheads connected to this in some way? If his train had been on time, he would have been standing next to Uri when the motorcycle roared past the hall. But the more he thought about it, the less likely it seemed that there could be any connection. He had no idea how Uri had got to Westminster, but it was almost certain that Leon had taken him there in the Jeep. If this were true, they could well have been followed. After all, both of them worked for a secretive Jewish revenge group, and many organizations would be only too keen to take this kind of retribution. On the other hand, if he, David, had been followed, a killer could easily have finished him off by now.

Slowly the fear subsided. He wondered if he should let the police know that he had an appointment with the dead man. But what use would it do? He didn't know any more than they did. Once they identified the victim and checked his security files, they'd put it down as a murder of one terrorist by another.

Meanwhile, he was within a few hundred yards of a target of his own, one that he had been tracking for weeks, one that he needed to see at close quarters. The better he got to know Muntz, the quicker he could discover what the man had done to his father, and the quicker he could do something about it.

The ambulances had gone by the time David returned to the hall. A few late-comers like himself were completing attendance forms for the receptionists in the foyer. As he approached one of the desks a policewoman stepped up to him.

'Excuse me, sir. We're investigating an incident which took place outside the hall earlier this evening. Might I ask you if you saw anything or if you know anything that might help our enquiries?'

'No,' he said. 'No. I've just arrived. What happened?'

'That's all right, sir. Sorry to have bothered you.'

David filled out his admission form, jotting down his name, address and professional affiliations. As he handed it back to the receptionist he had a sudden impulse to snatch it from her and go home to Kate. His brain was still in turmoil. The man he had arranged to meet had been shot, for God's sake. Why? Who by?

'Thank you, Mr Lewis,' the receptionist said. 'We are running late this evening, so Professor Muntz has not yet begun speaking.'

David nodded absently, not really taking it in. Uri and Leon were

163

very security conscious, so their lives must have always been under a threat of some kind. Perhaps Uri had been recognized by an enemy group, probably an Islamic organization. The PLO, or Hizbollah. And if Albert Levy was right, Muntz had no more to do with the *Turmfalke* project than David did, so David couldn't possibly be in any danger. He'd conjured the connection from long-forgotten magazines and books about the Second World War, or conversations he had overheard as a child. The whole thing was a figment of a very overwrought imagination.

He was about to turn around and make his way home when a hand reached out and took his arm in a firm, almost painful grip.

'Good evening, Mr Lewis. I believe this is what you Britishers call a coincidence, is it not?'

He turned and found himself gazing into the piercing eyes of the stocky man who had been so attentive to him at the DAW annual meeting.

'Good evening, Herr Streichner, this is a surprise,' he said, taken aback at the man's appearance.

'Why a surprise?' the German said. 'I am a member of the professor's personal staff, so naturally I accompany him on his lecture tours. But what are you doing here, might I ask?'

'Fräulein Winter suggested I came,' David said, as lightly as he could. 'It is our policy to learn as much as possible about the key people from whom we seek work, and she kindly told me about tonight's lecture. It was an opportunity I did not want to miss.'

'I am sure you will find the professor's views to be of the utmost value,' Streichner said.

The hall was almost full and buzzing with that air of expectancy engendered by people who look forward to hearing something about which they are already firmly convinced. He found an empty seat by an aisle near the back of the auditorium and waited for his second sight of Muntz. At one minute before eight o'clock, the tall, white-haired figure emerged from behind a partition and strode to the lectern, followed by a woman who introduced the speaker, apologized for the delay and took her place at a table behind the lectern. Muntz stood motionless, and the expectant buzz of conversation died away until there was absolute silence, suddenly shattered by Muntz's voice thundering from the public-address system, strafing the crowd like cannon shells, with an authority that forced ears to listen and brains to accept. From the first second the man wove a spell around his audience, speaking English as if it were his mother tongue, with only the slightest of dogmatic constructions to hint at his Germanic origin.

'What I tell you today applies to you, the individual, as powerfully as it does to the largest state on Earth. Its truth is present in our families and social groups, and in our commercial companies and our churches. When it ceases to be present, then the individual ceases to exist. The organization ceases to exist. The nation ceases to exist. I am talking about our wondrous ability to solve the problems of Nature and to make decisions to control the world in which we live. Man is a decision-making creature, set aside from the animals by this great gift. By Man, of course, I mean the genus Man, men and women who base their decisions on the three great artefacts of civilization: economics, politics and morality.'

Muntz paused, and David felt that the man was staring across a hundred rows of seats into his eyes. When he glanced at his neighbours he could see they were staring back at Muntz, mesmerized, bound together by the magic. A rivulet of sweat trickled down his spine as Muntz continued his theme, a whirligig of ideas about the need for pure thought to reach correct decisions, the dangers of dilution as groups enlarge, inter-act, inter-marry, inter-breed. There were no black people in the audience. No Chinese or Indians. No Arabs. And if there were any Jews, David could not identify them.

'. . . and thus we argue that racial purity is essential for the survival of any civilization, be it Bantu or British.' The speaker leaned forward dramatically, his hand pointing over the heads of his rapt audience, upwards, heavenwards.

'And this purity is dependent on this trinity of irreducible social elements. First and foremost of these is Economics. We make our decisions to keep ourselves and our loved ones alive, and that is the prime purpose of Economics. Secondly, we come to Politics. In its elemental sense, this is the aspect of other people's decisions that affects our survival. And thirdly we have Morality, the component of our decisions that affects other people.

'And thus, for each person we can construct a model in which Economics, Politics and Morality encase the ego in concentric spheres. When two people meet in harmony the spheres touch and merge in harmony. But if there are too many people, the spheres

165

become deformed and harmful, and only those with the purest of origins can survive the encounter, because our inner strengths are based on the values of cultures that go back thousands of years . . .'

At nine o'clock the deluge stopped, and as the audience applauded ecstatically Muntz stepped to one side of the lectern to let the chairwoman come forward to the microphone.

'Professor Muntz has provided us with a formidable challenge, sweeping away conventional barriers to our personal improvement,' she said. 'And now he will be pleased to answer a few questions.'

As if on cue, a middle-aged man in the front row stood up, and a young girl handed a radio microphone to him. After thanking Muntz on behalf of everyone in the hall he said, 'I believe that the theories you put forward tonight are to be published as a series of essays.'

'That is correct,' Muntz said. 'The book is entitled *Decisions Are My Heritage*, and it will be published by the Freyer Institute in September.'

As Muntz stepped back again the woman said, 'Advance order forms are available at the entrance.'

In the silence that followed, David felt his heart hammering against his ribs as his own question took form, but before he could stand another man was asking, 'How does the professor view the relative decision-making capabilities of various ethnic groups?'

'An interesting question,' Muntz said. 'To give you a brief answer, it is, of course, nothing to do with conventional perceptions of relative intelligence. Mankind exists in geographical and cultural environments that are diverse and specific to each race. The indigenous population of these environments are best qualified to make appropriate decisions on their home territory, so to speak. Thus, if my car broke down in the Australian outback, I would naturally prefer assistance from an Aborigine than a Chicago street cop.' This drew appreciative chuckles from the audience. 'My thesis on that topic is set out in my book *Towards a Better Understanding of Our Fellow Man*. I believe Mrs Hartley has arranged for copies to be available tonight.'

The chairwoman held one up and waved it vigorously. David took advantage of the brief pause and stood up. 'You say that Man is set aside from the animals by his ability to make decisions . . .'

Muntz was shaking his head and cupping his ears, and the audience turned to stare at David.

'The professor can't hear you, sir,' the chairwoman said. 'Could you use the roving microphone, please.'

The girl made her way to his seat and handed it to him. David swallowed, trying to clear his dry throat before repeating, 'You say we are set aside from the animals because we are the decision-makers . . .' He was holding the microphone too close, and his voice boomed around the auditorium, so he held it a little further away. Muntz nodded his understanding of what David was saying. '. . . but would you not agree that some animals are also superb decision-makers. Kestrels, for instance? *Der Turmfalke.*'

Muntz stared intently at David and at first made no reply. There was an uncomfortable silence, then he seized the podium microphone.

'This is an utterly stupid question.'

People turned again to stare at David, and the chairwoman said hurriedly, 'Perhaps there is someone else who has a question.'

The girl tried to take the roving microphone from David as several other questioners held their hands up for attention, but he held onto it.

'Why is it stupid?' David had not meant to shout, but the words echoed round the auditorium as Muntz whispered angrily into the chairwoman's ear.

'Would you please sit down, sir,' she stuttered, 'otherwise I must ask you to leave the lecture.'

'Why? Why should I? I asked a perfectly sensible question . . .'

There was a sharp tug on his sleeve. Two ushers were standing in the aisle looking uncomfortable but determined. David pushed past them and rushed down the stairs and into the street, choking for a breath of air. Carrigan and Levy would have to believe him now. Muntz was condemned out of his own mouth, using in his lecture the very phrase from the Commandant's Address to Students in the *Turmfalke* project, delivered in 1945.

Man is a decision-making creature, set aside from the animals by this great gift.

*

167

When the ringing tone stopped and the pay tone pinged in his ear, David jammed a coin into the phone box.

'Joe? It's David. Listen. I've just been to a lecture by Muntz, and someone's been killed –'

'Hi, David. Can you slow down a little? You're coming at me like a run-away Titan.'

David gulped for air. 'I've just heard Professor Muntz speaking in Westminster, and there's absolutely no doubt that it's him.'

'You've just heard who?'

'Muntz, for Christ's sake. Muntz. I have to see you. It's absolutely vital.'

'Well I can see you in the morning sometime.'

'I mean now, Joe. It's absolutely staggering. I have to see you right away.'

'Well, if it's that important, you'd better come over.'

Carrigan put the phone down, and Kate said, 'Why didn't you tell him I was here?'

'Jesus, how could I? He was sounding off like a bull moose. Something about this guy called Muntz and someone being killed. I just didn't get the chance. Anyway . . .'

'Killed? Who was killed?'

'He didn't say, but it sounds serious. Maybe you better stay until he arrives.'

'I don't think that would be a good idea, do you?' Kate took her jacket off the back of his settee. 'I shouldn't be here in the first place, should I?'

'The way things are, it doesn't matter. This is the world's only true platonic relationship.'

Kate looked at him steadily. 'Yes, but it's the thought that counts.'

V

Carrigan listened quietly to David's frenzied chatter, trying to piece together the fragmented bursts of information. Uri being killed right in front of him. Albert Levy and his records of Nazi criminals. The ferry at Andernach and the island of Röhmer Insel. The Freyer

Institute, Theodore Pökke, hundreds of identifiable names, proof of the *Turmfalke* conspiracy and finally the lecture, in which Muntz had damned himself by repeating the phrase used by the *Turmfalke* Commandant to his incoming students.

'It all fits together, don't you see? Even Albert Levy will have to admit that Muntz is the man we want, especially now that they've shot Uri . . .'

As Lewis continued his story, Carrigan began to feel out of his depth. During his work in Los Angeles he'd come against some very sick minds, and there was a dreadful logic in David's story that was all too familiar. Equally familiar was Carrigan's realization that everything David said about Muntz was based on a fantastic supposition, in which Muntz was assumed to be the man respon- sible and David merely looked for and found corroborating evi- dence. The name 'Ernst' on a photograph from a dream. Scrawled initials on an old Nazi document. Old railway warrants for unidentified SS officers. Muntz's perfectly legitimate connection with the Freyer Institute which owned the Röhmer Insel estate, which may or may not have been the site of the *Turmfalke* college and concentration camp. The whole thing was founded on a dream, made spuriously convincing by the subsequent discovery that the *Turmfalke* project, with its monstrous college and its inhuman prac- tices, had actually existed. In his anguish, David had certainly created a half-convincing theory, but a first-year law student would have no difficulty in ripping the strands apart. Carrigan knew he had to feel his way with infinite delicacy.

'It sounds incredible, David, but I can see how you've brought everything together. We'll have to go carefully on this one. Let's go through the whole thing again, but slowly this time. You've been talking so fast I'm sure I missed at least half of it.'

As soon as David left his house, Carrigan telephoned Kate. 'He's on his way home,' he said urgently. 'For Christ's sake be careful. He's at some kind of breaking point. I offered him some sedation before he left here, and he became extremely agitated. Wants to keep his mind clear, he said. When he gets home, just try and act normally.'

'But who is this person who's been killed?'

'From what I can gather, the guy was a member of some kind of Jewish reprisal group. Something to do with this Albert Levy fellow.'

'The one whose phone number we've got?'

'Right. I can't see any connection with David. These people are always blowing each other away, aren't they? It can't possibly have anything to do with him.'

'What's wrong with him, Joe? There must be something more you can do than tell me to act normally.'

'The only thing I know for sure is, he's absolutely zapped out. With a bit of luck he'll run out of steam and sleep it off. Best possible thing. Call me if you need to, and in any case I'll phone first thing in the morning.'

'Well, we all know David can sleep, don't we? It's his poor bloody wife who's awake all night. He's probably planning another visit to Germany right this minute. Honestly Joe, I hardly ever see him, and when I do he's always so preoccupied, as if he's living in another world.'

Carrigan tried to soothe her. 'I know it's a worry, but he's taken on quite a workload on top of everything else.'

'I just want to know what's going on. Things have been horrendous since you brought this dream of his out into the open.'

'I'm not so sure I have brought it out into the open.' Carrigan was silent for a moment. 'I wonder if he'd let me give him another session?'

'I don't think so,' Kate said. 'The last time I managed to discuss it he said you'd done your bit. Anyway, what good would it do?'

'I wish I could answer that, but the plain fact is, I don't know. I just think we should give it a whirl. You could tell him he would be helping me to finish a professional paper. That's not so far from the truth, as it happens. I have a number of people interested in my technique. Tell him he'd be tying up a few loose ends for the sake of science.'

'It might work, but I'd much rather you arranged it.'

'When are you and I going to see each other again?' he asked.

'Well,' she said, 'why don't we all meet for dinner?'

'I wasn't thinking of all of us.'

'I know you weren't, Joe. But that's the way it is.'

'OK,' he said. 'Let's settle for a working lunch. I'll bring a friend.'

VI

They met at a Sicilian restaurant in Trinity Road. Carrigan was accompanied by a girl called Laura who was brisk and businesslike. A research student from St Mary's College, she explained. She was, Kate noted, very attractive but without embellishment. Had Carrigan asked Laura along to make her jealous, she wondered? Either way, she found herself losing track of the conversation from time to time, as she watched the American move and talk. They shared some garlic bread, everyone laughing as Carrigan accidentally dropped a piece into David's wine.

'Before we settle down and get ourselves completely covered with olive oil,' David was saying to Laura, 'I'd just like to confirm that you aren't one of Joe's part-time assistants, you know, like a psychiatrist or an art teacher.'

'I only wish he'd let me be, but he's a very private person, aren't you, Joe?'

'If you mean as opposed to being a very public person, I guess I am.'

Laura turned to Kate. 'See what I mean. You can't get through to the bastard, and it's not from want of trying, I can tell you.'

'I'm sure you can,' Kate said. She hadn't meant to say it, but it just came out bitchy. 'Sorry. I didn't mean that the way it sounded. I think we all find Joe rather self-contained, don't we, David?'

'A bit flat, you mean?' When no one reacted, David sighed. 'Self-contained flat, geddit? Play on words. Pun!'

There were a few appreciative groans.

'I do feel a bit flat these days,' Carrigan said. 'There's a couple of things hanging in the air that I need to finish off. As a matter of fact, David, I was hoping you'd be able to help me over one of them.'

'You'll excuse me if I don't rush forward with naive enthusiasm, won't you?' David turned to Laura. 'I don't know if he's mentioned it to you, but I happen to have been one of Joe's patients.'

'Hey, come on.' Carrigan sounded irritated. 'You weren't a patient. I was just trying to help you sort out a couple of problems, that's all.'

'Yes, but now we both know that they aren't my problems, don't

171

we?' David said cryptically. 'Quite the opposite. They belong to everybody.'

'This sounds intriguing,' Laura said. 'You mean, they're my problems, too?'

'Not as such.' Kate hoped she wasn't sounding desperate, but she felt as if they were walking over a minefield, pushing David in front.

The waitress brought some hot towels to wipe their fingers, and for a minute they concentrated on cleaning up, then David asked, 'So what kind of help are you thinking of?'

Carrigan smoothed his moustache. 'I need another session with you. What we've been doing is not exactly a new thing taking each technique on its own, but it's certainly new to couple them together. I've been invited to submit a paper at Cornell in November. It would be very difficult to do that right now because I only have your visual material. I need to get you to talk about things, under hypnosis.'

David looked at him thoughtfully. 'Does that mean you might uncover some more facts?'

'Facts? Well, yes. I might.'

'And you'd let me have a copy of the recording you make?'

'Would that interest you?' Carrigan asked.

'It might do.' David sounded off hand. 'We never found out what sparked off my nocturnal ramblings, did we?'

'Nocturnal rambling? Are you a sleep-walker?' Laura asked.

'It certainly felt like it to me.' Kate forced a smile. 'David was having some very disturbing dreams, and Joe helped to stop them, that's all.'

'I have dreams about Joe,' Laura said. 'I don't know if he can stop them, but he certainly had a hand in starting them.'

As a joke, it wasn't much, but everyone chuckled politely. Beneath her smile, Kate realized that if Carrigan had brought Laura along to make her jealous, he had succeeded. She felt confused and vulnerable, but at least David had agreed to let Carrigan continue his sessions.

VII

When David was lying still and breathing steadily Carrigan plugged a remote pause switch into the tape recorder on his desk and opened a cupboard by the window. There was a second recorder inside. He switched both recorders on and sat next to David, occasionally operating the pause control of the desk recorder as he began asking questions, with David answering and making detailed sketches. The session took three hours, and at the end Carrigan poured himself a stiff whisky and went to sit in the sunshine on his patio, parts of David's recall floating unrealistically in front of his eyes like the original documents in the Bundesarchives that David's eidetic memory had revealed.

Daily reports

TELETYPE MESSAGE

From:	SS Standartenführer in charge of *Turmfalke* Project
Reference:	M ab/Mu/Gr.2944 – Journal No. 873/44.
To:	SS-Waffen Institute of Health and Hygiene/ Distribution List HF

Top Secret

PROGRESS REPORT ON MEDICAL FACILITY

Some of the subjects arrive in poor condition. It is both time-consuming and expensive for my staff to improve them to a state of physical health suitable for subsequent medical analysis. We find that priests and rabbis arrive in better condition, and attention should be paid to increasing the proportion of these subjects sent to us. In the meantime, rather than return unwanted specimens to Transport Section we have instituted a new system. We order twice as many subjects as we require in batches of twenty. When each intake arrives, all members are required to race through an obstacle course that we have installed in the camp. We keep the ten fittest and eliminate the others, so as to leave an optimum number. Apart from maintaining correct operational levels this has the added and beneficial effect of inculcating a degree of competitiveness in subjects, thus improving their attitude to the decisions they will finally face under laboratory conditions.

SS OFFICER IN CHARGE *TURMFALKE* PROJECT

(SIGNED)

STANDARTENFÜHRER

[CERTIFIED COPY]

David's vision of the *Turmfalke* project was disjointed and rambling. It was also horrifying, and it shocked Carrigan more than he would have thought possible, maybe because he understood the warped logic of medical men who could use a ruthless military machine to delve into the physiological condition of the human species. The temptation must have been enormous, once the all-powerful state had consigned non-Aryans to the bottom of the animal pack. From somewhere in his subconscious, David had dredged up such medical terms as hypothalamus and cerebral cortex ... vasopressin, thyroxine and adrenaline. How could he know about all this? Carrigan remembered a passage in one of his university medical books.

'... thyroxine is a long-term measure for dealing with stress, and adrenaline is short term. Adrenaline wins battles, thyroxine wins wars. As wars comprise a sequence of battles, so thyroxine and adrenaline are needed together in stress situations.'

The authors were thoroughly respectable, but the notions they propounded might well have taken form in *Turmfalke*, thirty years before their book was published. Carrigan wondered how much modern medical science owed to the Nazis and their obscene experiments into diseases such as cholera, and combat problems such as high-altitude flying, exposure to extreme cold, bullet wounds and other injuries. He went back into his interview room and unplugged the pause control from the desk recorder before turning to the still sleeping David. The edited tape that he gave David would run for about half the time of the version in the cupboard. He hoped the information it contained was harmless enough to help David find some way to resolve whatever was at the root of his problem without causing any more trouble. The full version was something he had to present to the one man who might be able to lay David's ghosts.

CHAPTER TWELVE

I

When Streichner went behind the podium after Muntz's lecture, he found the professor in a towering rage, striding around the dressing room and flailing his arms dementedly. The woman who had organized the British leg of his tour was cowering against a wall, speechless, not understanding a word of his tirade. When he saw Streichner, Muntz grabbed him by the jacket.

'Tell me how it happened, Josef. You are in charge of security. First someone is shot outside my lecture! Outside – my – lecture!' He said this with a tone of utter incredulity, as if there had been a breakdown in a divine plan. 'As a result, my lecture is delayed almost thirty minutes. And then this . . . this *Arschloch* jumps up out of nowhere and asks me questions about *Turmfalke*. Let's take it one at a time, Josef, can we? Who the devil is he? How did he get in?'

Streichner had never before seen Muntz in such a rage. The professor was normally able to deal with problems calmly and with a degree of good humour, but this *Turmfalke* thing seemed to have unbalanced him. Streichner thanked his protective saints that he could at least answer the professor's questions. He motioned the woman to leave the room. 'His name is David Lewis,' he told Muntz when she had thankfully closed the door behind her. 'He represents a firm of British consulting engineers who are quoting for improvements at Rosenheim. Apparently, a senior member of your administrative department suggested that he came tonight.'

Muntz stared at him, the veins in his head standing out like cords. Then the professor gave a sound that was half a bellow, half a laugh. When he spoke, he made a huge effort to get his voice under control.

'You tell me that an engineer who is concerned with a pharmaceutical production line can wander in here and start asking me questions about *Turmfalke*. Are you entirely mad? What the hell is going on?'

Streichner swallowed uncomfortably. 'We received a Loki report from America about this man Lewis. He visited a member of a US Army veterans' organization and began asking about *Turmfalke* and your links with the project. Then he turned up in Munich looking for a contract. He was given an interview because one of our regular consultants has linked up with his firm. Something to do with European competitive tendering. I instructed Oskar Hind to make enquiries and briefed the lads in Neuvolkgruppe to rough him up a bit.'

Muntz glared at the stocky man. 'Rough him up a bit?'

'To see if he made contact with any organization,' Streichner explained. 'We wanted to get him off balance.'

'And did he?'

'Not as far as we know. He made a phone call to Hind to report on his meeting with Frinkmann, as had been arranged. He made no comment about the incident.'

'Do you not think that was strange?'

'Sir?'

Muntz sighed heavily. 'A man gets "roughed up" as you call it. Shortly afterwards he speaks to Oskar Hind, and he does not mention an upsetting incident. Most people would.'

'I suppose so,' Streichner agreed.

'You suppose so.' The professor's voice dripped with menacing sarcasm. 'Well, you can suppose something else. It's quite obvious that, after all these years, someone working for Deutsche Arzneiwissenschaft Werke has released information about *Turmfalke* to this idiot, and I want to know who it is. Good God, man, don't you realize the implications for all of us?'

'I don't understand how such a thing could possibly happen, sir,' Streichner said defensively. 'Our security is absolute.'

Muntz stared at him. 'If there is one thing the Second World War should have taught the German people, my dear Josef, it is that there is no such thing as absolute security.'

'I will begin an enquiry into our arrangements immediately, Herr Professor,' Streichner said stiffly.

'An enquiry? Good. You have twenty-four hours. I want to know which organization this *Schwein* Lewis is really working for and who has passed this information to him. I want to know if there is any connection between him and the incident outside. This nonsense must stop. I'm cancelling the tour and returning to Brienzersee. Do you understand me, Streichner?'

Streichner stiffened his back and came to attention. '*Jawohl*, Herr Professor.'

When he returned to his office, he learned why a man had been killed outside the hall that night.

* * *

Loki Report

TO: *Herr Josef Streichner*
FROM: *Loki One*
Your Eyes Only
Be informed that one of our operatives intercepted a communication involving Uri Betmehl, member of a Mossad protection group assigned to Albert Levy and a Grade 1 target. I sanctioned removal of the target under the authority of Standing Order 232 of the Neuvolkgruppe Articles. This was effected in London. I note your instruction to be informed of any similar activity over the next three months.

II

The group met informally every few days in various cafés around Munich's Englischer Garten for black coffee, schnapps and reminiscences of the Second World War. Men and women with two things in common. They were Jews, and they had survived the death camps. Most of them were aged over seventy. A few such as Moritz Hubermann were in their fifties: they had been children when the cattle wagons rolled into desolate railway sidings inside the extermination centres. One group member, a self-employed writer, acted as a focal point, keeping the others informed about similar groups around Europe. Most of his news these days was concerned with the death of someone they all knew, but occasionally other information came through the loose network. He had received and discussed Albert Levy's first fax about *Turmfalke*, and this evening he had another to show everyone.

'Albert Levy is investigating something serious. That is quite clear,' he told his friends. 'Something to do with pharmaceuticals, eh, Moritz. Something in your own archives, perhaps.'

The DAW security manager smiled. 'There are many companies making pharmaceuticals, Martin,' he said.

'Feel free to use my facsimile machine whenever you want, my dear friend,' the writer said wryly.

Hubermann was intrigued by Albert Levy's request concerning *Turmfalke* so soon after he had met this engineer David Lewis at DAW's annual meeting. He had tussled with the wisdom of becoming involved, but something deep inside was affecting his judgement. If he was in a position to help Lewis without running any risk, so be it. But he had no intention of sending faxes if he found any reference to *Turmfalke* in DAW's records, as his friend was suggesting. The visitors' log for the following week included a note regarding David Lewis's second appointment with Fräulein Winter. If Hubermann found the references required by Albert Levy, he intended to pass them direct to David Lewis, who was obviously close to the heart of the matter. Maybe he could glean enough information to interest his friends when they next met for coffee and schnapps.

One of the signs of a problem in a well-run organization is that someone does something out of the ordinary. This can range from absenteeism to a request for a change in a duty roster. In the case of the head office security guard Conrad Klaus it was an unscheduled change from night duty to day duty for one shift. In his role as security consultant to the firm, Josef Streichner sent for the man on the pretext of checking his firearms-training. Klaus had been with the company for four years and had an exemplary record.

'It seems all is in order, Herr Klaus,' Streichner said after leafing through the man's personal file. 'However, I notice that you have spent the last three years on night duty. Would you not prefer to change back to the day shift?'

'The routine suits me well, Herr Direktor. I am a keen fisherman, and I spend many hours of daylight with my friends around the lake.'

'But not next Wednesday, I see,' Streichner remarked casually.

'Herr Direktor?'

'You have changed duty next Wednesday,' Streichner explained.

'Ah yes,' the guard said, nodding vigorously. 'I would have preferred not, because there is a coarse fishing contest that I will miss.'

'So why the change?' Streichner asked.

Klaus hesitated, not wishing to get his line manager into trouble, but it was, seemingly, an innocuous question. 'Herr Hubermann requested it, sir.'

'And who is taking your place?'

'No one, sir. That is, Herr Hubermann himself is taking my duty. He sometimes changes duties with us,' the guard explained helpfully. 'He says it helps to keep his hand in.'

'Perhaps it gives you an opportunity to take your wife out for the evening,' Streichner said as he dismissed the man.

Nothing out of the ordinary here, he thought. And he carried on thinking that until he turned to the visitor appointments file for the following week and saw that David Lewis had another meeting scheduled with the commercial relations manager on Thursday. He checked Hubermann's diary and discovered that the security manager had taken Thursday as a day's holiday. When he turned to Hubermann's confidential personnel file, he also saw the coded reference note that Moritz Hubermann was Jewish. He picked up the phone and called the company that had installed DAW's closed-circuit TV security system.

III

Fräulein Winter greeted David enthusiastically. 'I am pleased to inform you that Halkyn and Partners has been appointed to our list of approved consultants,' she said. 'We are preparing the tendering specification for contractors at Rosenheim, and we would like your firm to assist in this task.'

David was delighted. Evidently he had acquitted himself well in

Herr Hind's investigation. He would probably never know if it had been a way of checking his own honesty or Frinkmann's, unless Frinkmann and his staff applied for air tickets from Halkyn and Partners and then sold the tickets back to the airline. If this happened, he would politely inform Frinkmann that DAW's accounts department had requested full details on all expense transactions. That way, everything would be squeaky clean. And he would be working within Muntz's company, getting closer to the arch villain of *Turmfalke*. What could be neater than that?

'That's very good news indeed, Fräulein,' he said sincerely. 'How would you like to progress the contract?'

'I am arranging a series of meetings for you here tomorrow,' she told him. 'Have you booked into your hotel?'

The company had reserved a room for David in the Schloss Hotel at Grunwald on the outskirts of Munich.

'I'll be checking in when I leave here,' he told her.

'Good. I will send to reception a fax of the timetable by the end of the afternoon.'

IV

Streichner and Hind watched David on the bank of CCTV screens in the security control room as he left Fräulein Winter's office and made his way to reception, then took a taxi. As the taxi headed for the road to Grunwald, a grey Mercedes moved out of its place in the company car park. One of the TV screens changed to take in the images sent by a camera mounted on the Mercedes' dashboard as it followed the taxi.

'Where is Hubermann now?' Streichner asked.

Hind relayed his query into a high-frequency transceiver.

'Hubermann is sitting in his car outside Lewis's hotel,' he said. 'I presume they have arranged a meeting.'

'And you still do not know why he took over Klaus's night shift?'

'No, Herr Direktor,' Hind said. 'As you instructed, we filmed him making routine security rounds. He is, of course entitled to take over such a duty, and he has done so before.'

'It doesn't make sense,' Streichner muttered angrily. 'If he has indeed arranged to meet Lewis, he could have done it without going to all that trouble. We are missing something, Oskar. Play the recording again.'

The screens switched to a speeded sequence of time-lapsed video stills that showed Hubermann checking his security key positions in various parts of the headquarters building. In the twelve hours from six o'clock in the evening until six o'clock in the morning he made the scheduled total of eight rounds, checking in at each location almost to the second.

'Again,' Streichner said when the recording finished.

He was watching the third run when he noticed that one of the screens showed an empty desk throughout the sequence.

'Where is this?' he asked, tapping the monitor.

'That is the security man's desk in the corner of this room, sir,' Hind told him. 'The camera is behind your head, up there.'

'And what is the final location of the check routine?'

'It's in the basement, sir,' Hind said.

'*Gott in Himmel*,' Streichner shouted. 'The bastard never came back here. He spent all the time between his rounds in the basement. Have we got any cameras down there?'

'It was considered unnecessary,' Hind told him. 'All the basement contains are storerooms and building services.'

'What kind of storerooms?'

'House services use some for office consumables. The remainder are allocated to the communications division as studios and storage for the company archives.'

'*Ach!* The archives, of course,' Streichner said, with a savage understanding. Long ago he had lost the battle to have such sensitive corporate information stored in security bunkers. Company archives were always a major target for anyone indulging in industrial espionage. This was beginning to make sense, and he fully intended to make even more sense out of it. 'Who is in the Mercedes?'

'Walter and Pietre.'

'Get them some back-up. Tell them to observe what happens when Lewis and Hubermann meet and then bring Hubermann back here afterwards. No! Not here. I will meet them at the hunting lodge.'

'What about Lewis?'

'Leave him for the moment. I want to find out what the hell's going on with Hubermann. He may well be the key to all this.'

V

Moritz Hubermann was aware that the motorcyclist had followed him from his flat in Arabella-Parc to Grunwald. The rider was now lounging in the sun on the grassy mound in front of the Schloss Hotel, swallowing lager from a can as if he hadn't a care in the world. Maybe he hadn't, but a security man is trained to take note of such things. Another rider joined the first, and the two of them began examining each other's machines with that oil-stained enthusiasm common to bikers throughout the world. He turned his eyes back to the Munich road and saw David Lewis's taxi swerve into the hotel drive. A grey Mercedes drove past and parked in the courtyard of the nearby castle. At the sight of it, the colour drained from his face. It belonged to an unofficial fleet of cars paid for by DAW and used by a right-wing political organization. He opened his briefcase and stuffed the papers that were inside it under his shirt.

David was about to step into the shower when he heard the knock. 'One moment,' he called, pulling on a towelling robe. He opened the door, and Hubermann pushed his way in abruptly. 'Hey! What's this . . . ?' He began, but stopped when he recognized his visitor.

'Herr Hubermann! There was no need to bring it yourself. A fax would have reached me in time.'

Hubermann stared at him blankly. 'A fax?'

'I presume you've brought me the schedule from Fräulein Winter.'

'I know nothing about a schedule, Mr Lewis,' Hubermann said nervously. 'They are watching us both, but I don't think they know why I am here.'

'What the hell are you talking about? Who's watching us?'

The question astonished Hubermann. Lewis seemed quite unperturbed by his statement. He must surely realise that his activities had attracted attention by now. But there was no time to go into this.

'It doesn't matter. I have the documents your organization has requested . . .' Hubermann pulled a bundle of photocopies from inside his shirt and pushed them at David as if they were contaminated. 'It's all here. The research that made a fortune for the swine. Use it to condemn them, Mr Lewis.'

David was completely at a loss. The man was clearly very upset about something. Or was it another of Herr Hind's initiative tests for the Rosenheim project? Companies did the damnedest things during selection procedures.

'I'm not sure I understand.'

'For God's sake, take the papers,' Hubermann almost shouted. 'They are signed by Muntz himself. He'll be in Switzerland soon, preparing for a rally of fascist *schweinehunde* from all over Europe. You've got everything you need to know to put the bastard in prison, where he belongs.' He looked about, frantically. 'I need something to take outside with me. They might think I came here to collect, not to deliver. That's why I hid the papers in my shirt. It'll gain you some time.'

David stared at the papers. 'Muntz? These are from Muntz?'

Hubermann grabbed David's briefcase and emptied it on the bed. 'Is there something you can give me to throw them off the scent?'

It dawned on David that Hubermann was not simply agitated but afraid, and the fear was contagious. It focused his mind, sharply, and he selected a file.

'This is a copy of my company's proposals for a factory –'

'Yes, yes, at Rosenheim. It will serve.' Hubermann stuffed the file back into the briefcase. 'You must leave Munich, Mr Lewis. Make sure they do not follow you. Get out of Germany as quickly as you can. Get the papers to Albert Levy. He'll know what to do. Tell him . . . tell him Moritz Hubermann is honoured to help.'

Hubermann backed towards the door, nodding, almost bowing, at David. Then he was gone. A few moments later David heard the noise of squealing tyres and pulled back the lace curtain in time to see a grey saloon broadside into Hubermann as he was opening the door of his car. Hubermann was flung along the road and a skin-headed youth leaped from the saloon and pulled him inside, grabbing David's briefcase from the ground as the car wheelspinned its way into the main road. It all happened in a five-second blur, but David had time to recognize the skinhead as one of the two youths who had attacked him in Rosenheim. As the dust cloud rolled into the trees, he saw a black-clad motorcyclist staring up at his window.

CHAPTER THIRTEEN

I

Two days after David left for Munich, Peter Halkyn phoned Kate and asked if he had arrived back home. She told him that she had not heard from him since he had left for the airport, and Halkyn asked if any messages had been left for him, or if any mail had arrived.

'It's important, Kate,' Halkyn said. 'David sent us a fax saying we had been awarded a consultancy contract by one of Germany's largest pharmaceutical companies. The next day, I sent an acknowledgement to the firm's commercial manager, and she phoned me to say there had been a misunderstanding. I asked if I could speak to David, but she told me he had checked out of his hotel. Since then, we haven't heard a thing. I don't want to worry you, but it's not like David. He always keeps in touch. We're worried he might have fallen sick somewhere. Did he seem all right to you?'

'Absolutely,' she said brightly. 'He felt good about this prospect in Munich. I can't imagine what's happened, unless he decided to follow up some contacts he's developing in Italy. You know what the Italian phone system is like. He's probably faxing you a report every hour that's ending up in the Vatican or somewhere.'

Halkyn's chuckle lacked conviction. 'You're probably right. You will let me know when he gets in touch, won't you? I need to sort this pharmaceutical job as quickly as possible.'

'Of course,' she said.

Carrigan's BMW bike was not chained to the railings as usual, so Kate parked her car outside his house to wait for him. The row with David before he left for Germany had been the worst ever. It began when she quietly pushed the accumulation of several weeks' mail across the breakfast table, bills in one heap, letters from work in another and various other envelopes and packages in the third. Of course it had been a bad time to do it, but she hadn't expected the subsequent outburst.

'God almighty, not now. I've got other things to think about.'

'Well you'd better think about these. The BT one's written in the chairman's blood. Last time we forgot to pay the phone was off for a week, and we can't afford – '

'Don't bloody tell me what we can and can't afford. If you're so worried about money, why didn't you take up that advertising offer with your randy photographer friend and pay the damn things yourself?'

'That's beside the point, David. Some of these are from the consultancy. I can't answer those for you.'

'Why not?' he sneered. 'It's the day of the emancipated woman. Equal partnership . . . But if you can't cope, I'll deal with it all when I get back. Now, perhaps you'd be so kind as to hand me my briefcase.'

'Get the fucking thing yourself.'

She didn't mean to say it, but the words just spilled out of all the frustration and anguish she'd suffered over the weeks. David's face turned white with rage as he bunched his fists. For a horrified moment she thought he intended to hit her, but then his face crumpled, and he looked at her like a stricken child.

'I have to do this, Kate. Please don't be angry with me.'

Carrigan roared up an hour after she arrived, the bike sparkling in the sunshine. He spotted the car and came across the road, his welcoming smile fading when he saw her face. Without a word he took her into the house, straight to the living room and a stiff brandy, standing silent while she gulped it and held out the glass for another.

'I swear, if you were free I'd marry you this minute,' he said.

'I love David, Joe.'

He knew she would say it, but it struck deep. For a while he stood still. 'OK, so where is he now?'

'I don't know. Peter Halkyn says he left Munich without sending a message to the company. They don't know where he is, either.'

Carrigan wondered how much he could tell Kate about *Turm-falke* and David's obsessive research into the obscure and long-forgotten Schutzstaffel project. Sooner or later she would have to know, if she were to help her husband out of this thing.

'Look, Kate,' he said, 'there's not much either of us can do about things until David gets in touch. If anything happens to him, we'll find out soon enough.'

'I don't want to wait until something happens to him, Joe. We should do something now.'

'There's not a lot we can do.'

'I think we should phone the police.'

Her distress was heart-rending to Carrigan, in more ways than one. It would have been bad enough if he were a disinterested third party, but he was in love with her and had to see all her emotional energy directed to another man. The fact that the man was her husband, and his client, made it worse.

'They wouldn't take much notice. He's not really missing, and there are lots of reasons why he might not have phoned. Look, we need a break ourselves. A night on the town, maybe.' She began shaking her head, but he rushed on. 'Why not? We could take in some jazz, or a show. Have a meal. Then a fraternal peck on the cheek at your doorstep. You can trust me, lady. Honest.'

'I know I can trust you, Joe. It's me I can't trust.' But she smiled, and he knew she had accepted the invitation.

They tried very hard to have a good time. Their first stop was the Bull's Head at Barnes to hear some modern jazz. After that they went on a club crawl, finishing up at Angelo's in Westbourne Grove, where they consumed pitta bread, humus, taramasalata, calamari and afelia. Halfway through the second bottle of retsina, Carrigan asked the owner to arrange for a taxi.

'He can take you home, and then he can take me home. I can't take either of us home in this condition,' he explained to Kate over the bouzouki music. 'I can pick up your car tomorrow.'

'Let's have a dance,' she suggested.

It was all Greek, with little body contact, hands holding for a moment, neighbours joining in a line, laughter, plates smashing, lots of fun. Carrigan was absorbed in Kate, watching her move, responding to her rhythm. By the time the music stopped their cab had arrived, and they set off, sitting quietly apart in the back seat.

When the taxi stopped outside Kate's house he fumbled to open the door, but she didn't move.

'Wandsworth for the lady, like you said,' the driver reminded them impatiently.

'Actually,' Kate said carefully, 'the lady wants to go to Wimbledon.'

'All I know is, I've been booked to make a drop at Wandsworth, then Wimbledon.' The driver looked pointedly over his shoulder at Carrigan.

'Let's go to Wimbledon,' Carrigan told him.

'That's twenty quid, whichever way you look at it.'

When they arrived at Carrigan's house, Kate took his arm. 'I haven't seen your bedroom yet,' she told him.

'Tidy, it isn't,' he said. 'Bed's not made. Clothes all over the place. Typical bachelor stuff.'

'No Alice or Laura to help you keep house?'

'I have to be honest,' he said solemnly. 'No. I am all on my own.'

He led her up the stairs and into the bedroom, where she clung to him fiercely. 'I want you, Joe. Christ, I want you.'

'I have to go to the bathroom,' he said practically. Five pints of beer, the best part of two bottles of retsina and three cups of strong Greek coffee were demanding attention.

When he came back she was lying in bed, rich hair tousled over the pillow, fast asleep, the strain on her face barely visible in the dim light. He covered her and went downstairs to his study, where he played David's tape-recording, trying to fight his way through the horror of the dreams to the reason behind them.

In the morning he was making coffee when Kate staggered downstairs. She felt very confused, as memories of the evening filtered through a slight hangover.

'I'm sorry, Joe,' she said.

'What for?'

'Last night. I wanted you so much, and I let you down.'

'Rubbish.' He smiled at her. 'We both had a great time, didn't we?'

'Yes, we did.' David seemed very far away. Was it all over between them? She went forward and put her arms round Carrigan as he pressed the plunger into the cafetière. 'Could we try again?

188

Please Joe, but not here and not now. I need time to think about this, I really do.'

How could he say no?

'Sure,' he said. He needed some time himself.

Kate insisted on picking up her car from Westbourne Grove, leaving Carrigan feeling very hung over and very mixed up. At eleven o'clock he dialled the number for Albert Levy that Kate had given him. When Anna answered, he asked to speak to Levy. 'I am David Lewis's psychiatrist,' he said, 'and the matter is very urgent.'

Two hours later he found himself sitting blindfolded next to Leon in the Jeep, on his way to meet the old Nazi hunter. Despite his attempts to open a conversation, the young Jew did not speak a word to him during the journey. Anna greeted him tersely in the high-walled courtyard and took him up the stairs to meet Levy. The frail figure was hunched over documents and photographs, sifting methodically through the pile and making notes in pencil on a scrap of paper. He greeted Carrigan courteously enough.

'I must apologize if we all seem subdued, Dr Carrigan, but we have lost one of our friends,' Levy told him.

'I'm sorry,' Carrigan said. He knew that Levy was referring to Uri. 'It must be a bad time, but I badly need your help.'

'Something to drink, Dr Carrigan?' Anna asked.

'Anna insists I drink only lemon tea or decaffeinated blends of coffee,' Levy complained. 'I hope you don't mind. Personally, I find them most objectionable, but rather less so than Anna's displeasure.' When the coffee was poured, he said, 'I am told you are Mr Lewis's psychiatrist.'

'Yes, I'm treating David Lewis for a severe emotional disturbance.' Carrigan sipped the strong decaff coffee and controlled a grimace. 'To be honest I have no idea what's behind it, but its effect is considerable and possibly dangerous. He has talked with you, and I need to know anything he said that could give me a clue to his problem.'

'Dangerous, Dr Carrigan?'

'Yes. He could become violent.'

'Violent? Yes, I suppose that it possible.' Levy regarded Carrigan thoughtfully. 'You are the young man who has unravelled Mr

Lewis's dreams, so I suppose you know that he is troubled by the belief that he has uncovered the perpetrator behind a certain wartime project run by the SS. He has, in fact, indulged in a remarkable piece of detective work in tying together many previously unrelated strands.'

Carrigan nodded. 'Sure. But this detective work, as you call it, is doing him no good at all. His home life is under considerable threat, his job may be on the line, and he is beginning to lose control of himself. If you know anything that will help me get to the bottom of the problem, please tell me.'

The old Jew sighed. 'What can I tell you? Where do I begin? Mr Lewis is only partly aware of the significance of his discoveries. From the outset, he had the conviction that a certain SS officer who is now a respected businessman was in charge of the project in question. I have no need to tell an academic like yourself what such a preconception can do to an otherwise objective investigation. On the other hand, a number of his intuitive decisions have been entirely fruitful.' Levy motioned at the desk. 'A few weeks ago, for example, he said he had discovered the location of what we know as the *Turmfalke* project. Most of the photographs he took could be of any wartime military installation, except for these.' Levy fished among the prints that David had taken on Röhmer Insel. 'You see, this one shows a circular object partly covered by foliage, and this one shows a close view of the object, and the maker's name.'

'*I.A. Topf und Söhne, Erfurt,*' Carrigan read aloud. 'It looks like the door from some kind of boiler.'

'Not a boiler, Dr Carrigan. An oven. The firm Topf and Sons supplied ovens for the crematoria at Auschwitz and other death camps. The presence of such an artefact in Mr Lewis's photographs provides strong evidence that he did indeed visit the site of a concentration camp. Neither myself nor my staff can recognize the location, although we have extensive experience in such matters.'

'Is David working for you, or what?'

'Certainly not. The work he is doing is purely on his own account. We have merely furnished him with a little information.'

'But you must have seen how distressed he is,' Carrigan protested. 'It's got so bad his marriage is on the rocks. Couldn't you have persuaded him to leave things alone? Before this thing started, there was no way you could get the guy to take one step over the shoreline. Now he spends every possible working day in Germany. Next thing we know, he'll crack up completely. The man is suffering, believe me. His work, his marriage . . .'

When Levy didn't answer, Anna said, 'For some of us, the notion of suffering cannot be applied to work or marriage. Mr Lewis has to make his own decisions. We are merely a clearing house for information.'

'Sweet Jesus. I would have thought that you of all people would understand how important it is to, to . . .' Carrigan was at a loss for words, but Levy was not.

'To save an individual, Dr Carrigan? When one's loved ones have been torn from one's arms and thrown alive into ovens made by such firms as Topf, Didier or Kori in their tens and in their thousands and in their tens of thousands, I am afraid that the problems of an individual become irrelevant.' Levy began coughing.

'Please,' Anna said, 'you must not distress yourself, Albert. Dr Carrigan, I must ask you to leave.'

'Look,' Carrigan said desperately. 'Maybe I can't understand how you feel. Maybe no one can. But I have a responsibility for David Lewis, and six million dead Jews or twenty million dead Russians can't change that. I need your help, Mr Levy. David Lewis needs your help.'

Levy waved a hand weakly. 'You ask for something I cannot give. I am only a cipher.'

'I can't accept that,' Carrigan cracked back. 'I need to know why David had his dreams and how I can heal him. That's the bottom line, no matter what happened fifty or sixty years ago.'

Anna tugged his arm angrily. 'You will leave now, or I shall call Leon. You can see he's not well.'

Carrigan stood up. 'Yes, and I'm sorry. But neither is my patient.'

'One moment, Dr Carrigan.' Levy was pale with tiredness. 'In addition to the photographs you have seen, Mr Lewis sent me a brochure describing the activities of the Freyer Institute of Advanced Management Studies.' He fumbled among his papers and found the booklet that the dark-haired girl had handed to David at the castle overlooking the Röhmer Insel. 'We know that the Institute has several shareholders and that it owns the German pharmaceutical company of which Professor Muntz is the life chairman. As you can see, David has ringed the name of the organization that holds the largest single number of shares in the Institute. The Freyer Foundation of Neuroinformatics, based in Liechtenstein. Our directory of European businesses tells us that this Foundation is wholly owned by a shell company in Switzerland called the Falken Treuhandgesellschaft of which Professor Ernst Muntz and Professor Werner Blintz are the only trustees. Its funds are not open to any kind of scrutiny.'

'David went to see this guy Muntz give a lecture in Westminster,' Carrigan said. 'It turned out to be quite an unpleasant evening, as I'm sure you know only too well. I don't mind telling you it knocked David sideways.'

'Mr Lewis has convinced himself that Professor Muntz was the man behind the SS project he has been investigating,' Levy said. 'Although he had an arrangement to meet our friend Uri, we cannot believe that Uri's death has anything to do with this. Our people are always in considerable danger. However, it is clear that your patient seeks reinforcement of his theory. It may well be that he will continue to travel extensively until his problem is solved, perhaps to Switzerland or to Liechtenstein.'

'Shit!' Carrigan exploded. 'He's in no condition to go to the bathroom. I need more to go on than that.'

'I have already communicated with various sympathetic groups,' Levy told him. 'All I can do until Mr Lewis returns is alert them to give him any assistance he might need in the meantime.'

II

Loki Ten felt a warm glow of satisfaction. He was right, and he could prove it to his inept colleagues. He had accessed the complex computer programs at the heart of the Loki system to see why all the reports on the appearance of a subject called Lewis with grey hair and a connection with a project called *Turmfalke* had not been matched by the powerful data clustering algorithms. He discovered that whoever had compiled the instructions had included a cut-off point for words that were in frequent use. 'Lewis' was a very common name in both the USA and Britain, and 'grey' was also frequently used. The system had found several possible matches for its report and had simply given up after ten, as it had been instructed to do by its programmer. Loki Ten decided that this was a serious error. The subject, David Lewis, could and should have been noticed and investigated at a far earlier stage in the proceedings. In the close-knit community to which he belonged, his discovery would rank as a fine piece of analytical work.

He wrote a short but highly critical note for circulation and comment among the Loki community and sat back to wait for the reaction. He did not have to wait long. The memorandum from Loki One flashed on his screen within minutes. It had been copied to all Loki personnel.

Loki Instruction

TO: *Loki Ten*
COPIES: *All Loki Operatives and Advisers*
SUBJECT: *Unauthorized Access to Neural Processor*
Your report timed at 0330 hours indicates that you have gained access to the central processing unit of the Loki organization for an unauthorized examination of source code. Such access is strictly prohibited under Regulation 551 Section 45 Paragraph 3 of your contract. Your action could have caused the neural processors to crash, with serious consequences to the clients whom we serve and who pay us for our services. As for your conclusion that there is an error in the search strategy, please be informed that some of the finest minds in our organization constructed the system, and we utterly reject your criticism. It is recognized that you have acted in good faith, nevertheless it is our judgement that you are fined DM10,000 which will be taken from your current account by direct debit. If you breach regulations on any subsequent occasion your contract with Loki will be terminated with extreme prejudice.

Loki Ten stared at the message for more than an hour, sweating copiously until his Save-the-Wildlife T-shirt and Levi jeans were soaking wet. Then he slowly put his thumb in his mouth and began rocking back and forth, moaning in anguish. How dare they! How dare they expose him to ridicule on the network like this! Who did they think they were? Finest minds, indeed! If he hadn't told them what he had done, they would never have known of the poor programming. Stupid silicon bumpkins, that's what they were. Pissy-arsed, right-wing, stupid, silicon bumpkin bullies. They were trying to find out about David Lewis, were they? Whoever he was. Well, he'd show them. That's what he'd do. He'd show them.

CHAPTER FOURTEEN

I

David experienced a panic attack. His heart began to beat faster, and he could not get enough air into his lungs. He lay down on the hotel bed and closed his eyes, forcing himself to think logically about his situation. He realized he had been guilty of a classic error of the academic. He had been so taken up with researching the *Turmfalke* project that he had lost sight of the practical realities. And those realities included the fact that he was dealing with people who were wealthy and powerful. They were also ruthless. Hubermann had known this, and Hubermann had just been abducted, there in the street, right in front of him. And some fellow on a motorbike was staring up at his window. The hunter had become the hunted.

Carefully he rolled to the floor and crawled into the bathroom. He prised two screws from the mirror above the hand basin and crawled back to the window. By propping the mirror in the back of a chair, he could see into the street without being seen.

The biker was still there, leaning against the wall, a mobile phone clamped to his ear. He nodded every now and again, and twice stared up at David's hotel window.

David could not understand how Hubermann knew he was interested in Muntz nor why, in any case, Hubermann should try to help him. Hubermann's reference to an organization was also a mystery. All he could think of was that there had been a grotesque coincidence. Someone else was also checking the *Turmfalke* affair, and Hubermann had made a mistake. Perhaps it was Levy. But Levy had made his doubts clear. Either way, David realized that Hubermann's frantic warning could not go unheeded. He picked up the telephone, then put it down. The less the hotel staff knew, the better. He took the pharmaceutical reports and sealed them in an envelope with a scribbled note to Joe Carrigan, asking him to keep them safe. Taking his cue from Hubermann, he pushed the envelope inside his shirt, together with the notes about Muntz. He put everything he would need to travel lightly – his cash, credit cards, air tickets, passport and a few personal items – into his pockets and went downstairs to the reception desk.

'I'm expecting a fax message from Fräulein Winter of Deutsche Arzneiwissenschaft Werke,' he told the clerk. 'Kindly acknowledge receipt in my name. I'll pick it up before dinner.'

The clerk made a note on her pad, and David wandered into the lounge and through the empty dining room. No one was in the kitchen, and he made his way to the staff entrance at the rear of the hotel. He was about to step outside when he caught sight of another black-clad motorcyclist chatting casually with one of the chambermaids. He went back inside, feeling trapped. In the middle of his fear, he remembered something a business management lecturer had once said: 'When you can't think what to do, do the unexpected.'

He strode boldly out of the front entrance and walked to Hubermann's car, which was still parked near the motorbike, nodded to the biker and glanced at his watch. After a few minutes he said, 'Excuse me, sir. I'm expecting to meet my friend here. I believe this is his car. Have you seen anyone waiting?'

The biker looked uncertain. 'No one has been here.'

David waited a few more minutes, then said, 'Look, my name's Lewis. If he turns up before you leave, would you be kind enough to tell him I'll meet him in the castle.'

Before the biker could reply, David nodded and sauntered past the hotel towards the main entrance of Grunwald Castle. Once out of sight, he doubled back along the line of trees behind the hotel, controlling a powerful instinct to break into a run. The motorcyclist who had been parked near the staff entrance revved his engine and roared off to join his companion, and as soon as the way was clear David made his way quickly to the taxi rank on the far side of the hotel. Two cabs were waiting for passengers, their drivers enjoying a sociable cigarette in the sunshine.

'Could either of you take me to Landshut?' he asked. It was a town fifty miles north of Munich. One of the drivers blew a stream of smoke thoughtfully into the air.

'My mate's first in line, but he's off duty in a few minutes. I'd take you, but he'd lose a fare . . .'

In no mood to haggle, David passed a fifty Deutschmark note to the other driver and got quickly into the cab.

'I'd be obliged if you took the Munich road,' he said as the cab pulled out of the rank.

'That's the long way round,' the driver observed. David said nothing, and he picked up his radio mike and logged the journey to his controller. When he clicked off, David leaned across the seat and handed him a thousand Deutschmarks.

'I'm going to Zurich,' he said. 'That's so you don't call in with our change of plan.'

'That'll cover it,' the driver said laconically, stuffing the notes into his shirt pocket.

II

Streichner was sitting at a bare wooden table in the basement of his company's private hunting lodge when Walter and Pietre arrived with Hubermann. The security man's mouth was bleeding, and he winced as they threw him roughly into a chair. Walter passed David's briefcase to Streichner, who examined the contents. Then he took a knife and slit open the stitching. By the time he finished, the briefcase and its handle were in pieces. He stared at the rubble, and at Hubermann, then nodded to the skinheads who began ripping Hubermann's clothes off and giving them to Streichner. When Hubermann tried to stop them, they slapped his face viciously. In a few minutes he was naked and his clothes had suffered the same fate as the briefcase. Streichner lit a cigar thoughtfully.

'Well, Moritz. What's all this about, eh?'

Perhaps you have to be a death-camp survivor to know for sure when your time has run out. Or maybe it was the tone of finality in Streichner's voice. Either way, Hubermann felt the cold hand of death grab his insides. He knew if he tried to spit in the stocky man's face, his spit would let him down and the two bully boys would start beating him. Whatever they wanted to know, the only thing he could achieve now was to confuse them.

'There's no need for all this, Herr Streichner,' he muttered. 'I've been helping Mr Lewis get his contract with us, that's all.'

There is always a lie at first, Streichner thought, and this was not a bad one. Quite convincing. The method was to let the victim develop the lie until it collapsed in on itself. At least, that was the method if you had time on your side, which Streichner didn't. His sense of urgency was increased when his mobile phone chirruped. He listened impassively as one of the motorcyclists informed him that David Lewis had taken a taxi to Landshut, but had somehow managed to give them the slip. He disconnected and turned back to Hubermann.

'What I want you to tell me, Moritz, is what you took from the archives last night, that's all. We know you gave whatever it was to Lewis, so please do not insult my intelligence, Jew.'

'I don't know what you're talking about,' Hubermann said.

The skinheads raped him before Streichner set to work with the cigar. It was a sensible method to use, because when they disposed of the body the police would conclude there had been a sado-maschist gay murder. There was no need for a gag, because no one would hear, and they all got a kick out of the noises Hubermann was making. After an hour, however, Streichner was getting desperate. He only had one cigar left. On the other hand, Hubermann had only one eye. His lips, nipples and testicles were charred beyond recognition, and apart from his screams he had not uttered a word. Streichner lit up the remaining cheroot and blew the tip into a white hot glow. As he moved it towards Hubermann's remaining eye he was relieved to see the security man begin to shake his head vigorously and strain to say something. All Streichner could hear was a hoarse whisper, so he leaned down and moved his face nearer Hubermann. With a supreme effort, Hubermann arched his body and gobbed a lump of mucus into Streichner's mouth. The stocky man threw himself backwards, retching, and Walter and Pietre began kicking Hubermann's head. By the time Streichner recovered his composure, Hubermann was dead.

'*Ihr Arschlöcher*,' he shouted at the skinheads. '*Ihr Riesenarschlöcher!*'

III

It was almost midnight when the taxi reached Zurich. David paid the driver the last of his German money at a hotel in a small square by the strip clubs in Niederdorfstrasse, the kind of place where they open a charge-card account before they give you the key. The driver gave him a leering wink as he drove away – another tourist getting away from his wife for a few hours. Good luck to the fellow!

David unpacked, then realized he needed Swiss francs. The hotel night porter directed him to a cash machine at the end of the street, and he used his Amex card to withdraw enough money to cover his needs for a few days. Back in his room, he began reading Hubermann's files and learned that Muntz owned an estate called Falkenheim not far from Interlaken. He went down to the reception counter and asked the porter if he had a large-scale map of the area.

'Yes, sir. I know the canton well. Falkenheim is near Brienz, across the lake from the town. It is a private estate, I believe.'

'Will I need a car?'

'The trains are excellent. You go to Berne, then Interlaken and change there for Brienz. There is a ferry from the town to a landing stage at the foot of the cliffs below the estate, every hour during the daytime. That side of Brienzersee is very beautiful, and there are many walks to the high meadows in the mountain passes.'

At breakfast next morning, the receptionist came to David's table and handed him an envelope.

'We were asked to give you this first thing in the morning, without fail, Mr Lewis.'

He took the envelope automatically, his blood running cold.

'Who asked you?'

'I have no idea, sir. The night porter received a phone call at five o'clock.'

Sweet Jesus. Only the taxi driver knew where he was, but someone had evidently got to the man. They were probably watching the hotel right this minute. As the receptionist left the dining room, his hands began to shake, and then he realized that he wasn't thinking straight. If they had found him, whoever they were, they would surely not take the trouble to present him with a warning like this. He ripped the envelope open. The message said simply: 'Telephone the following number immediately and without fail.' He recognized a UK cellular phone prefix. Leaving his breakfast unfinished he hurried back to his room and dialled the number. After the usual inter-boundary switching noises, the other phone rang and an answering machine clicked on. The voice sounded distorted.

'Mr Lewis. Your life is in grave danger, and I am the only one who can help you. My name is Loki Ten. You will be concerned to know how I located you. This was achieved through a high-speed search of bank and charge-card databases and a scan of current usage. At 1158 hours last night you used your Amex card to book into your hotel in Zurich, and at 0036 hours this morning you withdrew one thousand dollars' worth of Swiss francs at a Bank of Switzerland cash machine. If I can accomplish such an investigation, others will eventually do so. At the end of this message you must tell me the fax number of your hotel and stand by the fax machine. You must do this without fail, or I will not be able to help you. Please leave your message immediately.'

The hotel fax number was printed on his room card, and when he heard the message beep he read it into the telephone, then raced downstairs to find the machine. It was behind the reception desk, already chattering out the first of two sheets of paper. The receptionist handed it to him. He read with horror that he had become the subject of an investigation by an organization called Loki that advised the security division of DAW.

'Owing to a fault in the surveillance routines,' the fax continued, 'much of the information gathered on your recent activities was not properly cross-referenced. It was therefore not reported. This mistake has been rectified, and your threat level to one of our clients (Turmfalke) has been upgraded. You are now designated as a target for a right-wing German death squad.

'I have decided to intervene for reasons that are of no consequence to you. If you wish to survive, you must stop using your current identity, bank, charge cards and passport. You must avoid contact with your wife, your business and your friends . . .'

The second page of the fax contained instructions to visit the Amex offices in Bahnhofstrasse where a charge card would be ready for him in the name David Louis. Loki Ten had chosen this name because it would be easy for David to remember and the spelling would by-pass any computer check for Lewis. The Personal Identification Number for this card was 9456. He must make a cash withdrawal of US$170,000. He should then go to a photobooth at the railway station to get two passport photos and take these to a certain Monsieur Crequelle at an address in Beethovenstrasse. For $10,000 in cash, Monsieur Crequelle would furnish him with a new UK passport.

When this was done, he should go to an address in Sprecherstrasse where a Herr Bluthner would provide him with a mobile data communication system for a cash payment of $150,000. He must use this equipment to establish contact with Loki Ten, who would guide him through the next few days until he had achieved whatever it was that he has set out to do. And he must hurry. And by the way, the extra $10,000 was for initial out-of-pocket expenses. When he runs out he should draw more, from any bank.

David carefully read the fax again. Did it make any sense? The whole thing was becoming tainted by unreality, but he had to take this second warning very seriously. If Loki Ten, whover he was, had meant him any harm, the harm would surely have been done by now. As he stood there, the fax machine clicked on-line and made a series of bleeping noises. The receptionist went over to it and pressed a few buttons, but nothing happened.

'What's the problem?' David asked.

'I don't know, sir,' she said. 'It seems as if the memory has been over-written. We've lost all our call records. Funny. That's never happened before . . .'

David left her pressing buttons and went back to his room. There seemed no harm in following Loki Ten's first instruction. After all, who would send someone to an Amex office if they were planning mischief? The worst thing that could happen was that Loki Ten was lying about the charge card, and there was only one way to find out. But first he had to post the documents that Hubermann had given him to Joe Carrigan with instructions as to how he could get them to Albert Levy. He was certain that Levy could and would use the evidence to bring Muntz and his fellow criminals to trial. That was Levy's purpose in life, after all. And David saw with great clarity that it was his purpose, too.

IV

The two black-clad motorcyclists had not been as sophisticated as Loki Ten in finding David. They simply asked the Grunwald taxi company which driver had just taken a British friend of theirs from the hotel by the castle. The controller told them that the driver concerned had called in after dropping his passenger in Zurich, around midnight, and that he would not get back to Grunwald until at least four o'clock in the morning. No, she didn't know where in Zurich, and even if she did she was not allowed to give such information over the telephone.

They set off towards Switzerland, keeping a few kilometres apart. There was very little traffic, and when the leader identified the cab as it passed him on the outskirts of Memmingen he phoned back to his partner. A few minutes later, the taxi driver's lights picked out a large object on the carriageway. He slammed his brakes and skidded to a halt only a few feet from what he saw was a motorcycle. The rider was lying to one side, moaning, and he took a quick look at the man before reaching into his cab for the radio. As he thumbed the transmit button another motorcyclist came roaring out of the darkness and braked sharply.

'There's been an accident. I think this guy's badly hurt,' the taxi driver called to the newcomer. 'See if you can help him while I call in.'

'No need to bother,' a voice said in his ear.

'Oh, so you're all right, are you?' the driver said with relief.

The first biker grabbed the mike out of his hand and ripped it from the radio.

'OK,' he said. 'Where did you drop the Britisher?'

'What Britisher?'

The second motorcyclist hit him in the stomach with a steel bar.

'We've got into a lot of trouble because of you, you bastard,' he said. 'So don't screw about. Where did you drop him?'

'Jesus,' the driver said painfully, as he struggled to catch his breath. 'Somewhere in Zurich He . . . just asked me to drop him off, and I did.'

The second blow knocked him to his knees.

'Not good enough, friend. Exactly where. And I mean exactly.'

The driver realized that whoever these two bastards were they meant business. What could he do? Maybe the guy was running off with someone's wife. Serve him right if these animals caught up with him.

'Niederdorfstrasse,' he wheezed. 'Hotel opposite the Black Cat Club.'

'Name?' the second biker asked.

'How the hell should I know . . .'

The steel bar hit him again.

'It's got a sign with a beer bottle on it,' he sobbed. 'That's all I know, as God's my witness.'

The second biker grabbed his face and dug his fingers into the man's cheeks.

'Money,' he said.

The driver nodded desperately towards the taxi. 'The box under the glove compartment. It's all there. You have it. Go on.'

They collected the money and told him to lie face down on the road, hands behind his back. As he mumbled fearfully into the concrete, they broke his neck with a final blow of the bar.

V

David signed his charge account to check out of the hotel and bought postage stamps from the hotel receptionist. He was pushing the packet of documents that Hubermann had given him into a federal postbox outside the hotel when he heard the bikes. They came out of nowhere and roared round the small square, frightening the pedestrians against the buildings and spinning round David in narrowing spirals. He scrambled against a lamppost and crouched in terror as one of the riders lifted his arm. The steel bar missed David's head by inches and clattered against the lamppost, the recoil throwing the biker off his course and wobbling into the other bike. David clutched his case and sprinted down the alley leading towards Limmatquai and the waterway beyond. He dodged through the ranks of parked cars and leapt onto a tram, perspiration pouring down his face. Several people stared at him disapprovingly.

'No ticket,' an old woman said sternly in English. 'Inspector fine many francs.'

The bikers had seen him get on board and were following closely. David closed his eyes and gulped air, desperately wondering what to do.

The old woman prodded him. 'Take,' she said, holding out a strip of prepaid tickets. 'Buy tickets always before getting on tram.'

'Thank you,' David panted. He had to fight an insane urge to giggle. Two lunatics were trying to smash his head in, and this old biddy was worried about tram tickets. She spoke bloody good English, too. That was Switzerland for you!

As the tram rattled its way towards the main railway station, two police bikes swooped into view, sirens howling. His persecutors opened their throttles and surged past, police in hot pursuit, vanishing up the hill towards the Polytechnic as the tram rumbled to a halt outside the station.

David smiled wanly at the old woman and tried to give her the tickets back, but she shook her head and showed him how to nick them to cancel the right amount for the journey.

'Buy tickets always,' she called as he stepped down into the street and made his way hurriedly towards the station and the photobooths.

The American Express office was already busy when he arrived and went to the enquiry desk. He gave his name as David Louis, realizing that this was a sensible alias for Loki Ten to have provided. Less to remember, apart from the different spelling. An assistant manager invited him into a private office and opened a file.

'If you will be so kind as to sign here . . . and here . . . and here, sir. Thank you. And if you can enter your PIN on the keypad here.'

David tapped in the numerals that Loki Ten had sent on the fax. The assistant manager looked at his screen, nodded and passed David an envelope.

'Everything is in order, sir, and may I wish you the compliments of American Express. If you should need anything while you are in Zurich, please do not hesitate to contact this office.'

'I need to make a cash withdrawal,' David said.

'Of course, sir. How much will you require?'

David felt as if a great finger was pointing at him out of the sky. This was it! He'd been set up. There was no way this Loki Ten nutter or anyone else was going to let him withdraw such an awesome sum of money, just like that. No way.

'One hundred and seventy thousand US dollars,' he said tightly. And waited for the Swiss fraud squad to jump out at him.

The clerk tapped his keyboard. 'Certainly, sir. If you'll just authorize it for me here, and here . . .'

Monsieur Crequelle was one of those elderly craftsmen who gives the impression that they have seen it all, done it all, and for whom casual conversation is an unnecessary waste of time. He took David's photographs and the $10,000, vanished into a back room and returned in ten minutes with a UK passport made out in the name of David Louis and bearing the stamp of the central passport office in Petty France. David looked at it hard, but could see nothing out of the ordinary. Monsieur Crequelle sniffed and opened the door for him to leave.

In Sprecherstrasse, Herr Bluthner proved to be a loquacious enthusiast of the art and science of digital globe-hopping technology, talking at speed in a broad German-American accent and with a computer salesman's terminology. He placed a large briefcase in front of David and opened it with a flourish.

'May I say, Mr Louis, that when I read your colleague's fax this morning I was delighted by his choice of equipment. It's the best we have in stock. In fact, it would not be an exaggeration to say it's the best in the world. Some of the modules cannot be used legally in Europe, of course, but possession is not against the law. I am sure you will use them with discretion.'

'I certainly will,' David said. 'Perhaps you'd better run me through the system.'

'Certainly, certainly. All you have to do is turn on the power,' Bluthner said. 'You can use any standard mains supply, and it has integral re-chargeable batteries that will last between six and ten hours, depending on use. The whole thing is menu driven, with icons to show the way, and your colleague has downloaded all the programs and datafiles you will need for full operation. The lid itself is an omni-directional satellite aerial. It scans the skies for the strongest signal and homes in on it. There is a telephone jackplug for line connection, of course, but you'll probably never need it.

Just open the case wherever you are, and the system tunes itself in, whichever direction it's facing. State-of-the-art technology. A wonderful piece of kit, wouldn't you say?'

'Wonderful,' David agreed. 'But what does it do, exactly?'

Bluthner looked at him blankly. 'Do? It does everything.' He began pointing out the features. 'You have here a neural array of Pentium chips accelerated to two thousand mega-Hertz and cooled by a high-conductivity heat sink. It contains twenty gigabytes of solid-state memory, thirty-two megabytes of random-access memory, a back-lit non-interlinked plasma colour display, a top-of-the-range sound and animation card, a digital camera for video-conferencing, and in this compartment is the smallest virtual-reality headset on the market, plus it comes fully installed with full business and communications software. In addition to that, your colleague has downloaded several dozen programs in source code whose functions are a complete mystery to me. I was instructed not to operate the equipment until you were ready for a test run.'

He looked at David like a puppy waiting for a bone.

'Go right ahead,' David told him.

Bluthner pressed the on-off button. For a moment nothing happened. There were none of the usual noises made by a hard disk powering up for action. Then the screen came to life to show a well-endowed young man having intercourse with a plastic doll.

'Wonderful definition,' Herr Bluthner said ambiguously.

As they stared in astonishment, the distorted voice that David had heard on his hotel telephone gave an echoing chuckle.

'Hello, David. Why don't you pay Herr Bluthner his money and take me away from all this?'

With his high-tech acquisition slung over one shoulder, and keeping a careful watch in case the motorcyclists made another appearance, David went into a shopping plaza to buy a bag and some casual clothes to replace the luggage he'd left in Grunwald. At the railway station he bought a single ticket to Brienz, next stage on his hunt for Muntz. The journey with numerous interchanges took him past tidy farms, lakes, waterfalls and dramatic mountains, snow still capping the peaks and reflecting the late spring sunshine. Resisting the temptation to open Loki Ten's briefcase in the presence of the

206

other passengers, David stared blankly through the train windows, oblivious of the view, conscious only that he was moving nearer to the beast who was responsible for the horrors of *Turmfalke*.

Three hours after leaving Zurich he arrived at Brienz and booked a room at the Hotel de la Gare. The hotel, the station and the ferry were within two minutes walk of each other, and after unpacking he wandered around the small town to get his bearings. A large tourist map showed the route taken by the ferries, with one landing stage on the lakeside directly opposite Brienz. He discovered a set of viewing binoculars in the park by the quay and spent several half-franc coins gazing across the water. The landing stage appeared as a small discontinuity in the shoreline, hedged by fir trees and cliffs. The turreted roof of a large building was visible about three hundred feet above the jetty, and a dark gash in the trees between the two buildings showed the line of a track which the map marked as a funicular railway. From the top of the cliffs, a series of waterfalls cascaded in and out of the trees and rocks. But although he scanned the neighbourhood for more than fifteen minutes, he saw no sign of life.

For the next two hours he sipped coffee in the hotel dining room at a table facing a wall covered by faded black-and-white photographs of old men with wrinkled faces. When he asked the manager who they were, the man shrugged. Just some neighbours from long ago. But David found himself wondering if they might not be ex-Nazis, like Muntz. This was, after all, a German-Swiss canton, and many fugitives from World War II had settled in neutral Switzerland, undetected and sometimes protected by the community. The faces peered back at him, hiding their secrets.

VI

Late in the night, the fly buzzed round his head and swung a steel bar at him. He flinched and yelled and began running down a long tunnel to get away from the noise, but it grew louder and louder until he opened his eyes and realized the buzzing was coming from Loki Ten's case. Stumbling out of bed, he opened the lid to see the handsome young man sitting on a terrace above a sunny coastline that looked decidedly Mediterranean. The man's face grew larger as the remote camera zoomed in, and the now familiar echoey voice asked him to turn the light on so they could see each other.

'I went to a lot of trouble to get this system to you, David,' the young man said. 'Why haven't you used it? Don't you want me to help you?'

'Not until I know who you are and why you're doing this,' David said. 'For all I know, you're trying to lead me into even more grief.'

'Who I am doesn't matter. It's what I do that matters, and I have not done anything except offer my help. You need my help, David.'

'I have to know what it is you want,' David said. 'There's no way I can trust you unless I can understand that.'

After a pause the young man asked, 'What is the worst thing that has happened to you professionally?'

It was an easy question to answer. 'I was overlooked for a partnership recently. Someone else got the promotion.'

'And how did that make you feel?'

David stared at the screen and smiled. 'I felt like killing the bastard.'

'Why didn't you?'

'Trouble is, I like him, and he was a good choice.'

'No. You hated him, didn't you? You were the better man, isn't that right? You could have killed him, but you didn't. I'll repeat the question. Why not?'

'Because,' David was almost shouting, 'because I'm not a bloody killer, for Christ's sake. I'm an engineer.'

'Exactly,' Loki Ten agreed. 'And I'm not a killer, either, but we both work for killers, don't we?'

'What the hell d'you mean?'

'Herr Professor Muntz is what I mean. I work for him, and you work for him — at least your company has been trying to get a contract to work for him, which is the same thing. So we have two things in common. We both work for a killer, and we share the sense of desolation and anger that comes when our professional colleagues treat us badly.'

'Who overlooked your promotion?' David asked sarcastically.

'It was worse than that. They overlooked my intellect,' Loki Ten said. The hollow distortion of his voice did not hide the transparent honesty of the statement, nor the sense of outrage. David was impressed. That had been exactly how he had felt about Stephen Carrickworth's promotion.

'You still haven't told me what you get out of this.'

The chuckle echoed into the room. 'You haven't figured it out yet? I'm mad, and I want to get even. And I need your help, as you need mine.'

It sounded reasonable. Perhaps too reasonable.

'I have to think about this,' David said.

'You haven't got time to think. I can delay one or two things, but Muntz has many people out there looking for you right now. Sooner or later they're going to catch you, wherever you are. Incidentally, where are you?'

'Nice try, Loki Ten,' David said, reaching for the power button.

'No, no, just kidding. Don't switch off,' the voice entreated. 'I knew where you were this morning, and you didn't come to any harm, did you?'

Loki Ten evidently knew nothing about the motorcyclists in Zurich. He certainly would not have arranged for them to attack David at the same time as he was supposed to be collecting a new passport and all the other items. One merit point to Loki Ten.

'I want to do something for you,' Loki Ten told him.

'What do you mean?'

'Something special. We're both having a bad time right now. I could upload some of my movies for you. They're great with the headset.'

David recalled the plastic doll.

'No thanks. Not my style.'

'Well, is there anyone you'd like to talk to? Your wife, maybe? The call will be perfectly protected from any monitoring.'

Despite the fact that it was the middle of the night, that wasn't a bad idea. Kate must be worried sick about him. He nodded, and seconds later his hotel phone rang. He picked up the receiver, and Kate said in a sleepy voice, 'Hello, is that you, Joe?'

'Kate? It's me.'

'David?'

'Yes, it's me. How did you get my number?'

'I didn't get your number. The phone just rang. David, where are you? Are you all right?'

How do you tell your wife you're on someone's hit list? 'I'm fine,' he lied. 'How about you?'

'Lousy. I can't yell at you any more, David. I just don't understand why you're not here.' She began to cry.

'Hey, stop that,' he said. 'You'll have me going in a minute.'

He heard her blow her nose. 'Are you coming back to me, David?'

'You bet,' he said, 'but I can't just yet. Can you trust me?'

The question pierced its way to the heart of things. She honestly didn't know, and it was her turn to lie.

'Of course I can, David.'

After he disconnected, he wondered why Kate had thought he might be Joe Carrigan.

CHAPTER FIFTEEN

I

There were five people at the conference table at DAW's head office in Munich. Ernst Muntz was at the head of the table. A heavy-set woman with dull brown eyes and the wrinkles of old age sat on his left. She was Irma Schumaker, one-time chief wardress of the women's section of Treblinka concentration camp. The thin man on his right was Viktor Fischer, who had been Hermann Goering's personal treasurer. Between them, Muntz, Schumaker and Fischer controlled several German-based companies that had emerged successfully from the ashes of post-war Germany, funded by stolen treasure and, in the case of the DAW group, given a flying start through the application of information collected by medical experiments on prisoners. Josef Streichner sat opposite Muntz. The young man next to him dressed in a cotton shirt and wearing beads round his neck was Harry Downer, chief executive officer of the Loki organization. Loki One.

Streichner had presented his report on the activities of David Lewis. He was hoping that the same deficiency in the security system that had led to his problem was keeping all knowledge of Hubermann's death from his colleagues. Not to mention the taxi driver whose unnecessary killing had led to the arrest of two members of the Neuvolkgruppe Action Brigade in Zurich. And of David Lewis's most recent disappearance in that city.

While Streichner sat sweating, Harry Downer explained why an unknown person had managed to penetrate so deeply into one of the many secrets they all sought, collectively, to hide. *Turmfalke*.

Muntz was trembling with suppressed anger, and Viktor Fischer was shaking his head perplexedly. The woman spoke first.

'You appear to be telling us, Herr Downer, that the security system we have spent millions of Deutschmarks putting in place can be breached by a single man in the space of a few weeks. Apart from his name and the fact that he works for an engineering firm, he is a ghost. He appears. We receive a low-level report from your friends in Loki. He disappears, only to reappear. Loki generates another report that your system fails to connect with the first, or the third, or indeed the fourth. Would this be a fair summary?'

Downer looked steadily at his employers. 'Up to a point.'

'And what point would that be, precisely?' Muntz asked him.

'The problem's in the specification that you gave us to set up the Loki system in the first place.'

'I don't think we follow you,' Fischer said in his dry voice. 'You were asked to construct a system that would alert us to any activity that would be or might be prejudicial to our security.'

'There you have it in a nutshell,' Downer said patronizingly. These old has-beens could never get their heads round the reality of his business. 'Would be or might be! We're dealing with a range of probabilities here, people, and when it comes to neural-processing time, probabilities cost money, real money. If you recall, you set some pretty tight budgets for my group. I warned you about it at the time, if you remember.'

Muntz looked at him balefully. 'Perhaps you could be just a little bit more explicit.'

'No problem,' Downer said blandly. 'It's like the old rounding-up, rounding-down routine. Take Blade Shearman. If they entered every till receipt from all their stores round the world into their company's central computer to the nearest cent, they'd need ten times the processing power they do now. Instead, they round every-thing up or down to the nearest ten cents. Saves a lot of bucks. So when we run a cross-reference on data fields in our reports, we cut off after ten matching records, otherwise we'd be flooded with use-less data and the machine would never finish a report. Have you any idea how many times the name Lewis figures in our databanks? Jesus, I never knew there were so many guys with that name.'

'You appear to be saying that we ourselves are responsible for this problem, Mr Downer,' Fischer said.

'Exactly. My team is made up of the best intellects in the world. We simply do not – repeat, not – make mistakes. If you want all this sorted, we'll need a budget of ten million, with an up-front payment of thirty per cent. That's dollars, by the way.'

'It sounds to me that you are trying to use the situation to your own advantage,' Frau Schumaker said tonelessly.

'Sure I am. It's business. You need to swing the probability set your way, and we need paying to do it. There's a helluva lot of work involved, believe me.'

They looked at him in silence, then Muntz opened a drawer, took out a Luger pistol and pointed it at Downer.

'Jesus, professor, there's no need to wave that thing around,' the American said. 'We can sort this out. Maybe we can cut it to five million. All we have to do is . . .'

The nine-millimetre bullet entered his mouth, ripped through his tongue, exited his neck and embedded itself in the wood panelling behind him. The noise of the shot left them all with a ringing in the ears. Outside the room someone ran to the door and knocked hard.

'Get out of here,' Streichner shouted as it began to open. 'There is nothing wrong. A demonstration. No need for alarm.'

The door closed silently. Streichner picked up a phone and keyed a security extension. 'Come to the main conference room immediately. Bring the removal equipment. Yes, and the cleaning kit.'

They sat impassively as three of Streichner's men wheeled a large carton into the room, zipped Downer into a black plastic body bag, lowered him into the carton, examined them all for possible bloodstains and shampooed the carpet. One of them found the bullet hole and eased the spent bullet from the wall with a knife.

'The panelling will be repaired overnight, Herr Streichner,' he said before he left the room.

'Was that not a little precipitous, Ernst?' Schumaker said to the professor.

'The man was a danger to us all, with his appalling attitude,' Muntz snapped. 'His elimination will focus the minds of his colleagues more sharply on our problem. And the first thing they must do is track down this David Lewis so that we can eliminate him. I am no longer concerned to know who he is, or with whom he is working, or who is backing him to investigate me, or why. He has inflicted his presence on *Falkenschloss* and at Röhmer Insel. He has infiltrated my company, and on at least two occasions he has been close enough to put a bullet in my head. Enough is enough. I am scheduled to attend the farming festival at Brienzersee on the first of May. Josef, I will travel there immediately, and we will conduct our business from Switzerland until this matter is settled. I would be most grateful if you, Frau Schumaker, would join Herr Fischer in choosing a replacement for Loki One. Pick someone who has the intelligence to understand that we are not playing games.'

II

When David woke up he spent several minutes staring at the metalled briefcase resting innocently on the table by his window. Memories of the conversation with the androgynous young man flooded back, but he could not shake off a conviction that it had all been another dream. Part of it was a phone conversation with Kate. Well, he thought, at least he seemed to be over all those nightmares, with their mystery and their terror. Here he was, tucked away in an inauspicious Swiss hotel on a clear, sunny morning, neglecting his work, running away from assailants, plotting and planning with Jewish Nazi hunters . . . It had to be a dream, despite the presence of the briefcase. He opened it and powered up. The screen came to life and displayed a menu, with choices for Work-desk, Personal Organizer, Games & Leisure, Internet Communications and Loki Ten. The computer said in a passably humanized voice, 'Good morning, David. Which choice do you wish to make?'

'Loki Ten. Message.'

'You have the choice of keyboard or voice-to-text.'

'Voice-to-text. I am about to shower and have breakfast. I will contact you at eight o'clock sharp, Swiss national time.'

'Your message is logged and transmitted at six forty-five A.M., Swiss national time,' the computer said.

When he opened the briefcase again, Loki Ten was waiting for him with an apology.

'I am sorry that I disturbed you last night. I was worried about you. I sometimes forget that other people need their sleep, and being in constant contact with colleagues in many time zones doesn't help, either.'

214

'Don't worry about it,' David said, and wondered what to say next. He used computer bulletin boards and information networks for his work, usually operating them with a computer keyboard. A voice-activated system was merely an extension of this, however sophisticated it might be, and this was sophisticated. But where would it get him? The only thing Loki Ten could deliver directly to him was information, and, as he had no idea what to do next in the hunt for Muntz, what use would Loki Ten's information be? Certainly, any warnings of danger would be appreciated, but would he get them?

'Your graphics and animation are superb, by the way,' he told the screen.

After a short silence, the young man said, 'Graphics? Animation?'

'I've never seen anything so realistic.'

'What gave me away?' The synthesized voice was emotionless, but David thought he detected an element of petulance.

'We've spoken twice now, with a four-hour interval. During the first connection, you were sitting outside what appeared to be a villa overlooking the Mediterranean. But it couldn't be the Mediterranean, because the sun was shining, while it was nighttime here in Switzerland. On the other hand, it can't be anywhere else either, because there's nowhere on earth where the sun casts shadows in the same place over a four-hour interval. You appear to be sunning yourself in the Villa Virtuali.'

The handsome face stared at him, and then the lips parted in a chuckle. 'Astute observation, logical deduction, correct conclusion, Dr Lewis. I will ensure that my sun moves the same way as yours from now on.'

David noticed the use of his doctorate. He took it as a compliment.

'Call me David,' he said.

'Thank you. That would be nice. I need to know something, David.'

'Fire away.'

'What is your objective?'

Good question, David thought. And he had no answer. Or, rather, he had too many answers, none of which made much sense on its own, all of which might be tied together by something hidden in his childhood. A few things were clear, though. He wanted to finish Muntz, and anyone connected with the man. He wanted to destroy him because of the evil he represented. He wanted to pull down the man and his organization. He wanted . . . His hands were shaking.

'I'm sorry, David. My question has upset you.'

David looked at the perfect, expressionless face and said, 'There's something wrong with me.' It was the first time he had admitted to himself that he really did have a problem, the first time that David the hunter had spoken with David the engineer. Joe Carrigan had skirted round that particular issue, but it was true. He had a problem.

'I don't understand.'

Neither did David, but he had every intention of trying. If he didn't, what was the point of anything?

'It's a long story, but it boils down to the fact that I have something locked in my head that concerns Ernst Muntz and a project called *Turmfalke*. Everyone thinks it's my overwrought imagination, and so do I, sometimes, but it's quite clear from what's been happening that Muntz has something to hide. And I think I know what it is.'

'So you're gunning for Herr Professor Ernst Muntz,' Loki Ten said.

'Yes . . . yes, that's exactly what I'm doing.'

'In my opinion,' said the computerized voice, 'there's nothing wrong with you. There's something wrong with him.'

Was it that simple? David wondered.

During the next few minutes, Loki Ten told David a great deal about the professor, his business and the organizations that protected him and others like him. As the information unfolded, so did the implications. David knew he was utterly out of his depth, in a position he associated with TV characters. Life-threatening danger. But it was all too real. And it was very, very frightening.

'There's nothing to worry about at the moment,' Loki Ten assured him. 'They have instituted cross-border checks for you, and they're trying to identify air flights, cash withdrawals and stuff like that, so I've laid a trail to Munich. They'll worry more if they think you've gone back to DAW heartland. I'm not sure how long this will be effective, because there's always a way of verifying this kind of information. But on balance, I'd say you had forty-eight hours or so before they realize you aren't where they think you are.'

'But they have no idea that I'm right where Muntz is planning to spend the next two weeks, have they?'

'Not yet. But staying close to Falkenheim and waiting for him is a mistake. Apart from anything else, there's absolutely nothing you can achieve on your own. I can get all the evidence you need to bring the whole lot tumbling down in every country they operate. Pack your bag, and get out of there.'

'I can't do that. I have to know why I am involved in this, and I intend to find out, otherwise it's all pointless. Fräulein Winter told me he isn't due here until the May festival, and that's in two days' time. I can go and have a look round before he arrives.'

'It's far too risky, David,' the voice told him, but David already knew that.

'I've got to try,' he said. 'I might find something at Falkenheim that'll help to put the bastard behind bars.'

'Behind bars? There are far better ways of dealing with a situation like this. For one thing, we could pass everything over to those Nazi hunters you know. They'd love to get their hands on a bunch of World War II sadists, not just Muntz.'

David began to say that he was only interested in Muntz, but he realized that this wasn't the case. Why choose one rotten apple from a barrelful of rottenness? But whatever else was true, he had to find out what was in Falkenheim, and he had no idea how to set about it. Maybe he should do what they least expected, as he had done with the motorcyclist.

'Well, I'm definitely going over there, and that's all there is to it,' he told Loki Ten firmly. 'I'll be all right.'

The simulated sigh was quite realistic. 'In that case there's a few things you have to do. You'll need a wrench, a No. 8 Posidrive screwdriver and a pair of wire cutters. Chewing gum would be useful.'

'What for?'

'The security system. You'll need to cut into some wiring and insulate the circuits.'

'I'm a plastics engineer, not an electronics expert.'

'No problem. My organization installed Muntz's security systems. I can tell you exactly what to do. It will give you an edge.

If you are not back here by six o'clock I will inform the police that they can collect your corpse from Falkenheim.'

'That's not very funny,' David said.

After haggling for secondhand tools with a reluctant garage mechanic and buying a pack of chewing gum from the post office, David went to the jetty and waited for the afternoon ferry. No matter how hard he tried to remain calm, the prospect of getting close to Muntz's home in Switzerland threw him into a breathless panic. But there could be no possible harm in taking a look at the place, and it might give him an idea of what his next step should be.

The SS Interlaken arrived in Brienz punctually at 1437 hours. The only passengers were several elderly ramblers who smiled a greeting before returning to their route maps. He took a seat in the main cabin from where he could see the far side of the lake as the ferry approached the shore. The first of his obstacles was clearly visible, a tall metal post with a motorized CCTV camera mounted on top. According to his new-found computer friend, the system was based on telemetry, images from all the cameras being radioed back to a base station at the house and broadcast from there to the Loki organization for twenty-four-hour monitoring. If any of the cameras began tracking David, Loki Ten would be able to see through his computer link-up.

The camera pointed down as the deckhand looped a mooring rope round a bollard on the landing stage and held the ferry steady while David and two other passengers stepped ashore. He tagged along with the ramblers as they made their way along the coastal path leading away from the Falkenheim estate, letting them take an increasing lead until they were out of sight. When the ferry vanished round the western headland he re-traced his footsteps until he could see the camera from a vantage position between the trees, still pointing at the moorings. As he watched it began to sweep across the lake until it was pointing in the opposite direction. He looked at his watch and waited. In five minutes it swung back, and in ten minutes it swung away again. Loki Ten's detailed information on Muntz's security system was correct about the timing, and this gave him the confidence to move quickly to the building to the left of the landing stage that housed the estate's hydroelectric generator.

Its discharge water swirled into the lake from a large black pipe. The water supply came through another pipe running into the back of the generator house from the woods. After listening for sounds of other people in the area, David took hold of the padlock on the door of the generating station and began levering it with his wrench. It resisted all his efforts, and he began looking at his watch feverishly as the time for another camera movement approached. When the lens started its travel, he pressed himself into a corner of the fencing, trembling as the adrenaline began to pump around his system. By the time the camera moved back, he was wringing with sweat, and every muscle seemed to be trembling. He was also talking to himself. 'Get a grip of yourself, you wimp. The bloody thing won't bite you!'

He applied himself to the padlock with a renewed ferocity, and it suddenly ripped away from the door, which swung open. He slipped inside and shut it behind him. The noise was almost unbearable, a combination of whine and roar from the shining, well-kept machinery that shut out all other sounds. The yellow-and-black fuse and junction box that Loki Ten had described was on the wall in front of him. The Posidrive screwdriver fitted perfectly, and in ten seconds he was staring at a rack of coloured power lines connected to the security supply cable. Any attempt to turn off the system or remove the fuses would sound alarms and activate a stand-by generator. He had to disable the motors of the external surveillance cameras and the window alarms by cutting three wires in strict sequence, and he had to do this when the cameras, which had been synchronized to avoid visual confusion in the control room, were all pointing to the west. He had to leave the internal cameras active, as they were in fixed positions anyway, covering all the rooms and corridors.

'No one notices when something doesn't happen,' Loki Ten had explained. 'Security guards hardly ever look at the screens anyway. We've done checks, so we know. They're a waste of time for preventative surveillance. Their main value is for analysing situations after something has gone wrong. When you've disabled the junction box in the generator building, I can hack into the system and see what's going on inside the house. Might be useful to keep an eye on you.'

As he stared at the circuitry, David forgot the colours he had memorized. He also had no idea which way the camera outside the building was pointing.

Taking deep breaths to control his nerves, he went back outside and peeped cautiously towards the camera, which seemed to look straight back at him. BOW. Blue, Orange, White. Blue, Orange, White . . . Bee, Oh, Double-you . . .

The black lens was like the eye of a malevolent snake.

It turned away and pointed along the shoreline leading towards Brienz, and David rushed back to the junction box. Separate Blue. Control trembling fingers. Snip. Press live wire into blob of chewing gum. Separate Orange. Control trembling fingers. Snip. Press live wire into blob of chewing gum. Separate White. Control trembling fingers. Snip. Press live wire into blob of chewing gum.

'Easy peasy,' he muttered.

The path leading into the woods was barred by a heavy steel gate, with a chain link fence running behind the buildings and enclosing the entrance to the old rack-railway he'd seen on the map. It passed between the trees at an impossibly steep angle, its two red wooden carriages parked at either end and linked by a cable. An electric fence had been installed to keep deer and other animals from blundering into the lower section of the disused railway. At close quarters, he could see that most of the insulated grips were fractured, and the wire was broken at one post and dangling uselessly into the soft earth. The fence was not a problem. Taking a final look round, he hoisted himself over it and stepped carefully up the planks of the walkway that ran alongside the rail cables.

By the time he reached the passing place in the middle of the system he was breathless and suffering from a sense of vertigo. Further along the track, he had to cross a bridge over one of the waterfalls rushing down the mountain. The handrail was covered with thick cobwebs, and the supporting timbers bent threateningly under his weight. He stood still for several minutes, his legs trembling and refusing to move until he managed to blank his mind in the way that Joe Carrigan had taught him over the weeks of therapy. Finally, he clambered the final feet to the upper rail carriage, where he slumped on a passenger seat in exhaustion. He stayed there for almost thirty minutes, listening to the forest noises and the constant rush of the water cascading down the mountain. At one point he shrank into the corner of the carriage when two men carrying gardening implements passed close by, talking about a local football team.

'. . . Kuyper, the silly sod . . . couldn't score if the kick-off was inside the goal. We'd all be better off if Heglin dropped him in a lump of cowshit . . .'

It was so normal that for the second time since Carrigan had helped him to unravel the sickness of *Turmfalke* David felt like turning back from his self-appointed quest. Perhaps Levy was right, after all. Perhaps some long-forgotten childhood impressions had implanted the whole thing in his head. He had certainly traced the SS college at Röhmer Insel, but he had to admit that this was largely through a series of coincidences. Yes, *Turmfalke* was real enough, and so were the names of the students he had uncovered, but Muntz was a different matter. A forename, Ernst, dimly recalled in a dream. A phrase in a lecture, given in English, that translated to a similar phrase used by an unknown college commandant to his incoming classes. Muntz's testimony at Nuremberg established the man's connection with education, but, although Muntz was obviously a thoroughly unpleasant man, there had been nothing to link him with any war crime. David saw with great clarity that he had reached a preposterous and wholly illogical conclusion. If he could only convince Muntz of this, the man would call off his hounds, and David's life could return to normal. As he sat and agonized over his dilemma, the matter was taken out of his hands by a smooth-haired dachshund that appeared from behind a row of bushes. It stopped and glared at him, one front leg held up in mid-step, then snarled, its lips flat against its teeth.

'*Anselm! Wo bist du?*' It was a woman's voice, high pitched, quavering. She came round the corner towards the disused rail carriage, wearing a floral housecoat with an apron over it. 'Ah, there you are, you bad dog. Come here at once, or I shall tell your master.'

Anselm took no notice, but her presence increased his boldness, and the snarling rose a few decibels. David pressed himself into the far corner of the carriage.

'What on earth is the matter with you, Anselm? Come along. It's time for your breakfast.'

Anselm darted a few steps forward, stopped and retreated, the snarl changing to a whine.

Realizing that his attention was firmly fixed on the rail carriage, the woman peered inside, shielding her eyes from the sunlight. When she saw David, she gasped and began calling.

'Manfred, Herman, come quickly.'

'It's all right,' David said quickly. 'There's no need to be alarmed.'

A man's voice called, 'Is that you, Frau Erika? What's wrong?'

'Come quickly. There's someone in here.'

David stepped out of the carriage as the two gardeners hurried towards it.

'Who are you? What are you doing?' one of them asked roughly.

'I was taking a short-cut from the ferry landing, and I lost my way, as you can see,' David said. 'Then I felt unwell. I'm not used to such exercise.'

'This is private property. No one is allowed in these grounds unless they have an appointment.'

'I apologize,' David said quickly, 'but the circumstances are unusual. I am an admirer of Professor Muntz, and when I learned last night that this was his home I'm afraid I couldn't wait to come here and see if he would be kind enough to let me pay my respects. I thought the ferry would be the best way, but as you can see I had to negotiate your funicular from the landing stage. I didn't know how else to get here. I certainly don't want to disturb him. If he is out, I will leave a message.'

The woman stared at him curiously, and David realized that he was covered with leaves, cobwebs and rust from the handrail. The gardeners muttered to each other for a moment, and the second one said, 'It is forbidden to be here. You must come with us.'

They moved towards him, two large determined men. The house-keeper hesitated, then said, 'At the least, sir, you had better come in and clean yourself. Perhaps Herr Hulbrecht would have a moment for you. He is one of Professor Muntz's personal staff.'

'Thank you,' David said, following her towards the house, the two men walking closely behind, followed by the dachshund. 'I didn't realize I'd got myself into such a mess.'

They accompanied him to a washroom and waited outside while he removed most of the muck from his walking shoes and shook the woodland debris from his clothes. He could hear them talking about him through the panelled walls.

'He is just someone who has lost his way,' the woman was saying.

'We have orders to keep people out,' one of the gardeners said. 'We could all get into trouble over this, unless we see him off the grounds right now.'

'He is an admirer of the professor,' the woman said. 'How can anyone get into trouble over that?'

'He looks harmless enough,' the second gardener said. 'I think you're right, Frau Erika, but I think we should ask Herr Hulbrecht what to do.'

When David came out of the washroom, they looked at him uncertainly.

'Thank you very much for your courtesy,' he said. 'If you would be so kind as to direct me to the road, I'll be on my way.'

'We would like you to see Herr Hulbrecht, sir,' Frau Erika said. 'Perhaps you would be kind enough to wait in the library while I find him. And perhaps also you would like some refreshment.'

David realized with concern that they would not allow him to leave until he been vetted by this chap Hulbrecht. But at least they were being hospitable, and he also realized that he was very hungry and thirsty after his exertions. Apart from being understandably defensive, these three seemed perfectly normal, and he could not believe he could come to any harm. He might as well make the most of it.

'That would be most welcome, but I don't want to put you to any trouble.'

'A pot of coffee would be no trouble, sir.' She smiled and ushered Manfred and Herman back into the courtyard before making her way towards the back of the house and the kitchens. 'Come along, Anselm,' she called to the dachshund, but Anselm stayed at the open door of the library, his nose twitching. If his master's friends were not frightened of the stranger, why should he be?

David bent down and held out his hand. 'Good boy,' he said. 'Good boy.'

Anselm's tail joined the nose in a twitch, and he cautiously approached the hand, which he sniffed and gave a tentative lick before moving closer and giving David's shoes and trousers a thorough examination. When all seemed well, he wagged his tail a little harder and followed David as he moved around the shelves examining the books, trying to calm his nerves. Some of the volumes were centuries old, bound in pigskin and hand-illuminated. There were sections on philosophy and natural science, with what seemed to his untutored eye to be first editions of Goethe, Wittgenstein and other writers, and more modern sections on business management. Nothing to suggest that the owner of the library was anything other than a wealthy, cultured and intelligent person with extremely good taste.

Anselm suddenly began whining gently and scraping at a door that was almost hidden in the centre of the shelving.

'You want to go in there, do you, boy?'

David found the brass handle recessed into the carved woodwork and opened the door to let Anselm scamper into a large study furnished tastefully with antique furniture. Oil paintings of Prussian officers were ranged along the walls, and two ancient battle standards were crossed on pikes above a massive leather-topped desk with an equally massive leather chair behind it. Anselm jumped onto the chair and sat upright, staring at David proprietorially.

'Is that your master's desk, Anselm?'

The desk top was clear, except for a set of pen holders and a folding picture frame with the photograph of a coldly beautiful woman, her hair coiled in the style of the 1940s. David looked at it with a sense of shock. As he reached out instinctively to pick it up, Anselm whined and wagged his tail again. The frame was heavier than he expected, and a closer inspection showed a catch for a hinged panel which opened to display a second photograph. Anselm barked excitedly and jumped up to lick the photograph, as if it were all part of a ritual that he had seen many times before. David looked at the photograph impassively before closing the catch and going back to the library in time to hear an angry voice outside the library door, a man berating a servant.

'. . . leaving him alone and unguarded. I will report you to Herr Streichner, Frau Erika, for this foolishness.'

David could not hear the woman's mumbled reply.

'I don't care how you treat strangers in the village. All strangers here are a threat to the well-being of Professor Muntz.'

The door was flung opened and a middle-aged man with intent, staring eyes came in. 'Hulbrecht,' he said bluntly, without offering to shake hands. 'Frau Erika says you are an admirer of Professor Muntz. To arrive uninvited here is most irregular.'

'Yes,' David said woodenly. 'I realize that now, but as I explained to your colleagues, the whole thing is an accident. I am staying in Brienz and overheard someone mention that this is where Professor Muntz lived. I know his work, and I thought it would be courteous to call. I see now that this is an intrusion, so I will be on my way.'

'Well, now you are here I shall ask the professor if he will see you. Quite apart from anything else, this is rather early in the day for him, and he has a busy schedule to follow. Your name . . . ?'

David felt his mouth dry out as if someone had stuffed chalk powder in it. Holy Jesus! Muntz was here. He wasn't supposed to be here until Thursday. He stared blankly at Hulbrecht.

'What is your name?' the man asked again.

He swallowed hard. 'David Lewis.'

'David Lewis?'

'That's right. Perhaps you would tell him that I have come with an apology.'

'An apology?' Hulbrecht repeated, uncomprehendingly.

'It's a bit complicated, but there has been a dreadful misunderstanding.'

Hulbrecht went slowly to the door and turned. 'The books here are very rare. Kindly do not touch them.'

CHAPTER SIXTEEN

I

Carrigan checked the room carefully. One bottle of champagne was in the ice bucket, and another was in the cold box by the writing desk. He had pondered for hours about the hotel. Should it be an old, romantic building with a four-poster bed, hidden away in the countryside, or a modern box near the airport? In the end he decided that a modern establishment in a small town would be ideal, anonymous enough to avoid unexpected surprises yet sufficiently up-to-date to let a couple settle down to enjoy themselves without attracting knowing looks or raised eyebrows.

He looked at his watch again. Six fifty-four. Half the ice had melted since he arrived, and the champagne was well and truly chilled. The flowers on the table looked good. So did the bed. He tried the piped radio again to see if he could tune to some suitable music, but all he got was a telephone chat show and the weather forecast.

The phone rang at seven twenty, and the receptionist said, 'Your friend has arrived, Mr Carrigan. She is on her way to your room. Please let Room Service know when to bring dinner.'

'Thanks,' he said. 'I guess half an hour would be fine.'

By the time he put the phone down Kate was knocking at the door. She was dressed in a hand-sewn leather vest over a loose-fitting silk blouse, with designer jeans clamped to her legs. Raven hair fell to her shoulders, emphasizing her pale face and luminous purple-black eyes.

The only sensible thing he could think of saying was, 'I've got some champagne.'

She watched as he fumbled with the foil and the wire. The cork refused to budge, and the condensation on the cold bottle made his hands slip uselessly.

'Fuck,' he said quietly.

'Let me do it.'

She took a towel from the bathroom and ran the neck of the bottle under the hot tap. When she twisted the towel round the cork it plopped out with a dull thunk. Grey vapour issued from the bottle as she filled the two glasses.

'Here's to you, and here's to me.'

'At the risk of sounding like a Noel Coward character, I'd prefer to drink to us,' Carrigan said.

She drank steadily until the glass was empty and turned towards the bed. 'Maybe we can do that afterwards.'

Luckily, he remembered that Room Service was due any minute.

Later in the evening, after a passable dinner which neither of them enjoyed very much, they made love violently and slept until midnight, then made love again, like two animals, putting all other matters out of their thoughts. At five thirty in the morning the telephone rang. Carrigan tried to see his watch, but couldn't focus his eyes properly. He picked up the handset.

'Yes?'

'Dr Carrigan. David Lewis has been arrested in Switzerland. Mrs Lewis must telephone a detective at Lucerne in exactly half an hour. I presume the lady is still with you.' The cold voice sounded like a machine.

'Who the hell is this?'

'The detective's name is Sergeant Henri Martin and his telephone number is 00 4141 218111.'

Kate began to wake up and mumbled, 'David?'

'Write that number down and repeat it to me,' the voice told him.'

'Now just one Goddamn minute,' Carrigan said. 'Who the fuck are you?'

'Who am I?' Unaccountably the emotionless voice conveyed passion, almost rage, without altering its tone. 'I suppose it would be true to say that I am the only friend that David Lewis has in the world. You, on the other hand are masquerading as his psychiatrist, and the lady next to you is his unfaithful wife.'

'Joe? Who is it? Is it David?'

227

'No it's not. It's some bloody lunatic.'

'Have you written down that telephone number, Dr Carrigan?'

'What d'you mean, he's been arrested?'

'He is in medical custody. He has been seriously injured. Write down that number.'

'Wait a minute.' Carrigan found the hotel writing folder. 'Give it me again.'

'oo 4141 218111. That's the police station at Lucerne. Ask for Sergeant Henri Martin. Read it back.'

'oo 4141 218111. Sergeant Henri Martin.' Carrigan said.

'Twenty-six minutes.' the hollow voice said, and the connection was broken.

Carrigan jabbed the hotel operator button.

'Yes, Dr Carrigan.'

'Who the hell told you to put calls through to my room at this time of night? Who was that caller?'

'I'm sorry, Dr Carrigan, but no calls have been put through to your room this evening. The last call you had was Room Service.'

'What on earth is happening, Joe?' Kate asked.

'I don't believe this,' Carrigan said. He got out of bed and went to splash water on his face.

'Don't believe what?' she called.

'Who did you tell you were coming here?'

'I assume you are joking.'

'Somebody told someone, and it sure wasn't me.'

'Well you don't think I'd be mad enough to tell anyone, do you?'

He held his head. 'No, no, of course not. Sorry.'

'So what's going on?'

'This weirdo phones to say David has been arrested in Switzerland. You are supposed to call a policeman in Lucerne at six o'clock. Apparently, he's been hurt as well.'

'Oh God,' she said.

'It's got to be some screwball joke,' he said. 'I just don't get it.'

'There's only one way to find out if it's a joke or not,' Kate said. 'Give me that number.' She picked up the phone and prodded the number for directory enquiries on the keypad. 'Switzerland . . . the police station at Lucerne . . . Thank you. oo 4141 218111.'

'Shit,' Carrigan said sincerely.

They dressed and waited nervously until it was time to make the call. It took several minutes for the police operator to trace Sergeant Martin.

'Good morning, Mrs Lewis,' a calm voice said. 'This is Sergeant Martin. I regret to inform you that we are holding your husband in custody at the general hospital here. He is accused of attacking a Swiss citizen and causing damage to private property. He himself has been badly injured. It would be of great assistance if you could come to the police station in Lucerne on the first available flight.'

CHAPTER SEVENTEEN

I

The library door opened and Hulbrecht came in, his eyes staring piercingly at David. 'Professor Muntz will see you now. He is waiting with one of his colleagues whom I believe you already know.'

Hulbrecht led the way to a modern extension in the west of the building and opened a sliding door into a well-equipped conference room. Muntz was standing by a dais, his tall figure almost dwarfing the thickset man standing beside him, Streichner. The man whom David had first met at the DAW annual meeting in Munich. The man who had been with Muntz when Uri was shot. Streichner was holding a file of papers. Hulbrecht showed David to a seat.

'What an intriguing person you are, Mr Lewis, or should I say Dr Lewis?' Muntz sounded brisk and businesslike. 'Fräulein Winter tells me you represent a firm of English engineers. Herr Streichner keeps meeting you in unusual circumstances. Our security advisers tell us you belong to some kind of Jewish revenge organization. On the other hand, Herr Frinkmann is convinced that you are an exceedingly fine engineer who can solve a technical problem for him. And now, to confuse matters even more, Herr Hulbrecht informs me that you have travelled all the way to Falkenheim with an apology for me. What are we to make of all this?'

'That's right,' David said. 'An apology.' Muntz's eyes were so pale that it was difficult to see where the whites began.

'What intrigues me most is your outburst at my lecture. Something about kestrels, I remember. A pointless question. Why on earth should you pick on such a creature to question my theory of decision-making? Why choose that particular bird?'

'For the same reason you did.'

Muntz cupped his ear. 'I beg your pardon. You speak too quietly.'

David tried to lean forward, but found it impossible to move.

His head and hands were locked to the chair. Something was happening that he couldn't understand, but he knew it was bad. Muntz was there, as he should be, but Herr Streichner was out of place. Streichner shouldn't be in this room. Neither should Hulbrecht. The woman in the white coat should be there. And there was a person at his side. His sister. Little Gerda. He wanted to see her, but he couldn't move his head. His mother had fallen onto the floor of the train wagon and didn't get up. And where was his father? Where was his father?

'*Papa! Papa!*'

David hurled himself at Muntz like a battering ram, sweeping projectors and microphone stands aside. Hulbrecht's nails raked his neck in a fruitless effort to stop him, and Streichner was a fraction too slow to get between David and his target. Muntz staggered back under the onslaught, putting up a surprising display of strength for an old man, but David's hands closed round his throat, squeezing with manic ferocity for a few seconds before Streichner reached him, two stubby fingers ripping viciously up and into his nostrils. It should have been all over then, but as Muntz clung to the lectern rasping for breath, Streichner and Hulbrecht methodically beat and kicked David to a pulp, only stopping when Muntz weakly waved his hand.

'No, no . . . That's not the way. We need his information. Clean him up and take him to the cellar.'

II

Loki Ten wrung his hands in anguish as the computer screen displayed the brutal assault on David. His enlarged hands feverishly wrestled with his games joystick, as if he could somehow convert reality into virtual reality, so that he could control what was happening, as he did with his video games. But the kicks and the blows continued until the tall man with white hair whom David had attacked waved at them. This must be Professor Muntz. He must have re-arranged his schedule. Loki Ten watched as they dragged David's body out of the conference room and into the corridor, following their progress on one camera after another, until they were laying David on a table in a basement room. His view showed him that the room was kitted out as an operating theatre, with instruments, gas cylinders and drug cabinets. Loki Ten realized that if he were going to save his new friend, he had to use his brain as well as his computer. Desperately he switched his voice synthesizer to a German translator and called Muntz's Falkenheim number. The old housekeeper answered.

'This is Loki One,' he told her. 'Inform Professor Muntz immediately that the police have been informed of a disturbance. They are on their way to the estate now. Everything must appear normal.'

'*Wass?*' she said.

Loki Ten carefully repeated his message. It was probably the most stressful thing he had ever done in his life. But it worked. He watched as Hulbrecht and his colleague strapped David to the operating table. Then the tall man with white hair left the table, picked up the house phone and listened, before turning to the others and snapping orders at them. In a few more seconds David was lying alone and still on the table in the basement room.

Sergeant Henri Martin's phone rang three minutes later in his office in Lucerne police station. It had taken Loki Ten that long to identify a Swiss police officer whose views were known by the Loki organization to be unsympathetic to right-wing organizations in general and to Nazi right-wing organizations in particular.

'Martin,' the sergeant said into the mouthpiece.

'Would I be right in assuming that you will pull out all the stops to prevent a murder from taking place in your jurisdiction?' The emotionless voice asked him.

Martin held the phone away from his ear and looked at it suspiciously. 'Who's this speaking?'

'My name is Loki Ten. You have heard of the Loki organization.'

'Yes,' Martin said.

'You haven't much time. A British subject is being held against his will in the basement of Professor Ernst Muntz's Falkenheim estate. He is badly injured and strapped to a table in a room containing prohibited substances for which the professor does not hold a licence.'

'Name two,' Martin said, scribbling notes.

'Morphine and potassium cyanide,' the voice said. 'The English-man's name is David Lewis. He has gathered evidence of Muntz's complicity in war crimes. Others are involved. If you do not get there within minutes, Lewis will die and so will his work.'

'I can't possibly . . .' Martin began.

'Take a car to Lucerne helipad. A private Jet Ranger will be waiting.'

'Loki, you say?'

'Loki Ten. You can get me killed with that information.'

Martin's phone clicked off. 'Brazzi, Valadié, Marner!' he roared. 'Car, out front. Now! You, Luther, radio an ambulance team to the Falkenheim estate at Brienz. Hurry.' He frantically keyed another number. 'Judge Rheinholt? It's Sergeant Martin. Yes, sir. I'm sorry. It's exceedingly urgent, sir. I need a search warrant for the Falk-enheim estate, Brienzersee . . . That's correct, sir. Prohibited sub-stances . . . I can have a police courier with you in five minutes.'

Police Sergeant Henri Martin and his team arrived at Falkenheim from Lucerne by helicopter less than forty minutes after Loki Ten's phone call. Streichner watched the Jet Ranger land in the car park as he was phoning his police contact in Geneva.

'There's no activity involving Falkenheim, Josef, I assure you,' the man was saying.

'In that case,' Streichner snapped, 'why am I watching three armed constables and a plain-clothed officer walking towards the front entrance this very minute? Get on it.' He slammed the phone down and opened the door.

'Professor Muntz?' the plain-clothes man asked him.

'No, I am not Professor Muntz.'

'I am Sergeant Henri Martin of the Criminal Investigation Branch. You are . . . ?'

'Josef Streichner, and you have no . . .'

'I have reason to believe that this property contains substances prohibited by law, and I have a warrant to search the premises.'

Martin motioned to the constables, and they moved forward. Streichner didn't budge.

'The hell you will,' Streichner snarled.

Another movement from Martin, and the first constable lifted the barrel of his Heckler and Koch carbine.

'We'll try the basement first, shall we?' Martin said pleasantly.

Streichner followed him. 'Look, there seems to be a misunderstanding. We have already informed the local police that a man broke in here and attacked Professor Muntz. We had to restrain him, that's all.'

One of the constables called, 'In here, Sergeant.'

As they went into the operating room, Hulbrecht came running down the stairs, stopping abruptly when he saw the policemen.

'There's a bloody ambulance here now, Josef. What the hell is going on?'

'That's a very good question,' Martin said, as he stared down at David.

'His injuries are very severe, don't you think?' he asked Streichner as the hospital team wheeled David out of the front door.

The stocky man shrugged. 'As I said, he attacked Professor Muntz.'

Martin's weary eyes took in the damage to the conference equipment. 'And the professor, how is he?'

'We have our own medical staff,' Streichner said. 'They will report to me as soon as they have examined him.'

Martin picked up one of the fallen microphone stands and replaced it on the dais. 'By the look of things you may soon be facing a manslaughter charge.'

'Rubbish. We were dealing with an intruder. I have already spoken on the telephone to your superior, Inspector Heilbron, and explained the situation.'

'Ah, Inspector Heilbron.' Martin sighed. 'I see. But do you have any idea as to why Mr . . .' He glanced at his notebook. 'David Lewis should attack your employer?'

Streichner shook his head. 'If you ask me, we're dealing with a madman.'

'Unless he recovers from your vigorous self-defence,' Martin said heavily, 'your supposition will remain untested. In the meantime my people will take statements, including one from Professor Muntz. If you know Inspector Heilbron you will also know that like all good policemen he insists on playing things by the book. I have no wish to return to my office with an incomplete dossier on this unfortunate incident.'

He scanned through the statements as the helicopter returned to Lucerne. The old housekeeper described how she had found a stranger in a disused compartment of the old funicular railway. He said he had been taken ill after climbing the mountain. Hulbrecht's version was hardly more illuminating. He had conveyed the visitor's request for a meeting to the professor who had magnanimously agreed to see him. Streichner's account described how a perfect stranger had wandered into the private estate on the pretext that he was an admirer of Professor Muntz. As a courtesy, Muntz had agreed to see him in the presence of his personal assistants. For no apparent reason the stranger had erupted into an unprovoked attack on the professor and had to be subdued. Unfortunately he fell during his attack and sustained injuries, for which he was about to be treated in the basement operating theatre when Sergeant Martin arrived. The local police had been called, naturally. Muntz's statement was totally useless, merely stating that he did not wish to prefer charges, either for personal injury or damage to property. Sergeant Martin's parting words to Muntz's staff were that the police themselves would be instituting criminal charges for the possession of the prohibited substances listed on his search warrant.

The sergeant arrived at the hospital as David was being rushed to emergency surgery, so he went to the restaurant for coffee. An hour later the senior surgeon joined him to report on David's condition.

'Starting from the head down, his skull is cracked in two places, but fortunately not too badly, and he has lost three front teeth. We've had to sew part of his nose back on his face. The right side of his neck is deeply lacerated by three parallel nail marks. The right collar bone is broken, his arms and shoulders are severely bruised and the left ulna is fractured in two places. He has five broken ribs and a ruptured spleen. His kidneys are bruised and one of his testicles may have to be removed. The good news is that only one of his legs is broken. Whoever did this should be given life. I've not seen anything like it in fifteen years of orthopaedic work.'

'Pretty bad,' Martin nodded. 'Did he have any injuries to his hands as if he'd been hitting anyone. Abrasions to the knuckles, for example?'

'No, they were clear when I examined him, apart from a bit of skin under the right thumb nail that I assume came from someone else.'

'You'll put all this in your report.'

'Sure,' the surgeon said. 'Plus the fact that his blood pressure is abnormally low and before he went under the anaesthetic he seemed to be in severe shock. But that's hardly surprising, under the circumstances. He may well have suffered brain injury. We'll have to keep him in intensive care for twenty-four hours at least before we know the true extent of the damage.'

Martin handed the doctor one of his cards. 'Thanks. Please telephone me the moment you think I can talk with him.'

III

Carrigan insisted on accompanying Kate to Lucerne. They drove from the hotel to collect passports and extra clothes, then took a Swiss Airways flight to Kloten airport, Zurich. They arrived by train in Lucerne at midday and booked into two single rooms in a small pension by the railway station and then took a taxi to meet Sergeant Martin at the Gendarmerie. He had a small room with two chairs for visitors jammed in front of an ancient wooden desk. Files were stacked in racks all round the walls. The only decoration was a stuffed fish in a glass case on one of the filing cabinets.

'Freshwater bass from Brienzersee,' Martin said in excellent English. There was a silence while he shuffled some papers. Neither Kate nor Carrigan felt like responding to small talk. 'This is a strange business. A total mystery.'

'Sergeant Martin, you said my husband is injured.' Kate only just managed to keep her voice under control. 'I want to go to him immediately.'

'He is in the best of hands, Mrs Lewis. I have informed the hospital that we shall arrive at three o'clock. You must understand that he is under sedation. I am happy to say that the latest report is that his condition has stabilized, but you must prepare yourself. He doesn't look very good.'

'What kind of sedation have they given him?' Carrigan asked.

Martin turned to him. 'I'm not a medical man, Dr Carrigan. You can be sure the hospital staff have done everything correctly. Do you always give such individual attention to a patient's requirements when he is outside England?'

'I'm not his general practitioner. I have been treating Mr Lewis to a course of therapy. I am a qualified psychiatrist.'

Martin's eyebrow's rose a fraction. 'I see. So Mr Lewis is suffering from a psychiatric illness.'

'I didn't say that. He has a problem, and I have been helping him deal with it.'

'In view of the seriousness of yesterday's incident, would you mind explaining what you mean.'

Carrigan glanced at Kate who nodded. 'Sure. But first I'd like you to tell us exactly what happened.'

'I don't know exactly what happened.' Sergeant Martin laced his fingers and stared broodingly at his files. 'I was informed of an incident at an estate near Brienz yesterday. Apparently, Mr Lewis attacked and injured the owner of the estate and was restrained by two of the staff. He also damaged an amount of furniture and equipment.'

'Are you talking about Professor Ernst Muntz?' Carrigan asked.

'Yes,' Martin said, surprised. 'Do you know him?'

Carrigan shook his head.

'How do you know who Mr Lewis attacked? The information has not been released.'

Carrigan summarized the events that started with David's dream. Martin listened intently, jotting notes on his pad and making comments. He underlined Albert Levy's name several times, and when Carrigan finished he closed his eyes and leaned back in his chair.

'It seems that we have a mystery that is two mysteries. One is the discovery of this so-called *Turmfalke* project, and the other is the problem of who operated the organization. If I understand you correctly, Mr Lewis learned of *Turmfalke* and uncovered proof of the existence of the college and death camp, partly by coincidence and partly through some remarkable detective work. He is convinced that Professor Muntz was the commandant, and yet, unlike the existence of the project itself, there is not a shred of evidence to support this view.'

'That's about the strength of it,' Carrigan agreed.

'I have no need to tell you how serious are these allegations.'

'Come on, Sergeant. No one is making allegations. I am reporting on a situation that affects a client. What Mrs Lewis and I want to do is help in any way we can, so that her husband can go home. You said no one was preferring charges.'

'I said that Professor Muntz was not taking action. There is still the matter of criminal trespass and damage. Not to mention your husband's own condition. He is in our custody and must remain so at least until I get his statement. That might take several days.'

'Why is he so badly injured?' Kate asked quietly. 'What did they do to him?'

Martin cleared his throat. What hadn't they done to him! Despite his many years of police work, Martin was still incapable of understanding that people could behave in such a way. A routine check on Streichner had shown he was a naturalized Swiss citizen who was born in Bavaria. One police memorandum linked his name with members of the Volkssozialistische Bewegung Deutschlands, a neo-Nazi group involved with the killing of one of Martin's friends in 1980 during a gun-running operation. Streichner was also suspected of having connections with the ultra-right-wing Munich-based political party Neuvolkgruppe. But all this was just a labelling exercise. It did not explain what kind of person could brutally beat someone like this.

'Well, as I said, the doctors are happier this morning than they were last night.'

Kate sensed his sympathy. 'I just want to take him home, Sergeant.'

David lay motionless in the intensive-care unit, linked by tubes and wires to an array of equipment monitoring heartbeat, brain and other functions. Carrigan noticed the dialysis machine pushed into one corner behind the bed. The duty doctor reeled off the list of injuries.

'. . . but I am more concerned with his lack of reaction. Normally a patient with such injuries would be conscious by now, and there's

238

nothing we can see that is preventing this. A number of factors point to a malfunction of the brain or central nervous system, but the small fractures of the skull are not serious enough to cause this, in our opinion. Mind you, he might be suffering a mild concussion caused by transferred or secondary trauma.'

'I think you're more likely to find that he's in a coma,' Carrigan said.

'Coma?' The doctor paused. 'You could be right, but it would be most unusual.'

'If I am right, Sergeant Martin might have to wait a long time before he gets his statement.'

Martin looked unhappily at them. 'I have no wish to extend this case, but I must have a statement.'

'You say Muntz is not gunning for David. You also implied that David might have a case for taking action against the thugs who beat him up. What if Mrs Lewis signs some kind of release, as next of kin. Would that help?'

Martin thought of his superior, Inspector Heilbron, and sighed again. 'It might. But there is still the possibility of my department taking its own action against one or more of the parties concerned.'

Carrigan pushed his advantage. 'Come on, Sergeant. That depends on you, doesn't it? As soon as Mr Lewis is fit enough, surely the best thing we can do for him is get him home.'

David's physical condition stabilized on the second day, and the arrangement they came to was that he could be transported by private ambulance to England and released into Carrigan's custody at the Swiss border, provided, said Martin apologetically, that all the State expenses were paid in full and on the understanding that David would eventually make a statement to Martin's counterpart in New Scotland Yard, a Detective Sergeant Fry, 'Just to tie up the loose ends for my report.'

Kate spent the rest of the day on the telephone to London sorting out how much of the costs would be met by David's various insurance policies, leaving Carrigan to wander about Lucerne. They linked up for dinner in a lakeside restaurant overlooking the town's mediaeval Wasserturm and the covered wooden footbridge over the river, neither of them feeling much like eating, making no mention of their night together. Carrigan was relieved when the outburst finally came.

'You absolute bastard.'

'If it's any consolation, I don't think there's anything you can say that could make me feel worse than I already do,' he said quietly.

'All that stuff you told Sergeant Martin, about this man Levy and David going mental over this bloody Nazi . . . How come I didn't know anything about this? If you'd confided in me, I just might have been able to help my husband, you know, like a wife is supposed to.'

The anger in her face made him feel sick.

'Yes. But equally you might have caused some kind of adverse reaction. There was no way I could judge.'

'Judge, he says!' People turned to look at them, and she forced her voice to a furious whisper. 'The one thing we both know that David needs is love. You can cut the crap about psychoanalytical root causes and obsessions. Nothing matters except love. Personally, I don't give a damn about the Nazis and what they did fifty bloody years ago. If you'd only told me exactly what was going on I could have talked David out of it. I know I could. But no! You just let me into some of the secret, and watched while David went screwing himself all over Europe, conveniently leaving the field free for you to screw his wife.'

'Jesus, Kate. It wasn't like that.'

She poured herself another glass of wine and swallowed it fiercely. 'No? Well that's exactly what it feels like.'

They sat miserably, and she started to cry. Neighbouring diners shuffled embarrassedly as she rushed onto the quayside. Carrigan threw some notes on the table and followed her round the corner where she was dabbing her eyes with a tissue.

'I'm sorry, Joe. That was unfair.'

'Not entirely. The trouble is that I've been conning myself about being objective over David. I fell in love with you the first time I saw you, and I've been conning myself about that too. I thought I could handle it . . .'

A polite cough interrupted him. The waiter from the restaurant was standing next to them holding a silver tray.

'Excuse me, sir, but you forgot your change.'

When the man had gone, Carrigan looked at the notes and coins and managed a wry smile. 'Well, thank God we can at least rely on Swiss efficiency and honesty.'

They walked back to the pension, and after a few steps she slipped her arm through his as if to tell him that she still needed his support. It made him feel a hell of a lot better.

CHAPTER EIGHTEEN

I

Loki Ten planned his moves carefully and wondered how long it would be before one of his colleagues on the network realized what he was doing. He laid traps in his data system to provide an early warning of approaching danger, then set about his final tasks as a Loki operative. The first of these was relatively straightforward: the destruction of Muntz's reputation. He prepared a press release to the news and business editors of major publications and broadcasting companies announcing the professor's retirement from all his official positions. He drafted another press statement purporting to come from Herr Dolland, DAW's chief executive officer, denouncing Muntz and distancing the company from what the man had done. The press announcements included a briefing paper for the provincial newspaper that circulated in and around Brienz.

His next step was to prepare a report to German and Swiss government departments and police headquarters containing an account of Muntz's involvement in *Turmfalke* and the manner in which he had secured the results of his experiments on prisoners for use by DAW. He included all the archive references necessary for any state prosecutor to mount an investigation, then he compiled a summary of all the documents for the DAW press office so they could prepare for the inevitable media onslaught. Loki Ten stored all this information in his computer's 'out basket' for simultaneous transmission to the various recipients through the Internet when the next and most intricate phase of his project was complete, the close-down of Muntz's finances.

The mutual untrustworthiness of the three business partners and wartime colleagues had led to an arrangement whereby each agreed that a secure Loki database should hold details of every bank account, shareholding and asset they owned. One heavily encrypted file contained their personal identification numbers for the banks involved. Another contained on-line authorization codes for their solicitors and stockbrokers. If any of them died the survivors would act as his or her executor, and Loki One was authorized to release this information to them. In this way they could maintain control of their business and also gain access to their dead colleague's wealth without resorting to the courts, a move that would lead to almost certain investigation by the authorities.

Loki Ten had cracked all Loki cyphers as soon as they were installed, just for a bit of fun, and now he used his knowledge to issue instructions to Muntz's banks and stockbrokers to sell all his assets, convert the proceeds to dollars and send tranches of the money to certain bank accounts and charities. He cancelled Muntz's charge cards and liquidated his pension funds. He stopped all standing orders and direct debit payments to telephone, gas, electricity and municipal authorities. And he informed the banks of Muntz's employees that no more money would be forthcoming from their employer.

The entire process took about six hours. It took a little longer to arrange the sale of Falkenschloss in Germany and Falkenheim in Switzerland. This was achieved through an international firm of estate agents who conducted their business through extensive telecommunication data networks. Both properties were owned by trust companies, and the relevant accounts were operated by electronic data transfer, so Muntz's signature was not required for any of the transactions involved. Only his PINs.

The complex system that had been put in place over generations to secure the professor's ancestral lands and wealth now began to act against him.

Loki Ten experienced an unexpected delay when the properties were offered to the market at low prices to encourage a quick sale, and various people and organizations around the world began bidding against each other. One large Japanese company wanted to acquire both properties as part of their plan to expand into continental Europe. Their chairman, Mr Nagashuru, was already in Germany with his family, looking for suitable locations. Not unnaturally they wanted to see what they were bidding for. Loki Ten hastened the process by using the security cameras on both estates to send video images of the exteriors and interiors to Mr

Nagashuru. He made a firm offer which was accepted by the estate agents acting, so they thought, under Muntz's instructions, and the purchase cash was sent by electronic fund transfer to a numbered Swiss bank account belonging to Loki Ten. While this was being resolved, one of his warning traps put a set of code numbers on his screen:

'Source code search for 52 55 51 49 31 10 initiated by 52 55 51 49 30 01'

This jumble of figures meant that the newly appointed Loki One had come looking for Loki Ten. He smiled to himself and began laying trails of data that would have the effect of a gale in a paperchase. They'd locate his address sooner or later, of course, but by then he would be long gone and working with the same system under an alias. The only way they could stop him was to shut the entire network down, and that would create havoc for a much wider group of Loki clients than Muntz and his *Turmfalke* friends.

When all this activity had been completed, Muntz's entire fortune had disappeared into financial limbo, and the man was a homeless pauper. It only remained for him to find out.

Loki Ten's final communication was directed at Muntz's partners in crime, Irma Schumaker and Viktor Fischer, advising them of the situation and warning them that Muntz's carelessness might compromise their own safety unless they took remedial action. This message was stored in his fax machine and scheduled for transmission after the press had received their information about Muntz. By Loki Ten's reasoning, a dishonoured, disinherited and disorientated Muntz may well become expendable.

II

For Muntz, the first indication that something was amiss was when his housekeeper Frau Erika failed to turn up for work the next day. Neither did his cook, and he sat for several minutes at his dining table in bemused astonishment, ringing the servants' bell and waiting for a breakfast that did not appear. But Josef Streichner did appear, waving the local newspaper.

'Why did you not tell me that you were doing this?' he shouted, slamming the paper on the table. 'After all these years, you should do such a thing to me.'

'Get a hold of yourself, Josef,' Muntz said. 'Where is Frau Erika?'

Streichner's face turned purple. 'You do this, and you ask about a housekeeper. Are you senile?'

Muntz was not used to being spoken to in this way, and he had no intention of allowing it to continue. He stood up.

'You forget yourself, Herr Streichner. I have yet to have my breakfast. Kindly leave me, and send Frau Erika. She is late. I have never known such a thing.'

'Leave you. Yes, I'll leave you, you bastard,' Streichner yelled at him. 'Although I'll be bloody lucky to get as far as the gate without being arrested. You've done for us all, you son-of-a-bitch.'

He rushed out, and Muntz heard his car over-revving as it fan-tailed along the drive and into the road. He went to the door of the dining room and called for Frau Erika, then Hulbrecht. There was no response, and when he picked up the telephone all he heard was a recorded message saying that the line had been taken out of service. Trembling with anger, he stalked to the garage, only to find that its door was locked. Hulbrecht, Streichner or one of the chauffeurs always drove him, and he had no idea where the keys were kept. He shook the door in a rage, then tried the phone again. Slamming it down, he went back to the dining room and sat down, plucking at his napkin, unable to understand or accept what was happening. It simply was not logical.

Ex-SS Standartenführer Professor Ernst Muntz took a deep breath and closed his eyes. His entire life had been devoted to the concept that everything was indeed logical. It was just that he could not see the logic of this. He forced his mind to travel back over the days and weeks to see if there was anything that could possibly explain his extraordinary predicament, and time after time one name kept floating into his consciousness. David Lewis. *Der verdammte Engländer!* Everything had been as it always had been, until those Loki reports about David Lewis, and until David Lewis had appeared in Munich and then in Falkenheim. A nerve began to twitch in Muntz's temple. So who the hell was the man? What had he done to cause this mess? Why had Streichner, a loyal and trusted retainer, shouted all those incredible insults and accusations? Where was his housekeeper, his cook, the gardeners?

A snuffling at his feet broke his concentration, and he looked down to see Anselm his dachshund looking up at him. He reached down, but Anselm backed away and ran out of the room.

What the hell was happening to the world?

His stomach reminded him how hungry he was, and he went into the servants' quarters to find some food. The last time he had been in the kitchens had been when he and Irena were children, and he wasn't sure exactly where they were. How he missed her still! She would have known what to do in these outrageous circumstances. Everyone did her bidding. She had only to turn those wonderful blue eyes on you, and you were her slave. He remembered the day she had taken the initiative. It had been in their secret room in the roof of Falkenschloss, among the jumble of discarded furniture and old paintings. She had commanded him to strip naked and stand before her, then she had removed her own clothes and watched carefully as his erection grew and grew.

'I have read about something called masturbation,' she said. 'I want you to do it. I want to see the seed of your loins.'

He had no idea what she was talking about, so she took hold of him and inexpertly brought him to a climax. Over the weeks and the months they got better at it, and he did it to her, and then one day she said she wanted him to put it inside her. Whenever he thought of the beauty of that moment, tears were born, and they came now, flooding his vision so he had to stop and wipe his eyes. *Liebe, liebe Irena*, who died bearing his child. His one true love, apart, of course, from the Führer. How could it all have ended as it did? It made no sense whatsoever.

He found the kitchens and began opening cupboards looking for the fresh bread rolls and cooked meats that Frau Erika served each morning, but all he could find was a plate of venison and some dried-up vegetables left over from the previous evening's meal. He wolfed it down savagely, vowing that this fellow Lewis would pay dearly for causing him all this trouble.

The food revived his spirits considerably. He would find out exactly how this idiocy had been brought about, get everything into perspective, and then act, as the commander that he was! He would telephone Dolland in Munich and instruct him to begin an investigation. Here in Brienz he would sack the servants and hire new staff. Striding vigorously upstairs he went into his office and picked up the telephone, but it was still not responding. Even the bloody telephone company was letting him down. Unbelievable. Streichner would go, the ungrateful bastard. He recalled that Streichner had waved the local paper at him during his outburst. It was still there, crumpled on the dining table. He smoothed it out and adjusted his spectacles. His own portrait stared back at him. The headline above it stated: '*Professor Muntz admits War crimes. Eminent resident conducted medical experiments on Jews: resigns as chairman of DAW.*' Below this, the paper reported a confession by Muntz, admitting the use of information gained by his wartime activities in the setting up of his pharmaceutical group. There were cross-references and corroborating evidence from a number of authorities, plus a quote from a DAW press spokesman saying that the company had accepted Professor Muntz's resignation and was beginning an inquiry that would prove that DAW had been unaware of any improper activity relating to the development of its products.

He read it again and again, hardly able to understand the enormity of what he was reading. This was not possible. The world had gone completely mad.

He was still sitting at his desk four hours later, reading, lips moving as he silently mouthed each word, when noises from the drive of the house filtered into his office and into his consciousness. Eagerly he strode to the front door, half expecting, despite everything, to see Frau Erika, to hear her explain that there had been a tragedy in the village, that the road to Falkenheim had been made impassable by a fallen tree, that the telephone lines had been brought down by a late fall of snow . . . But no. There in the drive of his beautiful home was a huge and vulgar American car, jammed against the stone base of the fountain, unable to negotiate the curve and disgorging a seemingly endless stream of Japanese children. A man and woman were gazing around, video cameras clamped to their faces. The man approached Muntz, bowed and said, 'Nagashuru.'

There was a long silence as Muntz struggled to speak. 'This is private property,' he managed to say in German. 'This is my home. It is not open to tourists. I must ask you to leave. Get out, at once, or I will send for the police.'

The man nodded happily, smiled and walked past him into the house, his family following.

'Streichner, Hulbrecht, this has gone far enough,' Muntz called distractedly into the trees. 'Come to me, immediately, do you hear!'

He was still calling when the police arrived and arrested him.

CHAPTER NINETEEN

I

David was flown from Switzerland and taken to the Westminster and Chelsea Hospital in Fulham Road where he remained in a coma. Peter Halkyn insisted on paying for a private room, and Kate stayed with him night and day, talking about the things they liked doing together, reminding him of their walks in the Lake District, their friends, anything but the horror that had come unannounced and uninvited into their lives. She took short breaks when the nurses bullied her, buying coffee and snacks from the cafeteria and dozing in a chair until she remembered where she was and went back to David. Carrigan stayed away but phoned many times to check on her, and on David.

On the fourth evening she came back to David's room to find one of the hospital patients sitting in a powered wheelchair by his bed, holding his hand. She thought he must be from the paraplegic unit, not quite able to control his actions, maybe even a little simple.

'Hello,' she said.

The large round face turned awkwardly towards her.

'I'm sorry. I did not mean to intrude.'

'You're not intruding,' she told him. 'In a place like this, it's people like me who get in the way.'

'He is your husband.' The statement seemed like a question, but his monotone was a little confusing.

'Yes,' she said softly. 'Yes he is.'

'Do you love him?'

It's funny how the questions of a child-like mind can get so quickly to the heart of things, she thought.

'Oh yes. I love him very much.'

The red-rimmed eyes stared unblinkingly through her.

'Do you love anyone else?'

Dear God, please stop this. She wanted to lie, but found it was impossible in front of this man-child.

'I . . . Yes I do, but in another kind of way. It's not easy to explain.'

'I am his friend.'

'Of course you are, my dear,' she said and promptly burst into tears.

By the time she had recovered her composure the patient had vanished and David was watching her with wide open eyes.

'Loki Ten was here,' he said. 'That bugger Muntz has got his comeuppance. The Swiss police have arrested him. Loki Ten gave all the evidence to the authorities, he said. Muntz is ruined, financially, socially, every way you look at it. His money, his home, everything. You can't say fairer than that. Are you all right, Kate?'

Before she could say anything he closed his eyes and fell asleep. She sat staring at him, not knowing what to think. He had spoken like the old David, but the madness about his dream figure, Muntz, was still there. She was still sitting silently when the nurse wheeled the telephone trolley into the room and plugged it into the junction box.

'Dr Carrigan is on the line for you, Mrs Lewis.'

She took the phone. 'Hello?'

'Kate, you're not going to believe this, but this guy Muntz, he's been arrested . . .'

'I know,' she said.

'You caught it too, then. Headline stuff. His entire organization seems to have collapsed in on itself, and all the business about *Turmfalke* is coming out of the woodwork. It was true all along. Makes me feel like a complete schmuck. If only we could get this through to David . . .'

'He already knows,' she told him.

'What?'

'He came out of his coma, and he already knows.'

'That's absolutely wonderful. Well, let's hope the news helps to get him on the mend.'

'I'm sure it will,' she said quietly, and hung up.

She gazed at David for a long time, and a slight shiver ran down her back. He looked absolutely normal, lying there. His colour had returned, and his breathing was deep and easy. But here was a man who had dreamed a nightmare that turned out to be true, and now he had woken from a coma and told her things that he could not possibly have known. She remembered his reference to Loki, and recalled that this was a Nordic god. There had to be a logical explanation for all this, but the shiver kept returning.

II

Three weeks after David's beating, Kate took him home to start his convalescence. Carrigan called round several times, staying to chat with David, and keeping Kate company for an hour or so. Their relationship stabilized into a warm friendship. The only thing still worrying Carrigan were the German documents he had found waiting among the pile of mail behind his front door, with the cryptic note from David to keep them safe until he returned from his overseas trip. They were safe enough, in the hands of Detective Sergeant Fry from New Scotland Yard who had taken a statement from him and was waiting for one from David.

Four weeks after they returned from Lucerne he decided that David had recovered enough for him to mention the undertaking he had given to Sergeant Martin about DS Fry.

'I think you're doing OK, but the important thing is, do you?'

'What kind of statement does he want?' David asked.

'Just tell him what happened, from your point of view.'

David looked at him blankly. 'But I don't know what happened, apart from what you've been telling me.'

It was the first sign Carrigan had that David was suffering from amnesia. In the next few minutes he learned that David had also forgotten about *Turmfalke* and the beating he had received from Streichner and Hulbrecht.

'I don't know what to make of it,' Carrigan told Kate. 'In one way it might be good, because he certainly seems more relaxed. It happens a lot in accident cases. A kind of self-protection. Maybe he'll be able to settle down to work more quickly without all this business clogging his mind.'

251

'I hope you're right,' Kate said. 'Peter Halkyn is being absolutely marvellous. In fact he said it was lucky the DAW thing happened when it did, otherwise the firm would have been caught out, along with DAW's other suppliers. DAW shares have plummeted, and they're in real financial trouble.'

'He's probably right. By the way, I'll call this pal of Sergeant Martin's at Scotland Yard tomorrow. What we need is for him to take a statement from David right now and back it up with a medical report. The statement won't be worth anything, but the Swiss will be able to tie up their bits and pieces then, and David can get on with his life.'

Carrigan hoped he sounded more confident than he was feeling.

Kate wondered if she should tell him that David apparently knew about Muntz's arrest before coming out of his coma, or about the statement that had arrived from David's bank showing a payment into a new joint account of ten million American dollars. But the whole thing was so unnerving that she kept the information from Carrigan and David.

Two days later Detective Sergeant Fry sent David's statement to Switzerland, and Sergeant Martin acknowledged it with a personal note to Kate in which he sent his hopes for David's full recovery. As winter approached and the physical healing continued, David took up the reins of his business again, working out proposals for potential clients in various European countries. Carrigan put his notes and tape-recordings on his work with David in a cupboard. He reduced the number of calls he made to the Lewises and settled down to routine, devoting his time to research.

III

Loki Ten's new location was a rented ground-floor studio flat overlooking a seaside town. From his windows he had a view of a small bay and harbour across red tiled rooftops, with gulls swooping and calling overhead. It was nothing like the Mediterranean villa he had constructed for himself inside his computer, with its terrace and swimming pool, but when the autumn sun moved across the sky he was able to examine how the shadows changed, and he spent some time reconstructing his villa program so that his virtual sun did the same. He felt a warm glow of gratitude to his friend David Lewis for suggesting this improvement. From time to time he peeped into David and Kate's bank account to see how they were spending his present, but neither David nor Kate made a withdrawal. Eventually, Loki Ten began to worry about his friend. David had been very, very ill, after all. Perhaps he was still poorly, even though Professor Muntz had been ruined. Loki Ten thought it would be sensible to keep an eye on things.

IV

It happened again. Carrigan's telephone bleeping in the middle of the night. Kate's panic-stricken voice.

'Joe . . . wake up please, Joe.'

He fumbled the phone round to his other ear. 'Kate? Is that you?'

'Come round, Joe. Please. I can't handle this.'

He swung his legs to the floor and sat upright, groping for a robe. 'Tell me.'

'It's David. He's had another dream.' She was groaning in anguish. 'Come and help me, Joe.'

When he arrived Kate was barely capable of opening the door. Inside the hall he embraced her fiercely, holding her upright, feeling her terror.

'Hey, come on,' he whispered. 'What's wrong?'

'I can't go through this again, Joe. You know I can't.'

'How is he?'

'Fast asleep. Can you believe that? He screamed for his father, Joe, just like last time. It's starting all over again. You have to help us.'

Us. That was the first time she had used the word. It had always been 'him' and 'me'. A sea-change in their marriage. That was good. Very good. He made hot, sweet coffee, well laced with brandy, forcing her to sip it down before it cooled. 'I'll do the best I can, I promise,' he told her.

*

It was indeed like starting all over again. David had absolutely no idea that anything could be wrong, and Carrigan had to coax and cajole him into another session of therapy.

'It's Kate you should be looking after,' David insisted. 'She's pretty washed out these days, if you hadn't noticed. Not sleeping too well.'

'I know,' Carrigan said. 'And between you and me I'm keeping a close eye on her. But she's got this notion that you're unhappy about something, and she wants me to go into it for you. The plain fact is that it will almost certainly do her a lot of good if she thinks I'm treating you.'

'Unhappy? Why on earth should she think that? As a matter of fact, I couldn't be happier. Some silly sod at the bank has whacked a small fortune into our account. They're refusing to admit it's a mistake, so I've transferred it to a deposit account. When they do sort it out, maybe they'll let us keep the interest. Paying a friendly shrink to unravel things for Kate ain't going to be a problem.'

At least he said 'friendly', thought Carrigan.

'I'll do a deal with you, David. I'm working on a new technique to delve into people's innermost souls. Let me have a go with you, and I'll not only waive my enormous fee, I'll buy you a crate of the finest bubbly. That's an offer I know you can't refuse.'

'Sounds good. When do we start?'

'We already have.' Carrigan smiled. 'I've got you on my side, and that's the first step. Let's go for the next one.'

He took the sketch pad and charcoal sticks from a cupboard.

'You sketch your patients, do you?'

'It's for you,' Carrigan said. 'I plonk you in deep hypnosis, and you draw what you see. Simple. All you do to start the ball rolling is swallow this magic potion while I make three wishes.'

David looked at the pill suspiciously. 'What is it?'

'Don't ask me to pronounce the medical name. It'll relax you as I do my number with the deep, soothing voice.'

He watched as David swallowed the sedative, then began the routine, calmly talking, using the key phrases that had lulled then overcome David's conscious mind during their first sessions together in the spring. Half an hour later, although David had made no sound, Carrigan knew it wasn't working. He tussled on, feeling as if he were bouncing off a physical malevolence.

254

'Sleep . . . you need to sleep . . . to relax. You know you can relax. And we'll travel together through the darkness in perfect safety . . .'

David lay still with his eyes closed, but he was not asleep, and Carrigan decided to take a gamble. Without a pause in his words he took a hypodermic and charged it with a mixture of diazepam and a mild barbiturate solution. He then gently rolled David's shirt sleeve high enough to show the brachial vein. He dabbed the spot with a steriswab and slipped the needle under the skin, firmly discharging the contents. The plunger was almost home when David opened his eyes and looked curiously at his arm. There was the briefest of pauses, then he went berserk.

The needle was ripped bloodily from Carrigan's hands and hurled across the room to smash against the marble fireplace. Carrigan felt himself lifted effortlessly, and for an all-too-brief second he was flying after the hypodermic before crashing into the hearth in a jagged heap of limbs and antique fire irons. He scrambled into a corner to defend himself against the sudden fury, but there was no need. He saw David crouched pathetically by the upturned chair, tears streaming down his face, saying over and over again in a little-boy voice, *'Papa! Papa! Papa!'*

V

The sketch was flawless, the best David had done. A carved wooden picture frame with folding sides opened to show the face of a beautiful woman in her early thirties, hair wound tightly about her head in a luxuriant coif in a 1930s style. The frame was standing on a large desk, and in the background David had depicted a number of other picture frames, ranged on a wall, with a shadowy, indistinct figure on each and what seemed like a heraldic device with an arrangement of flags. But everything was subordinate to the woman. Carrigan gave David a second sheet, hoping to see the same kind of development as before, but David merely reproduced the sketch. In an hour he drew three, each exactly the same as the other.

'Is this all?' Carrigan asked quietly.

Although David made no sound, Carrigan felt the resistance

again, pushing back. He persisted, and after a while David took up the charcoal and began again. It was the same sketch, but instead of drawing the woman's face he left an empty space in the frame. This time his hand was trembling, so the lines were less clear, and this time he was making unnerving groans, sweat pouring from his face. Carrigan realized he had gone as far as he would ever manage to go with his patient and began to bring him back.

One thing was clear to Carrigan. The key to David's problem lay in that picture. But having the lock without the key was no use whatsoever. Although the odds were hardly favourable, Albert Levy was Carrigan's only hope of unearthing the root cause of David's problem. Anna answered his call and told him that she would not put him through to the old man.

'I understand exactly how you feel about my involvement,' he told her, 'but I'm begging you to tell Mr Levy that I called. David Lewis has quite literally risked his life to solve the kind of problem that you deal with, and I believe he desperately needs your help to solve his own.'

She returned his call next day, and once again Leon took him to meet Levy, resentment oozing from the young Jew. Anna was waiting in the enclosed stone courtyard to take him up the rickety stairs to Levy's rooms. She didn't say one word of greeting, angry disapproval stamped on her stubborn features. Levy was sitting in pyjamas and dressing gown, propped in bed, the scar on his face shining with sweat. Although the windows were open and the room was full of flowers, Carrigan could smell the old man. It was the kind of smell that comes shortly before the body finally runs out of steam.

'If you need information, Dr Carrigan, I shall do what I can.'

Carrigan steeled himself and shook his head vigorously. 'You know very well that I need more than information. I need your practical help.'

Levy sighed. 'Tell me what you think I can do.'

'It's not that easy. I don't know what you can do. I just want to tell you what's happened, and if you can see a way through the problem, fine. If not, I won't trouble you again.' He put David's sketches on Levy's bed. 'Maybe we could start with these.'

'Anna, will you fetch us some coffee, and this time perhaps you can give Dr Carrigan a rather more palatable blend.'

'I would prefer to stay, Albert.'

'I know you would, my dear, but Dr Carrigan's violence stems from a love for his patient. He is hardly likely to use it to harm me.' He turned to Carrigan as a reluctant Anna went back downstairs. 'Tell me what has happened to bring you here again.'

'You'll have heard about Muntz being arrested.'

'Yes, but all we know is what the newspapers tell us.'

'David discovered where Muntz was living, an estate near Brienz called Falkenheim. He went there, and according to the police he attacked Muntz and was badly beaten up for his pains by two guys called Streichner and Hulbrecht. They nearly killed him. He's over the physical problems, but he's got no memory of recent events, and something else happened in Switzerland. Christ knows what, but my guess is he had a violent trauma in Muntz's house. He certainly went berserk and then into a coma there, and the only things I have to go on are the papers in that envelope and these sketches he made a couple of days ago.'

He laid out the sketches and watched as Levy looked closely at them through his magnifying glass.

'They are very fine sketches, Dr Carrigan, but I see nothing of significance in them.'

'Neither do I. All I know is that David was right about Muntz from the time his nightmares began, and this photograph will explain how. If we can find it, maybe I can begin to put the pieces together and help David get over whatever is causing his illness.'

Anna came back to the room with a tray of coffee. It tasted as bad as it had on his previous visit, but Carrigan gulped it down and put the cup back on the tray. 'Lovely,' he told Anna. 'Best coffee I've ever tasted.'

She managed a slight smile.

'And what is in your other envelope?' Levy asked.

'David mailed me a pile of German documents from Zurich. They are part of the evidence that put Muntz away. I had to hand the originals over the police, but I took copies. I can't read German very well, but they date between 1944 and 1947. The first set seem to be the results of some kind of laboratory experiments, and they're all signed by Muntz. As you can see each one is stapled to a variation of the same data, only the second set is all printed on DAW note-paper. They're signed by Muntz and countersigned by W. Blintz, whoever he may be.'

Levy slowly leafed through the documents, his face impassive. He leaned back and closed his eyes. 'Did Mr Lewis say how he acquired these?'

Carrigan shook his head. 'Nope. He just asked me to keep them safe. What are they?'

'Do you believe in the Devil, Dr Carrigan?'

The question took Carrigan aback. 'To be honest, I never really think about it.'

'So much evil . . .' Levy blinked his eyes several times. 'These documents confirm your patient's nightmare in its entirety. They are post-mortem results from the project we know as *Turmfalke*. Not the usual kind of post-mortem, but detailed analyses of physio-logical changes in the human body under extreme stress and of attempts to counteract the stress by chemical means. Only God knows how much pain and terror these results represent, but they appear to have been put to good use.'

'What do you mean?'

Levy smiled wanly. 'We have here a meticulous account of a pharmaceutical fraud, signed by the two perpetrators. The infor-mation they cut and probed from poor shrieking wretches was – I believe the word is "laundered" – and used to provide apparently legitimate evidence of the testing of ethical drugs launched by DAW after the war. This evidence is enough to convict them of war crimes before any judicial court of inquiry.'

'That's all very well, but it's not any help to David,' Carrigan muttered.

Levy sat still for several minutes. Carrigan had begun to think he had fallen asleep when he spoke again.

'There is a possibility I can add to your information, although there would be no guarantee it would help Mr Lewis.'

'I'll take anything you can give me, Mr Levy,' Carrigan said.

When Carrigan had gone, Levy reached for his address book, looked up the name of Isadore Absolom and then insisted that Anna bring him the phone. He dialled the number and spoke in German, a language that Anna also spoke fluently.

'Isadore? This is Albert Levy . . . Shalom. Shalom . . . I'm fine, and you? Good, good. I have a favour to ask, old friend. Your friends Jacob and Edith Lewis, their son David was adopted was he not? No, no, I understand, but this is very important, Isadore, believe me. I need to know . . . A great favour, yes . . . I now have a facsimile machine. Perhaps your friends could send anything of importance to me. It is urgent, Isadore . . . Yes, it would be good to see each other once more.'

CHAPTER TWENTY

I

Carrigan was in his front garden polishing his motorbike when the courier stopped outside his house. The driver looked appreciatively at the machine.

'That's a classic, that is.'

'My pride and joy,' Carrigan admitted.

'I'm a Harley man, myself. Can't beat a Harley.'

'Not unless you've got a BMW.'

The driver sniffed. 'Matter of opinion. Your name Carrigan?'

'Joe Carrigan, yes.'

'Thank Christ for that. Everybody's out today. Got a delivery for you.' He opened the side door and eased out a large carton with Customs stickers plastered on it. 'I'll need some ID.'

Carrigan fished in his pocket and pulled out a wallet of credit cards. 'What is it?'

'Dunno,' the driver said peering at the cards. 'We picked it up from a hotel in Switzerland, is all I know. Sign on this line here.'

He drove off at speed, leaving Carrigan to carry the carton inside. It contained a large black briefcase. He opened it, and the computer screen switched on to show a handsome young man standing in what appeared to be an African jungle with his hand stretched out in greeting.

'Dr Carrigan, I presume.'

As few American schools deal with the history of British explorers, the joke was lost on Carrigan. Wrongly assuming that the image was some kind of screensaver, he tapped the keyboard.

'The keyboard is disabled at the moment,' the young man said. 'Would you mind sitting down so I can see you better.'

Carrigan peered closely at the briefcase and saw a tiny lens set in the open lid. He sat down.

'This is cute.'

The young man gave a hollow laugh. 'I have not heard such high technology described as cute before.'

'Well, you presume correctly. I am Joe Carrigan. Who should I presume you are?'

'My name is Loki Ten. I am a friend of David Lewis.'

'Ah,' Carrigan said. 'Loki Ten.'

'I would like to ask you a question, Dr Carrigan.'

'And I'd like to ask you a few, you son-of-a-bitch . . .'

'My question is important.'

'Really. Is it the same kind of question that makes you phone people's hotel rooms in the middle of the night and insult them?'

'Are you David's friend?'

'Yes, I'm David's friend,' Carrigan snapped.

'If you are his friend, why did you and Mrs Lewis go to bed together?'

Carrigan leaned back, as if to avoid a rotten smell. 'OK, I know you called the hotel to help David. I suppose I should thank you for that. But all this other stuff is none of your business. Quite apart from anything else, how did you know where we were?'

'That is not relevant,' Loki Ten told him. 'What is relevant is whether or not you are David's friend. I meet very bad people in my work. I do not think Mrs Lewis is bad. Are you bad, Dr Carrigan?'

'You like getting down to the bare bones, don't you. Yes, I'm bad. I've been bad for a very long time. Bad at taking orders, bad at my work, bad with my relationships.'

'That is not what I mean,' the mechanical voice said. 'Do you hurt people?'

'We all hurt people, pal. All of us. Unless you're the exception. Do you hurt people?'

There was a long silence.

'I do not think that I hurt people.'

'Well hurrah for you, my friend.'

After another silence, the young man said, 'You are right to disbelieve me. What I do sometimes causes people to be hurt. But I want to help David.'

'And you think I don't? Jesus Christ, I seem to be spending all my time trying to help him, but it ain't easy. And sitting in front of talking briefcases doesn't make it any easier, believe me.'

'You are David's friend, then?'

'I'd certainly like to think so.'

'You are looking for something that will help him. What is it?'

Another mystery! How did this animated computer character know so much? What else did he know? Carrigan needed time to think.

'How does this thing work? It's not plugged into anything.'

'That is not relevant.'

'Humour me.'

Loki Ten explained about the satellite technology that linked them together. Carrigan only half listened to the descriptions of solid-state electronics and neural networks. His brain was racing to distil everything he knew about this Loki Ten character into simple factors that would help him do the right thing. It boiled down to one question: was Loki Ten friend or foe? He interrupted a detailed description of heuristic computer programs.

'I need to get hold of a photograph. I'm sure David saw it when he was in Muntz's place in Switzerland. A photograph of a woman in a wooden frame. That'd be a tough one for a computer to solve, I guess.'

'Would you like to see what happened when David went to Falkenheim?' the toneless voice asked him. 'I recorded his visit on the security cameras.'

Carrigan was impressed. 'Can you really do that?'

The screen flickered for a few moments, then Carrigan found himself watching David being accompanied by a grey-haired woman and two men to the door of a large house. A small dog was trotting at their heels. The screen flickered and the view changed to a library. David was looking at the shelves. Then he bent down to pat the dog, which scampered to a section of books that turned out to be a door into another room. The next sequence showed David picking up an object from a desk. Carrigan almost shouted.

'Stop. There. That's it. Can you zoom in on it?'

'Yes, but the clarity will not improve because . . .'

'Never mind that, just do it.'

Carrigan made Loki Ten play the sequence several times, until he was sure of what David had been doing.

'There's something else in that frame. Another photograph.

That's what set David off. I know it did. But what the hell . . .'

Carrigan stopped. He knew what the photograph was. He had seen David's drawings of it many times.

'Can you help me to get that picture frame?' he asked Loki Ten.

'Why?'

Carrigan went for the simple explanation. 'It will help David.'

'I do not believe my system is capable of discovering the picture frame. It is improbable that individual items have been entered on the Swiss police computer system.'

'What are you getting at?' Carrigan demanded.

'New owners have moved into Falkenheim, and everything that Muntz owned has been taken into police custody. I'm looking to see which depository they used, but I don't think even that has been entered. Very inefficient. I suggest you telephone Sergeant Martin and see if he can help.'

Martin was sympathetic, but there was nothing he could do. The Muntz case was due for its first court hearing, and everything was ultra-sensitive. No, he had not made a personal examination of Muntz's property. That was someone else's department. A picture frame, probably wooden, with a photograph of a woman? He'd make enquiries, if that would help . . .

CHAPTER TWENTY-ONE

I

Ernst Muntz was kept in solitary confinement in a high-security remand prison near Berne. He was treated with scrupulous courtesy by his guards who maintained a twenty-four-hour vigil. Every meal was closely examined, and all possible means of suicide were removed from his cell, the walls of which were discretely padded with tough, energy-absorbing material. Washbasin taps were opened and the lavatory was flushed when sensors detected the need. A warm-air dryer that could be directed all over the body obviated the need for a towel. His prison clothes were made from fabrics that could not be unravelled and twisted into a rope. The visiting room was separated from the cell by bullet-proof glass, and conversation was conducted through a microphone and loud-speaker system monitored by the guards. Not that Muntz received any visitors. Streichner and Hulbrecht were also on remand, and no one from his company or anyone else that he knew had bothered to come. The only contact he had with the outside world was through his solicitors, who were the only people other than the guards allowed into the secure area.

To the guards, it did not appear to have dawned on Muntz that he was finished. He treated them like servants and flew into rages if the slightest thing upset him. He threatened that their own careers would be over once he got out and told his friend Inspector Heilbron from the police department how badly they had treated him. When one of them finally lost his composure enough to inform the professor that Heilbron had also been arrested, he flew into yet another rage.

Life was made no easier for Muntz when, a few days after his arrest, his lawyer arrived to inform him that the account with the firm of solicitors who had acted for his family for generations had been closed. From now on, the State would be providing his legal services. The next day a pimply and inexperienced young man arrived at the prison and spent hours asking the same tedious and unnecessary questions that he'd gone through the first time round. The fellow seemed incapable of understanding even a simple fact, let alone linking two facts together.

Two days later, Muntz was horrified to be informed that yet another firm of solicitors had been appointed by the courts, their fees paid for by a Christian charity.

'This will save State money,' the prison governor told him.

His anguish at the prospect of going over the same ground for a third time was rendered all the more unbearable when two young, officious women wearing tailored suits walked into the cell with the guard. One of them had a slight squint and a rather mannish appearance. The other wore her blonde hair scraped back, and her tight jacket emphasized rather than concealed her bosoms. Despite himself he was reminded of his darling Irena. She had the same cold beauty, the same slightly disdainful expression, and it offended him deeply that another human being could make him miss his lover so keenly after all these years.

'We'd like to get straight down to business,' the mannish one said. 'Can we begin with this confession that you now claim you never made . . .'

And so it started again, on and on. Muntz was answering all their predicable questions like an automaton, when the one who looked like Irena turned to the guard.

'Would you mind getting the professor a glass of water? He doesn't seem well.'

Muntz looked at her in surprise. 'There is nothing the matter with me.'

She simply stared at the guard until he let himself out of the cell. The mannish woman stood up.

'We need a moment together alone, Ernst,' she said conspiratorially. 'You have not been forgotten, but you must be strong.' She went behind him and put her hand on his shoulders, sympathetically. 'Your friends are striving to clear this slur on your good name. It affects them too, you see.'

Her colleague nodded and reached across to take his hands, holding them tenderly.

'I knew they would not desert me,' Muntz said, almost pathetically.

She tightened her grip on his hands. 'I know, I know.'

The other woman stroked his hair and his cheek, then took hold of his face, but what seemed like a caress turned into a vice as she slipped her arm round his neck. He was too bemused to struggle at first, but when he saw the hypodermic needle being held under his nostril he began lurching from side to side. They held on until he tired himself and couldn't struggle any more, and then the long needle was slipped up his nose and forced through the thin bone covering the sinal cavity. Despite a long and distinguished relationship with other people's pain, Muntz could not believe it could be as hellish as this, a searing explosion of agony, and the cruel grip of the dreadful women, watching dispassionately as his brain reacted to the poison. There was no relief, no hope of respite, only a terrifying realization that it would go on for ever.

The women let go of him carefully, and the one who had reminded Muntz of his sister reached into her bag for a tissue, carefully dabbing into his nostril to remove a trace of blood. When they were satisfied that everything was ready, the mannish one called for the guard. By the time he arrived, they were both patting Muntz's face and slapping his hands ineffectually.

'I think the professor has had a heart attack,' she said. 'Hurry, get the doctor.'

The inquest discovered that it was indeed a heart attack that killed Muntz, but no one asked why the guard had gone out of the cell for water when there was a supply of perfectly drinkable water at the washbasin.

II

Sergeant Martin phoned Carrigan a week after Muntz's death to let him know that he had found the wooden picture frame and was taking steps to send it to Carrigan. He would be grateful if Carrigan did not publicize this, as he was taking short cuts in police procedures. The frame arrived a week later, with a note from the sergeant giving Dr and Mrs Lewis his respects. Carrigan stared at

266

it for a long time, then looked for the compartment that he had seen David open on the video recording. And there it was, as he knew it would be. The photograph from David's nightmares. Hitler and his greeting to dearest Ernst. And *Turmfalke*. It wasn't the last piece in the jigsaw, but he mentally slotted it into place. All he needed to know now was how David knew of its existence in the first place. He did not have long to wait.

The following morning Leon arrived in the Jeep and stepped into the house with a perfunctory greeting.

'Good morning, Dr Carrigan. I was hoping you might have a few moments to spare.'

'Sure,' Carrigan said. 'All the time in the world.' He led the way inside, and when they were sitting down the young Jew, declining the offer of a coffee, opened his briefcase and took out a thick envelope.

'Mr Levy hopes this will help to solve your patient's problem. Many people have gone to a great deal of trouble to bring the information together.' Leon's expression made it clear that he regretted being one of them. All this trouble for one man.

Carrigan opened the envelope and took out several sheets of paper containing a long list of code numbers and names.

'*Totenschein?*' he asked.

'A record of death certificates. Each prisoner taken into the *Turmfalke* camp was completely documented throughout his or her time there. Look at the end.'

Carrigan saw an entry ringed in red ballpoint. 'What's this?'

His visitor frowned impatiently. 'It would be quicker if you were more fluent with your German. That is the only prisoner out of more than seventeen hundred who did not have a death certificate issued.'

'*Krankengeschichte 387b: Hajo Kneiper, 5 Jahre*. I don't follow.'

'It's a project case number, Dr Carrigan, for a male child aged five years.'

He pulled a small white envelope from his pocket and handed it to Carrigan. 'I might say that this document took almost as much trouble to unearth as all the others put together.'

It was printed in German, with old inked writing and a number of indecipherable rubber stamps. Two names leaped at him: Jacob

267

and Edith Lewis. Hajo Kneiper was also hand-written, on a line labelled Child's Name.

'It's an adoption certificate,' Joe muttered. 'You mean my client started life as this kid Hajo Kneiper . . . ?'

'It seems a logical conclusion.'

'But how on earth did he get out of that bloody camp when no one else managed it?'

'Who knows. He's probably the only patient you have who has been orphaned twice over.' The young man stood up. 'I'll leave you to your work. Mr Levy wishes me to say that he sincerely hopes this information will help Mr Lewis. Of course, it all depends how you choose to use it.'

Carrigan caught the antagonism. 'You don't sound as if you share his concern.'

There was no ready smile to hide the anger. 'You've stuck your nose into something that is none of your business. God knows why Mr Levy took your part, but he did. That meant we were all obliged to get involved. The Second World War was over a long time ago, and we have other problems to deal with now.' He pushed the front door open. 'I hope you're satisfied . . . and when you read *Krankengeschichte 387b* I advise you to have a bottle of brandy in your hand. You'll need it.'

Carrigan sat for a long time after he had left, then he called the Lewises' number. Kate answered.

'I don't want you to ask any questions,' he told her, 'but someone has helped me to sort out what's been crucifying David. If you both agree, I reckon I can start building instead of breaking down.'

'That's wonderful,' she said. 'We've been trying not to go under, but David doesn't understand what's happening. We're both exhausted.'

'Well, with some hard work and a little luck we should be able to end it for you.' He managed to imbue his voice with a buoyancy he was far from feeling at the moment.

'Joe,' she said softly. 'Thanks for staying with us.'

'You're very welcome, lady.' He heard her put the phone down, and after he replaced his own he went to the drinks cupboard and took out a bottle of Cognac. Leon sounded as if he knew what he was talking about when it comes to drowning sorrows, he thought as he pulled out the stopper and settled down to struggle through *Krankengeschichte 387b*. It didn't take very long, but by the time he had finished translating it the brandy bottle was empty.

GROSS-ROSEN KONZENTRATIONSLAGER, FEBRUARY 1945

It was a dull and bitterly cold morning when the cattle train arrived at the sidings. Steel-helmeted guards jerked open the rusty doors and yelled at the half-frozen occupants to get out, pulling them onto the hard earth, careless of injury. No one noticed the smell of sickness and death that rolled out of the carriage with the dazed newcomers. It was part of the nightmare fabric of the place, in keeping with the bare, twisted cherry trees that the first commandant had planted along the path connecting the station with the camp. The avenue of trees was to honour a visit by Heinrich Himmler in 1943, but they had never blossomed. Before the station was built, the previous commandant had used the area to bury ash from the ovens.

Once the pathetic figures were lined forlornly in front of the trucks, Kapos clambered inside and threw out the bodies of those who didn't make it. When they finished, there were more corpses piled on the ground than prisoners standing. Prodded by the guards the few hundred survivors began shuffling painfully past a group of immaculate SS officers sitting at a desk by the gate leading into the death camp. Those who had the strength tried to straighten their backs and swing their arms, hoping to get into the queue that meant a few more days of precious life. Some were herded to the left and some to the right. A small number found themselves sent to a separate group where two men in civilian clothes checked their papers.

Rabbi Harold Kneiper was one of those selected, a fit-looking man whose normally happy face was drawn with fatigue and marred by a gathering bruise below the left eye. He had tried to lift his wife's body from the carriage and been struck with a rifle butt for his pains. In his arms he held a girl child, Gerda, aged three years. His five-year-old son Hajo stood silently by his side, both children too exhausted and hungry to cry. Thin lines of tears trickled down Kneiper's face. When the trio arrived at the desk, one of the officers looked at them for a moment and then consulted a memorandum headed with the arms of the Waffen-SS Institute of Health and Hygiene. He tied a label to Kneiper's right wrist and one to each of the children. 'Go to the train,' he said flatly, before turning his attention to the next in line. Kneiper took his little boy by the hand and shuffled back the way they had come. Each guard they passed checked their labels before letting them proceed, more often than not with an unnecessary prod from a rifle. Only when they reached the train did Kneiper look at his label. All it said was: *SS Turmfalke – For forward transit. Röhmer Insel Konzentrationslager.*

APRIL 1945

The handsome young SS-Standartenführer nodded casually as the laboratory assistants stiffened to attention. 'Is everything ready?'

'Almost, Herr Professor,' the laboratory technician said from behind the apparatus. 'We have been having some difficulty with the timing mechanism, but it works well now.'

Muntz lifted a hand to the row of new student officers in the gallery at the back of the laboratory, waiting with no small measure of excitement for their first experience of the famous Professor Ernst Muntz at work. They brought their heels together respectfully.

'What case are the young officers about to study today?'

'Case 387b, sir. The Kneiper family. The children have been told that they are to help their father in a game.'

'Good, very good.' Muntz cast a practised eye over the two children strapped next to each other in separate chairs. They stared back at him with the slack, vacant look he always associated with Jews under stress. But they did not interest him. Only the father.

The senior SS nurse came into the laboratory. 'The subject is waiting in the anteroom, Herr Professor.'

Muntz turned his pale eyes on the students. 'What you will see in this laboratory demonstrates the most important and central part of your studies. It is here that you will experience the most sophisticated experiments in human understanding since Pavlov's studies. He, of course, was obliged to study the lower forms of life, as befits one who is a member of a subordinate species.' He paused, appreciating the smiles and chuckles arising from his clever allusion to a gifted but nevertheless Jewish scientist. 'That is why I have chosen to place the Führer's personal gift to me here, to remind all who come that no library, no lecture hall, no precious theory, can measure up to the power of practical and constructive experimentation in a well-equipped laboratory.'

272

He turned to the signed photograph of the German leader on the wall in front of the two children.

'To our dear friend, Ernst. May your "Kestrel" show us the way – Adolph.'

His 'Heil Hitler!' was immediately echoed by the students. Then he followed the senior nurse through the door to the anteroom where Rabbi Kneiper was waiting.

'Ah, Herr Kneiper. So pleased to meet you at last.' Muntz ignored the silence and offered the chubby man a cigarette. 'No? Then you are wiser than I. It is the one vice I allow myself, although some would have it that incest is a sin. I wonder what you think about that as a parent, as opposed to your rabbinical calling ... No matter. Tobacco from the Balkans. Wonderful! I may tell you that the only two decent things to come out of that rabid hell-hole are tobacco and horses. I'm a cavalry man myself, you know. Always loved riding. Riding and hunting. Do you hunt, Herr Kneiper? My own obsession is falconry. In particular, my kestrels are renowned for their speed and accuracy in the stoop.'

At the word 'kestrel' Kneiper raised his eyes briefly.

'I see you understand,' Muntz said vigorously. 'Kestrel! One of the world's most efficient hunting machines. But more than that, Herr Kneiper, much more than that. It is also one of the world's fastest decision-makers. What other animal can spot the whiskers of a field mouse from the clouds and kill it before the beast can scamper a metre towards its burrow. That, as you might imagine, is why I chose it for our codename.' He paused and rubbed his hands together, changing the pace of the experiment. 'My colleagues have looked after you well, have they? And the children.' Kneiper's silence continued. 'Good, good, because it is very important that you are all three fit and well, as I am fit and well. Because today we are engaged in an important project, you and I. We are examining the physical nature of the decision process in the adult of the human species. To put it another way, we are seeking to understand the nature of stress and thus to enhance the ability of those who lead to make decisions. It follows that we must know as much as possible about the entire process. The physiology, the chemistry. You can understand that, can't you?'

Once again Kneiper kept his silence, but Muntz continued regardless.

'In my laboratory through that door you will have a decision to make. It is a very simple decision, as you will see, and we will give you thirty seconds in which to make it, which I think you may find to be rather on the generous side.' He stopped his chuckling when Kneiper mumbled something. 'I beg your pardon?'

Kneiper cleared his throat. 'The Allies are advancing into Germany, and the Russians preparing to attack Berlin. Why do you continue this nonsense?'

Muntz laughed delightedly. 'Oh really, Herr Kneiper, you must pay no attention to these rumours. History shows that the tide of battle rises and ebbs, but be in no doubt as to the outcome of this war. The Third Reich is invincible, and we continue our work on that basis.' He glanced at his watch. 'Now this is what I want you to do. When you go through there you will see your two little children.' He looked down at the file. 'Gerda and Hajo. They'll be sitting in front of you perfectly unharmed, you may be sure, although we have been obliged to strap them into their seats for reasons that will quickly be apparent. Behind each little head is a pistol, set to fire automatically one half-minute after I press my red button here. In front of the children are two buttons, one for Gerda and one for Hajo. Now, if you decide to do nothing, both the pistols will fire, but you may choose to save one of your children by pressing the appropriate button. Naturally, if you press both buttons you will merely fire both pistols. And now, if you are ready . . .'

Muntz stretched his arm across the desk and pressed the red button. Kneiper stared at him aghast.

'You can't do this . . . you can't! Not to my little children . . .'

'Oh, come now,' Muntz said reasonably. 'If I'd left you in Gross-Rosen the three of you would be dead by now. This way you can save one of your brood. But hurry. You only have twenty seconds left.'

Kneiper lurched to his feet and burst through the door, closely followed by Muntz and the senior nurse. He felt his pulse hammering, building a terrible pressure that crushed his heart. Two pairs of frightened eyes in little heads clamped to those dreadful chairs, watching him, voices piping *Papa! Papa! Papa!* Two buttons, but which one saved which child? He couldn't think. Couldn't move his limbs under that awful pressure that was about to burst his brain as the large second finger of the wall clock juddered past 6 ... 5 ... 4 ... 3 ... 2 ... 1 ... And then he half fell, half leaped the distance to the nearest button, pressed it, heard a strange faraway *plop* and felt something warm and wet on his face.

Blood of my blood. Flesh of my flesh. My little innocents ...

The SS nurse knelt by Kneiper's hunched and shuddering body and injected his left arm.

'The usual autopsy, Fräulein,' Muntz said briskly. 'Blood-sugar levels, adrenaline, extracts from the main organs, et cetera, et cetera.'

He was pulling off his white coat when the nurse called, 'Excuse me, Herr Standartenführer, but there is something of interest. The boy has fallen into a trance.' She was holding Hajo's arm, about to use the same hypodermic needle.

Muntz peered closely. 'Indeed he has.' He placed one hand on the child's head to pull an eyelid back, and a tuft of hair came away from the front of the boy's scalp. He examined the flesh thoughtfully. 'This is most interesting. Put the subject in Cubicle 6. I must see how this develops.'

'With respect, Herr Professor. The cubicles are full.'

Muntz turned to go. 'In that case, have him sent to Professor Blintz at Andernach General Hospital under my authority. I will examine him there in two weeks' time ... that is, if the Russians or the Americans don't come along and spoil our arrangements. Not to mention the English, the French, the Jews ...'

As his laughter echoed down the corridor, the SS nurse thought she was lucky to work with a commandant with such a fine sense of humour.

EPILOGUE

When he was satisfied that David was recovering both physically and mentally from the nightmare of *Turmfalke*, Joe Carrigan returned to the USA to take a post as professor of diagnostic psychiatry at Cornell University. A few months later, he received an envelope from England. It contained a photograph of a baby captioned '*Joseph Lewis, 15th March, 8lb 4oz*', together with a note from Kate that said simply, '*David is getting better all the time. Thank you for everything you have done for us. David, Kate, and your name-child.*' The next day he bought a silver frame and placed the photograph on his desk. If a new student asks if the baby is his, he smiles a little, sighs and says, 'I wish!'